THE CRASHER

THE CRASHER

SHIRLEY LORD

WARNER BOOKS

A Time Warner Company

A Brandon Tartikoff Book

Warner Books, Inc., 1271 Avenue of the Americas, New York, NY 10020

Visit our Web site at http://warnerbooks.com

 A Time Warner Company

Printed in the United States of America

First Printing: April 1998

10 9 8 7 6 5 4 3 2 1

Library of Congress Cataloging-in-Publication Data

Lord, Shirley.
 The crasher / Shirley Lord
   p. cm.
  ISBN 0–446–52027–6
  I. Title.
 PR6062.O724C7 1998
 823'.914—dc21   97–39164
                                                          CIP

Book design by H. Roberts

To my husband

I am indebted to the late, great, brave Brandon Tartikoff, who inspired this book. Thank you, Brandon. It was a joy to know you.

My thanks to Maria Quiros, the San Francisco design consultant for the excellent crash course on fashion designing she gave me one lovely Labor Day weekend in the Napa Valley; to Eliza Reed, vice president, business development, Oscar de la Renta, for her advice and diligent fact checking; to Michael Gross, author of *Model*, an informed guide to the world of modeling; to *Washington Times* correspondent Elaine Shannon, author of *Desperados, Latin Drug Lords, U.S. Lawmen and the War America Can't Win*; to Tom Constantine, DEA administrator, for facts and figures about international drug trafficking; to Ann Landers for her words of wisdom; to Washington attorney and author Ronald Goldfarb, and Adam Zion, assistant district attorney, Kings County, for their patience and help in ensuring certain portions of this book are legally correct; to Beth Harmon, marketing manager of the New York Public Library for her guided tour; to my son Mark Hussey, professor of English, Pace University, and his wife, Evelyn Leong, adjunct instructor, women's studies, for help with Ginny's early education.

I also especially want to thank my dedicated agent, Owen Laster, my brilliant editor Maureen Egen (both of whom know how to guide and spur a writer on . . . and on and on to better work) and my powerhouse of an assistant Zina Berthiaume, who typed and retyped this manuscript so perfectly without once losing her radiant smile.

The last person I want to thank is the most important. It is fair to say this book owes the most to my husband, A. M. Rosenthal, for his encouragement, support, and always (being the genius of an editor and writer that he is) insightful advice.

THE CRASHER

PROLOGUE

He obviously hadn't remembered her name.

"Madame Designer," he'd mockingly called her, through thin, spoiled lips.

She'd made a point of telling him she knew who he was. "Mr. Stern," she'd said more than once, with obvious deference.

"Arthur—call me Arthur," he'd replied, with the leer she remembered from their first meeting.

What a big-headed fool she'd been, sipping champagne at the reception, her confidence climbing as no one challenged her right to be there.

She'd congratulated herself that once again, despite increased nerves, she'd managed to crash this important party so successfully, the party she'd hoped would change her life and put an end to her crashing forever.

The young girl shuddered. It had changed her life all right, in a way that even in her worst dreams she could never have foreseen.

False smiles, arch movements. There had been plenty of both, as she'd tried to impress the fashion magnate. She'd even walked in a certain way to emphasize the sensual swirl of silk around her legs, as she'd accompanied Mr. Stern so lightheartedly to the darkened upper hall.

In total control, she'd thought she was, her body the perfect mannequin to show off the dream of a dress she'd designed for the evening's grand affair.

Who cared that there might be an invitation in the way she turned her shoulder to allow one of the pale slender straps to slip slightly, but not too far, onto her pale, cool arm? Not she. Mr. Stern would recognize her style, her flair, the cunning construction of her dress. That was all that had mattered then.

Who cared that he was married? That was the point, or rather his wife, Muriel Matilda Stern, was the point; the influential wife who really held the purse strings, who was known to prefer to stay home, allowing her husband to roam to discover new talent for their fashion empire.

This new talent had been so sure she could handle the passes, the leers, the suggestive innuendos of all the Arthur Sterns of the world. She'd encountered enough of them at events she'd crashed in the past. Hadn't she always handled them before?

But no, not this man she couldn't; not this time she hadn't.

She gagged as she thought of her futile struggle as Stern had pinned her to the wall, ripping her precious dress as if it was a rag, wasting no time in his fierce attempted rape.

But then had come the startling distraction—shouts from the end of the hall, a gunshot. Stern had turned; they'd both turned to see two men violently fighting, one using maniacal strength to push the other over the balustrade. There had been a high scream of fear and a horrifying crash of body, bone, matter on the marble floor below. It had all happened in a matter of seconds.

Could the victim still be alive? The girl cowered back in her hiding place, the scream again filling her head. She was shivering so much, she felt she could go into convulsions, like the homeless woman Johnny had made famous in his columns. Johnny. She sobbed silently. He would never forgive her.

She wrapped her arms around herself, trying to calm down, but it was impossible.

Where was Stern now? Looking for her or denying her existence as he rearranged his perfect tuxedo and restored his sangfroid?

And where was the other man in the fight, the perpetrator, the shadowy figure who'd disappeared so quickly through the narrow door she herself was now hiding behind? Who was he?

She had to be wrong about his identity. She was imagining things; she'd only seen him in silhouette, and yet there was something that tugged at her memory, something significant she knew she should remember. What was it? And where was he now? Waiting for her below, in the darker dark?

Stop the panic.

Her dress felt wet. With sweat? Or was it semen, blood? How long did she have before her hiding place was discovered? Not long. She was in shock, but she had to get out—now. But how?

Wait, you know this place, the warrens, the maze of corridors, the doorways that never held doors, the unexpected exits around forgotten corners.

A week, a carefree lifetime ago, came to mind, when she'd worked as a volunteer for *Vogue*'s One Hundredth Birthday Party. Sulkily she had gone in and out, indoors and outdoors, like a slave laborer, fetching, carrying, backward and forward. Yes, she knew this place.

She tensed, hearing voices, footsteps getting closer. Heels. Her stiletto sandals were off in seconds. She maneuvered herself down the narrow inside stairwell, one, two, three flights down into the old giant of a building, the grating hurting the soles of her feet.

A door at the bottom screeched as she pushed it open. She froze, as still as an owl. A solitary dim lightbulb hung in the corridor stretching ahead. Was anyone waiting in the shadows? She saw figures who were not there, but slowly, as she inched along, hugging the wall for protection, recognition was coming back.

Twice left, past a row of wooden filing cabinets, which carried a sad, old smell of cedar and wallpaper primer, immediately right past a thin tall door, another long corridor, left, left again and there was the fire door.

She had been warned before, it would set off an alarm if she tried to open it, but it was the only way out for her now. She knew she would find herself in Bryant Park, no longer covered by the huge fashion tent, the tent from which she had been ignominiously rejected the year her dreams had been so optimistic and fresh.

The door was heavy and awkward, but it opened without a sound. She looked to the left, to the right. No one. She came out running, across the park with a blustery rainy wind blowing a sense that the ocean wasn't far away.

Some island
With the sea's silence on it.

Browning, *Pippa Passes*.

One of her father's favorite poems. Why was it suddenly in her head? Crazy. She was running in Manhattan, the noisiest island on earth. The noisiest, nosiest, and yet, please God, let it be true, the most private, too.

Her breath was a continuing sob, her feet were getting cut. She ran on and the rain helped hide her wild flight. She stopped for a second to put on her sandals. Even in this neighborhood people would remember a sobbing young woman running in a torn silk dress. But no one stopped to stare; no one turned around.

She had no idea how long it took her to reach her walk-up loft apartment, so beloved only a few hours before.

She double-locked the door and threw herself, still panting, groaning with a leg cramp, across her white divan. The pain in her feet and the thought of dirt and blood spoiling the immaculate piqué surface brought her back to reality.

She staggered to the bathroom, looked in the mirror and wept again. She was disfigured, disgraced, swollen with crying, her eyes small slits in a face she hardly recognized.

She ran a hot bath, pouring in the expensive bath oil she usually rationed out drop by drop, but as she soaked, the terror came back.

Had the man who crashed on the marble floor lived? How could he have lived?

Who had pushed him?

Would they find her? But how could they know who she was?

She wasn't on the guest list. As usual, she had gate-crashed the party, but this time with a definite purpose: to put an end to her problems.

Her mother had often said her raging ambition would lead her into real trouble one day. Now it had come true.

She was finished. She would move to Florida to be near her parents. She would work for her father as he had always wanted her to do. She would never design or make another piece of clothing in her life. She would sell her sewing machine. She would live simply, quietly. She was finished.

Limping back to the divan, she saw one of her sandals, but not the other. It must have fallen off on the way home, but she had no memory of it happening. Somehow she had managed to bring back her tiny evening purse. There it was, damp, carelessly thrown on the hall table as if she had just returned home like a normal partygoer.

She opened it and saw her best lace handkerchief. Beneath it was a cloakroom ticket.

It was only then, as the phone began to ring, Ginny remembered her cloak, the spectacular one-of-a-kind Napoleonic cloak she had spent weeks making, for what was to have been such a momentous occasion.

She had arrived wearing the cloak. She had left it behind in the cloakroom of the New York Public Library.

1990

CHAPTER ONE

1645 EAST CLARENDON, DALLAS, TEXAS

"How old was Ginny when she stole the sheepskin car seat, Virginia?"

"Oh, Graham, don't say that. She didn't steal it; she . . . she borrowed it to make a lamb's costume for the school's nativity play . . ."

Outside the living room door Ginny fumed. That old story! She couldn't believe it. She'd been planning to give them a surprise and add a little sparkle to their evening, but as so often happened she was getting a rude surprise herself. What exactly was her father trying to prove this time?

"Borrowed, stole. What's the difference? She cut it up so it was unusable afterwards. Hey! I've got gin!"

"Damn! Graham, you're not fair. You take my mind off the game by talking so much and telling us all your stories, then you always win." Ginny heard Lucy Douglas giggle, but she bet she wasn't really amused. Her mother had told her Lucy hated to lose and so did her drab husband.

Since moving to Dallas in '88, her parents had drifted into these Sunday night gin games with the Douglases. Her mother wished they hadn't, although it had started because Dad loved playing the game and so did Lucy, who worked at Neiman Marcus, where her mother also worked as a fitter.

A chair squeaked and Ginny heard her mother say in the cheery-trying-to-be-pleasant-at-all-costs tone she knew so well, "Let's have some coffee, shall we?" Ginny clenched her teeth. Please, Dad, don't go on with the car seat story. She didn't have much hope.

"So what was I saying? Oh yes, well it was when we were still in San Diego, so I suppose Ginny was about ten, eleven."

"Nine and a half," Ginny murmured.

On the way to the kitchen Virginia shot Graham a warning sign to shut up. Everything he said would be all over the alterations department in the morning. She'd warned him before, but as usual he took no notice.

"Seems Ginny didn't get the part of Mary or even one of the angels in this nativity play, so what did she do? She didn't sulk or moan. She got the car seat—she's like her mother, good with the needle—made it into this lamb's costume, then, plucky kid, went uninvited to a rehearsal wearing the damn thing and one, two, three, convinced the teacher that to add authenticity to the stable scene she should bleat her way throughout the performance, right in front of blessed Mary, too." Graham whacked his leg with gusto. "How's that for chutzpah? How's that for showing initiative, something, I might add, Ginny knows I always highlight in my courses as one of the crucial elements for success."

Initiative! Virginia groaned. So that's what he was calling it now.

Lucy screamed with laughter. "What a character. If she was like that at ten, what will she get up to at twenty?" Virginia wanted to hit her. "Where is Ms. Sweet Sixteen, anyway? Out on a date, I s'pose?"

Ginny had had enough. Taking a deep breath, she opened the door.

"Here I am, evening Mr. Douglas, Mrs. Douglas . . ."

She struck a pose in the doorway, hand on one hip, cane in the other, five feet seven inches and still growing. She tossed her head back and winked, before giving the startled group the benefit of her most mischievous grin.

Her mother gasped, "What on earth . . . ?"

With every strand of her generally tousled chestnut hair hidden out of sight under a curious black turban, her slanted cheekbones made more so with powder blush, her dark eyes—inherited from her Italian grandmother—made still darker with kohl, Ginny Walker was wearing—could it really be possible—the jacket of her father's old-fashioned tuxedo. Belted tightly around her tiny waist, the jacket ended well above her knees, her lanky legs in shiny black tights looking as if they reached up to her armpits.

Trouble, she looked like nothing but trouble. A line from her favorite Bette Davis movie, *All About Eve*, came into Virginia's mind. "Fasten your seat belts. It's going to be a bumpy night."

Sure enough, even as Graham was giving Ginny his usual mixed signal of aggravation and reluctant admiration, half smiling a fatuous smile while shaking his head sorrowfully, Ginny plumped down on the sofa and said, "That's right, Mr. and Mrs. Douglas. I learned everything I know about initiative from Dad. Did you tell them, Dad, about that other time in San Diego, when the Von Karajan concert was sold out and you, eh, pretended to the old Mother Hubbard at the box office you'd given the tickets to me and I'd lost them?"

As her father's face reddened, Ginny rocked backward and forward, a determined look on her face. There was no stopping her now. "Of course, I didn't know then Dad was pretending, that there never had been any tickets, otherwise I wouldn't have bawled my eyes out as he made me empty my pockets to find nothing there . . . and the kind old Mother Hubbard wouldn't have taken pity on us, would she, Dad? She gave us some standing room tickets meant for others in the line just to shut me up."

The smile was gone from Graham's face. "Ginny, watch that loose tongue of yours." He suddenly realized what she was wearing. "And who gave you permission to wear my jacket? What do you think you're doing? What d'you think you look like anyway?"

"Practicing for my audition in *Ginger and Fred*, Dad . . . I'm the tallest in the class, so I'm trying out for Fred." She gave him a coquettish look. "I wanted your opinion about the look before I asked permission to borrow it for the big night . . ."

As Graham growled something about putting the cart before the horse and the Douglases made polite titters, Ginny got up and tap-danced around the room, the taps on her shoes and the tap of the cane on the wooden floor reverberating through Virginia's head. When she reached the door she bowed low to the ground. "Good night, ladies and gentlemen."

Jim Douglas made a halfhearted attempt to applaud, but when nobody else joined in, he stopped. There was an awkward silence as they heard Ginny run upstairs. "I'll get the coffee," said Virginia, and "Where's that coffee?" said Graham, simultaneously.

"Ginger and Fred?" Virginia didn't need to look at Lucy Douglas to know she thought her daughter belonged in a straitjacket.

"Ginny's in a modern dance class at Dallas High," Virginia snapped over her shoulder.

"Oh, does she want to be in show biz now? I thought she wanted to be a dress designer?"

Graham's face was still red. "Certainly not." He struggled to regain his composure. "She's top of her class in math. When she graduates, she's going to business school, to get a degree in business administration." He straightened his shoulders. "She'll eventually join me."

"Over my dead body," Virginia murmured. She was so upset, reaching up for the precious coffee cups she only used when they had company, she dropped one, the handle breaking off as it hit the countertop.

Upstairs, at the small sink in her bedroom, a lifesaver in the rented house with only one bathroom, Ginny slowly, painstakingly, began to remove the kohl with Johnson and Johnson's Baby Oil. Before she was halfway finished, her tears were helping the job along.

What a fool she'd made of herself . . . and in front of prissy, gossipy Lucy Douglas, of all people. How could she have let her mother down like that, giving away the family secret that her father had always conned his way through life?

Ginny stared at the black streaks on her face. Not half an hour ago she'd felt so excited, applying the newly acquired kohl, managing to stuff her unruly hair into a skintight, olympic-style bathing cap that gripped her skull so tightly, it made her cheekbones look more prominent, tying her pièce de résistance on top, the black turban she'd made out of the control tops of her mother's old panty hose.

She'd set out to make everyone laugh with her Fred Astaire act, to help her mother, who wasn't that keen on playing gin—or for that matter having the Douglases over. As usual, because of her father, it had turned into a nightmare.

Why did he constantly humiliate her with his well-worn stories? Why was he always illustrating his own cleverness with stories about escapades her mother believed showed up her worst trait, an overpowering determination to get her own way, no matter what, rather than flashes of brilliant initiative learned at her father's knee?

She was spent, worn out, the way she always felt after any confrontation with her father. There were more and more of them these days as the subject of Her Future loomed nearer.

She knew when it was coming. Usually at breakfast. Often on a Monday, her father's favorite day for making pronouncements, the day the fathers of most kids she knew were in a rush to get to work, dashing to their cars or the subway, or a seven-thirty or eight o'clock bus to get to an office, a plant, a business.

Her father was different, and how she'd grown up hating that fact.

It was her mother who went to work. Her father worked from home—wherever home happened to be—and most Mondays he acted the way she supposed most wage earners did, sighing about the onset of another week of toil ahead, sitting at the breakfast table as if he was the chairman of the board.

What bullshit as Toby, her best friend at Dallas High, would say. Monday was no different from any other day of the week for her father. He would go into whatever room of the house he'd designated as his "office" and dictate his daily output of words of wisdom into his "Memory Minder." Later he would take hours, starting and stopping the machine, to listen, before finally typing out, almost word for word, what he had already dictated.

It was a terrible waste of time, but Ginny had long ago given up hope of trying to persuade him to type his thoughts directly onto the typewriter.

"Think of the correspondence course as a classroom," he would pontificate. She could repeat it word for word. "When the material arrives through the mail, it is essential the pupil can 'hear' as well as read what the teacher is teaching. So I must first hear what I am going to teach—the tone is almost as important as the information."

Quentin Peet, the nationally acclaimed columnist, her father's idol, would then be brought into it. "I am sure Peet must dictate his pieces," her father would say. "Every word resonates like no other writer's in the world. I am sure that's his secret."

Well, bully for Mr. P. As far as Ginny was concerned dictation was for secretaries, but there had never been enough money around in their lives for that kind of luxury.

California, New Mexico, Colorado, Texas. During her short life they'd lived in four different states and seven different cities. Toby thought it sounded terribly glamorous and she'd let her think it, but it wasn't, no sirree. It wasn't glamorous at all. It was hell on earth.

Just before moving to this dreary house near the Marsalis Park Zoo, they'd been living in Denver, and that was where the horrible, lurking suspicion that had been building inside her turned into reality.

Her mother, trying to hide the fact, had been crying over the electricity bill, and like a thunderbolt, as if God himself had spoken, Ginny had suddenly known, absolutely known for certain that the Walker School of Advanced Learning was a failure, if not a sham, that despite growing up hearing over and over again that it was their passport to prosperity, it never had been, nor would it ever be.

Heavy rain began to beat against the window. At least that would drown out the smell of the monkey house for a few hours. Ginny threw off the tuxedo jacket, undressed and jumped into bed to finish her math homework. At ten o'clock at night, still only in October, she was shivering, dreading another Dallas winter, with only a gas fire in her room.

"It rarely rains and is never cold in Texas," her father had said two years before as he outlined the reasons for their move to the area of his "new opportunity."

As she turned out the light Ginny's resentment and anger returned. Just like the Walker School of Advanced Learning, that had been a lot of bullshit, too.

When the Douglases left, Virginia could just imagine what they were saying as they drove home. "Is that what he teaches in his How to Succeed in Business or whatever he calls his courses, to lie and steal and crash? No wonder his daughter's such a kook. He probably cheated at gin, too. He probably always cheats, then calls it chutzpah or initiative."

The car seat story was all too true. Virginia hadn't been amused or impressed when it had come out. On the contrary, she'd wanted to punish Ginny, to make her realize that taking someone else's property was stealing, that to go anywhere where she wasn't wanted was undignified. To her fury, before she could do anything, Graham had not only told Ginny he was proud of her, he'd rewarded her with a wonderful present, her first sewing machine, using some of the money they'd put away for medical emergencies.

Ancient history though it was, Virginia thought about it as she washed up the supper plates, and it made her boil all over again. As if the sewing machine hadn't been enough. As usual, she'd been the one paying for the lease on the car and so, of course, for the car seat, too.

It was all uphill and tonight it was all too much. How could she ever give Ginny a normal life, growing up with a peripatetic father who had itchy feet as soon as responses to his local ads ran dry, whose "School of Advanced Learning" would have led them into an advanced stage of poverty without her paychecks?

On the wall was the set of kitchen knives Graham's sister Lil had sent them last Christmas. How horrified Lil would be if she knew what she, Virginia, wanted to do with them right now.

After "Dear Friend," Graham Walker's opening letter to new subscribers began with the homily, "We don't wake up on the wrong side of the bed. We wake up on the wrong side of the brain." Ever since she could remember Ginny had always tried to sleep flat on her back.

Now it was one of the few left of her father's many dictates she thought might contain an element of truth. Certainly on this day of days, when she'd woken up on her stomach, with her head buried in the pillow and the wrong side of her brain definitely in control, not cooperating in any way with what she had to do.

Two weeks had passed since the stormy morning-after-the-Douglases-night-before. She'd apologized profusely to her father, more to please her mother than anything else, knowing she could twist him around her little finger, providing he never suspected how she really felt about his "life's work."

It wasn't her father she worried about. It was her overworked, overburdened, wonderful mother, who didn't deserve a brat like her for a daughter, or a control freak like her father for a husband. Toby knew how much she needed her mother, particularly now, when her support would be so essential when the Big Showdown finally came: business school versus liberal arts at the community college or, her most longed-for dream, allowing her to become an intern, apprentice, gofer, or whatever the lowliest job was called in the world of fashion design.

How crazy her mother would think she was if she knew that was what today was all about.

For the third time, Ginny squeezed hard with finger and thumb the small tube of adhesive in her left hand, as in her right, she held, trembling between tweezers, a set of Supreme Sable Lashes. Again nothing came out of the tube.

As she had been expecting with every tick of her bedroom clock, her mother called from the bottom of the stairs, "Are you nearly ready, Ginny?"

Her brain suddenly gave her a break. Of course, the stupid tube needed to be pierced. The explicit instructions, propped up against the mirror, that she could probably recite because she'd read them so often, had omitted that obvious piece of advice, because it hadn't been written for morons like herself.

As she was about to use the thin end of the tweezers to go to work, her mother called again. "Ginny!" She got the message. Her mother was about to take off without her.

"I'm coming . . . I'm coming."

It was too bad. There was no time left to add the Supreme Sables. She should have given them a trial run, but she'd been too concerned that once on, they wouldn't come off, and she couldn't see herself getting away with them at Dallas High, where patience for her "originality" was definitely wearing thin.

As the car horn blared outside, Ginny looked again in the mirror. It only showed her down to the waist, but she thought she'd accomplished what she'd set out to do.

With the Fred Astaire turban again covering her hair, this time worn with an electric blue velvet sheath she'd made, Scarlett O'Hara style, from curtains she'd found in a yard sale, large round herringbone earrings made from overcoat buttons, and a lightly penciled brown mouth, she did look different, perhaps even "head turning," which was cousin Alex's greatest compliment.

The Supreme Sables, at the considerable investment of five dollars and seventy-five cents, would have added the perfect finishing touch, but che sarà, sarà. She had learned—literally at her mother's knee— when to stop crying over spilt anything and when to get on with life.

Because Alex had told her more than once that you don't have to be a Boy Scout to know how important it is to Be Prepared, she popped the lashes and adhesive into her small black sewing kit, which today would double as her purse.

One more look in the mirror.

Would the most famous designer ever produced in the United

States—well, at least in Texas—notice how the turban emphasized the shape of her head? If so, it would be worth the headache it was already creating. Would Paul Robespier, once Paul Roberts, back in Dallas with his first American collection after ten successful years in Europe, realize how original her cut-on-the-bias sheath was? If he didn't, the day still held plenty of promise. Thank goodness it was a school holiday. There had never been a day to match this one.

She felt the same nervous excitement she'd had before diving from the top board in the school diving competition. She'd won then. Diving into something totally different today, she told herself, she'd win again. Her hands were shaking as they'd been up there on the board. Surely, a good omen?

The car horn blared once more and she raced down the stairs of the boring little beige house, light-years away from the world to which she was headed. It was a world, Ginny knew, where women thought nothing of spilling their breakfast orange juice on ermine bathrobes that cost seventy-five hundred dollars a throw, where every stitch her mother made to fit colossally wealthy (often colossally overweight) Texas matrons into colossally expensive creations cost more than her father usually earned in a day.

Ginny opened the car door and nonchalantly tossed a coat on the back seat, her mother's coat.

Guilt brought her excitement down a peg. They'd often shared the coat, the warmest one in the house, but her mother didn't know she'd made an adjustment or two to make it look more fashionable—well, on her. With lapels removed, the coat now opened wide in front to show off the vivid blue of her dress. She had also shortened it an inch or two to show off what she considered were her best features, long, shapely legs.

As the car backed out slowly, although it was too early for any mail to have arrived, both mother and daughter looked at the mailbox. Neither realized she was doing it. It was an involuntary action, because there was a special significance about the Walker mailbox. Regularly empty or regularly full meant all the difference between staying put or moving on to "another more profitable location," as Graham Walker put it.

It was the reason the size of the mailbox was the first thing Ginny looked at when they arrived at a new address. Too large and Ginny feared it would never look full enough to satisfy her father, so she took her time unpacking all her bits and pieces, in case they'd soon be on the road again. However, she always found a place to set up her precious sewing machine.

How her mother put up with all the packing and unpacking over the years she would never understand, but then there was so much about her parents she didn't understand and probably never would.

In a flood of affection Ginny attempted to give her mother a kiss as she backed the car onto the road. "Oh, I'm so thrilled, so thrilled . . . thank you, oh thank you, there's no other mother in the world like you."

It was true. For weeks Ginny had been thinking of a way to smuggle herself into Paul Robespier's much publicized Fashion Show of the Year at Neiman Marcus. Just when she'd decided to hitchhike to the store at dawn to try to get in through the staff entrance with the cleaning crew, her mother had suddenly told her she could come with her, "providing you keep yourself quiet."

Virginia turned to smile at her only child. Her loving expression changed immediately.

"Ginny, why on earth are you wearing that again? You look like . . . like something from another planet—like one of those ETs or whatever they're called. Oh, Ginny, really, I just can't believe you."

"I thought you liked it," Ginny said defensively. "I got the idea from a late night movie . . . something Adrian made for Joan Crawford in . . ."

"Adrian! Joan Crawford! I really can't believe what I'm hearing. All month long you talk about your longing to see Robespier's collection, nagging me insane to sneak you in somehow and then, when you finally drive me into the ground to get your way, you appear in . . . well, I don't know what to call it, except as you've just described it yourself . . . in something out of the ark. Adrian . . . Joan Crawford—they've both been dead for years!"

Ginny concentrated on swallowing to stop angry tears from ruining her makeup.

Virginia sighed heavily. There was no way she could disappoint Ginny now. "All right, stop feeling sorry for yourself. All I'm going to say is, looking like this, it's even more vital you keep your promise to stay in the background. It's going to be a madhouse anyway. There's a waiting list a mile long hoping for cancellations."

On the expressway she continued. "Ginny, I don't understand why you want to make yourself look like a freak. You've got such lovely hair. Why on earth d'you want to hide it?" Her voice was soft, low, the way it was sometimes when she sat on her bed at night to tell her wonderful stories about life in the world of fashion. "You can sew beautifully . . . if I can get some *Vogue* patterns . . ."

"I hate sewing! I hate patterns! Mother . . ." Ginny couldn't help it, her voice broke as she tried to explain. "Don't you understand, I want to be original, to look different. It's the only way I'm ever going to get anywhere in fashion. Alex says . . ."

"Alex! What does he know about fashion? He's as off-the-wall as you are. Originality is one thing, but . . . but . . . looking like a weirdo . . ." Virginia sighed again. It was no use. It was never any use, particularly if her too-smart-for-his-own-good nephew, Alex, had given Ginny his seal of approval.

Since childhood Ginny's idol had been her ten-years-older cousin, and her mother well knew that no amount of parental disapproval, disdain, or detraction had ever been able to topple Alex off the pedestal Ginny had created for him.

Neither of them spoke again until they reached the exit for Neiman Marcus. Then, "Remember Ginny, you've got to stay out of sight." Virginia paused, then added sharply, "None of your tricky business."

"I swear, I swear, no one will know I'm there, but if there is a chance . . . the slightest, tiniest chance, could you introduce me to Monsieur Robespier, pleeese?"

Virginia tried not to laugh. It was out of the question, but she wasn't going to have another scene now. "Ginny, I hardly know the man. He's only asked for me because most of the women coming to the show are my regular clients and if they buy anything he knows they'll want me to fit them. I really don't know, Ginny, but I'm certainly not going to let you anywhere near him if you don't take that . . . that monstrosity off your head."

Ginny thought of the adhesive and lashes in the sewing kit. If the turban had to come off, the Supreme Sables had to go on. Otherwise she'd make no impression on anyone, let alone Monsieur Robespier. She'd just look like everybody else.

*　　*　　*

"Just a fraction—less then half a millimeter—nothing less, nothing more. Yes, *absolument,* that will do it. *Parfait.*" The instruction was snapped out imperiously in an accent that still owed more to Paris, Texas, than Paris, France.

Behind a screen at the back of the large mirrored fitting room, Ginny saw her mother, pins in mouth and hand, drop to her knees in her usual urgent way, to begin to make minuscule adjustments to a fishtail hem, which slithered across the pale carpet like a fat black snake.

It wasn't the only fat snake in the room. Mrs. Heathering Davison, of the Turtle Creek Davisons, like so many women Ginny had seen being fitted by her mother, was giving her a hard time, fidgeting, swishing her tail and letting out exasperated sighs at the waste of her valuable time. But that wasn't the worst of it.

The hard ache of disappointment and disillusionment which lodged in her chest like a brick had to be related to heartbreak. It had begun to develop long before Mrs. Heathering Davison arrived to throw her considerable weight around and insist she had the first claim on Virginia Walker's time.

It began when, ordered by her mother to stand behind the back row of chairs surrounding the auditorium, and then behind one of the topiary trees, shaped in the form of a peacock (Paul Robespier's logo), Ginny had endured—it was the only word for it—sixty minutes of watching the worst clothes she had ever seen in her life.

Either Paul Robespier Roberts was a master fraud, pulling skeins of wool over the eyes of every fashionable woman in Texas, and the world for that matter, or she, Ginny Walker, had to accept that her mother was right. She could sew, but as far as her fashion sense was concerned, she was a freak, not an original.

Now she was marooned, stuck, hidden behind a screen until her mother finished, and God knew how long that was going to take. To try to calm down, Ginny did what Alex told her opera stars did to relax their nerves before going on stage. She opened her mouth wide in a huge silent yawn. It didn't help.

She dropped her head onto her lap. There was nothing worse than knowing you yourself were to blame for being in a situation you'd give the moon to get out of.

It was embarrassing to think she'd planned to parade before Robespier before her mother could stop her, to hear the homegrown maestro exclaim, "But she is ravissante! Who is this young girl with such style?"

"Ginny Walker, Monsieur Robespier. I am the fitter Virginia Walker's daughter. I was hoping . . . when I finish school . . . I would love to work for you. To become your apprentice."

"But *bien sûr* . . . the way you have coordinated your colors . . . the line of your sheath, I can see you have a natural talent. And your turban! It is superb! Here is my card. I insist, Madame Walker, your talented daughter contact me when . . ."

Ginny swallowed hard. She would throw up if she continued to dwell on how far she had allowed her fantasies to carry her. Trapped, unable to move, unable to speak, let alone scream, she was an unwilling stowaway stashed behind a screen, because it was she, and nobody else, who had begged and pleaded and worn her mother down into agreeing she could attend this rare occasion and watch the great Robespier at work.

She would never read *The Dallas Morning News* again as long as she lived. "Local Boy Turned Maestro," the fashion page had headlined. "Robespier returns from Europe in time for the Crystal Ball with a special collection, dedicated to the fashionable women of Dallas—Robespier, the talented Texan who has spent the last decade learning at the feet of the great masters, Givenchy, Chanel, Patou."

It was really hysterically funny. To think she'd been dreaming of learning at the feet of Robespier, of impressing him so much he'd ask her parents' permission to make her his apprentice and take her to study with him in Paris, instead of going to business school.

In the mirror Ginny saw Mrs. Heathering Davison swivel her ample hips to see her back view. She stuffed her fingers in her mouth to stop giggling. No dress could do much for Mrs. Heathering Davison's derrière, but this one, besides emphasizing the positive, also accentuated every inch of her body's negatives. How could it not?

She started to reorganize the structure of the dress, but gave up. Some things were beyond salvation. The dress belonged in a chamber of horrors—or a circus, along with Paul Robespier himself, who might have learned something at the feet of the masters, but it certainly wasn't how to design clothes. More likely how to shine shoes. His were so shiny he could surely see his face in them.

Ginny looked at her watch, her frustration growing. If only she hadn't persuaded her mother to smuggle her in to see Robespier's collection . . . if only she hadn't had to hide behind this screen when her mother was summoned to carry out alterations on the four Robespier nightmares Mrs. H.D. had ordered, if . . . if . . . if!

Alex was right. Her life was full of *if only*'s, because, as her cousin frequently chastised her, she was not selective enough. She tried to cram everything in, when, instead, she should focus on what was really important, on things which would use and improve her natural talents.

Like right now, when she could have been at the NorthPark Mall with Toby, waiting for Cindy Crawford to check out the local chic for MTV, a chance in a million, the promo had said, to be filmed live "Where America Shops."

It had been a toss-up between seeing an actual couturier in action (particularly a Texas-born, Paris-trained one) and hoping to make a major impression on him—or joining Toby and the NorthPark crowd, hoping to be plucked out by Cindy as one of Texas's youngest most stylish, most chic.

The wonderful realization had come that she could fit in both.

She looked at her watch again. She could still do it if they left now. Without thinking she let out an exasperated sigh, every bit as loud as the ones uttered by Heathering Davison, following it up inexplicably with one of her allergic sneezes.

Ginny got to her feet sheepishly, about to slink away to the exit, as Robespier marched up to the screen and screamed, "Who is this? What are you doing here?"

To her horror, her mother began to say all the things she'd fantasized hearing.

"I do apologize, Monsieur, but this is my young daughter, Ginny. She—she is such an admirer of yours, she begged to be allowed to see your genius at work. I am really very sorry."

Ginny looked at the floor to fight off another fit of giggles. Everything had happened so quickly, she'd never removed the turban.

She was blushing. She could feel the creepy crawly blush spread from her collarbone as Robespier obviously swallowed every word, and began to smile, showing pale pink gums above a row of achingly perfect small white teeth.

"Come out from your hiding place. Bring your chair. Ah! What an interesting . . . chapeau." Now Ginny really didn't know where to look.

It took another agonizing thirty minutes before the fishtail was declared fit for human consumption.

"Do you still want to go to NorthPark? I'm exhausted."

"Mother, you promised . . . you promised . . ."

"Oh, God. Oh, well, I'll drive you there, but I'm not coming in. If you find Toby, let me know, then you can go home with her."

"You really are the best mother in the world." Ginny hugged her, although it was obvious her mother didn't want to be hugged. "I hate you having to put up with people like that," she said, in a small apologetic voice.

"People like that!" Virginia mimicked. "I thought you wanted to run off with 'people like that'—people like Paul Robespier, the genius."

"Genius! Ugh! I've never seen such hid-e-ous clothes. If it wasn't for you Mrs. Heathering Derrière wouldn't have been able to move a step in that joke of a dress."

Virginia shook her head reprovingly. "Ginny, don't be rude." Then, "Do you know what that dress cost?"

"Millions."

"Not quite, but the alterations alone cost nearly five hundred bucks."

"I can't believe it." But Ginny was no longer interested in what Robespier was able to get away with. She caught sight of the time. "We've really got to get going, Ma. MTV will be there any minute."

"I'm not moving until you take that thing off your head."

"But Robespier said . . ." They both started to shriek with laughter.

"Okay, Mother, you win." She pulled the turban off so violently, half the swim cap ripped as it came off, too. With her mother still howling with laughter, Ginny opened her sewing kit purse to flourish the box of Supreme Sable Lashes. "These cost a fortune, too, five dollars and seventy-five cents. Mrs. Heathering D. will never be chic, however many millions she spends, but I bet these will get me on MTV!"

Virginia found a parking spot at the huge NorthPark Mall and Ginny leaned over to get the camel hair coat from the back seat.

"Who told you you could borrow my coat?"

"I thought you did."

When Ginny got out of the car and nervously put the coat on, Virginia didn't know whether to laugh or cry.

"Don't you agree . . . it's . . . better this way?" Ginny looked in anguish, waiting for her mother's reaction.

Her mother shook her head resignedly. "Yes, baby, it looks great. You can have it"—she started to laugh again—"for your birthday. Now don't be long. It's been quite a day and we've got to get home to get your father's supper. You've got forty-five minutes max to be one of MTV's chic."

Ginny's face lit up, a mixture of relief and excitement. She blew an airy kiss to her mother. "Wish me luck," she yelled, striding off, as if she'd just been given the world.

Virginia watched Ginny cross the parking lot in her renovated coat. She bit her lip. The feeling of defeat was back. Like father, like daughter. However hard she tried to explain things to Ginny, there were too many indications she had inherited or absorbed Graham's tenacious (or pigheaded, depending on how you looked at it) determination to be noticed and make a mark on the world, no matter what it cost.

Once Virginia had thought she could make a mark, too, growing up in Hollywood, designing for the movie stars. It had taken a while to accept she couldn't design dresses, but she could make the cheapest piece of junk off the rack fit and flatter even the worst figure faults. She'd encountered them all.

Ginny had more imagination than she'd ever had—too much, if it was possible. Virginia sighed. Ginny had done wonders to her old camel hair coat. She'd cleverly used a zipper as ornamentation on the blue sheath, too, à la Moschino—but that didn't mean she could be a successful designer. She didn't want Ginny to experience the hurt and humiliation she'd gone through, waiting for customers who never turned up.

It was ironic, for while she'd managed to drown her dreams, Graham's had grown larger with every passing year, but not their bank account.

How enthralled she'd been in the beginning when he'd talked about his ambition to leave his job, teaching English lit at an undistinguished West Coast school, to become a modern day Socrates, "earning fame and fortune, teaching my unique brand of wisdom by mail."

How she'd hung on every word as he'd talked and talked and talked. "I can teach, but I also know how to learn," he'd said. "Not such a common gift as you might suppose. I can find something of value in practically everything." And, indeed, he'd confessed that while he studied the leading political and foreign pundits of the day, especially his number one, Quentin Peet, also included in his scrutiny were columns by "Dear Abby" ("already a multimillionairess"), the writings of Dr. Seuss, and the original texts of Dale Carnegie.

How impressed she'd been with his studious appearance, not knowing then, of course, the amount of time he devoted to choosing the kind of eyeglasses that strengthened his air of scholarship, the fastidious attention he paid to the size of knot in his tie, the amount of trouser leg he allowed to cover his shoes. No wonder Ginny was so clothes-mad.

She was sick of hearing Graham say "Clothes maketh the man," contemptuously dismissing those in academia whom he accused of deliberately setting out to look as rumpled and disheveled as possible "to be more in touch with the unkempt youth they attempt to teach."

No wonder Quentin Peet was his role model, appearing on television, immaculately dressed, even when just back from a war somewhere, epitomizing, said Graham, "the way a leader should look."

Well, Graham Walker was no leader. It had taken five states and five "partners" in as many years to learn that Graham had proposed and married her just at the time his sister Lillian told him, for her son Alex's sake, she could no longer help support him in his dreams.

She'd found Lil's old letter jammed in the back of Graham's desk. "It's God's will that you've met Virginia, for much as I love the idea of living as you describe it, a 'Walt Whitman life of freedom, traveling on unknown roads to unknown adventures,' now I have this new job with the art gallery, as a widow bringing up a son, I know I must stay put for his sake."

She had never confronted Graham with the letter. What was the point? And, in any case, at that time she'd been so full of optimism. "It takes time for pioneers to be recognized," he would say, "to get the big break that brings all the rewards."

Virginia jumped as she leaned forward and accidentally blew the car horn. It sounded like a bugle call, an alert to rescue her only child from the world she'd become so used to, a world of rented homes, leased cars and a nervous stomach at the end of every month as their bank balance went down and their bills went up.

Her mouth tightened. Already she could recognize the signs. Gra-

ham was restless; she'd caught him poring over the map again; seen him
hang up the phone hurriedly when she came into his study. Responses
to his ads hadn't been good, she knew that, but this time she'd demanded and he'd promised her in writing he'd give Dallas at least three
years before moving on. This time she'd written down something, too.

No matter what "extraordinary opportunity" beckoned in some
other "prime location," she wasn't going with him. Not this time. Not if
he broke his word before at least three years were up. She was earning
more at Neiman Marcus than she'd ever earned.

She tried to stop herself thinking it, but she couldn't. If Graham
left them, financially Ginny and she would actually be better off. If she
didn't have to pay for Graham's small ads and endless printing and mail
expenses, she could easily pay the rent on the horrible little hovel they
were in and everything else that she and Ginny needed.

If Graham had the gall to bring the subject up, she'd let him know
at once—one, two, three—that she and Ginny were staying put in Dallas. At least she prayed that if and when the moment came, she would
have the guts to say and do it.

The problem was, despite everything, sometimes he could still convince her all was not lost, that one day he would be recognized as the
visionary she'd once been so certain he was.

If she only had herself to consider, she knew she'd be a camp follower forever, but it wasn't just herself. It was only recently she'd begun
to realize there wasn't a moment to lose to begin planning a future for
Ginny.

Her eyes misted over as in the distance she saw Ginny march around
the corner of the huge store. Her nearly-sixteen-year-old-going-on-
thirty-year-old daughter did look like a million dollars in her hardly recognizable camel hair coat, but there again Ginny had taken something
that didn't belong to her. Her values were all mixed up. Where on earth
was it going to lead her? One day into real trouble.

She must have dozed off, because to Virginia's surprise she saw
Ginny reappear around the corner. She looked at her watch. She hadn't
been gone for more than twenty minutes. She must have arrived too late
for Cindy Crawford and MTV.

Poor Ginny. She'd take the disappointment very badly. Virginia
could only hope, without much confidence, that at least it would be a
lesson to her not to try to cram all her dreams into one day.

As her daughter walked slowly toward the car, her demeanor expressing total defeat, Virginia was struck by how tall she was. Wait a minute. Virginia had a wonderful idea. If Ginny only grew a couple more inches, there was a job that could offer her the opportunity her brains and looks entitled her to, a job that could move her into the kind of circles where she might meet someone . . . someone who could give her the million-dollar life that Virginia knew, from a lifetime of listening to her clients, existed outside the fitting room.

Ginny could become the perfect runway model. She had always been skinny—essential to show off a designer's clothes. She had good posture, lovely skin, her own mother's deep dark eyes, a wonderful smile, and Graham's thick chestnut hair. She wasn't exactly pretty, but she was—or could look—cute, impish.

As Ginny approached, desolate and downcast, she was amazed—and furious—to see her mother looking so cheerful. How could she, on the worst day of her whole life?

"They wouldn't even let me in the door, Mother. There were thousands there. They—"

"Oh, never mind, Ginny. There'll be lots of other things . . ."

This was impossible. Her mother didn't understand what she was talking about and obviously didn't care either, probably concentrating on what she was going to cook for supper.

They drove home without exchanging a word, although Virginia didn't realize it. She was too busy thinking about the future she had just dreamed up for Ginny. From now on she would pay much more attention to what Ginny ate, her nutrition in general, exercise, poise and, yes, despite the opposition she knew she would encounter, Ginny's often crazy dress sense, too, all to help groom her for her future life on a famous designer's runway.

In the house, as she quickly made a salad and pasta, Virginia decided she wasn't going to say a word about her plan—yet. She didn't know what Ginny would think, but she could hear, as if he'd already said it, Graham's reaction: "Mindless! My daughter's going to use her brains, not her body. She's going to get a business degree, so she can run her own courses for the Walker School."

"Don't count on it," she muttered. "You may be in for a big surprise, Professor Higgins."

Ginny hardly touched her dinner, but Virginia wasn't taking her to task—yet. Poor Ginny, she'd had a miserable day. When Toby called around eight, despite Graham's frowns (he loathed phone calls in the evening, unless they were responding to his ads), Virginia was happy to hear Ginny talking and finally laughing upstairs. The young were so resilient; they soon forgot their disappointments.

By nine Graham had already gone upstairs to bed. He'd left all the lights on in the den, off the dining alcove, the space he used as an office.

What a mess it was, with papers all over the floor. She knew better than to attempt to tidy them up. He would accuse her of losing the one paper that was essential for his work, his life, their livelihood.

On his desk was a piece he'd been researching since learning, to his fury, that the U.S. postal rate might go up to twenty-nine cents in the new year. Disastrous for his kind of business. He'd sent President Bush an impassioned telegram explaining how counterproductive to the economy the increase would be. When that produced no response, to Virginia's increasing frustration, he'd wasted two weeks studying the U.S. Postal Service since its inception.

She picked up the heavily corrected manuscript he'd told her he intended to send to his God, Quentin Peet, expecting him to use the information in one of his columns. Why he thought Peet would be interested she had no idea, but that was Graham all over, full of confidence—or was it bluster? As far as she knew, Peet rarely responded personally to her husband's frequent missives, although she'd seen the occasional acknowledgment from Peet's office.

"Are you going to stay up all night?" he called from upstairs.

"I'm just reading your masterpiece, dear, on the Postal Service." She didn't bother to hide the sarcasm in her voice. He probably wouldn't notice it anyway.

She was right. "Good, good. Take your time. This is something Peet will really thank me for. It's of vital national importance."

Virginia grimaced. Oh, sure, Professor Higgins. I bet he can hardly wait.

"Good evening, Mr. Peet."

"Glad to see you back, Mr. Peet. Where've you come from this time? We've missed you here at Twenty-One."

"Good evening, Walter. Good evening, Bruce. None of your God damn business where I've been. Don't you guys ever read a paper? My son here yet?"

"Yes, Mr. Peet." The young manager looked around the comfortable sofa-and-armchair-filled lounge. "At least he was here a minute ago . . ."

Peet gave a cursory glance down the long room. A military-looking man was smoothing his mustache as he studied the stock market machine; a vivacious, curvaceous redhead in a low-cut dress sipped champagne and appeared to be watching an ice hockey match on TV, while two business-suited companions watched her.

"Perhaps he's on the phone."

"I don't doubt it." Peet curled his lip disdainfully.

With his head of thick dark brown hair, slim, well-exercised body and lightly tanned, brooding face, Quentin Peet never seemed to age. At fifty-nine, going on sixty, he still turned heads when he entered a room, not because he was one of the most famous journalists of his era, or certainly the most handsome, but because he exuded energy, power, and a word overused to describe him—magnetism.

At the 21 Club in New York, one of the most famous restaurants in the world since its days as a speakeasy back in the 1920's, Quentin Peet eschewed the much sought after first-floor restaurant just off the foyer, with its racy red-checkered tablecloths, sporting memorabilia covering much of the ceiling, and brass plaques announcing where the rich, famous and infamous had sat over the years. Most people clamored to sit there, and be seen, squeezed together in some discomfort and no privacy, but not Quentin Peet. He had never believed in being one of the crowd. He was one of a kind, a leader of men, and as many foreign potentates—not to mention journalistic competitors—had lived to regret, woe betide anyone who underestimated him.

Now he bounded upstairs to 21's gracious second floor, where, he knew without asking, his usual corner table would be awaiting him. Here, tables were spaced farther apart and the decor was much more to his liking.

With its gleaming dark wood, rich velvet curtains, soft lighting on crisp white damask, silver and crystal, the second-floor restaurant was, for him, reminiscent of London, which, after New York, was his favorite city by far. There, his only child, Johnny, had been born during sunny years when, his fame just beginning, he had been appointed his paper's youngest bureau chief, a reward after winning his first Pulitzer Prize for his reporting from Vietnam.

He hadn't been seated long before Johnny, aka John Q. Peet, rushed across the room to join him. "Sorry, Dad, I was—"

"On the phone, making a date to meet some babe after dinner with more boobs than brains." His father spoke in a matter-of-fact, clipped voice, as if the matter was already closed.

At twenty-five, Johnny showed a slight resemblance to his father, although it could easily be missed if you didn't know they were related. His father was dark. Johnny was fair. They had the same handsomely shaped head, the same straight nose, but the "take-no-prisoners" fierceness present in Quentin Peet's face was totally absent in Johnny's. His mouth was gentler, or weaker, depending on how you looked at it, and there was a hesitancy, a slight droop to the shoulders, more noticeable when he was with his father, that conveyed uncertainty, vulnerability, something he deprecated about himself, although he knew women were attracted by it. Not for the first time Johnny felt a flash of irritation noting there wasn't a trace of gray in his old man's hair. Goddammit, it was as thick as ever, although his own appeared to be actually receding.

In less than five minutes Quentin Peet's favorite cocktail, a Rob Roy on the rocks ("Chivas, light on the vermouth") was before him.

"What are you drinking these days, son?" Before Johnny could answer, his father laughed, a dry, humorless laugh. "I suppose you know you give away the kind of women you're dating in your choice of drinks. Please God, don't let it be Perrier on the rocks tonight. I can't face the thought of running into you again with Ms. Health Club 1990, with her sweaty, hairy underarms and what d'you call 'em? Fab abs?"

Johnny laughed in the same way, similarly unamused and unappreciative of the crack. "I'll have a margarita on the rocks, not frozen and no salt," he said defiantly to the hovering waiter.

He hesitated, gauging his father's mood, then decided to plunge right in. "I'm seeing Dolores again."

"The Bolivian bombshell? God save us. Does your mother know?"

"No, why should she? I said I'm seeing her, not marrying her."

"Well, just make sure that's not on her agenda. She's a disaster waiting to happen. For once your mother and I agree about something. She'll milk you for all you're worth and then some."

Johnny ignored the barb. Dolores was a spendthrift, but apart from the fact she was also sensational in bed, she had her own inheritance and was, if anything, more generous with him than he was ever able to be with her.

Following the usual pattern of dinner, an infrequent occasion because of his father's heavy travel schedule, Johnny knew the real reason for the meeting would not come up until they had ordered and the first course was well under way.

Perhaps his father knew, perhaps he didn't. In any case Johnny reckoned he wouldn't care a damn that the reason he always made a date to meet somebody after these command performances was because, no matter how good the food, he was too jittery to eat, then found he was ravenous as soon as they parted company.

Now he sat on the edge of the banquette, toying with his fork, watching his father throw down twelve malpaque oysters. He loved oysters, too, particularly in the late fall, as now; but as usual his appetite had disappeared.

"Great pieces from Saudi Arabia and Kuwait." He said what he knew his father expected him to say, but all the same he meant every word. His father had a magical way with words, whether at home or abroad clarifying the most complicated situations in a way that from a lifetime of listening to and reading endless letters of admiration, Johnny knew, made readers feel they had unraveled the problems of the world for themselves. It had always been hard being Quentin Peet's son and it wasn't getting any easier.

Peet grunted. "Mr. Hussein thinks he's going to get away with it, but he isn't . . ."

"I thought that we told him . . ." Johnny stumbled, trying to remember the American diplomat's name. As he often did to cover up his forgetfulness, he rephrased his sentence, "I thought our woman in Baghdad assured Hussein in the summer that we weren't going to interfere, that Washington has no treaty obligation to defend Kuwait?"

"Damn fool woman. I told State, Gillespie should never have been appointed there; wrote it, too." Peet leaned back and looked long and hard at his son. "Mark my words, the Security Council is sooner or later going to pass a resolution to authorize all members of the U.N.—and I do mean all members—to use force to expel Iraqi forces from Kuwait, if they haven't withdrawn by such and such a date. This is something they haven't done since Korea in the fifties."

There was a sense of pent-up excitement, mixed with impatience, about Quentin Peet. Johnny wasn't surprised. The old man liked nothing better than a fight, a confrontation, a war, another opportunity to be at the forefront of something most people would give their all to escape from, including Johnny himself. He swallowed a sigh. "You mean there could be a war?"

Peet didn't answer.

"What's going to happen, Dad?"

"That's what I should be asking you, son."

Here it came. Johnny pushed his oysters away.

"When the hell are you going to get off your ass? At your age, d'you know what I was doing? What I'd already done?"

"I know . . . I know . . ."

"Don't you 'I know' me!" Peet's brows met thunderously together as he puckered his forehead in rage. Once Johnny would have ducked for cover. Now he didn't need to, but he still slumped back against the banquette, head down, waiting for the onslaught to continue.

"Suez, Saigon, the Soviet Union—I'd already covered all of them at your age, not for my health and not for the travel section of *The New York Times* either."

Johnny winced. Since his father had arranged an internship for him at the *Times*, it was a constant cause of friction that one of the few bylines he'd achieved had appeared in the travel section. He'd written a piece about Puerto Rico after going there with Dolores to visit some of her cousins, and he'd been thrilled, even if his father hadn't been, that the travel editor had liked it.

It was just his luck that shortly after the piece appeared, Hurricane Hugo had ferociously hit the island on the way to devastating the Carolinas; and it was his father, not he, who'd flown down there to write a tearjerker about the four-billion-dollar path of destruction, a piece which had been reprinted all over the world.

Well, so he hadn't thought of doing it; his mind didn't work that way, and in any case he was far too low on the totem pole at the *Times* to be able to go wherever he wanted.

That, of course, was the reason for tonight's dinner. After almost two years at the paper, although he'd become a staff reporter, he hadn't climbed far up the greasy pole. He knew there wasn't anything he could say that would satisfy his father, but he had to say something.

"Dad, I'm trying, but you must know, I've told you before, I'm . . . I'm not you and I'm never going to be you. You're unique. Everyone knows that. Nobody expects another Peet like you." He wasn't about to tell his father that he still dreamed of smelling out a story that would turn him overnight into a Woodward or Bernstein, that he could be tenacious, too, if and when he was interested in something, but nothing and no one at the *Times* had come close to lighting his creative fuse. He was sure it was his fault, but it had been nothing but grind; and now there was the nightmarish suggestion of Albany.

Albany! How was he supposed to get excited about going to Albany, where, okay, he'd probably get the occasional front-page story, reporting on some dreary piece of legislature, even "above the fold" as the other reporters dreamed of achieving, but where he'd die of boredom in a cultural desert, not to mention the lack of any sophisticated girls about town.

His father's expression didn't change; he still looked stony, his mouth set in a grim, disappointed line as their main courses arrived, lamb chops for him, with a half-bottle of claret, swordfish and another margarita for Johnny.

In his customary way Quentin Peet attacked the meat hungrily, drinking down a glass of claret as if he were dying of thirst. Then, as if he could read Johnny's mind, he said much too calmly, "Max tells me you're not too keen on going to Albany?"

Before Johnny could answer, his father continued, his voice low, icy, "If you don't go, you know you'll have cooked your goose, don't you? You don't turn down jobs at the *Times*; you take them in Patagonia, Peoria, Patchogue, Peru . . ."

"Paris?" Johnny tried to laugh, to defuse the miserable atmosphere, but his father refused to be deflected.

Eyes blazing, he said, "I repeat: Patchogue, Peru . . . you go there and you turn the fucking place into a story, a hundred stories, you deluge the desk with stories until the place comes alive and somebody begins to think that perhaps it wasn't such a bad idea having old Peet's son there after all. You use this"—he jabbed Johnny's forehead painfully— "this . . . this . . . this . . . your brain or whatever's left of it after fucking yourself into a stupor every night."

He stopped eating to stare at his son. "I shouldn't tell you this. You should have worked it out for yourself, but nobody is sent to Albany as a penance. It's a prize—for showing some talent, a place where some of the best people on the paper proved themselves, Johnny Apple, Frankie Clines, Steve Weisman . . ." Quentin Peet reeled off a list of impressive names. Johnny knew better than to show he wasn't buying it. He listened attentively as his father continued, "Albany's about power, sonny. It's where the money trail begins . . . money and power . . . If you ever have the luck to be appointed Albany Bureau Chief, I'll know you've inherited my genes."

Johnny couldn't think of how to respond to that. There was silence, his father waiting expectantly. Before he could make some kind of intelligent answer, Quentin Peet lost patience. "Okay, then, you go to Albany and write a fucking funny story for the travel department," he exploded. "About the Rome of the North." He paused to chew the last piece of meat off the chop. "You do know there is a Rome near Albany, don't you?"

By the time coffee came, Johnny felt as if he'd been tossed around in a cement mixer. He could hardly think straight as his father spelled out for him his dismal future life on the *Times* if he didn't accept the Albany post. "They can't fire you because of that union deal made back in the sixties, but you'll be shunted into one dead-end job after another."

"Perhaps I should leave now?"

"Where would you go?"

"Oh, I don't know, television, a magazine."

"*Vogue?*" sneered his father.

As so often happened at the end of a terrible evening, his father abruptly changed the subject. "Pity Dolores isn't Colombian."

"Why?" This was a surprising switch.

"I've got a hunch there'll be a lot of interesting stories coming out of Colombia now. If Dolores was Colombian, she'd be able to introduce you to the place, might inspire you into a little action, to get on the case."

He drained the last drop in his second glass of wine. "There's a war going on down there, a particularly nasty, violent war that few people realize is happening. D'you know the drug kingpins carried out nearly three hundred bombings last year, killing nearly two hundred people, not including those on the Avianca jet they probably blew up? And what kind of news was it here? Not even an m head story. I tell you these drug lords live in the kind of luxury the United States has forgotten ever existed. I think I'm going to pay a little visit to Bogotá myself to see what I can cook up."

It was nearly ten o'clock. "Time to go, son. I've hardly seen your mother since I got back from the Middle East. It's a wonder she remembers who she's married to."

It was a well-worn joke that always made Johnny shudder inside, because it was so near the truth.

As they went downstairs, his father threw an arm casually around his shoulders. "Good to talk to you, Johnny. It's always good to get together and—"

He stopped as, at the bottom of the staircase, an attractive, stocky, Italian-looking man opened his arms wide and said, "I can't believe it! QP himself. I called you earlier this evening. You're just the man I want to see."

"Mario!" Quentin Peet allowed himself to be embraced in a bear hug, then said, "You're just the man I want to see, too. Meet my son, Johnny. Johnny, meet the governor of our magnificent state, Mario Cuomo . . ."

As Johnny shook the governor's hand, his father winked at him. "Governor, I want you to remember Johnny. In a couple of months you may run into him up in your neck of the woods. He's with the *Times*, you know, and they're dangling the Albany Bureau under his talented nose . . ."

1993

CHAPTER TWO

Johnny Peet would never admit it, but the intensity of Dolores's moods, her volatility or seismicity, as he liked to describe it to himself, always turned him on.

Perhaps it was because she was the antithesis of his very proper, low-key mother, Catherine Ponsoby Peet, who, in and out of the hospital with a tricky heart valve, never complained, although she had plenty to complain about. Perhaps it was because he'd inherited from his father, at least, the desire to live dangerously, if nothing else.

Whatever it was, although his common sense occasionally warned him his parents were right and Dolores could easily lead him over a precipice, tonight, as on many nights, his common sense was nowhere to be found.

He was already excited with the events of the day, so much so he realized he could even be reckless enough to talk to Dolores about spending the rest of their lives together.

In the hallway of her exotic East River apartment, sublet from a Third-World member of the U.N., she'd met him like a tigress, spitting out her fury that he was half an hour late, although punctuality was hardly what she was known for.

He'd recognized the signs. Tonight, the fourth night of the new year, she was dying to be tamed . . . and he'd been dying to tame her, on the floor just inside her front door, before he'd even thrown off his overcoat, across the bar in the living room, where she'd run, pretending to ignore him, pouring herself a glass of champagne, and finally on one of her own prized Chinese Chippendale dining chairs, where he'd pulled her to sit astride him, and where they'd rocked together so violently as they came, the chairback cracked with a sound like a rifle shot.

Now she lay langorous, still, on the white suede chaise longue in her bedroom. Naked, she was as white as the suede, as white and as curvaceous as a swan, Johnny thought, and just as unpredictable.

Unlike most women he'd known, Dolores had never sunbathed and the pallor and smoothness of her skin from top to toe showed it, emphasizing the black curls surrounding her head like a halo and the tiny neat triangle of black pubic hair, which, she'd told him more than once, she would let grow into a beautiful bush just for him—he had only to say the word.

Even after such a wild hour, his penis reacted to her lightness and darkness, but he wasn't ready again, yet. He looked forward to the next game she would most likely play, acting like an innocent, aloof little princess, making him wait for it, hoping he would even beg a little.

Before that, he had something to tell her, something to discuss, and on the phone she'd said, in her usual mysterious Mata Hari manner, she had something to discuss with him, too.

He went to the bar to get more champagne and grinned at the unholy mess they'd made as they'd wrestled to find each other, sweeping everything on the countertop to the floor, an upturned bottle of Cristal still dripping out its contents.

He cleaned up and took another bottle from the fridge. Dolores only drank Cristal. Dolores wanted and expected only the best. It was one of their major problems. She wouldn't even consider flying business class, anywhere, let alone coach.

He came back to the bedroom with two glasses. She was reading *Time* magazine. "Recognize her?" she said.

He gave her a glass and, sitting on the chaise longue at her feet, looked at a full-length photograph of a stunning Brunhilde of a woman in a bikini, only her face hidden in shadow.

"Yes, I do . . ." He looked at the caption. The name meant nothing to him. He laughed. "I recognize the face . . ."

Dolores pinched him hard.

"All right, all right. I recognize the body. Once seen, never forgotten.

I know we've met, but I can't remember where or who she is and frankly right now, Ms. Scarlett, I don't give a damn."

Dolores made a soft, purrlike sound, which meant she was sated with sex and happy. "I'm glad you don't remember her. I thought you were bowled over by her when I introduced you last summer. Then she was called Rosa Brueckner, but apparently that wasn't her real name. If you read the story you'll understand why."

Johnny lazily lay back, his eyes closed, in heaven, feeling Dolores's softness, inhaling the strange, slightly orangey, slightly musky fragrance made specifically for her in Paris by someone she said made fragrances for Chanel. "I don't want to read any goddamn *Time* articles . . . I don't want to read anything right now. Would any man in his right mind?" He reached back and made contact with her perfect, full nipple, massaging it until, as he guessed she would, she pushed his hand away.

"What did you want to discuss?"

He sat up and clinked his glass against hers. "*Next!* magazine has been after me again. Don't know why. Certainly not because of my tell-all stories from Albany . . ."

Dolores giggled. She knew only too well she'd come back into his life just in time to disrupt it. For more than eighteen months, it had cost him a fortune trying to keep in touch with her, commuting to the city from upstate New York, often to find she was out with somebody else.

All the same he'd tried to follow his father's advice and turn the place into a story, but the result was that the Albany Bureau, thank God, had gone to someone more worthy.

He'd been lucky. Between the Gulf War and the drug wars in Colombia, his father had been too busy to pay much attention, and by the time his periscope focused again on his only son and heir, Johnny had found himself some kind of niche on the paper, working for the Weekend section, writing profiles or stories, like the one appearing yesterday, about fashionable food in the nineties, post-nouvelle cuisine.

Dolores was playing with his hair. He hoped he was wrong and there wasn't the beginning of a bald spot at the back; even more, he hoped she wouldn't find it.

"So what did they say?"

"I had lunch there today. Beautiful offices, beautiful girls . . ."

She removed her hand abruptly. He grabbed it back and put her fingers in his mouth. "Mmmm, delicious! Nobody as beautiful as you, my swan." He sat up to drink more champagne. "It's a little like a ballet, this job market. Two steps forward, two steps back. This is about the third call I've had asking me to come in . . . so this time I went and round and round the conversation went . . . 'We like your recent Weekend pieces,' one says . . . 'We know you know the world,' another guy says. 'Are you interested in investigative pieces, like your father . . . or would you like a regular people profile type of assignment?' 'Look, you asked me to lunch,' I said. 'What do you have in mind?' "

"Did they talk about money?" Dolores was shocked, or so she said, by how little she considered he received from the *Times*. "Pocket money," she called it.

"The ball's in my court. They've asked me to come up with a proposal."

"So come up with one . . . a million dollars a year with no limit on expenses . . ."

Johnny laughed, although he knew Dolores was totally serious. She was so far off the ground, no wonder his parents disapproved.

The idea of working for *Next!*, which was fast becoming a hot read, intrigued and excited him, although how he would ever break the news to his father—that he might consider leaving the *Times* for such an upstart magazine—was beyond his comprehension. But then, with no promotion in sight, he didn't know how long he could go on doing what he was doing at the paper. The idea of his own column . . . investigative reporting . . . covering what he wanted to cover, instead of following orders from a female editor who didn't bother to conceal her lack of admiration for his work; who wouldn't be intrigued, excited?

Dolores pulled his hair. "Listen to me, Johnny, ask for a million and maybe you'll get seven fifty and in return you'll investigate and . . ."

He turned to bury his face in her neat little triangle, his tongue on its own tour of investigation.

She tried to push him away, but she showed she didn't really want to.

It wasn't until about one-thirty they thought about dinner. As far as Dolores was concerned that meant Le Cirque or La Grenouille or, at this time of night, caviar, foie gras, and more Cristal from the fridge.

Johnny picked up *Time* as she went to the kitchen. Wow! Now he remembered Madame Brueckner and yes, he had been bowled over. He'd

been in the Hamptons with Dolores and gone to one of her Latino mul-
timillionaires' estates for lunch.

La Brunhilde Brueckner had been one of the guests, and Dolores and
she had fallen into each other's arms like long-lost sisters, although it
turned out they'd only met a couple of years before, when Dolores had
been living part of the time in Los Angeles. She'd told him Rosa wasn't
a playgirl. On the contrary. Apparently she was considered to be one of
the most brilliant financial consultants around.

So what piece of business had she landed to merit attention from
Time? As Johnny began to read, his interest grew. This was the kind of
story he would have given anything to write. This was the kind of story
every journalist would want to go after. Indeed, Rosa Brueckner wasn't a
playgirl and besides that, her interest in the richest of the rich had nothing to do with making more money for herself.

Rosa Brueckner, the story revealed, was an undercover agent for
the Drug Enforcement Administration, working under this pseudonym
for two and a half terror-filled years, operating a sophisticated money-
laundering operation on the West Coast, through a network of bank
accounts and shell companies. So successful had her double life been,
she had penetrated the cocaine industry more deeply than any DEA
agent before her, leading to the recent arrest of Luis Uchobo, top
money manager for the drug lords of Cali, Colombia.

"Brueckner's triumph is a milestone for women in federal law enforcement," Johnny read, "boosting the morale of her sister agents, much
as the performance of military women during Desert Storm buoyed their
female colleagues."

"This is incredible, swan." Johnny took the magazine into the
kitchen. "Is she really a friend of yours? I'd love to see her again."

Dolores stuck out her tongue. "I bet you would."

"No, seriously . . . according to this piece she's been married for quite
a few years to someone in the DEA, but she pulled off something few
people ever live to see, trapping all those murderous drug guys . . ."

Dolores finished arranging a container of Beluga in a well of crushed
ice. "I know, I can hardly believe it. It sounds as if everything was just a
front . . . her gorgeous home in Beverly Hills, her jet . . ."

"Jet?"

"Yes, jet!" Dolores's dark eyes opened wide in appreciation. "It was
gorgeous—in green and gold. She gave me a lift once to Vegas, said she

was meeting some men who had more money than Fort Knox. I wanted her to introduce me . . ." Dolores smiled at Johnny coquettishly. "Before you swept me off my feet, of course, but she said they were too deadly." She gave a mock shiver. "I thought she meant deadly boring . . . but I guess from reading this she meant it literally."

"In a way, I can't believe *Time* running this story. Her mission may be accomplished, nabbing this big fish for the government, but surely she'll have to pay for it now everyone knows who she really is."

"That's what I thought, but they don't give her real name and you can't see her face . . ."

Dolores giggled again, as Johnny pretended to reel back. "Who needs a name or a face with a body like that staring out of the page? Next time we go to California, can we look her up?"

"She may not even live there anymore. In any case, she's married . . . so don't get any ideas . . ."

One idea was still uppermost in his mind: to make a commitment to Dolores. But something held him back.

"I wonder if my father knows her?"

"I'm sure he does, baby. I thought you said your father knows everybody."

Johnny promised himself he'd ask him at the next opportunity. *Time* had broken this big story, but that wasn't the end of it, he was sure. With somebody as intrepid as Rosa Brueckner, there would be other missions, other mountains to climb, other incredible stories to write. For *Next!?* Why not?

As they ate and drank, Johnny held Dolores's hand and occasionally leaned across to kiss her. "What did you want to tell me, swan?"

She looked sorrowfully at the piece of foie gras on toast she held in her perfectly manicured fingers.

There was a dramatic silence he knew he wasn't expected to break.

When she raised her beautiful head to look at him, her eyes were liquid with tears, but even that didn't warn him of what she was about to say. "I'm broke, Johnny. I've run out of money, my inheritance. I don't know how it happened. I'm not even sure I can pay my rent next month and . . ." A tear rolled down her pale cheek. "I think I'm pregnant. We're going to have a baby in the summer . . ."

*   *   *

Over three thousand miles away, outside Lausanne, in a small, private Swiss clinic, *Time* magazine had just been delivered to Suite 42/43.

Although the occupant of the suite, the clinic's most important patient by far, could have written the story himself, give or take a few unimportant details, his eyes, the only part of his face not hidden by bandages, followed every word slowly, painstakingly, as if to memorize them.

He'd never met Rosa Brueckner, although her name had come up once or twice over the past couple of years. It was easy to say no woman would ever fool him, but he seriously doubted it. It was the oldest problem in the world. The reason regimes that had everything going for them, from Perón's Argentina to Hitler's Germany, collapsed. Greed. Too much, too easily, too fast. People at the top got lazy, slack and, zap, it was over.

He'd been expecting something like this Brueckner-Uchobo fiasco since that asshole Pablo Gavira turned himself in to the Colombian authorities on the promise he wouldn't be extradited to the U.S. The American press had gone orgasmic over the story, with that fucking correspondent, Quentin Peet, who thought he was a cross between Sir Galahad and James Bond, divulging that Pablo, the idiot, was being held "in his hometown of Engivado, ten miles from Medellin, in a 'prison' so luxurious, Buckingham Palace might be found wanting in comparison."

Gavira would have to be exterminated; Uchobo, too, if the chance came up. As for the Brueckners of the world, death was too pleasant a punishment for them. There were other, more meaningful kinds of living-death to remind them to stay out of other people's business.

He'd been promised the bandages would be off today. He didn't seem to be in any hurry, which surprised and relieved the highly qualified plastic surgeon entrusted with the job.

No one had expected him to be such a model patient, forced because of his special circumstances to stay in one place for nearly ten days, but he enjoyed being unpredictable. It kept people on their toes, and after the first painful seventy-two hours, he'd realized it was the first time in years he'd had plenty of time to think, to plan.

Outside his corner suite sat Hugo Humphrey, six feet eight inches of brute force, whose handshake was enough to give those chosen to experience it nightmares for months. Hugo had been with him in the operating theater to ensure the surgeon kept his word and used only a local anesthetic.

"Surgery is performed inside the nose under a local anesthetic to prevent the patient from bleeding as much as he would under a general anesthetic. This also keeps the face as natural-looking as possible while the operation is in progress."

That information had been the determining factor to go ahead. He'd never lost consciousness in his life. It had been the one thing about the face change that had bothered him. All the same, not trusting anyone, he'd told Hugo to watch everything from soup to nuts, only warning him not to get rough with the doctor if, as he'd been told might occur, he ended up with black-and-blue eyes for a few days.

As it happened, he hadn't, which, having read everything he could on rhinoplasty, was evidently a sign of the surgeon's ability. No bruises weren't just an indication of good healing capacity, which he knew he had from the life he'd led; they reflected the surgeon's skill. Nose bones have a good memory. Those advising him on such matters had chosen well, a surgeon who had handled the delicate nose bones with such finesse, they would never resume their previous position, a surgeon who, because of his own checkered past, would never talk.

Soon, another heavyweight guard would relieve Hugo for a few hours, but there was no one as dedicated as he was. In his opinion, another of Hugo's major assets was his keen antipathy to women.

Lucky Hugo. Although no woman would dare try to fool him, he sometimes wished he could leave them alone, too. Would his new nose and the few other alterations just carried out make him more attractive to women? As if he cared. His old nose had never stood in the way of his conquests. How could it when he was, as Randela had once described it, "literally filthy rich." The delicious, but far-too-smart-for-her-own-good Brazilian had pointed out one day that truckload after truckload of dirty crumpled dollars, pounds sterling, lire, yen, pesetas, and marks pouring into Colombia from drug deals had given new meaning to the phrase, just as a new one—money laundering—had had to be invented to make use of it.

If Randela had had the sense to shut up and to stay alive, how surprised she would be to know that it was she who had first given him the idea that, when it became expedient to take on a new identity, he should go to a plastic surgeon.

He could remember it as if it were yesterday. They'd just made love and he'd noticed something different about her thighs. There was simply less of them, and finally she admitted she'd had some body work done, some thigh trimming, from the most famous slicer in the world at that time, a Doctor Ivo Pitanguy in Rio de Janeiro, so deft with the knife, according to Randela, women flew to him from all over.

He'd thought it was her national pride speaking, but he'd checked it out and sure enough, Pitanguy was indeed then the top doc in that field.

Hugo knocked and put his head around the door. "The doc's here, wants to see you. Okay, boss?"

The man who didn't believe in words when actions would do nodded.

"How are you feeling?" asked the doctor.

He nodded okay, to the doctor, too.

"Good, good. This morning you will see your new look for the first time. I think you will be pleased. In three to four weeks when everything is perfectly healed, your new profile will look as if it has always been in residence." The doctor examined the bandages. "Very good. In about an hour then." He paused. "Any questions?"

"I'll be leaving today." It wasn't a question. It was a statement.

When the doctor left, the patient smiled. New profile was a good description of what lay ahead. He'd been giving a lot of thought to his profile in general and his name in particular during his layover. Of course, in common with the other patients in the clinic, he was using an alias, one of many he'd used over the years.

Now he'd made a final decision. Just as he had reduced the large nose he'd lived with all his life, so it was time to reduce his extra-long, difficult to pronounce real name, the one he'd been born with in Georgia, Russia, sixty years ago.

For the life of respectability that was imminent he would shorten it to one syllable, one that everyone could say—and remember—a name with resonance.

When he arrived in New York with his new profile, his name would simply be Svank.

Bumper-to-bumper to the Queens Midtown Tunnel, and Ms. Ginny Walker, eighteen this past December, poked her tongue out at the huge billboard, which nobody could miss and her mother had been raging about for months. It was the first time she'd had an opportunity to study it, so for the moment the intense traffic jam didn't bother her.

YOU'RE GOING TO NEW YORK DRESSED LIKE THAT? Charivari, the Manhattan fashion business, was asking the provocative question in fifty-foot-high letters.

"Well, yes, as a matter of fact, Madame Charivari, I am," she thought, "and it may interest you to know, if you catch Elsa Klensch's fashion coverage on CNN tonight, she will probably describe me as one of those 'dressed to kill' at the New York fashion shows today."

The ad really upset her mother, who after all was a major player in the fashion business these days, working for Scaasi, one of the few celebrated custom designers left. According to her mother, Scaasi evening dresses were the price of a station wagon, but then, Ginny figured, they did need an awful lot of expensive fabric. His most famous client, Barbara Bush, First Lady until she'd been replaced in January by Hillary Clinton, was apparently svelte in comparison to some of his others.

Her mother thought the ad was offensive, condescending, but Ginny, after a few minutes staring out of the stationary cab, decided it didn't bother her. If it made women take a second look in their suburban mirrors before setting out for the big city, she was all for this kind of confrontation.

It was part of the "say-it-as-it-is" New York challenge, something she felt physically—energizing, yet terrifying—every time she saw the incredible Manhattan skyline just waiting to devour her. It didn't happen often. Only on the rare occasions, as now, when she crossed the East River by cab.

The subway was her usual loathsome mode of transport, suffocating, but usually swift, delivering her for the last eighteen months to the drudgery of Pace business school. There, as usual because of her December birthday, she was the youngest in the class; and because of her height, also as usual, she was among the tallest, towering over all the lumpy girls, and, alas, many of the guys.

They'd moved to Queens in the fall of '91, after a disastrous few months in Boston, where to her excruciating embarrassment she'd discovered her father was using "Harvard" in his "business" address, although they'd lived miles away from the college and, of course, had nothing to do with it anyway.

It had been the worst time of her life, but at least it could go down in Walker history as the year her mother had FINALLY HAD ENOUGH.

Unemployed, hearing through the pins-and-needles network about an opening for an experienced fitter at Scaasi, Virginia Walker had left the house one morning, glowing references in hand, taken the shuttle to La Guardia, and storming the couture citadel, despite stiff competition, walked away with the job.

Her mother had announced now she was the one moving on to a "new opportunity"—in New York City—and, thank the Lord, was taking her daughter with her. The Walker School could move, too, with its founder and chairman of the board, or it could stay exactly where it was—in no-win "Harvard" country.

Ginny had been on cloud nine, thinking they were going to live in Manhattan, but it was financially out of the question—certainly for the first few years, Mother said. She'd felt a lot better when she'd realized that Queens, although a borough of New York, was actually situated on Long Island.

In *People* magazine she'd read that it was where Donna Karan, another of her fashion idols, had grown up—"miserably," nicknamed "Popeye" and "Spaghetti Legs"—for obvious reasons. Describing herself as a "social misfit," Karan hadn't joined in the usual school activities, longing for the day when she could focus on something she was good at, fashion designing. Ginny found it comforting. And with a mother also in the fashion business, Karan and she seemed to have a lot in common.

It was Fashion Week in New York City and if the traffic ever allowed her, Ginny was on her way to see the show of another American designer she was wild about, Calvin Klein.

The tiny beads of perspiration she kept wiping from her upper lip with her best linen handkerchief had nothing to do with any heat in the taxi. There was no heat.

No, nerves were responsible for her rare sweat, because she didn't actually have an invitation to Klein's show. She was going to crash by masquerading as somebody else, somebody Charivari would never dare question about fashion standards. She was about to take on the identity of no less a personage than Elise Marathaux of French *Elle*.

It was a piece of cake. First, to look like one of the fashion flock you couldn't go wrong with black, black, and still more black. To add the necessary French Elise touches, she'd chosen a pimple-size beret, sheer-as-glass black hose and clunky black half-boots. The French were mad about clunky half-boots.

Everything had seemed all systems go at home. Now, with the journey taking so long, she didn't feel so confident. She gingerly stretched out her legs to examine her stockings for flaws, willing them not to run. Buying them from a stall on Queens Boulevard had been a major risk.

Next she consulted her compact to inspect the angle of the beret. Her tiresome hair wasn't helping it stay where she wanted it to stay. When they got nearer, perhaps she should take the beret off and start all over again. If only they were nearer . . . if only she'd brought something to read . . . if only she'd brought a sketchpad to doodle something for her class tonight.

She dug her nails into her palms. No more *if only*'s. She'd sworn, once in New York, she'd never have to say that to herself again.

She'd encountered fierce parental opposition over her evening classes at the Fashion Institute of Technology, FIT to the initiated, where she'd been taking as many courses as she could in everything from basic pattern-making to yarn and cloth manufacture, printing and dyeing.

To pay for the classes, thanks to total family uninterest in her real career choice, which was to be a fashion designer, on Saturdays and Sundays she sold lamps, china and glass at that other national institution, Bloomingdale's. It meant she was "unavailable" to accept any exotic invitations over the weekends, but che sarà, sarà, and in any case those had yet to come her way.

The taxi lurched forward so suddenly her latest most prized possession, large black-rimmed glasses, slid off her lap onto the floor and only her outstretched hands saved her—and her hose—from landing there with them.

"Easy, please sir, easy!"

Angrily she used her damp handkerchief to wipe away a minuscule piece of dust from the frames. They carried the Klein name. Natch!

These days designers were into designing EVERYTHING.

Alex, her best friend, advisor, not to mention first cousin, who ages ago had "loaned" her three hundred bucks toward FIT, was the one who'd opened her eyes to the ENORMOUS importance and influence of those at the top in the fashion business.

"The most important designers today aren't those who just 'dress' people," Alex had said deprecatingly, "but those who affect the way people live, think, behave. Who d'you suppose, Ginny, put all those Monday-to-Friday pen-pushers into cowboy gear on weekends?"

"Who?"

"Ralph Lauren, of course, changing the look of America."

He'd shown her a clipping from the *Wall Street Journal*, which stated that Ralph Lauren's after-tax income was now about thirty million dollars a year and climbing; that Lauren was a revolutionary—"like another little man, Napoleon, five feet nothing without his built-up heels," Alex said, "changing not only fashion, but home furnishings, house, car, and garden design, fragrance, even the shape of bagels."

Calvin Klein was another Alex example: "Klein never has to ask the price of anything." It was one of Ginny's favorite Alex expressions, especially the way he said it, with a thrilling mix of cynicism, envy and approval.

No, Klein didn't even have to ask the price of a Georgia O'Keeffe, her favorite artist at the moment. Would Calvin ever know or, better still, care that they shared a love for Southwestern art?

Ginny looked at her watch. This was turning into a fiasco. She leaned forward anxiously. "Is there any other way you can go? To get out of this traffic?"

The driver growled something unintelligible, and for the first time Ginny realized he was wearing a turban. Just her luck to get a Sikh off the boat from India.

Now she was getting worried about the taxi meter. She'd estimated it wouldn't cost a cent more than twenty bucks from Queens to Bryant Park, where for the first time some of the New York shows were being held in a huge tent pitched beside the New York Public Library. Every time she glanced away for a second, she could swear the meter shot up another dollar.

Although he didn't know it, Alex was the one who'd decided her to take the plunge and try to crash the Klein show today, because he'd told her he was going to be there. A tad condescendingly, she thought, he'd promised to tell her "all about it." Was he in for a big surprise.

"What you wear says a lot about who you are—or want to be—and so does the way you arrive wearing it. Even Grace Kelly had to be taught how to emerge 'flawlessly' (Ginny loved that word) from car or carriage." She had never forgotten Alex telling her that. It was the reason that today, a walking fashion statement, she'd splurged on a cab.

Thank God for Alex. He'd always been her biggest booster, even when she thought she might have gone too far. "Pushing the envelope"—that's how he described her most daring designs—although he didn't hesitate to be a severe critic, too.

A reefer coat she'd made that terrible summer in Boston, out of a new bath towel, had received one of his more scathing comments, and not just because he knew she'd got into such trouble at home. Her mother had told her, with an almost bare linen closet, if she wanted to take a shower in the future, she'd have to dry herself with the coat!

Her father didn't like Alex. Even if they didn't see him for weeks and sometimes, to her despair, months, every time Alex called to say he was in the vicinity, her father made the same cracks. "He's too smooth for his own good" or "He's always on to something," accompanied by a sour expression which spoke volumes, despite the fact that Alex was the only child of his beloved sister, Ginny's Aunt Lil.

That was where part of the problem lay, for Lil, or Lillian, as her father always called his sister, had worked for the Walker School in its early days in California. When it started to move around the country she'd quit, saying she couldn't uproot with a young son to take care of. Her father had apparently always blamed Alex for losing his sister's services, which just showed what a cockeyed way he had of looking at things.

It was peculiar and cruel, Ginny thought, considering what a sad early life Alex had had, having lost his father in a car crash when he was only two or three.

Years ago, one wonderful summer when they'd just arrived in Denver, Alex had arrived in a red sports car, all grown up, tall, dark and handsome, there to "help out" at the Walker School himself. At least that's how Ginny dimly remembered her father describing it. Far more clearly, she remembered their disagreements over "the content and substance of the courses" and one morning she'd woken up to find Alex gone. She'd been brokenhearted, but it was only the first of many rumpuses between her father and his nephew, and after a while things calmed down and, thank God, Alex would once again pop back into their lives. As far as Ginny was concerned, it always seemed just in time to guide her in the right direction.

Without Alex's input, for instance, she wouldn't have gone so quietly to business school. Both her parents knew that.

They'd been sitting round the dining table in Queens that fall of '91, still surrounded by unpacked boxes, in their usual state of just-arrived chaos when, to her father's irritation, Alex had turned up.

The touchy subject of Her Future had arisen, and Alex, who knew all about it from Aunt Lil, jumped into the fray with "having a business degree can be a wonderful insurance, Ginny, no matter what career path you finally take."

He'd winked to take the sting out of his words and later, helping her with the washing up, he'd whispered, "give yourself some time, Gin. Go to the blankety blank business school, get your degree—you know you're the little Einstein in the family. Then you can tell the parents to stay out of your life, you've done what they wanted you to do, now it's your move . . . you can stick it to 'em."

The moment she'd heard it from him, business school had begun to make sense, and she'd said so. Had her father been appreciative? Of course not. He'd been furious that it was Alex, not he, who'd changed her mind. You didn't need to be a brain surgeon to understand why.

Jealousy. It was all about jealousy—for lots of reasons, many of them to do with her. Although she knew it drove her father—and to a lesser extent, her mother—wild, why did she sing Alex's praises and quote him so constantly? It was easy to answer.

Who had taught her to swim, to dive, to ride a bike, to catch a butterfly, to dry her tears when she didn't make the square-dance team (and then make her realize knowing how to cha cha cha was much more cool)? Alex, of course, not her father and not her mother either.

She'd figured it out a long time ago, reading a book about the formative years—*From Childhood to Puberty*. It was sheer luck that hers had mostly been lived in California with Alex close by.

While her mother went to work and her father was, as she grew up to accept, "busy behind closed doors, not to be disturbed, writing, studying, working on a new course," it was Alex who'd shown her how to turn ordinary days into adventures, who'd introduced her to a world seen through his especially sophisticated eyes.

Ginny didn't exactly know what Alex did in what he called the Wall Street trenches. Whatever it was, since her eyes had been opened in Denver to the true worth of the Walker School, in her opinion he was infinitely more qualified to give and sell advice than her father.

Alex's own financial situation, as he was the first to admit with a Paul Newman shrug, swung like a pendulum from rags to riches, riches to rags, but at least when he did make a mint, he'd told her, he didn't need the services of the good old U.S. mail. Of course, it was a dig at her father, but she didn't blame him for that.

The meter was twenty-five cents away from dollar number fifteen, but at last the traffic was moving; in fact, the cab was zipping fast through the tunnel.

"I can't make a U-turn, miss. D'you want me to drop you on the corner of Fifth and Forty-second or go up to Sixth and come down?"

Now he was telling her. But how could a Sikh taxi driver know how essential it was that she arrive exactly at the Bryant Park entrance and not have to burrow through the garrisons of gawkers always surrounding entrances and exits at fashionable events.

Ginny looked at the meter, then at her watch. Her timing was perfect. Not too early. Not too late. Although her half-boots were killing her (maybe that's what Elsa's "dressed to kill" compliment really meant), she decided she could always limp to tonight's class at FIT. The boots (bought by her mother in a Chanel sale) needed breaking in anyway.

"Go up to Sixth and come down."

No backpack today. She'd read that Anna Wintour, the unutterably chic editor of *Vogue*, never carried a purse, but she was never going to be that confident. Money, powder and a lip pencil were essential. As she didn't want to spoil the line of her black wool wraparound coat by adding a pocket to carry those vital impedimenta, she'd "borrowed" her mother's evening bag—black, unshiny moire, so it didn't shout "P.M."

As the taxi waited behind an idling Mercedes, Ginny settled the outrageous fare (twenty-four dollars plus three dollars tip) before it finally pulled up exactly at the entrance to the fashion tent.

Despite a hiss and a glare from the turbaned one, she took her time getting out, placing first one long, sheer-stockinged leg firmly on the pavement, then the other, bending her torso slightly forward, head held high, slightly smiling but—unnoticed, she hoped—gripping the taxi seat like death to propel herself out of the cab with one graceful movement, without leaving the coat behind.

It wasn't easy, but as usual Alex was right about how posture and grace always attract attention. Her arrival was marked by a few flashbulbs going off and she knew without looking left or right that the gawkers were wondering who she was. (So, in a funny sort of way, was she, knowing that in a few moments she intended to use the name of someone she'd never set eyes on.) She'd never been photographed arriving anywhere before, unless you counted the wedding of her mother's close friend, Alice Turner. She certainly didn't.

She approached the newly carpeted (already dusty) steps with the same slight smile as another photographer flashed, and a perfect candidate for Charivari, in grubby leather jacket and sloppy jeans, murmured, "Sorry, could you give me your name?"

It was a great moment, but she blew it, saying too hurriedly over her shoulder, "Ginny Walker." Even to her, it sounded like "gin and water." Too late she realized she should have practiced using the name of the French fashion editor, her passport into the show.

It was already ten minutes past showtime, yet she was amazed—and horrified—to find hordes of people, as many men as women, of every age, color and fashion peculiarity, pushing, shoving, forcing her to rush along with them down a wide entrance hall, lined with booths offering free Evian, free newspapers and even hair-color forecasts from Clairol.

It was Armageddon. Even if she wanted to linger, to soak up every molecule of her first New York fashion show, it was impossible. If she stopped short, she was sure everyone would trample her into the floor.

It wasn't at all what she'd expected. There was no way anyone could see what anyone else was wearing, let alone show off any fashion style of one's own. There was no way she could find Alex to see his startled admiration at the way she looked.

Figures of speech came to mind: a pride of lions . . . a gaggle of geese . . . more like a herd of elephants trampling wildly on as they did in that wonderful old movie *Elephant Walk*. In common with Alex she was mad about old movies. They were so inspirational.

"Move . . . show your tickets . . . show your tickets . . . move!" bellowed tough-looking guards.

Buyers, editors, hip and chic nobodys like herself were waving little green tickets, except she didn't have a little green ticket. She was acid-green with envy, but not deterred. Heart-skipping adrenaline pushed her forward. Nobody seemed to be taking the green tickets, which added to her up-yours optimism.

A strong bebop beat of music started up from behind a huge white wall at the end of the hall, the magic wall which stood between the charging elephants and the arena and runway where the action was obviously about to begin.

Somehow she'd ended up sandwiched between an oversized black man—he had to be at least six foot six—wearing an odd cocoon-shaped cloak and an older woman with hair so sleek and close to her head it reminded Ginny of her old labrador who'd died in Boston.

It was as if they were glued together. They all made a frantic rush for the opening in the white wall. The guard stationed there obviously knew her companions, because as she copied them, waving her arms about, pantomiming important lateness, he ushered them inside to darkness.

"This way, Miss mumble mumble . . . Mr. mumble mumble." To Ginny's frustration she couldn't hear the names, but both haughtily followed the guard's pointing finger, without a care in the world. They were "known"; they took it for granted good seats, perhaps the best seats, were waiting for them in the packed-from-floor-to-rafters huge tent.

The guard put up his hand like some prison warden as Ginny attempted to follow them, putting on her best bored, superior expression. Before he could ask her for anything, let alone a little green ticket, she peered bleakly over the audience at an imaginary seat assignment.

She couldn't believe her luck. With a scream of excitement, she spotted Alex across the runway, talking animatedly to a man as assured-looking as himself.

"Alex, Alex," she yelled, but of course in the din there was no way he could hear her.

"Ticket, seat number."

Ginny looked in her mother's moire purse in a bored, disgusted way. Then, well rehearsed in Queens, lifted her hand dismissively, as if green tickets were totally unimportant, saying in a charming French accent, "I'm Elise Marathaux, from French *Elle*."

The guard looked, if possible, more bored and disgusted than she did. "You'll have to go back to the front. I don't have the checklist here, miss. You saw the sign. Check at the desk first if you don't have a ticket."

"But this is im-poss-ee-ble! The crowds . . . it is im-poss-ee-ble," she said again, in impeccable pigeon French. "I am Elise Marathaux." She pointed to Alex. "There is my art director."

There was a hiss from behind and a heavy, henna-streaked woman cut in front of her. "Annie Jourdan," she said, handing the guard a green ticket. "*Elle* magazine."

Ginny swallowed hard. Could she die now, please, and go straight to heaven?

The guard looked at the ticket; looked at Ginny, then at Madame

Henna. "Is French *Elle* in your row?" He made it sound like 'ell. He in-dicated Ginny. "She's from your French crowd."

Heavy henna looked at her in distaste. "Who are you?"

With a deep breath, trying one more time, "Elise Marathaux."

"No, you're not. She's already here . . . down there." She glared at Ginny as she pointed an accusing finger. "This isn't the first time people have tried this." She turned to the guard. "Check her ID. Call Security. It's time you caught on to these imposters . . ."

There was a blast of music as a spotlight illuminated a model step-ping onto the runway. To Ginny she might as well have been on the moon.

Heavy henna looked torn between wanting to take her seat and making sure Ginny was put on death row. Calvin Klein won. She walked in the direction of her row, shouting over her shoulder to the guard, "See you take care of her."

Like a wannabe Elise Marathaux, Ginny pointed again to Alex. "That's my cousin. I'm sure he's saving my seat for me."

"I thought you said he's your art director."

A miracle occurred. Alex looked up and straight in Ginny's direc-tion.

She waved frantically, shouting again, "Alex, Alex."

He saw her, but what did he do?

He gave her a perfunctory wave, then looked back at the runway, in-dicating with his body language a total lack of interest.

She was stunned, her desire to see the show wiped out. Alex had turned his back on her. She couldn't remember feeling more lost, more bereft. Tears welled up in her eyes. Now, she wasn't acting.

"Sorry, miss. You can't come in without a seat number. See for your-self, there isn't one left in the entire place."

The guard must have seen the look of imminent suicide on her face. He became human, almost fatherly. Although she no longer cared about anything, he said, "You won't see much, but you can stand here in the doorway if you like."

He was right. She couldn't see anything or anyone, and no one, thank God, could see her, as deflated as an overcooked soufflé. At least he wasn't calling for Security to lock her up.

She mumbled her thanks as he walked away.

She had played hooky from business school for nothing. It reminded her of that terrible day in Dallas when despite all her efforts to stand out in a crowd, she'd failed to be discovered either by Monsieur Robespier or by MTV.

This was far worse. Her best friend, her longtime confidant, her own cousin, had not only neglected to come to her aid, he had publicly spurned her. Blood thicker than water? She would never feel the same about Alex again, she was sure.

"If I tell you the stock market will likely go higher this year, but also higher volatility can be expected and maybe a two hundred fifty to six hundred correction during the summer, what would you say are the reasons for the wider price swings?"

The Wall Street forecaster, who came to lecture to the business class at Pace University every month, looked around the room with his customary lack of enthusiasm.

Ginny put her hand up. "More money is pouring into the market, but investors are nervous due to growing signs of economic weakness."

There were the usual hostile currents blowing around her, but she lifted her chin and plunged on, realizing as she spoke that despite attempts to correct it, there was still a residue of her father's pompous, professorial tone in her voice. Tough luck. "The fat profits realized from currency conversions by multinational companies like Svank Securities, carried out when the dollar's value was declining, will dry up as the dollar's value rises."

"Exactly, Ms. Walker."

It was as easy as raising a hem to her. She didn't care two cents that her grasp of business would never win her any popularity contests among the other would-be tycoons, people whom she hoped—after graduation—never to see again.

FIT was so different from Pace. At FIT everyone was so into getting his own construction right, no one thought about one-upmanship—certainly not at evening class anyway. Perhaps it was different being a full-time day student, when everyone had a chance to do real design, when the best got shown at a fancy annual event, attended by retailers and the fashion press. Ginny tried not to think about it.

She was working around the clock to get her finance degree locked up as soon as possible. She was getting there faster than even she'd expected, but oh, she was so tired. At Bloomie's last weekend she'd told a customer who couldn't read the price on a particularly hideous lamp that it was far too expensive and she shouldn't consider buying it. Luckily she'd thought Ginny was joking and laughed her head off, but she didn't buy the lamp and Ginny shuddered to think of her supervisor ever hearing about it.

Esme Jee, also in lamps, had become a good friend, making up for the loss of Toby in Dallas, whom she still missed from time to time. Esme and she were drawn together by a similar financial/parental predicament. Like Ginny, Esme still lived at home, but at least home was in Chinatown, which Ginny thought had to be incredibly fascinating, although Esme denied it. Because of her twenty-hour work days and nights, so far she hadn't even been able to visit Esme or her cheongsams, which apparently were passed on from generation to generation, some with real gold thread. Imagine.

Esme wanted to study art history and maybe teach or write, but her parents, like Ginny's, insisted she go to business school. At least Esme's father only wanted her to become an accountant. Ginny's still had this half-baked idea that on graduation she might start a jolly little Walker School of her own, "aimed at the young market," while her mother thought she should become a model! Incredible how obtuse parents could be.

Something stung Ginny's cheek. A paper dart landed on her lap.

She glanced with supreme indifference across the aisle. Just as she'd thought. Robb Sinclair was sitting there with a self-satisfied smirk, the one he often wore above his silly tuft of fair beard, which never seemed to sprout more than a handful of hairs.

Ginny had given him some Miracle-Gro for Christmas. He'd given her a packet of ghastly false talons in return, which was fair enough. Since beginning her heavy-duty time at the Space Asylum, as Pace University was called by some of its inmates, she'd taken to biting her nails.

There was something different about Sinclair today, but she couldn't put her finger on what it was and she certainly wasn't going to give him the satisfaction of glancing at him again.

Out of the thirteen guys and nine lumpy girls in her class, Robb Sinclair, who to his credit also wore an earring in his left ear, was the only one who halfway measured up to her criteria for passable.

As she had always done on landing anywhere in the nation, she had taken her time to make a critical survey in both the looks and brains departments of her new colleagues. The results had been dismal. Ginny had quickly come to the sorry conclusion there was no chance of a kindred spirit girlfriend among the females, let alone any love interest among the males.

Because she was tall—yes, Mother, I know that's an incredible advantage in the world of brain-dead models—she usually ended up dating Jolly Green Giants, the kind of men whose gray matter seemed centered in their shoulders. Or alternatively who were so square, there was no way they could fit into, yes, she'd admit it, her demanding circle.

In one of his "cute" tailor-made courses for those five feet or under ("How to Overcome that Disadvantage"), her father quoted from a medical survey that in the job market tall people generally got chosen over short people, but for what jobs? House painter? Tree doctor? It hadn't been her experience that the taller the man, the more intelligent or certainly the more exciting. To be fair, she knew most guys thought she was "too intense, too ambitious," both commendable traits in her opinion.

Over the months Sinclair was the only one to redeem himself by showing he had a mad sense of humor and some understanding of what she was all about. Yesterday he'd even commented that she was wearing kohl around her eyes. He'd recognized it because his mother worked in a beauty shop and was into "experimentation," whatever that meant.

As the lecture ended and she strolled out, Robb grabbed her arm in the hall. Her uninterested stare collapsed when she looked at him.

"What d'you think?"

She clapped her hand over her mouth to stop screaming with laughter. Robb Sinclair was wearing kohl, badly applied but still unmistakably ringing both his eyes. He winked and grinned at the same time, which she had to admit was an attractive combination. Grudgingly, she told him she admired his guts for trying something different.

"D'you want to have a coffee, a drink?"

Why not? She had several hours of studying to do at home, but she felt jaded, worn out. Putting it off for half an hour wouldn't jeopardize her business future.

"Okay."

Maybe this would lead to a real date. Her problem was, she didn't know whether she wanted it or not. There had to be someone out there, someone more than the halfway passable Robb Sinclairs of the world, guys who, if they didn't have Alex's knowledge and sophisticated looks, at least acted more like her role-model cousin, despite his many faults.

She had been trying to concentrate on Alex's faults because weeks and weeks had passed without a word from him, not one word since the Klein debacle. His phone didn't answer and she certainly wasn't going to ask her parents if they knew where he'd gone.

Ginny was used to his coming and going like the Scarlet Pimpernel, but this time she was really hurt. She'd started to act like the other Scarlett, the "I'll-think-about-it-tomorrow" O'Hara one, as far as her cousin was concerned.

But think of the devil (as she did every day), who should be waiting outside Pace when she sauntered forth with Sinclair? It was Alex Rossiter himself, standing beside the snazziest car she'd ever seen, long and pointed, more like a missile than an automobile, in a wonderful shade of sad green, the color of the moors where Laurence Olivier agonized over Merle Oberon in *Wuthering Heights*.

In one way she wasn't sorry that Sinclair was beside her; in another she was acutely embarrassed that Alex should see her accompanied by a guy wearing definitely non-chic eyewear. In broad daylight Sinclair looked like a freak.

"Hi, Ginny." Alex opened the car door as if he were her regular chauffeur. "Hop in. I've come to run you home."

Sinclair, alas, didn't know it, but there was no contest.

"Sorry, Robb, some other time. This is my cousin from . . . from out of town," Ginny mumbled. "I don't get to see him very often."

He winked and grinned at the same time again, but this time it wasn't attractive, and she noticed that when he turned abruptly away, he slouched as he moved down the street.

Even though the passenger door was open and Alex had already moved in to take the wheel, Ginny hovered on the sidewalk, rather than throw herself onto the seat as, alas, she knew she usually would have done. She bent down to give Alex the stare Sinclair said she was famous for in class, the one which terrified the inmates, although they'd never admit it. It didn't terrify her cousin. He reached over and pulled her down.

"Get in before I get a ticket."

She tumbled in, glad she had on a new skirt she'd made up from some ginger-colored leather Esme's family didn't want her to wear. It went beautifully with her chestnut hair, but she hadn't yet worked out the color scheme for the jacket.

As he zoomed them uptown, with no explanation for his long absence or apology for anything, Alex started snapping questions at her like a machine gun.

"Why didn't you tell me you were going to the Klein show?

"Why were you so late?

"If you'd arrived ten minutes earlier, I'd have taken you to one of the best seats in the house.

"Why are your priorities always so mixed up? Why on earth didn't you tell me you wanted to go?"

She was so taken aback by his onslaught, she couldn't think of a thing to say.

As they crossed over to Madison Avenue and passed Fifty-seventh Street and the exit for the Queensboro Bridge, Ginny finally asked, "Where are we going?"

"You'll see."

So now he was treating her like a ten-year-old. All right, Mr. Rossiter, she knew how to give the cold-shoulder treatment, too.

Alex checked the one-of-a-kind missile into what she considered to be a one-of-a-kind garage, charging for a few hours what would be a week's house rent in Queens.

Clutching her by the arm as if she were an escaped fugitive, Alex literally marched her a block or two down Fifth Avenue into a classy hotel called the Sherry something.

In the ultra hushed and plushed lobby (with two, not one, Versailles-type chandeliers), there was a large, very closed-looking door with *Private Club* engraved on a gold plate, beneath what she first thought was the double intertwined C of the Chanel logo. It wasn't a C. It was a large, double intertwined D.

The door couldn't have looked more closed, with "keep out" in invisible ink written all over it, but Alex opened it as casually as if it were his own front door. Immediately before them was a luscious-looking, deep pile, dark purple carpeted stairway. They descended down, down, down to arrive in another lobby with a beautiful antique porter's desk where Alex casually scribbled his name in a leatherbound visitors' book.

"Is this called the Two D's?" she whispered, to show him how observant she was.

No, she learned, this strictly private, subterranean club was called Doubles, buried so far beneath Fifth Avenue and East Fifty-ninth Street that not even the most superintelligent beaver would be able to find it.

It was so velvety and plumped-up cushiony, it was like being encased in a jewel box from Tiffany's, which was only two blocks away, but at street level, of course.

It was also the kind of place where her mother would immediately start looking for the fire exit. There was no sense of time or place here, no noise, no trace of climate, of day or night.

Ginny sat stiffly on the edge of a fat cushioned banquette, waiting for something momentous to happen, still trying to hold back her forgiveness. The problem was, now she wasn't altogether sure who was in the right and who was in the wrong. At that moment the most delicious-looking piña colada appeared before her.

Where was all this glamorous treatment leading? As she took a sip she decided to push her suspicions aside. There was, after all, something deliriously sinful about drinking the most exquisite drink in living memory at barely five o'clock in the afternoon. And to think that less than thirty minutes ago the extent of her expectations had been a cup of coffee or a glass of jug wine with Robb Sinclair.

"Sorry I haven't been in touch," Alex said abruptly. "Some urgent business came up in Europe—I had to fly to Switzerland right after the Klein show."

If this was Alex doing penance she decided she'd put up with his offhand behavior and bad moods—providing they didn't crop up too often. To help give the ugly, suspicious side of her nature a slight concussion she took another swig of the piña.

She waited. Silence, then, swinging a carefree arm around her space on the banquette, Alex continued, "I'm so proud of you, Ginny. I hear you're on the way to becoming the youngest person at Pace ever to get a B.A. in finance—and in record time. Congratulations!"

As she had already been told this was probably so, she nodded with what she hoped was humility, laughing giddily the next second when Alex added, "with your father taking full credit, of course."

"Of course."

The piña colada couldn't drown out her real problem, which was that once again, in no time at all, Alex was mesmerizing her. She had never met anyone remotely like him, who could make her laugh hysterically one minute and the next, trigger her into a serious debate on the Dalai Lama. With her limited social circle she didn't suppose she ever would.

Alcohol sometimes made her father maudlin, melancholy; and just occasionally it had that effect on her. Before the tears she felt lurking plopped into her regal glass, Alex gave her a squeeze and to her surprise said, "After working your guts out, you deserve something special. Name your desire . . . I've just closed on a big deal, so the sky's the limit."

For a minute she had lockjaw, then, thank God, remembering her parlous state, came to her senses. "Retail math, merchandising planning and gross margins." She couldn't believe she'd said it.

Alex looked put out. "What are you talking about? I thought you'd say a trip to Paris, an Hermès bag, a . . . a . . . oh, I don't know, young women are a strange breed."

"It's some courses I long to take at FIT . . ."

"But you're already taking courses there and turning into a salesgirl on weekends to pay for them . . ." The way he said "turning into a sales-girl" was not complimentary.

She wasn't deterred. Seeing a shining light at the end of a long, dark tunnel, Ginny began to develop a speech in her head on how incredibly valuable she'd discovered FIT to be and how terrified she was she wouldn't be able to afford to go there much longer without some extra financial help.

Alex removed his arm and sank back into the cushions. "You know your parents think I influence you too much, don't you, Gin?" He could change the subject faster than a cloud covered the sun.

"Well, you do influence me. What's wrong with that? They should be thrilled I have you as a role model and not some creep who doesn't know a . . . a . . . Hockney from a . . . a . . ."

"Hallmark," he supplied instantly. Then, "Hold it. Hold it right there." He took a camera from his pocket.

"Why?"

"I love that look of yours." He snapped away. "It's the bored, aloof countenance of a cheetah."

"Oh, Alex, I do love you."

She did, too. Pretense and poses hadn't a chance. Her parents were right. He did influence her too much and she did care for him too much. It had always been like that, ever since in her distant memory she remembered first meeting him when he came to visit with his mother, her father's clever sister. How old had she been? About four, so he must have been fourteen or fifteen, thrilling her even then with his devilish smile and sophistication. If only he wasn't her cousin . . .

"And I love you, too, cheetah, but . . ." His voice was unusually serious. "I worry about you. You're brainy, creative, as cute as a button, but just when you should be having the most fun, you're all work and no play. You're too choosy."

She was so shocked by this switch in direction, she took a long sip of the delicious drink to prepare for the worst.

"It's not altogether your fault. Graham and Virginia have brought you up to look down your nose too much, to be too picky. For instance, why don't you go out with this Robb character you told me about? You might find he has hidden depths."

She'd forgotten she'd told Alex about the creep, forgotten she'd embellished Sinclair's winks and hanging around to make it sound as if she was the much sought after prey of a Tom Cruise look-alike, tycoon-in-the-making kind of character. How embarrassing.

In a little-girl voice she despised, she said, "I thought I told you he's already tied up." She couldn't resist adding, "or down, if you ask me. He wanted to break it off, but . . ." she paused, trying to think how a Tom Cruise tycoon-type personality would handle a three-way situation. It came out in a rush. "He's engaged to the daughter of some trillionaire who's going to set him up in business and I wouldn't let him do . . ."

She couldn't finish the sentence, because Alex was laughing so hard. She tried not to laugh herself, and instead began to fume. "Stop it, Alex. Stop making fun of me. I'm not picky; I'm not choosy."

Alex poked her in the ribs. "What's the long face for? Wasn't that Robb—the Tom Cruise look-alike—with you, coming out of class?"

"I haven't the slightest idea."

"The fair Tom Cruise, the one trying to grow a beard for his next part? The one with the brass ring in his ear?"

Now she was half crying, half screaming with laughter. Alex put a light hand across her mouth. "Shush, you'll get us both thrown out of here. Time to get down to business."

The cloud was back across the sun. She was right to be suspicious. Why was Alex, a Wall Street heavy, carrying a camera? Why had he turned into a shutterbug this afternoon? She tensed up. Now she was going to hear the real reason for Alex picking her up.

"This fashion design business is infecting your whole personality. I mean it's taken over your life." He looked at her reflectively. "I met a model the other day in Europe—in Düsseldorf, to be precise. She was home visiting her family."

"How cozy." She hoped he got the lack of enthusiasm in her voice. She leaned forward as his arm encircled her space again.

"It was Claudia Schiffer on her home turf." Alex gave the laugh she usually adored, short, slightly mocking at the absurdity of life. "She was discovered dancing in a Düsseldorf disco, you know. She's absolutely gorgeous."

"How cozy," she said again, immediately feeling foolish.

Despite the "your-parents-worry-I-influence-you-too-much" garbage, was it possible Alex was acting as an emissary of her mother in bringing her to his jewel box of a club?

"Remember when I told you once what constitutes the real importance, influence, of a top designer today?" He wasn't expecting an answer. "Well, Ginny, there's a new era of influence emerging, my little duckling . . ."

She was too depressed to remind him she'd looked like a bored cheetah half a glass of piña colada ago.

"The supermodels, they're beginning to replace movie stars as icons, influences, and they're earning incredible bucks, huge bucks because"—another Alex laugh—"they are huge; they're literally titans of beauty. Schiffer told me she's five eleven, and Christy Turlington and Cindy Crawford—"

"She's much shorter and has a mole," Ginny interrupted sulkily.

"And thanks God for it every night. How much d'you think these beanstalks are getting for a sitting?"

"A sitting?"

"A photo shoot."

"I haven't a clue." Couldn't her superperceptive cousin realize her anger was so heavy, it was hanging in the Doubles air like a bomb waiting to explode?

Of course he realized, but he was so secure he made matters worse. He chucked her under the chin.

"Don't do that!"

"D'you know why I did it?"

No answer.

"You have a dream of a chin, a pointy little chin which makes you—"

"Pretty!" she snarled out the word, having heard her mother say it more times than she could count and now certain where her faithless cousin was headed.

She had been too carefully raised to watch for behavioral clues, slip-ups in speech, any kind of evidence of a moving day around the corner, not to be able to sniff "trouble," even from her once-beloved A.

"No, you're not pretty," he went on as smooth as silk, "well, not conventionally so, but you have a cheeky urchin look, emphasized by that pointy chin of yours, which, as I've explained to your perceptive mama, might make you eminently photographable."

The bomb exploded. "I can't believe it; I can't believe that you're actually talking about me becoming a model." Ginny took a good slug of her drink. "For the one and only time in my life I agree with my father. I'd rather do anything, serve hamburgers at McDonald's, spray scent at Bloomingdale's or make selling lamps there my lifelong career, than strut along a runway. It's brainless, it's mindless. I want to use my brain, not my body. I thought you understood I want to be a designer."

The tears were out in the open, one fast after the other down her cheeks. She no longer cared.

Apparently neither did Alex. He leaned back, as cool and as unperturbed, Ginny thought, as Sam Shepard as Chuck Yeager in *The Right Stuff*. For the first time she was tempted to slap him across the face, hard.

"How d'you plan to go about that?"

Playing for time to think of an answer that would finish the discussion, Ginny took another long sip and made a disgusting slurping sound as she dredged up what was left at the bottom of the glass.

Alex beckoned and another piña colada appeared.

Ginny protested, but he ignored her, repeating the question. "How do you intend to become a designer?"

She was ready. Well, almost. "I'll start as a design assistant, a gofer, a dupe maker, a fitter, anything with one of the fashion greats."

Alex raised an eyebrow sardonically. "Who d'you have in mind?"

Before she could start on the list, Alex put his arm around her, not just the banquette, and because it was so unusual, she wanted to burst into tears and have him kiss every tear away. Instead, she shut up like a tortoise and sort of withdrew her head (and pointy chin) into his shoulder.

"Listen to me for a minute?"

She brought out her tortoise, duckling, cheetah head to nod yes.

"After meeting Fräulein Schiffer I looked at the economics of what's happening to lucky girls like her. I did some research on the kind of money they're making. I tell you it shocked the pants off me. I had no idea! These top girls are very young, under or just over twenty, and they're making millions. I told your mother she's both right . . ."

Within his arm, he felt her stiffen, then relax again as he continued, ". . . and wrong. I don't agree at all that you should ever step on a runway—or at least not until you've begun to earn hundreds of thousands of dollars and the top designers are begging for you."

She was raging again, but said nothing.

"She understands that you want to be a designer and she thinks one day you will be—and a successful one, too."

His words startled her so much, she sat upright. Mother thought she could be a successful designer? Since when?

"I think so, too, but you're going to need capital, lots of capital. Ideas alone do not a successful designer make. Even a talent like Carolyne Roehm never made it, despite having so many of her then-husband's millions behind her."

She was beginning to feel less betrayed and took a furtive sip of colada number two. It was twice as good as the first. She wanted to purr or quack or make some kind of cheerful cheetah sound.

"Mother has a problem," she said slowly. "She reads too many romantic novels. She thinks once I'm up there strutting my stuff, some multi-zillionaire will come along and sweep me away to never-never land."

Alex said earnestly, "It's not on the runway you'll meet Mr. Zillionaire—" He broke off as a stunning pale brunette in a dark red, beautifully cut velvet suit glided across the floor of the still empty restaurant to a far dark corner. She was followed by a heavyset, equally pale man.

Night people, Ginny thought with awe, glamorous, gorgeous people who are super-pale because they never see the sun and only appear after dark.

As Alex continued to stare after them, Ginny said, "Wow! What a beauty. Who is she? She looks like a prima ballerina . . ."

Alex grinned. "Prima donna's more like it. That, my dear, is Dolores Relato Peet, out of money, but not out of luck."

Ginny stared enviously at the couple, now engrossed in each other. "What d'you mean?"

"She was about to be sued earlier this year for not paying her bills, said she was going to declare bankruptcy, but then Quentin Peet's son came to the rescue . . ."

"*The* Quentin Peet?"

"One and the same. I heard somewhere Peet senior took a very dim view of his son making an honest woman of the divine Dolores. I'm not surprised, seeing what's going on over there . . ."

"You mean that's not Mr. Peet's son she's with?"

"No, my dear, it's not. Now look at me." Alex tilted her chin in his direction. "I repeat, you don't belong on the runway. As I've pointed out to Aunt V., to your mother, it's as a model, like Schiffer, in magazines, the top magazines, that you belong. Your mother's right, you do have model potential, taller than average, a great bod—"

Ginny wasn't mollified. "I'm an ectomorph as opposed to a rounded endomorph. For months mother's been watching every forkful of food I put in my mouth . . ."

"Good for her." Alex laughed. "To go on, you have natural animal grace and . . ." This time when he chucked her under the chin she didn't object, "an adorable pointy chin."

She loved the way he was describing her, but where was it leading? He probably thought she was still angry when she didn't answer. It wouldn't hurt.

"Seriously, Gin, you may have the kind of looks that can put you up there with the big money-making girls. You may be able to make the kind of money you'll need to set up shop on Seventh Avenue. Then, with your business degree, you can cut it like it's never been cut before."

Was it the piña coladas? Dollar signs were dancing before her eyes and she could see a shining white salon with one huge sunflower decorating the reception area of Virginia Walker Fashion, Inc., or should it be Ginny Walker Fashion? V.W. wasn't bad either, except for its Virginia Woolf connotation, which to her related to the kind of floaty, flimsy, greenery, yellowy clothes she loathed.

"We won't know whether you have it or not until you sit before a professional camera, so first we have to find you a photographer, because so far a photographer hasn't found you. We have to get you a contact sheet to take to the top model agencies . . ."

It all sounded so easy, but somewhere behind the colada mist was still a modicum of common sense.

"I haven't the time," she moaned. "For these last exams I have to study harder than ever and still manage to get to FIT and Bloomingdale's . . ."

"Forget FIT and Bloomingdale's," Alex snapped. "You don't need FIT now, and perhaps, with your kind of creativity, you never will. You hire people to do that kind of dog's work."

What did he know?

Alex stood up. The discussion was over. For a second he hesitated, looking again in the direction of the corner where Quentin Peet's daughter-in-law was nuzzling the ear of somebody who apparently wasn't her husband.

Ginny stood waiting, hoping Alex would go over, so she could follow, be introduced and get a closer look at the woman's slinky suit.

No, he wasn't going. Alex took her elbow and guided her out into the vestibule, where still no one was manning the desk. Nobody came running after them with a bill, either.

"I want you to start experimenting with looks, hair, makeup, this weekend and I'll look into photographers." Alex appraised her. "How tall are you? Five eight, nine?"

"I'm not"—hiccup—"sure. About five eight, I think."

"I'd say you're a tad more, but in any case get into the habit of wearing three-inch heels or higher. In fact, that's what I'll buy you for being such a good girl. We'll go shopping on Saturday."

Goodbye Bloomingdale's. Esme's sweet face came to mind. It was quickly blotted out by Claudia Schiffer's.

As they climbed the staircase to the real world, Alex went on, "I want you to burn every pair of sneakers you own . . ." He heard her gasp and turned around to give her his most wicked smile. "That is, until you're regularly on the cover of *Vogue*. Then you can wear them to a ball for all I care. Then, but only then, like Schiffer, you can wear what you like."

CHAPTER THREE

539 EAST 55TH STREET, NEW YORK CITY

"Ginny, it's for you."

This was embarrassing. She had only been in this lovely woman's unlovely apartment for about forty-five minutes. Her suitcase was not yet unpacked, her sewing machine was still cluttering up the tiny hall, and already she was monopolizing the telephone.

"Hello?"

"Hi, Ginny, it's me, Es . . . *crackle* . . . *crackle* . . . How are you?"

"Who? Sorry, the line is terrible."

"Esme . . . *crackle* . . . *crackle* . . . Jee."

Ginny didn't want to say she couldn't hear her because then she would ring again. "I'll call you back." She longed to hang up and go down to the street, where she knew there was a pay phone.

"I'm on a cellular . . . *crackle*." The line went dead.

Esme had turned out to be a wonderful friend, but, Ginny had to admit, their relationship was now clouded by jealousy. Hers. Esme wasn't speaking to her family anymore. Rather, they were not speaking to her, because she'd escaped from Chinatown, literally out of her bedroom window, to move in with Ted something, a guy in real estate, loaded with money and, according to Esme, incredibly attractive.

Her family wouldn't have cared about her running away "to live in sin" if Ted had been Chinese, Esme had told Ginny, but he was Caucasian, and, worse, Jewish. They told her that unless she gave him up, they would consider they no longer had a daughter. It didn't seem to faze her. Although she wasn't sure she really loved Ted, apparently they had this extraordinary sexual thing, which had completely taken over her life.

Ginny hadn't met Ted yet, and she wasn't sure she wanted to, unless he had a best friend or a brother. She tried not to think about it, but every so often she asked herself why Esme and not me?

It took an hour for Esme to call back. By then Ginny's mother's old friend, Sophie Formere, aka "the salt-of-the-earth," had insisted on helping her carry her precious machine into the box of a second bedroom, one day to become famous, Alex predicted, as the "first Manhattan home of the celebrated model Ginny Walker." She had also unpacked her suitcase, which didn't take long because she didn't believe in accumulating clothes.

Instead, as an undiscovered (to date) fashion designer, she preferred to accumulate interesting fabrics, and her suitcase was full of bits and pieces. As her portfolio of designs, also in the suitcase, clearly showed, if the fabric "said something," however small the piece, there was always something she could use it for. She also collected assorted things other people might not view as accessories. Safety pins, for instance, which she was working with right now on an asymmetrical dinner dress.

Ginny went into a slight decline when the phone rang again at eight-forty. It was, of course, Esme, this time in a phone booth on the way to a party.

Brought up in a home that considered any calls after seven-thirty in the evening to be nuisance calls or ones delivering very bad news (or else!), Ginny knew she sounded sharp, although Mrs. Formere was still sweetness itself when she handed her the receiver.

"I've only just moved in. How did you know where to find me so soon? I was going to call you this week."

"I called your number in Queens, which, 'at the customer's request' "—Esme tried to imitate the operator's voice, without success— "redirected all calls to a 301 number. I spoke to your father, who told me where you were."

"What did he say?"

"That the Walker School of Advanced Learning is now based in Washington, D.C., so, as your modeling career is about to begin, your mother arranged for you to stay with an old friend, who's acting as chaperone."

Chaperone! She could die! Only Esme, bless her, could utter the word in this day and age without sneering or laughing her head off.

Alas, it was true. Her parents had just moved to Maryland, not D.C. (her father was still incapable of telling the truth about his real location), and Sophie Formere, God help her, was supposed to be her chaperone, as well as giving her a free roof over her head until she started to earn all the big bucks she kept hearing about.

It had taken months of on-and-off warfare, but her mother had finally caved in, believing, she told Ginny, that this time the Walker School was joining forces with another "learn-by-mail" outfit in Chevy Chase that promised long-term stability. Leaving Ginny behind had seemed impossible, until Sophie Formere's offer of guardianship allowed the umbilical cord to be cut.

"Hello? Are you still there?"

"Yes." Ginny lowered her voice. "It's a bit embarrassing, Esme. I'm staying with this friend of my mother's. I've only been here a couple of hours and already you've called twice. She's going to think I'm a phone hog."

Esme didn't get the hint. "I'll talk fast. I think I've found a photographer for you, someone my family knows really well. Ted and I bumped into him at a party over the weekend. He used to do paparazzi stuff, but now he's working regularly for magazines and big-time ad campaigns. He's just been asked to do a job for *Glamour* . . . they're looking for someone with a different look. I showed him that picture I took of you when you left Bloomie's and he—"

"What kind of look?" She could see herself in Mrs. Formere's hall mirror. Her hair looked tatty, her skin not at its best, her delightful pointy chin down, as opposed to up for optimism.

"Well . . ." Esme was a tactful girl. Ginny knew she probably wasn't going to tell her what *Glamour* was really looking for. They liked doing those "before" and "after" stories. Tonight, she was definitely in the "before" category.

"It's hard to describe over the phone. I said you'd call him and make an appointment. His name is Oz Tabori. He's Rumanian and he's definitely about to make it really big." Esme gave her his number and Ginny, relieved to get off the phone and move away from her reflection, went into the kitchen to make some coffee for Mrs. F.

There was no doubt her mother had chosen well. Sophie Formere was perfect for the chaperone role, a mother-hen type, who, clucking around, must have asked her a dozen times in the space of an hour, "Are you sure you have everything?"

Ginny expressed her joy and appreciation a dozen times back, inwardly groaning. There was no need for Mrs. F. to know that, in fact, she had nothing . . . at least nothing that she wanted. No man, no sex, no job, no real home.

Stop! No self-pity either, she told herself. If she hadn't become a successful, money-earning model, let alone a supermodel, in six months, no matter what anyone said (especially Mr. Alex Rossiter) she was going to forget the whole idea and comb Seventh Avenue for a job, any job, even sweeping up debris from the floor in a fashion house.

But if she had to stay with Sophie F. for six whole months, would she be able to resist cutting off the fringes she saw everywhere? Mrs. F. surely had to have a fringe fetish. They were on everything: lamps, sofas, antimacassars (a pale lavender one in the living room might make an interesting collar on a plain black dress). Her fingers were itching to get to the scissors.

It took ages to escape from talking about what the salt-of-the-earth described as "the good old days," way back when she worked as a fitter with Virginia in San Diego, days Ginny was pretty sure her mother wouldn't describe that way.

When Mrs. F. began to describe her present "very important" job, Ginny stood up.

"Please excuse me, Mrs. Formere . . ."

"Oh, do call me Sophie, dear."

"Er, Sophie, I must wash my hair. I'm seeing a lot of photographers tomorrow."

"Oh! I do hope there's enough hot water . . ." Fuss, fuss, rush, rush. Sophie was so kind, Ginny kept telling herself, but how on earth was she going to put up with it?

Alex was supposed to pick her up at nine sharp the next morning to take her downtown, where many of the hot photographers lived in a kind of exclusive commune.

Nine A.M. arrived and departed; so did nine-thirty, when Mrs. Formere—er, Sophie—still talking and smiling, went about her business with a gentle reminder to Ginny to double-lock the door when she went out to become the model of the decade.

At nine-forty someone phoned on Alex's behalf. "He's been called into an emergency meeting." The voice was so languid (and sexless), it took away any anxiety over the word "emergency."

"A photographer's agent will be calling you shortly, so don't leave the phone." Pause. "His name's Sam Swid . . ."

"Swid as in S-W-I-D?"

"Yep." Click.

By noon nobody had called; so, thanking God for Esme Jee, Ginny called the Wizard of Oz and spoke to an answering machine with such loud Heavy D background music, she could hardly hear the message. Just as she was about to hang up, the earsplitting sound stopped and a voice that sounded as if it belonged to a redwoods man with thick fatherly beard boomed over the line.

It was Oz himself.

He seemed to know who she was. "Come on down," he said, "about five-thirty, six. I should be through by then . . ."

As she was leaving in the late afternoon instead of the morning, she scribbled Sophie a note, in case her "chaperone" thought she'd been kidnapped. Sam Swid hadn't called. To Hades with him and all the other promise-breakers in the world.

After putting on and taking off everything in her wardrobe, she finally decided to wear a drop-dead two-piece white suit, made from a double-damask tablecloth she'd found on sale at Bloomingdale's. It was deceptively simple, definitely bosom enhancing—a necessity for her optimistic size A and narrow frame.

She couldn't afford it, but she took a cab because she wanted to arrive in as pristine a condition as possible, and already she was sweating her makeup off through nerves and an unexpected heat wave outside.

She didn't know how to get to Tribeca and there was no one around to ask. The problem was the taxi driver didn't know and didn't care to ask, either. She only found that out after being driven round and round in circles. So much for her perfect daily budget, carefully worked out with all the expertise of her finance degree. It was already used up by the time the driver discovered Oz's address. He screeched to a halt with a smile of triumph on his money-grabbing face as if he'd discovered the source of the Nile.

It was well after six. Would Oz still be home?

Ginny sighed. Of course, his studio would have to be on the top floor. She staggered up five flights of irregular stairs, massive blasts of Heavy D getting nearer.

Blinding light and deafening sound poured through a wide open door. She had arrived. After two or three blinks, she saw she was in a huge loft, white walls, white floors, whiter-than-white everything, probably making her double-damask look dingy.

At the far end, through tall, curtainless windows, she saw a dramatic panorama of docks, boats, cranes. New York Harbor? For a crazy minute she forgot where she was. The light was so bright, the white so dazzling, she had to put her hand over her eyes to scout the huge space for Oz or any sign of life.

It was there all right, in a far corner, where, their backs to her, a bunch of people were scrutinizing something laid out on a table.

Layouts? Polaroids? She knew little about the steps leading up to the finished product, the glossy, better-than-life picture in a magazine, the only kind Alex wanted her to consider.

She looked around. There were a couple of really sleazy pictures on one of the walls, nudes with tongues hanging out, just asking for it.

She was scared, could feel her heart thumping against the wired bra top of her jacket. She wished she was back safe among the fringes, waiting for Sam Swid's call.

There was a burst of laughter, so raucous it managed to be heard between drumbeats. A tall, thinner-than-a-rake guy with supernaturally pale skin and sleek jet hair held back with a comb, turned away from the table and spotted her. He was in black from top to toe, which made him look like a vampire. Ginny wondered if he was the famous photographer Steven Meisel, who only ever wore black. Did one photographer, who'd already made it, visit another, who was about to?

Somebody said, "Hel-looo, there. You must be . . ."

"Ginny Walker." She tried to sound confident.

Like a Martha Graham choreographed slow-motion ballet the group at the table turned, one by one, to look at the interloper. Now she could see why they'd been so engrossed. The long table was covered with food, mounds of food, technicolored shrimps and lobsters carelessly spilling out from giant clam shells, golden loaves and silver fishes, rich brown Japanese baskets (gorgeous) full of tactile, perfectly shaped vegetables and fruit. To photograph? To eat?

Tall and skinny ambled over, followed by a burly bearded man in jeans and button-down shirt. Remembering the voice on the phone, she placed her money on the beard and gave him what Alex called her best "tail wagging" smile.

She lost.

"I'm Oz," said tall and skinny. "Don't tell me. I'm good with names. Ginny Walters?" He turned to the beard. "She's brand-new."

As she corrected her name, "Thought so," said the beard. "Who's she with? Looks like Elite with those fascinating, slightly crooked teeth."

"I like the Audrey Hepburn chin, too. With the sixties coming in again, well you never know . . ."

So that was the accurate description of her pointy chin, but *you* never know *what*? The bearded one was as chatty as Mrs. F., but not *to* her—about her.

Oz, giving her a lank hand to shake, and the beard started to spout off about her looks in a car salesman sort of way. "Natural . . . original . . . too little color . . . a sort of hidden raciness . . ."

Another man chimed in. "Too thin."

How dare he! Didn't these terribly "in" people know one couldn't be too rich or too thin?

They had to be on something, but Ginny was still too scared to move and run. It was as if she was glued to the excessively white floor, not knowing what to expect, except perhaps to be offered some grass.

"Take a roll of film on her, Oz."

"Go stand on the no seam."

She was still glued. What was he talking about? Oz put his hand on her arm and guided her to a vast sweeping sheet of seamless paper.

"Drop your skirt, please. Just—boom—right there where you're standing."

Had she heard what she thought she heard? Her mouth, Ginny knew, had formed an exact O as she stared at a deeply tanned woman who had materialized beside Oz. Even in her terror Ginny noted there were both straight pins and safety pins stuck in the woman's white shirt, as white as the room, rubber bands around her wrists, no makeup, hair scrunched unbecomingly back, all business. Was she about to be raped by a lesbian?

The tan cracked into a smile. "Trust me. I'm Lee Baker Davies, a stylist. Your jacket is long enough—you'll still be decent. I want to see your legs. We're looking for great legs for Hanes. Your arrival could be divine providence."

Not for her. This was intolerable. Now she could see a couple of girls, who had to be models, standing by the table, either minus their skirts or wearing the shortest minis in fashion history.

She'd always considered her legs to be pretty good, but her father's voice was loud in her ears, going on about joining the meat market. "No, not today." She was amazed how firm she sounded.

"She's right. Not today. Tomorrow." Oz smiled at her. He had a terrific quirky smile. His teeth, although also slightly crooked, were not in the least bit fascinating, but then they didn't need to be.

"Let's talk," he said vaguely.

The Heavy D din had ceased. Now there was a babble of voices and she could see plumes of smoke curling up and smell the sweet sickly smell of marijuana.

The sun began to go down, its great glow outside the window making everyone around the harvest festival table look rosy. No one took any notice of her, so she took a plate and filled it with the photogenic fruit and vegetables, trying to look as if she belonged there. The conversation was fascinating.

"Serena was my booker," one skirtless, gorgeous redhead who looked about ten feet tall was saying to another ten-footer, this one ice-blonde. "She wanted me to go with her when she opened her agency, but I knew it wouldn't last. She hasn't the brains for the long haul and getting the best contracts. She just took the money from one of those fat short zillionaires, who let her stay in the black for as long as she supplied a different beautiful girl every night. As soon as one hooked him, he closed the agency down."

"I'm going to Click . . ."

"Eileen is suing . . ."

"When is she handing over?"

"Never!"

"Enjoying yourself?" Oz's hand encircled her waist, then moved up casually to her right breast.

"Don't do that."

He ignored her, his hand staying awhile in forbidden territory before moving slowly back to her waist. "Tomorrow, come back tomorrow. Bring a selection of things. Esme's snap was okay. You do have a new look, maybe the one I'm looking for."

"How . . . how . . . sorry, how do I get uptown by subway or bus from here?"

"Where d'you hang out?" He saw the tanned one striding toward the door. "Lee, are you going uptown? Will you give Ms. Puritan a lift?"

"Sure thing."

Before Ginny knew it, having promised to be back at ten in the morning with a selection of clothes, she was sitting with Lee Baker Davies in a sedan with a Big Apple sign in the window, going fast uptown.

"You're really new to this business, aren't you?"

Ginny huddled in the corner with her hands crossed in front like a prize fighter. "Well, yes."

Although she hadn't asked her, Lee Baker Davies started to explain in a headmistressy way, exactly what being a stylist meant—"a sort of fashion interpreter, someone who helps the photographer get what the client's looking for by choosing the clothes, putting the right things together, adding, taking away, you know, that sort of thing." Ginny nodded dutifully.

Before Baker Davies dropped her off, she said, with all the concern of a maiden aunt, "Are you dead set on becoming a model?"

There was a long pause. "Well, not really. Eventually I'm going to be a fashion designer."

"That's good." Ms. B.D. sounded as if she meant it.

"Why?"

"It's a tough business. You look like a sweet, unspoiled thing."

Ginny could feel herself blushing. "I'm tougher than I look."

"Just don't get your hopes up too high, and if you do have what it takes, don't believe everything everyone tells you. I think you need to work on your look. You must have a certain look. That doesn't mean you aren't cute, but . . ." Baker Davies leaned across and, to Ginny's alarm, kissed her on the cheek. "I hope I see you again." Thank heavens she hadn't tried to kiss her before, when they first got in the car. She would surely have slugged her.

"Here's my card. Call me if you need any help in this hell of a city and for God's sake stay away from drugs."

As if anyone had to tell her that! Ginny was about to tear the card up, but luckily looked at it first. *Harper's Bazaar*, it said, *Lee Baker Davies, Contributing Editor.*

Determined not to waste any more money on taxi drivers as ignorant of Manhattan as herself, Ginny spent a couple of hours that evening, with Sophie's help, researching the city's transit system. It was something, she thought wryly, her father would thoroughly have enjoyed.

At eight-thirty the next morning, with Sophie waving goodbye from her front door as if she was going off to war, Ginny—in jeans, T-shirt and positive attitude—left, carrying her most avant-garde designs in one of Sophie's garment bags.

It was lucky she allowed so much time, because the subway was sluggish. She lost her way once or twice changing trains and didn't arrive at the Tribeca studio until five minutes to ten.

Oz was ready to go to work, which included, Ginny swiftly learned, a wide variety of passes—as he adjusted her positions, asked her to look at Polaroids of herself, and turned up in the makeshift dressing room behind a screen whenever he asked her to change.

Nevertheless, in ten days, after hours of playing hide-and-seek with Oz, evading his most blatant pounces, Ginny had enough pictures to create a contact sheet to show the model agency lucky enough to represent her.

She wore her own designs in all the shots, a keyhole swimsuit in denim (that was the most perilous Oz session of all), a body-molding, long-sleeved bodysuit in oilskin, and her double-damask "Ms. Innocence" dress, as Oz called it.

There were also two close-ups, one with her hair slicked as close to her head as Oz slicked his, another with her hair blown out in a voluminous cloud by a freelance hairdresser who'd dropped by.

Hairdressers, makeup artists and an endless procession of wannabe models with their "books" dropped in to see Oz throughout the day, all hoping he would add them to his repertoire of sources. Soon, he told Ginny, he would have enough money to build a reception area and hire a receptionist to block anyone without an appointment.

"The pictures are sensational," Oz exclaimed, and Ginny agreed with him, particularly the way her clothes looked.

Sam Swid had been on the phone, noticeably relieved when she told him she was busy being photographed by Oz Tabori. "He's okay. He's okay," he said eagerly, as if she was looking for a reference.

And where was cousin Alex, the man responsible for her taking this six-month diversion out of her fashion-designing agenda? The man who'd started her on what she hoped would not turn out to be a model goose-chase?

"Gin, darling, we have the worst luck, but just as you're starting a new life, so am I," Alex called from the airport. For one terrifying moment she thought he was going to tell her he was getting married, but no, thank heavens, he was about to go into a new partnership with a Swiss tycoon.

"Sorry, puss, but I hear from Sam all is going well?"

She hadn't the energy to say it was no thanks to him. "Yes, I can't wait to show you the pictures."

"Soon I'll be able to buy them in all the best magazines. See you in three months. Take care."

"Height 5'9" (actually 8½", but Oz said it didn't matter: all the models exaggerated). Bust 34A. Waist 23". Hips 34". Shoes 7b. Hair chestnut. Eyes—she wanted to put topaz, but Oz insisted on green-hazel. This was her model curriculum vitae.

B.A. in finance? Brilliant fashion designer? School diving champion?

Oz laughed the quirky laugh she'd grown to like when she suggested adding these not inconsiderable assets.

"Honey, when *Vogue* or *Bazaar* book you to pose in a pair of Ralph Lauren's jodphurs or Karl Lagerfeld's backless suit or a dab of Calvin Klein's Obsession, they don't give a damn that you were on the diving team or that you dream up your own clothes . . ."

Dream up your own clothes! She longed to correct him, but what was the use.

It was D Day. Following a call from Oz, she was going today with her contact sheet to see and be seen by someone at Ford Models Inc., the most famous model agency in the world.

Oz told her it wasn't too important what she wore to the interview; more important was how she held herself, to remember to look as tall as possible (in three-inch heels—at least Alex hadn't forgotten to buy her a pair), her posture . . .

Ginny didn't believe him. She still believed in what Alex told her a long time ago: What you wear and how you wear it says a lot about who you are.

It was beginning to get seasonably cool, so she could wear a little two-piece number she'd just run up in a light jersey. It was an experiment which had turned out incredibly well. Because her arms were so skinny, she'd set the sleeves in a different way, so they were extensions of a continuous line. They looked like floating wings and prevented the top riding up when she lifted her arm, holding on in the subway or flagging down a cab. Surely Eileen Ford would appreciate something as original as that.

One of the marvelous things she'd learned about Ford was, they not only gave models with the most potential room and board, they groomed them and taught them useful little things, like how to use a finger bowl. Because of all the drugs pervading the industry, they also apparently heavily chaperoned "their girls," but in a professional way, not like the smothering, suffocating, fringe-laden atmosphere surrounding her now.

As Oz had warned her, there were a lot of wannabes in the waiting room at the agency. Ginny gave them a quick survey and felt she didn't have much competition. The one sitting next to her was the worst dressed of the lot. An obvious blonde with strange slanting eyes, she looked as if she was wearing a sugar sack, which did nothing for what Ginny suspected was a superb body underneath.

She was such a warm, friendly girl, who introduced herself as Poppy Gan, that Ginny was embarrassed. Should she give her some dress tips? No, of course she couldn't without appearing to insult her. Instead, they talked about movies and men, Poppy saying with a giggle, "they're all little boys at heart."

It was a very long wait, so Ginny began to confide her hopes of eventually becoming a dress designer. She told Poppy more than she meant to, but Poppy was enthralled, admiring her new-style sleeves and saying she'd love some for herself.

Finally, at eleven-thirty, Ginny was summoned inside. She wasn't nervous. She reminded herself that she was in a more fortunate position than most models. With a finance degree she could negotiate a contract, although in the beginning she knew she would have to accept the standard—but only for the first few months. She intended to make that clear in a charming way.

To her disappointment she discovered she was not seeing the great founder of the agency, Eileen Ford, but her daughter, who everyone said would be taking over in the not too distant future.

Ginny smiled confidently and made sure her sleeve fell gracefully as she extended her hand to say hello.

Unfortunately Katie Ford looked up very quickly, then down again. Perhaps she was shy. It must be difficult following her star of a mother. Ms. Ford put her hand out for her pictures. There was quite a long pause. Ginny was sure she was noting the style of the clothes and she could hardly wait to tell her she'd designed them all herself.

Have patience, Ginny. Although she was sitting straight, something she no longer needed to be told, the selector of future supermodels was actually slouching behind her desk, perhaps to make applicants less nervous.

At last Ms. Ford looked up. "Sorry," she said, "I don't see it. It's not here."

"I don't un . . . un . . . understand?" Ginny stuttered.

"There's no distinct look. These are attractive pictures. You're an attractive girl, but I'd forget about being a model if I were you. There's something . . ." Ms. Ford hesitated, and in Ginny's desperate humiliation, she clung to the thought she was going to mention the clothes, but no, to her despair Ford said bluntly, "Your features are too anonymous."

Did anonymous mean forgettable? Ford looked at the pictures again. Ginny was so disbelieving, she still expected her to change her mind.

She buzzed her secretary. "Is Nancy around?" She nodded, then stood up, indicating the shot in the long-sleeved bodysuit. "Can I see your hands?"

Slowly, not understanding what it all meant, Ginny extended her hands, no longer caring that her sleeves were doing everything expected of them.

"You have good hands. If you grow your nails we may be able to get you work as a hand model. I'll show your sheet to one of our chief bookers. Call her when your nails are longer."

Ms. Ford sat down, head down. Under her desk Ginny saw she was wearing leather thonged sandals.

Good hands! She wanted to use them to strangle the woman. She didn't know how she was going to get out of her office. She wanted to ask for another opinion, for the senior doctor, Eileen, to look at her case, not to leave it to the poor judgment of the junior. Ginny opened the door, still not able to accept that her interview was over.

Poppy looked up anxiously as Ginny hovered. "How was it?"

Ginny looked back at Katie Ford, still thinking she might change her mind. "Are you all right?" Ford asked solicitously.

Ginny swallowed hard. Poor Poppy. To think she would now have to endure the same treatment. "Yes, I'm all right. Now you're going to see a real superstar, Poppy Gan. She has more than great hands." She laughed hysterically. She was being sarcastic. In fact, she didn't know what she was saying, but Poppy looked thrilled, squealing, "Oh, thank you, Ginny. Thank you so much."

"Well?"

It was Oz on the phone the next day, the worst twenty-four hours of her life. In Sophie's hall mirror, Ginny saw her eyes were red, with one of her "good hands" now practically bereft of nails.

Sophie had been so worried by her sobs she'd called her mother, who'd immediately demanded she take the shuttle for some TLC in Maryland, but that was the last thing Ginny wanted to do.

"Why haven't you called me?" Oz at his most autocratic. "What happened?"

She told him in staccato sentences. She sounded in complete control. "Asshole!"

"Who, me?" Her self-esteem had never been so low.

"Don't be stupid. Now I know what I'm hearing must be for real. Ford isn't making it anymore. You'd better come on down here immediately. I just can't believe what I'm hearing. Those shots were sensational."

She lapped up every word, thinking of the thonged sandals beneath the desk. What were Ms. Ford's toenails like?

"Come on, Ginny. I want to talk to you."

When she didn't answer, Oz sighed long and heavy into the phone. "Wear that slinky, snaky bodysuit. I'll send a car for you around eight. We'll go out and have some fun for a change."

It took a lot of Sophie's Clinique Concealer, but she put on a brave face and her oilskin, although now that it was fall, it felt clammy under a coat.

"Where are you going, Ginny?"

Sophie had no business asking her, but after her heavy sobbing act, Ginny admitted she had reason to worry.

Trying to put Sophie's mind at rest, she was all false smiles and optimism. "I've got a date . . . with an editor. Don't wait up for me. Everything's going to be okay."

And that was what Oz kept saying over and over again in the Tribeca bistro, where another Big Apple sedan had deposited her. "It's my mistake, Ginny. I should never have sent you to Ford. You're an Elite girl, just as Bruce said."

Bruce? Oh, yes. The Bearded One.

Oz leaned over and cupped her face in his hands. "Cindy Crawford was originally turned down because—"

"—of her mole." How many more times did she have to hear that story?

As she drank too much wine, Oz was making life sound better and better. "Before you see Casablancas, I want you to go see an editor at *Elle* tomorrow, or one day this week. She called me today about a beauty sitting . . ."

The bistro was near his studio. It seemed to make perfect sense to stroll back there, with Oz's arm slung affectionately around her shoulders. Everything she liked about him was emphasized; everything she didn't like, she'd forgotten.

As they climbed the stairs, his hand, beneath her coat, stroked the back of her oilskin, moving down to her behind. She liked it—a lot. Would she end up in bed with him? Probably. In fact, she was looking forward to it, in a groggy sort of way—until they reached his front door, the first time she'd ever seen it closed.

Sitting on the floor outside was an exquisitely pretty black girl. A shawl loosely draped around her shoulders revealed a bikini top and a sarong, which showed yards of glossy black leg. There was an overnight bag all too clearly beside her. Was Oz upset? Not that much.

"Well, this is a surprise. When did you get in?"

"Landed a coupla hours ago . . ." She had a soft, singsong Caribbean accent. "An' I came right ov'r like you tol' me to in Jama'ca."

Unlocking the door Oz said, "Ginny, meet Ursula. Ursula, meet Ginny. Let's all go in for some grass and see where it leads us, shall we?"

Group sex? She was never going to be that drunk. She had too much catching up to do on the twosome kind first. Her tiny fire of desire fizzled out. "Not tonight, Oz. I've got to get some beauty sleep for the beauty sitting."

He knew her well enough not to give her an argument; instead, he put her in a cab. "I'll set everything up. Now don't give Ford another thought." He obviously couldn't wait to race back upstairs.

"In interviews and court papers Miss Duke's friends and former employees describe a lonely old woman who grew more and more isolated from others and dependent on Mr. Lafferty in her dotage. As her health declined, her natural suspicion of people's motives grew and she changed her will four times in the last three years of her life . . ."

Quentin Peet swung his legs up onto the desk and pushed the newspaper away. So now there was going to be a criminal investigation and Mr. Lafferty, the lucky butler, was going to have to fight for control of the 1.2 billion-dollar-fortune Doris Duke had left in his hands.

Peet sighed heavily and leaned back in his favorite chair, his writing chair. He knew about suspicion and changed wills all right. Suspicion corroded feelings, stifled trust, and in the end created hatred, no matter what one did to prove allegations were unfounded.

He'd stood on his head to prove to Cathy he still loved her, that he was still faithful. In his own fashion he had been faithful. Only his body, never his mind, had been involved with other women, when he'd allowed himself the occasional fuck after a long and particularly dangerous mission.

Okay, so in recent years he hadn't missed her when he'd been away. Did any partner in a thirty-year-plus marriage still miss their spouse when they got off the domestic hook for a while? He didn't believe it.

And Cathy, that fastidious, perfectly groomed woman, hadn't wanted to go with him much after the first few years. She considered she'd done her bit, roughing it as the wife of a foreign correspondent based in the Far East and the Philippines. She'd liked the servants all right, then damn it, with England's crazy quarantine laws when he received the first of many rewards, the London Bureau, at first she hadn't wanted to leave the dog! Perhaps he shouldn't have fought so hard to persuade her. Perhaps it would have been better if she'd stayed home. Then she wouldn't have gotten pregnant, then they might never have had a child.

Peet could feel his anger building up again. He looked at his watch.

It was too early, but after the events of the last few days, he needed a drink. He got up and poured himself a stiff scotch.

All right, so he'd been too damned busy to miss her, but, funnily enough, right up until the end he always believed he loved her, despite her maddening waspy habits, despite her hypocrisy, showing to her equally well-bred friends only a damned stiff upper lip about his long absences abroad, while endlessly breathing heavily and tearily into the phone to him.

He'd often told her he'd prefer her to scream like a banshee and get the pent-up resentment out of her system, but her water-in-the-veins hoity-toity parents hadn't brought her up to behave like that, and in recent years she'd used her "delicate health" as a special weapon to torment him.

Now she was gone. All the years of trying to be as decent a husband and father as he could, while doing his job to the best of his capacity, were wasted. She'd left every penny of her Ponsoby money to the son born in London, to Johnny. He still couldn't believe it. Almost a million and a half after taxes, to a wastrel son who hadn't had the decency to let even a week go by after the reading of the will, before quitting the *Times* and telling him he was going to write a column for *Next!* magazine, of all disgraceful publications.

He would never forgive Cathy for slapping his face so publicly from beyond the grave. Never. He probably would find it hard to forgive Johnny, too, although he'd seen for himself how stunned Johnny had been by his mother's will, as stunned as he'd been himself.

Or had he been putting on an act? Was it possible he'd misjudged Johnny all these years, thinking of him, often ruefully, as a fairly bright young man of average talent and ambition, who'd never set the world on fire, but who, nonetheless, was decent, honest, caring?

Peet poured himself another scotch. Had his son changed since his marriage to Dolores, the wildcat from Bolivia, whose claim to fame was a publicly aired threat of bankruptcy at twenty-one? Had Johnny changed or had he always been Machiavellian, cunning, hiding an array of objectives beneath his easygoing, softhearted manner?

He couldn't believe it. Not because he was his son. Because he, Quentin Peet, who'd unveiled some of the most brilliant, duplicitous characters in the world, was too smart to be fooled. "But," a voice nagged in his brain, "your own wife fooled you. Despite her being equally horrified over Johnny's marriage, she still preferred to leave what remained of her inheritance to him and not to you." It was an act of revenge he didn't deserve.

He heard the fax machine going in the other room and soon after, the phone began to ring. He ignored both, staring grimly into space. Finally, he picked up *The Racing Form* and scanned the day's runners. Perfidy was running at Aqueduct at 8 to 1. It seemed an appropriate choice. He leaned over to call his bookie.

Finito. It was all over. Ginny Walker was never going to be a model, let alone a supermodel. She had just been insulted for the last time and it had given her great pleasure to tear her much-mulled-over contact sheet into shreds and shower them over the so-called style editor's head.

She should have done it before. After all, she and it had been seen now by three "top bookers" at three "leading model agencies," as well as by four editors, all with different titles, but the same job, flesh assessor, at four women's magazines.

Her paper shower had gone to a particularly well deserving assessor with acne at *Harper's Bazaar,* who'd had the gall to say to her face, "Sweet, but a shade too ordinary for us."

There was coffee in a paper cup on her desk. Ginny was tempted to wash away literally the editor's hypocritical expression of regret by pouring that over her, too. The editor must have read her mind. She moved the cup, and Ginny turned on her three-inch heels and marched away.

No more tears. THERE MUST BE NO MORE TEARS.

She would never set foot in Oz Tabori's studio again; she would never pose again; she would never read a stupid women's magazine again. To add colossal insult to horrendous injury she had also learned in the last week that Ford had actually signed Poppy Gan. There was no justice in the world. It was months short of her six-month deadline, but she was on her way to Seventh Avenue in the morning.

By the time she collapsed in a heap at Sophie's, although her bravado had dried up, a slow-burning anger remained, at the world in general and photographers, model agencies and magazine bookings editors in particular.

"There was a call for you." Sophie was such a doll; she made it sound like a proposal of marriage.

"I don't care. I'm not calling him for a while." Mr. "Everything is going to be okay" Tabori was dead and buried as far as she was concerned.

"It wasn't a him. It was a her. It was . . ." Sophie put on her reading glasses. "A Miss Baker Davies, contributing editor of *Harper's Bazaar*," she finished triumphantly.

So the butch stylist had already heard about her aberrant behavior. So what? Ms. Baker Davies could congratulate herself on her all-seeing eye and pat herself on the back that she had known before anyone, including Ginny Walker herself, that her face was anonymous, sweet, but ordinary, lacking that certain "look" factor needed in the great money-making faces of today.

"Aren't you going to call her back?"

"No."

"Oh, Ginny, dear, I think you should. It could be important."

Was Sophie trying to tell her what she knew only too well? That she had been taking her hospitality without contributing anything to hearth and home? Ginny didn't really think so, but she was super-sensitive on the subject, and her Bloomingdale's savings and dowry from the parents were running awfully low.

All the same, she wasn't going to call the stylist just to hear "I told you so" and run the risk of being kissed, even on the cheek. "No," Ginny said again brusquely and went into her box and shut the lid. .

The evening stretched before her. She had to get away from Sophie's reproachful eyes. She called Esme; and to her relief, Esme told her she had a night off from Ted—he'd gone to a business conference in Toronto.

Ginny rented an old Bette Davis movie, *Now Voyager*, and they watched it, eating pizza and drinking kir on the king-size bed in the king-size apartment Esme now shared with Ted in the upper eighties.

Bette's suffering in the movie made Ginny relax enough to pour out the story of her non-supermodel splash, endless rejections and feelings of total inadequacy.

"But you never wanted to join the brain-dead model set," Esme exclaimed. "Remember how you told me over and over you were only going through the motions to please your mother and Alex, your genius of a cousin." Ginny didn't like the sarcastic way Esme referred to Alex, but forgot it when she continued, "You were born to be a designer. Don't waste another second thinking about something you never wanted to do in the first place. Get into designing—go to Seventh Avenue."

Because of Ted's money, Esme only went to Bloomingdale's as a shopper now. "You're needed out there," she told Ginny soothingly. "There are tons of clothes, but they all look the same. Go to it, Gin . . ."

By the time Ginny left the apartment, she'd shortened one of Esme's recent purchases, critiqued a toque hat (suggesting Esme wear it back to front), and altogether—with Esme's encouragement, the kirs and Bette Davis—felt like a reasonably okay person again, even if a slightly hungover one.

There was a message in capital letters by Sophie's phone: "MS. BAKER DAVIES CALLED AGAIN. SHE KNOWS WHAT HAPPENED AND SAYS NOT TO WORRY IT HAPPENS ALL THE TIME. SHE KNOWS OF A JOB FOR YOU WITH A DESIGNER, EVERARD GOSMAN. PLEASE CALL IN THE A.M."

Underneath, in red pencil, Sophie had written and underlined, "Please wake me up if I'm asleep when you get in or make sure to see me in the morning. I know Gosman. This could be good." Dear Sophie. Dear Ms. Baker Davies.

Ginny rolled into bed and dreamed Bette Davis's lover, Paul Henreid, was trying to make love to her in a canoe.

Sophie woke her up with a cup of coffee, apologizing that it was only just after seven, but, "I was so worried I'd miss you."

Ginny was instantly alert. Good God, Gosman! Baker Davies had called about the possibility of a job with Everard Gosman!

Sophie bubbled over with excitement. What a loving, kindhearted chaperone she'd turned out to be. "I spoke for a long time to your friend, Ms. Baker Davies. She really likes you, you know." Sophie missed seeing Ginny's grimace. "Everard Gosman needs an assistant. Of course, he's not really a designer." Seeing Ginny's frown, Sophie added hastily, "I'm telling you this now because in this business you may hear him dismissed unkindly as a merchandiser."

"*Quoi?*—excuse my French."

"That's what people are called who copy other people's designs," Sophie explained carefully, "but Gosman is so good, his copies of French couture at low prices are amazing. I hear the stores are lapping them up. As usual it's only the jealous ones who call him that."

Certainly Lee Baker Davies, apparently one of Gosman's oldest friends, never did. When Ginny called her back an hour later, she asked to meet her for coffee to see her portfolio. She then gave her the third degree about her basic pattern/dressmaking knowledge and business experience.

Thank God what Ginny had learned at FIT and a B.A. in finance were enough to impress Lee. In twenty-four hours she'd arranged an interview for Ginny with Gosman, who hired her on the spot at twenty thousand dollars a year. (She could probably have gotten more, but it didn't even occur to her to ask until she waltzed home—if you can waltz on the subway.)

That weekend she went to Maryland to tell her parents her good news, and on Monday morning she joined Everard Gosman at 554 Seventh Avenue, spitting distance from the BIG INFLUENCES: Lauren, de la Renta, Karan, Klein . . . also only a few steps from Lou G. Siegel's kosher restaurant, where chicken livers on toast were to become her favorite meal, WHEN she had time to eat an actual meal.

Ginny Walker was in heaven and so was Mr. Gosman, who knew he'd never had it so good, because from that Monday on she set out to be *absolument* indispensable and so she was . . . a girl Friday, Saturday and every other day of the week if he needed her.

He needed her, all right. During a twenty-minute "training session" Ginny discovered how desperately disorganized he was, with phone calls coming in one after the other, people rushing in and out with "urgent" written all over them, and Gosman yelling instructions so fast all his words ran together.

The Wizard of Oz was still pursuing her. Ginny couldn't imagine why, unless it was that pride thing of his, because he had made it clear she was the only girl he'd ever photographed who'd refused to go to bed with him. Also, he was still convinced his pictures proved what a wonderful model she could be.

Those in charge of making it come true hadn't agreed. That was all there was to it. He could call everyone involved "assholes" until the earth froze over, but it wasn't going to change anything. One day he'd get the message. Goodbye, Oz, forever. Today was the first day of the rest of her life, her wonderful new life in the fashion industry.

As she rushed into the showroom, half an hour early, as eager and friendly as a wirehaired terrier, Gosman was prancing around with *Women's Wear Daily.*

"Read it. Read it, little girl. Learn something about your boss." As he kept it firmly in his hands she didn't have a chance until the phone demanded his attention. It was a story about a Gosman copy of a Valentino dress ($325 vs. $3,050), with what Ginny supposed Mr. G. took to be an admiring quote from a retailer: "He's a Xerox machine on legs. He remembers every detail and never runs out of ink."

Some of the staff were openly snickering, but obviously Mr. G. was proud of the piece, because later that morning he sent Ginny out to find a narrow black frame, so it could join the other framed clips on his wall, ones that chronicled his chutzpah and craftsmanship with headlines like COPYCAT CHAMP, INSTANT "COUTURE"—GOSMAN STYLE.

As far as Ginny could see, the press had been reporting his espionage for years, because he'd never bothered to hide it. He attended the Paris shows with a sketchbook, returning home to the U.S. to transform his sketches in a matter of days into three- and four-hundred-dollar best-selling copies of the multithousand-dollar French designs.

Ginny couldn't understand why he was so peculiarly proud of his reputation as a first-class copier. Ironic, because while he boasted about what, after all, was stealing someone else's work, he hid the fact that he actually designed originals all the time. On his desk were piles of sketch pads, many filled with new ideas.

Why? Was he scared to try out anything that was all his own? She was too new a girl on the block to suggest he give it a go.

"I want nine dollars off 705," he yelled one morning as she brought him his daily apple juice and baby aspirin (something to do with warding off heart attacks).

Mauve Smith, one of the male assistant designers, was nervously "walking through" 705, a short, pouffed-out silk taffeta dress from the new collection, just arrived from the factory several congested blocks away. This shape was "borrowed," Ginny gathered, from Christian Lacroix, a new French designer.

Mauve rapidly went through the cost (for interfacing, china silk lining, buttons, zipper and, of course, the five yards of fabric).

Gosman threw up his hands in disgust when he heard the fabric cost twenty dollars a yard. "Howd'y'thinkwecanmakeanymoney." Ginny often didn't understand him, but this was a familiar cry.

She ran outside. She had been seeing fabric reps the third day after her arrival, simply because there was no one else available to see them.

In several cases she'd asked for a sample five-yard cut because "it said something."

She ran back. "This is available." She handed Gosman a shimmering synthetic shantung, which, expecting the questions that now followed, she had already tested—"howdoesitsew?" . . . "howdoesitpress?"

"Beautifully," was the answer to both. "And it's eight dollars a yard."

Gosman held the swatch to his head as if it was an icepack.

"Whycouldn'y'findsomethinglikethisMauvellove it . . ."

Mauve looked at Ginny as if she should crawl back under the stone she had just come from. Gosman growled to no one in particular, "letmeseeitmadeuptell'mtoshrinkthemarker . . ." Ginny already knew he always slowed his sentences down when it was expedient. "Get it back by two," he said carefully. "No, you can make that three. I'vegottagotothe-dentist." Thank God for his root canals.

"Shrink the marker" was a key instruction—and something of an art. She'd learned that at FIT. It meant interlocking, or placing the pieces of a pattern together, tighter and tighter, to get as much out of the material as possible in order to make more profit on the final product.

Ginny put up her hand. "I'll take it."

She adored going to the factory. It emphasized the fact that she now belonged on Fashion Avenue, dodging the rolling racks of next season's dresses, inhaling the smells of chicken and rice, cigars and traffic exhaust, peering in the dozens of little storefronts selling zippers, leather and passementerie to the trade, running fast in sneakers (hers) or some days clacking along on three-inch heels (also hers), seeing micros and miniskirts mingle with yarmulkes and saris.

She also adored arriving at the grimy old factory building, handing over the dress sample from the sample pattern maker at the Gosman office to the factory production pattern maker to "dupe." It thrilled her to watch the massive automatic cutting machine (which looked like giant shears) slice through many different layers of material, each layer fitting exactly on top of another, to produce the pieces that would sew into ten duplicates of a ready-to-wear dress. It was like watching ten giant club sandwiches being made.

Today, as she waited for the elevator in the bleak stone corridor outside the showroom, Mauve came out with Frank, one of the senior tailors. (Because Gosman was also known for his "couture" suits, he employed two full-time tailors, plus a couple of freelancers.) Ginny smiled, but they were stony-faced and stood one on either side of her. They started pushing and shoving her hard, one to the other.

"Stop that." But they didn't stop, and Mauve said very clearly, "We're getting tired of you, little miss smart-ass. If you don't want to end up getting mugged one sad night by all the ugly people out there, you better keep that trap of yours closed tight from now on."

"Is that a threat?" Her voice was steady, although she wasn't.

"No, it's a promise," the other guy, Frank, said with a sneer.

When the red light went on to indicate the elevator's arrival, they gripped her arms so hard, she yelped with pain. "Look at your black-and-blues tonight, smart-ass, and know that's nothing to what you can expect to see on your face if you keep this up."

The elevator was almost full, but they pushed in with her and continued the gripping routine all the way down. She was in such a state of shock she didn't utter a word. Although they let her go with one more shove on the avenue and watched her rush away, she didn't stop looking over her shoulder all the way downtown.

She was wet through with panic. She hadn't a minute to spare, but she grabbed a cappuccino at a grimy-looking coffee shop on the corner, trying to calm down before facing the factory production pattern maker and asking him to shrink the marker and run up a quick dupe.

There hadn't been any more pushing, shoving and pinching, but every time she had the misfortune to run into either goon, she got her quota of filthy looks and muttered epithets. She didn't need to hear them. The bruising on her arms hadn't just been black and blue, it had been royal purple.

She was still indispensable, but she no longer made the mistake of putting in her three cents when anyone else was in the room. Mr. Gosman may have noticed a difference but he never said a word, and she was still frantically busy from entry to exit, with often a twelve-hour day in between.

Only on weekends could she relax. If she wasn't working on a super-creative design for herself, Esme, or Sophie, she loved curling up with a bunch of *Women's Wear Dailys*, carefully collected from Gosman's wastepaper basket at the end of every day. She devoured them as thoroughly as her father ever devoured Quentin Peet; and she also breezed through the magazines and social columns that Mr. G. let her borrow—

Town and Country, Avenue, New York magazine, *Vanity Fair,* stuff like that.

Gosman put paper clips on the pages showing photographs of women wearing his clothes. There were always lots of paper clips.

There was only one pinprick in this form of recreation. The emergence of Poppy Gan as a leading member of society. "Poppy Gan shows the flag at Bulgari's soirée," read a T and C caption, "wearing a clever shift from the workshop of Seventh Avenue's latest arrival, Jam Tollchin, a designer to watch." Clever shift indeed! It was something Ginny knew she could make with her eyes shut.

When it was announced that Poppy was the latest contender to be the new Guess? girl (where Alex's pal from Düsseldorf, Claudia Schiffer, had first made her mark), it seemed she was never out of the papers, especially *WWD,* photographed at parties, happy, carefree but, thought Ginny, still abominably dressed, despite now being seen in the company of some of the country's richest, most powerful men.

Women's Wear Daily spotlighted what Ginny called "fashion in action," reporting through its pick of the best parties around the country what the most fashionable were wearing. For some designers it was like receiving a brilliant review every day.

Why did Poppy's constant appearance in the papers annoy her so much? Because she couldn't see what it was Poppy had that was so special? Because the words "anonymous" and "ordinary" still tolled away in her head?

It hadn't taken long for a bitter truth to dawn: wearing her own creations, however witty and wonderful, along the grubby, drafty Seventh Avenue corridors, was never going to get her anywhere as a designer.

She needed to be seen in *Women's Wear Daily* herself, wearing her own designs, but how could she make that happen, with her limited social activities?

It was one of the reasons she started to seek out Lee Baker Davies. She moved in quite a few circles and seemed to regard Ginny as her protégée, which was fine by her, except for the occasional goodnight kisses.

Ginny wished she could tell Lee about the goons at Gosman's, but, of course, she couldn't, because Lee would certainly tell her best friend Everard and she would certainly end up in the emergency ward after Gosman warned the goons he knew all about their brutality.

In any case, things were looking up. Not only was the Mauve Monster leaving Gosman, he was leaving New York City to move to San Francisco, where, the word was, he had a fabulous new job with the Gap.

Mr. G. had implied in his usual monosyllabic way that as soon as Mauve was gone, she was to be promoted from "gofer" to "doer," which Ginny hoped would mean assistant designer. No mention of a raise, but one thing at a time.

Sure enough, one weekend there was a reason to celebrate. The promotion was hers, and a five-thousand-dollar raise went with it. Lee insisted on taking Ginny out—to swanky Mr. Chow's—along with Marilyn Binez, an artist friend. Later, they were all invited to a party in Chelsea, where Lee swore there would be no trace of Oz Tabori or anyone like him. Alas, thought Ginny, probably no trace of *WWD* either.

Ginny brought the subject up. "Lee, how can I get my designs in *WWD*? How can I get to some of these parties where my clothes can be seen? What are the best parties anyway?" She started to giggle to hide her embarrassment, but hoped Lee would take her seriously.

Lee loved the question, and between sips of Chinese beer and nibbles of dim sum, outlined what should be on Ginny's wish list to attend. "The annual opening of the Costume Institute at the Metropolitan Museum, the opening night of the Metropolitan Opera, the Literary Lions gala at the New York Public Library, er, the Botanical Gardens fundraiser, er . . ." She waved a chopstick in the air. "Private recitals, art shows, private movie screenings given by David Brown, book parties by Tina Brown . . ."

"Aren't they married?"

Lee's thin arched eyebrows arched higher. "Of course not, Ginny. David's married to that icon Helen Gurley Brown of *Cosmopolitan* and Tina's married to her equal in brilliance, publisher Harry Evans."

This was beginning to bore Ginny, but Lee was on a roll, enjoying herself, educating the hick from the sticks about who and what mattered. She ticked off more names with her chopsticks. "Parties at Mortimer's, owned by a genius called Glenn Bernbaum, who attracts the best crowd with delicious food at bargain prices; anything with a sniff of a de la Renta, Buckley or, of course, Brooke Astor presence . . ."

Ginny started to fidget, but Lee was oblivious, going right on. "Ginny, you should know there's a set calendar for women who spend and spend on clothes. From January to March your original parkas should be seen in Gstaad, St. Moritz, Vail, or Aspen. Next, it's all happening here, where your one-of-a-kinds should be seen at the A-list parties in New York, Washington, and Los Angeles till June. It's Europe from July Fourth to Labor Day—"

For a diversion Ginny knocked over a glass of water.

Lee got the message. "Okay, okay, that's enough for now, but seriously, as I've been telling you for ages, you've got to get out and about and be seen in your clothes." She turned to Marilyn. "She's a hermit."

Marilyn, who'd been hungrily eyeing Ginny's silver birdcage-like jacket with inside-out seams, asked, "Did you design that?"

"Of course she did," Lee answered proudly.

"Could you make me one?" Marilyn asked nervously. "Would you like to see my paintings? Perhaps you'd like one—in exchange for a jacket like that?"

What a spot to be in. Ginny looked around, trying to think of a tactful answer to Lee's portly artist friend, who should never wear the jacket, or anything like it, designed as it was for someone like herself without many curves. In that second, who did she see coming through the restaurant door on the arm of a polished, distinctly foreign-looking potentate? None other than Poppy Gan.

They made direct eye contact. Poppy hesitated. Ginny waved, hoping to distract Marilyn.

Poppy's face brightened. She moved toward their table. Mr. Polished pulled her back. She whispered in his ear. Followed by an entourage, including a couple of giants who looked like bodyguards, he went to the right, where a large gleaming table awaited.

"Hi, I can't believe my luck. I've been looking for you everywhere. You're the girl who recommended me to Ford. Where have you been hiding yourself . . . eh . . ." Poppy obviously couldn't remember her name.

"Ginny Walker. Yes, I heard Ford signed you. Congratulations." Ginny introduced her to Lee and Marilyn.

"How lovely to meet you. What a fabulous surprise, Ginny. I wanted to send you a big present, but I didn't know where you lived. I've never forgotten your sleeves. Are you a dress designer yet?"

Ginny hesitated, then, as she muttered something about working for Gosman on Seventh Avenue, Lee said smoothly, "She's going to be very soon."

Poppy wasn't listening. She squealed, "When can I see your collection? Is that gorgeous jacket you're wearing one of yours? Is it in the stores yet? I'd looove to get one or two—perhaps in brighter colors? Svank"—she waved her hand vaguely to the right—"my friend, he wants me to be a fashion plate, to get on something called the best dressed list." She giggled as she said in a stage whisper, "He's going into retailing or something like that . . . buying stores, you know."

She was like an adorable, overexuberant puppy. Ginny had forgotten how much she'd taken to her in Ford's waiting room. It seemed like a hundred years ago.

Lee scribbled something on a card and gave it to Poppy. "Give Ginny a call. Here are her work and home numbers. I'm sure she can help you."

Ginny was flabbergasted at Lee's pushiness. Also, looking at Poppy, she realized there was something about the way she wore clothes that suggested she couldn't wait to take them off. She was a beauty all right, but because her magnificent breasts appeared to start somewhere up by her shoulder blades, even the fairly demure dress she was bursting out of tonight, all buttons and bows, turned her into a juvenile delinquent. No wonder she was squired by so many men.

Across the room her "friend" was staring in their direction, impassive. It made Ginny uneasy, but Poppy chattered on about how much she loved Mr. Chow's and what had they ordered and what were the specials on the menu and how she had to be careful not to eat too much because Chinese food slipped down so easily, she quickly got "bloated" and— Ginny indicated that one of the giants appeared to be coming over to collect her.

Poppy shrugged, then with a quick glance over her shoulder, fluttered away with a "promise to call."

Lee said accusingly, "You didn't tell me you know Poppy Gan."

"I don't, but I intend to."

"Do you know who she's with?"

Ginny shook her head with cool indifference. "His name sounded familiar, but I didn't quite get it . . . Shank, Swenk, something like that."

Lee laughed in her most annoying, patronizing way. "Now I know you're reading too many *Women's Wear Dailys* and not enough *New York Times*. Quentin Peet just wrote a fascinating story about him landing on the U.S. scene like a comet from outer space." As she spoke, Lee twisted in her seat to look again in Poppy's direction. "I thought it was Svank, but I didn't believe it until Poppy mentioned his name. According to Peet he's one of the most powerful industrialists in the world, although

not much is known about his industries. I don't think his move into retailing has been in the papers yet. That's really exciting. I must tell
Bazaar. No wonder Poppy wants to please him. This could be your lucky
day, Ginny."

She was thinking the same thing. There was a lot she could do to
help Poppy. For a start, she could streamline her spectacular curves.
Obviously this was something this particular "friend"—Svank, now she
remembered his name from business school—wanted, and she couldn't
say she blamed him. Poppy ought to be kept under wraps for her own
good.

In return, Poppy could help her get invited to at least some of the social stuff they'd just been discussing. Her imagination was working over-
time. They could both show off her clothes. *WWD*, here I come, Ginny
thought excitedly.

Before they left Lee said, "Don't you think you should get Poppy's
number? In case she doesn't call?"

There was something off-putting about Poppy's table. "Don't worry,
she'll call."

"She may not." Lee stalked over to Poppy. Ginny could see her hand
Poppy her card. In a few seconds she was back, looking annoyed. "They
weren't very friendly. One of the goons just said, 'She's in the book,' but
I don't believe it."

"What did Poppy say?"

"She didn't; she looked distinctly nervous to me."

"Well, she'll call."

Ginny was flying, an almost forgotten adrenaline pumping through
her. She hadn't been at the party in Chelsea for more than a few minutes
when she was introduced to Ricardo Vicarno, an artist from Milan, in
New York for the first American exhibition of his work.

They shook hands for the longest time; they couldn't stop looking at
each other. His eyes are the same color as mine, Ginny thought; no,
darker, really dark green-brown.

Although they sat and stood and sat again, she didn't concentrate on
what they talked about so animatedly for more than an hour. His work,
her work, New York, Milan, mountains, shadows, swimming in cool
lakes. Lots of words, but more meaningful, lots of silences.

Lee came by to say she wanted to go home and so did Marilyn. She hovered, obviously unhappy that Ginny was not going to leave with them. Ginny walked them to the door with Ricardo, his arm around her waist.

"Can I get you a taxi?" he asked, with Marcello Mastroianni charm.

"They have a car, a Big Apple," Ginny said too quickly. She couldn't wait for them to go.

For some ridiculous reason Lee cried out angrily, "Don't forget Poppy's going to call."

Poppy? Was it possible she'd already forgotten about Poppy, and her bold plan for the future? Yes, it was possible. She'd forgotten everything.

The lights dimmed and people started dancing to Latin music. Ricardo moved close, closer toward her. She didn't want to hear the music; she buried her head in his shoulder; she didn't want to see; she closed her eyes. She only wanted to be aware of the slight roughness of his chin on her cheek when she lifted her head, the faint aroma of cologne as he moved his arms tighter around her and the giddy, mind-bending sensation of sexual arousal as he suddenly kissed her hair.

They stopped dancing and stood, their arms around each other, looking out at the empty street. Somebody jostled them and a glass of red wine spilled on her priceless jacket. She didn't say a word or feel a thing. No rage, no sorrow, only a sense of diving off the high board as, hand in hand, they went to find a bathroom and found a bedroom instead.

There was no need for words, no need to fear not knowing what to do. She just thanked God there was a key in the door, a key Ricardo turned in the lock.

She noticed his hands. They were the way artists' hands should be, fine, slender. He slipped her jacket from her shoulders. She wasn't wearing a bra; she rarely needed to wear a bra. He looked at her with such wonder, for the first time she was proud of her body and not her clothes.

He cupped her small breasts, pushing them up toward him. He bent his head of thick dark hair down to kiss and then deeply suck her nipples. She was weak; she was totally gone, open, wet, longing for him. So this was what being in love meant.

Oh, please, Ricardo, now. I don't want to wait any longer.

He lay her down on the bed and began to kiss her, her face, her ears, her neck. His fingers were cool and strong; he searched for and found her response.

It was the most beautiful night of her life.

*   *   *

When Ginny woke she was alone in a strange bed in a foreign, bare, bleak room with not a fringe in sight. She could still feel Ricardo's hands. She ached, she didn't know how, but yes, it was a physical ache to feel them again. She wanted him. Cheap love songs about want and need and longing played through her mind. She felt so lonely, she couldn't move. She wanted to weep and moan into the pillow. Where was he?

The door opened and Ricardo came in, laughing like a boy, although now she could see gray streaks in his hair, fine lines on his amazing patrician face. He was carrying her jacket.

"Sleepyhead, your jacket is ready. I cleaned it at my studio. Put it on. Now I want to take you there." His Italian accent made every word sound poetic.

It was incredible. There was no trace of red wine, but she didn't want to put her jacket on; she didn't want to put on anything. She wanted to put off getting dressed for as long as she could. She wanted him back in bed with her now, this instant.

She pouted. She held out her arms, but he only laughed again. "They want the room, *cara*. Let's go home to my place."

It was shameful. She could hardly walk along the street, she was longing so much for what had gone before and what she knew was only minutes away.

It was a perfect winter day, cool but not cold, with a brilliantly blue sky and valleys of golden sunshine, a time when she usually loved to walk everywhere, but feeling the way she did, this walk was too long and Ricardo made it longer. Every so often he stopped to swing her around or lift her high into the air like a child.

He had rented a big loft in Chelsea. It reminded her of one of her favorite advertisements—for a man's fragrance, a Spanish one by Paco Rabanne, where a gorgeous bare-chested man was on the phone, sitting in a studio on a rumpled but pristine white bed, obviously talking to the girl who'd just left it.

There was a smell of turpentine, cologne, coffee and expensive cigars; piles of canvases; sweaters, pants, belts hanging topsy-turvy all over the place.

Ginny sat demurely on the bed, forcing herself to smile. He stood over her, powerful, wonderfully powerful; he held her head between his hands and slowly brought her tight against his jeans.

It began again, the delirious ascent, descent, ascent, descent into a world she'd never known. Thank God, she'd taken Esme's advice and months ago started on the pill "in case" one night "it" happened.

Around four in the afternoon the phone rang and her gorgeous bare-chested, bare-everything man picked it up with his girl still in the tousled bed. He spoke in rapid Italian, but Ginny still caught *cara* every so often. Perhaps she caught it because after the first few minutes he stopped stroking her hair, her breasts, which he had told her over and over were like delicate exquisite flowering buds.

The phone call went on and on. It doused her senses like cold water. She didn't want to leave, but she got up and slowly dressed in last night's fancy clothes, waiting every second for him to stop talking and rush over to bring her back to his side. He was so engrossed, he didn't even seem aware she was still there.

She crossed the room and went to the door. She opened it and, without leaving, banged it noisily shut. Her hatred for the person on the other end of the wire was frightening. Ricardo looked up, still speaking, but he still didn't seem aware of her. He was upset about something, someone?

With a painful lump in her throat she walked out, sure he would follow her. Perhaps he was talking to his mother, perhaps she was ill; then she remembered he'd told her the evening before he'd lost both his parents in a car crash. At one moment she had nearly asked him if he was married, but the moment had passed and she hadn't wanted to break the magic spell.

She played a game with herself. If there was a cab cruising by when she reached the street, she would take it. If there wasn't, she'd go back up the stairs and wrest the phone away and kiss him passionately. Of course, a cab was cruising by. Like a sleepwalker she got in. By the time she neared Sophie's, she knew she had to start looking for a place of her own. It was bad enough taking a broken heart home; taking it to somebody else's home was impossible.

A vivid blonde was waiting at a stoplight. She reminded her of Poppy. It was hard to believe she could forget her plans for Poppy Gan, forget about dressing her to improve her fashion image, as in turn Poppy helped promote her clothes. It was unimportant now.

The next day, with no word from Ricardo, she called in sick, pretending to Sophie that she had stomach flu. In a way she did. Her stomach was violently upset—until one o'clock, when a bunch of dark velvety violets arrived with a card, which said only, "Will you . . ." By six o'clock she had received four more bunches, each with a card carrying only a few words. She laid them out on the coffee table. "Will you . . . have dinner with . . . me tomorrow night? . . . love Ricardo . . . call 808-3592."

In Sophie's hall mirror as she dialed the number she saw her face. It was glowing, full of anticipation.

So began eight weeks of a roller coaster life, soaring to the sky, descending to the bottom of the earth. "It's that elevator feeling," said Esme, with all the wisdom of her relationship with Ted. "There's nothing to beat it." That was for sure. On the rare days when there were no calls, she crashed down to the depths, certain he was never going to call again.

He was evasive on the subject of other relationships, only saying he had once been married and was very attached to his two sons, who lived with their mother. There had been other calls while she was in the loft. She didn't leave. She waited, however long they took, and Ricardo always had a lot to talk about. "Business," he would invariably say when finally he put the phone down.

"Monkey business?" she once teased. He didn't like it. She spent the rest of the day trying to cajole him out of a foul black mood. There were others equally black, but soon forgotten in bed, when he blamed his moodiness on the pressure of getting ready for his exhibition.

She was exhausted, living between his calls and their dates, on the edge of her emotions. She even fell asleep a couple of times at the office.

He was so loving and thoughtful the days before his big show, talking about a life together in Milan, buying her an enormous book about Italian cities and their art collections, encouraging her to start Italian lessons.

Finally the day of his exhibition came. She tried to stay in the background, but to her joy, he said he wanted her always to be in "viewing distance—my view."

The gallery was packed. It seemed a big success, ten paintings sold in the first thirty minutes, although "You never know what the critics are going to say," he had warned her the day before. "They smile with their lips, but their pens are as sharp as daggers."

Afterwards there was a big party at a nearby Italian restaurant. Lee and Marilyn were there, with Lee still wearing a disapproving smirk. "Don't believe everything you're told," she had the gall to say. Ginny decided she would not invite her to the wedding.

Around midnight Ricardo pleaded a terrible headache. He looked white, strained.

"Let's go home," Ginny said. "Let's get away from all this noise and tension. I'll massage you."

"No, no, no. I have to be alone. When I have these headaches—only a few times in my life—I know I have to be alone. I take a special drug. I will be out for twenty-four hours, then I am myself again."

She had no alternative; and with a headache herself from too much red wine, Ginny didn't protest too much when he put her in a cab with a soft, gentle kiss.

It was the last time she ever saw him.

The next morning a huge bouquet of roses was waiting for her at the office, with a card signed simply Ricardo. When she called, the phone was busy, then didn't answer in the late morning or the afternoon.

At seven o'clock, she was about to go down to the loft, dressed in the oilskin bodysuit he loved, her freshly washed hair loose and fragrant around her shoulders, when a letter arrived by messenger.

It was brief and to the point. He would always love her, but he would be ill if he did not return to Milan to his wife and adorable sons. He hoped she would forgive him and understand a father's devotion.

"You have told me you want a place of your own. Please move to my loft. I had to rent it for a year and there are several months left. It will give you time to find what you want and, believe me, *cara*, I want the best in the world for you," said the last paragraph.

She caught a cab down to the loft. She couldn't accept that he wouldn't be there, but he was gone, and so were all the things that belonged to him.

Only a bunch of violets in a Murano glass suggested he had left thinking of her—and one remaining canvas, an abstract of a cool deep lake, with shadows, cast by tall mountains, sweeping across it. "For Ginny," said the card. "I will never forget the last two months."

"Neither will I," she said to herself, but he had his wife and sons to help him recover. She was alone, miserably, terribly alone.

1994

CHAPTER FOUR

MUIR CASTLE, SCOTLAND

It was cold for May. "Bloody cold," the Brits would call it, and they'd be bloody right. Although—as planned—it was a moonless night, Alex could still see his breath puffing out like wash from a boat.

Also planned and paid for, an inflatable dinghy was waiting on the riverbank. With Angus, who still described what they were doing as "a jolly lark"—another example of the incomprehensible British sense of humor—he pushed the dinghy into the dark, fast-moving water and clambered aboard.

A scene from a James Bond movie came to mind; he couldn't remember which one, but dressed in black with balaclavas pulled over their faces, he reckoned they must look like Bond types, if not 007 himself, lean, strong, fearless, ready for action.

Alex's hands, despite lined leather gloves, were freezing, but rowing would cure that. Gripping the oars, it took them less than fifteen minutes to cross to the other side of the River Tweed.

He glanced at a recent acquisition, a luminous Rolex watch. They were exactly on schedule. For some reason, tonight he'd expected to feel more apprehensive, because this job was for a new and most important client. But, no, he was his usual cool, calm, and collected self, totally in control of his body functions, unlike Angus, who frequently peed in his pants when he felt they were in danger.

It had happened a few months before, again in Scotland, when they'd set off the house's main alarm, newly connected to Perth police headquarters. How they'd laughed in London the next day, reading that as the HQ was at least fifteen miles away, the police had taken nearly half an hour to get there.

Now they ran swiftly through the deep shadows of old trees until they reached the walls of Muir Castle, the eighteenth-century family home of the Duke and Duchess of Kirkburghe.

During the last month, they'd joined hundreds of tourists traipsing through the castle. They had been there to carry out their usual reconnoiter plan with Crisp, who, but for a hangover, would have been with them tonight. Crisp wasn't reliable. This was the last time he'd get any work from Alex. Crisp always thought he could hold his drink without effect, but he couldn't, although on the wagon he was among the best.

While the tourists pushed their noses against the glass cases holding precious artifacts and stared like zombies into one roped-off grand room after another, the three of them, once together, twice each on their own, had toured in their own inimitable way, to learn the floor plan, to check exactly where the required "merchandise" was located, to mark where the alarms were and to seek out blind spots away from the security cameras. At the dress rehearsal, it had been as cheering as ever to find that their sketches and notes, made mostly from memory, were practically identical.

Muir Castle, like so many stately homes in Great Britain, had been opened to the public by Their Graces to help pay the punishing maintenance bills, but "open to the public," railed the press, was the reason the recent spate of robberies had been so successful. Few aristocrats were equipped to deal with the professionalism of this new type of thief, who, they guessed, was "stealing to order."

The press was right on target, but so far—despite the hue and cry over the recent major art theft from Luton Hoo (alas, not their job), home of the Queen of England's husband's godson, Nicholas Phillips—nothing had changed, as far as they could see, in terms of extra security. Phillips blamed the theft on the publicity surrounding a movie crew he'd allowed (in return for a sizable fee) to shoot scenes around the house for a movie with the improbable name of *Four Weddings and a Funeral.*

Quentin Peet, who happened to be in London working on a major story about a drug bust at London Airport, appeared on CNN to mock that supposition, stating it had nothing to do with the movies; it was undoubtedly the work of the same kind of professional, who knew that Luton Hoo possessed the most incredible collection of Fabergé eggs in the world, and also knew exactly how to get hold of them for a particular customer, who was ready and waiting to buy.

Peet was impressive, Alex grudgingly had to admit that, but even Mr. Super Sleuth had no idea what was really behind this era of major heists, and he'd never be allowed to know, either.

There were two hundred rooms in the castle, but tonight they intended to pay an in-and-out visit to only two. Angus began to drill neatly and fast around a lock on a heavy door on the east side of the building. Open sesame.

Inside, they walked swiftly along a gloomy corridor, so ice-cold, their breath danced before them. Alex briefly wondered about the temperature of the Kirkburghes' living quarters. Ice-cold, too, he'd bet, remembering a night he'd recently spent in a stately home in Hampshire, where the sheets in the guest bedroom had been so cold and damp, they'd steamed from the hot-water bottle he'd had the sense to order before saying goodnight.

Up a short flight of stairs, two lefts and they were outside the display rooms, which held what they'd come to collect—silver objets d'art, rare enameled ornaments, and three special pieces of heirloom jewelry. While he dealt with the alarm, Angus made short work of the locked door, taking out a lighter drill to open the cabinets inside.

He now slipped on thin silk gloves to carefully extract two remarkable clocks, one by Fabergé, the other by Cartier, a necklace like a lace web of brilliantly cut diamonds by Boucheron, a twenty-eight carat blue diamond, another lacelike bracelet of golden pearls and coral and, from the third cabinet, a collection of eighteenth-century gold and enamel snuffboxes, which had come to the family's treasury of possessions straight from the craftsmen in Bilston over two hundred years before. Each item went into its own specially designed velvet pouch and all pouches went into a large, soft attaché case.

"Shit," Angus hissed, as in turning he tripped over a carpet runner, which hadn't been there on earlier fishing expeditions.

In trying to save himself, he shot his gloved hand through the glass of an adjacent cabinet. As the glass shattered, a penetrating alarm went off. They both grabbed objets and jewelry they hadn't planned on taking—waste not, want not—then fled down the stone corridors as the alarm continued to shriek and lights began to go on behind them.

It was a close call. Neither of them calmed down until, agonizingly trying to keep within the speed limit, they turned off the A699 onto the A68, the main north-south trunk road to London.

By the time *The Evening Standard* arrived at Alex's rented flat late the following afternoon, with headlines about "The Muir Castle Raid, Planned With Commando Precision," much of the haul was already on its way to his new client in Switzerland. Although he didn't know who the client was, he'd been told that the man was immensely powerful and rich. The new client had noted not only his professional work, but also his excellent knowledge of priceless, beautiful things.

Alex had enough sense to know it was best not to inquire into this mysterious gentleman's identity, but the hint of enormous benefits to come had piqued his curiosity. Through his own network of contacts he had learned there was a new demand for thieves with his kind of fine-art knowledge, because there was a new use for stolen masterpieces—in art and recently in jewelry, too.

It was drug related. He didn't know exactly how. Not ransoms, not egos, not a demand for Van Goghs to hang on drug czars' walls. He'd been told very clearly, if he wanted to stay alive, not to wonder why; just do the job and collect. That was okay by him.

If he had to move into the art world, that was okay, too, although diamonds for drugs suited his modus operandi better. It wouldn't be long before he would be called to discuss his future. He couldn't wait.

He yawned. He was too tired to go to the Eaton Square party with the A-plus guest list. It was, after all, just more work.

The invitation had described "snoozing" entertainment—a piano and cello sonata by some obscure Eastern European group before dinner, followed by more of the same after—yet he'd accepted because of the jewelry he knew he'd see there, spectacular, important pieces, some perhaps "entailed," out of the vault for the evening, or what he called "conscience items," costly gems, given by an erring husband or wayward lover, to right the balance on the scales of a dipping relationship.

The jewelry at these grand parties bewitched him; the women who wore it did not, most of them with faces redrawn so radically by surgery, they reminded him of the wives of Lot. Silly fools. Little did they know this was his opinion of their expensively maintained looks. On the contrary. He was a much sought after escort and house guest, the ladies doting on him to such an extent that after only a few months of zeroing in on the best quarry, he was able to keep an up-to-date dossier on the way they lived their lives, their habits, their movements, and, of course, where they stashed their valuables. It might easily be a year or so before he used this scrupulously recorded information, but it was as good as money in the bank.

He called Eaton Square to make his regrets, made himself a vodka martini—"shaken, not stirred" à la Mr. Bond—took it into the small, austerely elegant bathroom and soaked in a hot tub, full of Penhaligon's salts, sipping a cool sip from time to time.

If he wasn't out "working" a party, he usually liked to be alone the night after a big job, letting down, slowly relaxing with the things he most appreciated. What would he relax with tonight? The work of an erudite scholar? Mozart, or Elton John on his fabulous sound machine? No, something more amusing. He would watch *To Catch a Thief*, one of his favorite old movies.

As he watched Cary Grant and Grace Kelly on the Riviera, Grace wearing one more glorious outfit after another, he thought about Ginny.

He promised himself he would call her soon to see if, with her heart at last on the mend (he'd love to fix that goddamn Italian swine), she sounded stable enough to help him—inadvertently, of course—with an interesting American project he thought it was time to pursue. Yes, Alex decided, he'd call Ginny tomorrow.

Ginny was fantasizing, sitting at her number one assistant designer's desk, surrounded by swatches of material, a pin bag at her waist, doodling, dreaming of what might have been and what might still be.

She saw herself arriving at the Gosman showroom in her belted, smoky-gray suede suit (her most recent knockout design), interrupting a passionate embrace between her boss and one of his most ardent fans, a wealthy, over-blonded, crocodile-skinned Palm Beach widow. Both gasp, then extol her appearance.

"You see, darling Everard, you don't have to worry," the client says happily. "You can retire and come with me to Florida, leaving the business safely in Ms. Walker's talented hands . . ."

"Ginny, Mr. G. wants a walk-through of 854 on the double."

"It needs a fuller vent," Ginny murmured automatically. To come to life, she drank what remained of her cold coffee, then sauntered into Gosman's office.

Since being officially appointed number one assistant designer, Ginny believed Gosman and she were almost buddies and, as Lee told her at least once a week, she had indeed become "totally indispensable" again.

With bursts of his own "don'ty'worrygaly'candobett'rthanthatdago" lingo, Gosman had unwittingly been a figurative shoulder to lean on in the early days of Ricardo's abandonment. With Alex still in Europe, Ginny didn't know what she would have done without him, when without warning, her eyes would fill with tears and, with no comment, he'd hand her huge, crisp, white handkerchiefs across the desk. He also provided the best antidote for grief—work, work and still more work, without complaining when she didn't get around to all of it the same day.

Just as well. Back then, workaholic weeks had been followed by periods of such apathy she could hardly get dressed in the morning, especially when she stayed in the loft Ricardo had left behind as a going-away present.

In just a matter of days Ricardo's Chelsea sublet would be up and, thanks to the sentimental heart of the owner, an expatriate painter who lived most of the time in Dublin, she would become the full-fledged, rent-paying tenant for one year, with a right-to-renew clause at the end.

Ginny never dreamed she would end up renting Ricardo's loft. After his departure, she'd drifted into using the place as a base for apartment hunting, mainly to escape from Sophie's kind but overpowering fussing.

Time slipped by; friends started dropping in. She bought a ten-foot dark green rattan screen to hide the tiny kitchen. She finally hung Ricardo's shadows and lake painting on the west wall, where late afternoon real shadows added to its beauty. Without realizing it, she began to take possession . . . and then came the phone calls. From Ricardo.

Fifteen times she'd hung up on him. Then, like the violets arriving with one word or a few words at a time, she began to reply, never letting her guard down, sometimes courteous, sometimes not, always brief. Only too well did she remember Ricardo's marathon calls, the ones she'd sat through with such a fixed look of indifference.

Who was sitting or lying in bed with him in Milan, as with one hand he held the receiver, while with the other he touched, stroked, caressed . . . who? Oh, hell, who cared! Did she? Yes—and no.

Did she now look forward to the calls? Yes—and no. She didn't trust him; she didn't trust men in general. Over and out.

He'd begun to talk about coming back to see her. Of course, by then, she would have moved. He'd never find her. All the same, when the lease came up for renewal, she knew she'd sign it, despite the increase in rent. It was only for a year with an option to renew and Ricardo probably wouldn't come anyway.

On the subway going home she began daydreaming again. This time she was in Arthur Elgort's studio, one of *Vogue*'s most chosen photographers. "Adorable, wonderful, fantastic," he screams. "You're just the face Lancôme is looking for to replace Rossellini."

She climbed the stairs to the loft with nonstop applause in her ears, modestly following her "bride" down the runway, a particularly innovative one in gunmetal satin with a bouquet made of pastel leather "roses." Flowers deluge her as a headline flashes: THE COUNCIL OF FASHION DESIGNERS ELECTS GINNY WALKER DESIGNER OF THE YEAR.

The reality of no fresh food in the fridge and no energy left to call for takeout extinguished her fantasy life as she unlocked the door. Without taking off her raincoat she threw herself on the bed she'd shared so many times with Ricardo less than a year ago. As soon as she was the real tenant she'd loan or sell the bed to Barbara at the showroom, who was moving to an unfurnished studio. She'd buy herself a waterbed, supposed to be good for soothing exhausted bodies. She was exhausted all right.

She closed her eyes. The phone rang.

Six-thirty P.M. in New York. Half past midnight in Milan? She stared at the instrument, willing herself not to pick it up.

"Hello?"

"Ginny! How's my favorite designer? What are you wearing? What did you design for that old thief Gosman today? Where are you going tonight?"

"Alex!"

As she heard her cousin's voice, all tension and tiredness disappeared. "Alex!" she cried again. How she wished it wasn't just his voice in the room. How long had it been since his last call? Weeks and, like now, it had come at a particularly low, depressing moment.

He'd been in Paris, she remembered, and hearing her flat tone, he'd flooded the wires with his unique brand of sunshine. "It sounds as if it's raining in New York. You'd better come to Paris," he'd said, as if it was as easy as catching an uptown bus. "I may be able to get you something with Givenchy. I hear he desperately needs a new première d'atelier flou . . . you know, the key pair of hands in charge of fluid fabric, as opposed to the tailoring type. I'll check it out, call you back and help you get a ticket." He hadn't called back, not until now, and, of course, no ticket had materialized.

She was growing up; she hadn't given Alex's suggestion more than two seconds' thought. She'd given up expecting miracles from anyone, but especially from Alex. Nevertheless, there was still no one who could change her outlook on life so immediately.

Before she could reply to his rapid-fire questions, he asked another one. "What are you doing on Monday?"

"When is Monday?"

"The day after this Sunday, little donkey head." His warm, wonderful chuckle came over the line so clearly, she bit her lip, realizing how much she missed hearing it. "Are you busy?" he went on.

She was rarely busy, except at work, but ironically only yesterday she'd been asked for a date on Monday, when the wizard of Oz had arrived in the showroom without an appointment.

"Just passing by . . . hear such great things about you," he'd said, and then, like his most powerful lens, he'd looked her over. She'd been half amused, half flattered that for whatever reason he still had a thing for her. Later that afternoon, he'd called to say he was covering a fancy charity event on Monday and would she like to join him at the press table?

She'd said no automatically, regretted it, thought about phoning to say she'd changed her mind, then in the frenzy surrounding the changes to 854 had forgotten all about it until now.

"Well?" Alex's impatience was loud and clear. "Well?" he said again. Aunt Lil had proudly told her mother he was so successful now, he wasn't prepared to wait for anything. "If he wants something, he wants it NOW." What else was new? Alex had always been like that.

"No, I'm not busy," Ginny replied slowly. "Why? Where are you? D'you still want me to fly to Paris? To see Monsieur Givenchy?" She laughed, but there was a tinge of sarcasm in her voice. Alex didn't seem to notice.

"No, I'm in London, leaving tomorrow. I have to go to a black-tie charity ball in New York—for DIFFA, Design Industry Foundation for AIDS. Not your usual old boiled-chicken-on-a-plate Plaza do. It's downtown, but strictly A-list. I want to show you off to the kind of chic, original women who'll have their tongues hanging out when they see your clothes. Get busy with the old needle and thread, Ginny, m'dear. You must really look fabulous. I'll call you when I get in tomorrow." Ginny stifled a giggle. Was she still daydreaming or did Alex now have a distinctly British accent?

"Are you still there, old girl?"

Old girl? This was hilarious.

She couldn't wait to see what Alex would be wearing to match his new hoity-toity vowels. Spats? Plus fours? A monocle? Nothing would surprise her, but whatever he wore, he'd still outshine everyone.

For five minutes after she put the phone down, Ginny was ecstatic; then reality socked in. Was this one of the few promises Alex was going to keep? Why should this call be different from any of the others?

Ginny flicked through her limited wardrobe. She didn't have anything anywhere near resembling a ball gown, let alone a fabulous one. She could devote her weekend to creating one, but would she really have an opportunity to wear it? A ball gown was one article of clothing she didn't need on her beat.

For the first time in months she thought about Poppy Gan. Poppy had never called her after their strange meeting at Mr. Chow's and she'd had much too much Ricardo on her mind to think about calling Poppy.

Somewhere a delicate shoot of ambition stirred, like a tender perennial bud breaking through after a hard, cold frost. Perhaps Poppy Gan would be at the A-list DIFFA benefit. Perhaps not, but there would be other Poppy Gans there, perhaps even *Vogue*'s editor in chief, Anna Wintour, who was known to like downtown more than uptown.

As pessimism alternated with optimism about Alex keeping his word, Ginny forgot she'd ever been exhausted. She liked to nibble during the early stages of a design, so she went to the fridge. There were only two shriveled oranges and a bottle of witch hazel inside. It didn't matter; her mind was turning so fast now, she didn't have time to be hungry. She was remembering something special, hanging with other Gosman relics in a storage cupboard at 554, near where the lugubrious sample pattern maker, Moses Akkaroff, stood making muslin sample patterns all day long.

In minutes Ginny was in a cab on the way back to Seventh Avenue. Was it still there? The old Gosman copy of a Christian Dior sheath in Halloween pumpkin-colored sateen? It had to be—and it was.

She tried the dress on, first the right way, then back to front, so its décolleté neckline swooped down her back, exposing every vertebra, to hover just above the cleft in her buttocks, while the tiny buttoned-up back became the demure Victorian front, giving no hint of what lurked behind. She started to work in earnest.

To hell with Alex. To hell with DIFFA. Whether she went to the ball or not, this was a fascinating project. She stayed up working all night, having more fun than she could remember having in a long, long time.

Alex confirmed the date the next evening. He sounded jet-lagged and irritable. "What are you putting on your body?"

She described the dress, adding just to provoke him, "I went into Axman's, the tony butcher's shop around the corner, and—"

"What the hell for?"

"I asked if I could buy the huge cream-colored paper chrysanthemum hanging in their window, just above the baby lamb chops in their little paper cuffs . . ." Ginny paused dramatically, imagining the look of disbelief on Alex's face. "I thought I'd wear it on my head at the ball. It's exactly the right shade and—"

"Absolutely not," Alex roared. "Not with me as your escort you don't. Ostentation is O-U-T. I thought you knew that."

"From brass to class?" asked Ginny innocently. She'd just read the phrase in *Women's Wear Daily*.

"Yes," Alex replied grudgingly. "The word to aim for is—"

"Civilized," they said together.

He allowed himself a short guffaw. "All right, Ginny. So we're both reading the same trades now. So you know you don't go around looking like a lamb chop, or a spring chicken either."

He was in a very different mood when he arrived to pick Ginny up. "Ravishing." He appraised her thoroughly, front and back. "Absolutely gorgeous, Gin, my dear. Now, I wonder what your mentor has brought you to wear instead of a paper flower. Shut your eyes."

He guided her to face the papier-mâché mirror over the fireplace (which Mr. Landlord from Dublin warned could never receive a fire unless she wanted the place to burn down). Ginny felt Alex's cool fingers on her neck. For a second they were Ricardo's fingers and a rush of sex blazed between her legs. It went as soon as she opened her eyes, gone with the sight of the astonishing necklace, fitting like a collar, around the high neck of her Walker-Gosman-Dior triumph of a dress.

Diamonds, they looked like diamonds, but, of course, they couldn't be.

"Oh, Alex, I've never seen anything so beautiful, but you shouldn't have—they look incredibly ex—"

"On loan, Ginny, m'darling, so don't get too attached to them. They're on loan from Harry Winston. I want you to show them off tonight; no one could do it better."

He twirled her around and she felt radiant, ready for anything, as full of anticipation as, not so long ago, she'd felt all the time. How wonderful it was to have Alex back; how beloved the necklace made her feel.

For a second Johnny thought Dolores had come to join him after all. Through the crowd he caught a glimpse of a tall, slender, dark-haired girl, laughing up at a tall, handsome guy with English-looking sideburns.

As he moved toward her, he realized it was a hopeful figment of his imagination. This girl, in such a sweet, decorous, unlike-Dolores dress, didn't look like his wife at all; she didn't even have any bosom to speak of.

He smirked when the girl turned her back to him. What a perfect dress to describe a woman . . . two-faced, misleading, totally deceptive, because while the front was pure Miss Goody Two-shoes, pearl-buttoned to the neck, the back, so low-cut it only just missed the crease in her behind, was straight out of a bordello.

Johnny yawned. He was tired, that was his main problem, tired because of too many restless nights after too many rows with Dolores, tired of slammed doors, locked doors, empty apartments, let alone empty refrigerators. When and where was it going to end?

Although nowadays he often turned up alone at events like this one tonight, he'd noted he was rarely asked, "Where's your wife? Where's Dolores?" the way most people began a conversation when one half of a couple appeared without the other, particularly a relatively newly wed couple. It disappointed him and, for some reason, tonight added to his depression.

How long had they been married? Not even eighteen months. He swallowed a sigh. There was no sign of Dolores getting pregnant again, if—and it was an if that troubled him more and more these days—she ever had been pregnant that January of '93, when he'd proposed and promised to help take care of her debts. She'd lost the baby because of all the stress, she'd said, stress caused by people clamoring to be paid, not willing to be patient. He'd believed her then. Did he believe her now? He didn't know what he believed anymore.

He would feel guilty for the rest of his life that his mother had managed to wheedle out of him what a financial hole he was in, trying to persuade him to delay the wedding. He would forever feel that in tying the knot, in some way he'd hastened her death. Adding to his guilt had come the shock of learning she'd left him virtually everything, to make sure that with Dolores on his back, he wouldn't sink like a stone.

To his horror, he felt his eyes misting over. He missed his mother, much more than he ever dreamed he would. She'd been his anchor, and from her letter, written to him just before she died, he knew now that for years he'd been hers.

"Like your column, Johnny . . . going to write about us tonight?" A stranger was grinning expectantly at him, as if they were lifelong friends. Who "us" referred to, he didn't know or care. He grinned back and moved on.

People he didn't know were accosting him more and more these days, not in the awed, respectful way he'd seen strangers approach his father, but as if they knew him and liked him because they read his column. He liked that. He liked that a lot, providing they didn't want to enter into a discussion about why they did or didn't agree with his point of view.

Thank God, he liked his job, was crazy about it, in fact; although with his mother gone, it appeared he had no one to tell who would be remotely interested.

So far *Next!* seemed to like him, too, although at the last lunch with Steiner, his boss, he'd implied he was looking for a big cover story from him "one of these days." Steiner and he both.

He hadn't taken the bait, hadn't even blinked an eyelid to give away the fact that at last he thought he might be on to something. He was far too cautious even to admit it to himself. One step at a time . . . Rosa Brueckner style.

At least he could thank Dolores for Rosa, or Rosemary, to use the name she'd been christened with. Working on a story about modern-day heroines for *Next!*, just for the hell of it, he'd persuaded Dolores, on one of the days they weren't snarling at each other, to try Rosa's old number in California. To his amazement the number still worked and the next day she returned the call.

Dolores had reluctantly introduced "her husband" over the phone; he'd congratulated Rosa on the *Time* piece, said he wanted to include her in something he was working on for *Next!* and in February, when Rosa, now using her real name, Rosemary Abbott, had business that brought her to New York, they'd met.

"How come your number still rings in Beverly Hills?" was his first question to her.

She'd laughed, but there'd been no laughter in her eyes. "The trials from my job are still grinding on. It's going to take years before it's all cleaned up. That's why the DEA keeps the number operating. It's incredible, but despite the publicity, traffickers still call, hoping they've come to the best place to do their laundry."

"Aren't you scared?"

"Sure, sometimes, but if they wanted to kill me, they would have by now." She'd spoken in a matter-of-fact way, as if she was discussing normal working conditions. "There's a lot of macho behavior out there, guys who don't want to believe they were outwitted, double-crossed by a woman . . ." She'd smiled an understanding smile as he'd shaken his head in dazed admiration, adding, "I come from a law enforcement family. Both my parents were detectives and my husband's with the DEA. It makes a difference."

He'd never told Dolores about the meeting. He didn't hide it from her. He just didn't tell her, and at the time she'd been away, skiing in Aspen with Ash, one of the quartet of empty-headed, too-rich-for-their-own-good young women Dolores liked to hang around with; although in her case, Johnny was the one who ended up paying the bills.

But why hadn't he told her? Because despite being older than he remembered from their brief meeting in the Hamptons—about forty, he'd guessed—and wearing unattractive steel-rimmed glasses and a dowdy woolen suit, Rosemary Abbott was still one gorgeous hunk of woman, and Johnny knew there was no way Dolores would ever believe that after only five to ten minutes, Rosemary's looks were the last thing on his mind.

She was an avenging angel, burning with a passion to "rid the world of drugs, destroyers of humanity."

"Can I help?" It had seemed a natural thing to ask.

She'd looked at him long and hard. "Maybe you can." That mirthless laugh again. "You certainly come with good credentials." She knew about his *Next!* column; she probably knew everything there was to know about him, and then she'd admitted she'd only agreed to see him because she was such an admirer of his father and all he was doing to bring to justice those at the top in the drug business. "I would love to meet him one day." What else was new?

He'd been pissed off, but he didn't think he'd shown it. It was the cross he had to bear; and if it produced contacts like Rosa-Rosemary, he told himself, it was worth it.

"D'you know what I mean by *Trace* magazine?" she'd suddenly asked him. He did not.

"It's an international showcase of stolen property, circulates in about a hundred countries to alert would-be buyers not to touch. The new reality is, by the time it's stolen, it's already too late for any alerts."

"I don't . . . I don't get you."

She'd looked carefully around the restaurant on the Lower East Side, where she'd suggested they meet. It was empty except for a forlorn-looking girl waiting for somebody by the window. "There's been a spate of major thefts in Europe during the last couple of years . . . masterpieces, art, artifacts, jewels . . . expertly planned, no arrests, nothing to date retrieved. *Trace* issued photographs and gave details of about eighty million dollars' worth. Nothing turned up because the thieves weren't out there looking for buyers. These things were stolen to order—by order of the drug czars."

"My God, but why?"

All business and factual a moment before, suddenly Rosemary had changed, become vague, quiet, as if she'd said too much. "I've got to go," she'd said, although their main course had just arrived before them.

Why had she changed? Startled, Johnny had looked around, not seeing any reason for alarm. The forlorn girl had been joined in the window by another, equally drab-looking, that was all, but Rosemary had started to stand up. He'd insisted on getting her a cab and in the end they'd traveled uptown together.

Again asking her what he could do to help, before getting out on East 80th Street, she'd told him, "Keep up to date with stolen property—through *Trace* and the Art Loss Register, you know that international data base . . ."

He didn't, but he soon would.

"Then keep your eyes open. You go to all these fancy parties with Dolores. Every so often the ego of these guys gets the better of them and they can't resist flaunting something that will give them away. London's still the clearinghouse for this international fine-art loot, but New York's not far behind. What about that Long Island break-in over Christmas on the North Shore? A Goya, a Flinck, and what else? It's been two months and not a peep . . . where d'you think the robbery squad is now?"

He knew he'd looked baffled, but she'd provided the answer. "Nowhere, my friend, absolutely nowhere. They're still waiting for the ransom note, which I can tell you will never arrive. Check it out and keep in touch."

He went back to his office after that to get the Brueckner *Time* piece out of the file and reread it. One paragraph chilled him, thinking of how suddenly Rosemary had shut up in the restaurant.

"The woman in money laundering is a very important phenomenon in Colombia," he read. "The men are running the cartel, but women, professional women, are in control on the money end. For this reason Rosa Brueckner was perfect, able to develop a woman-to-woman trust, rather than the male macho thing."

Johnny thought of the two women in the window, so nondescript he couldn't remember a single thing about either of them. But something had alerted Rosa or, he corrected himself, Rosemary.

He hadn't heard from her since, although he'd called and left a couple of messages. She'd been right, of course. There was a veil of mystery surrounding the North Shore burglary of Stimson Court Place, once the home of a Vanderbilt.

He'd gone to play cards with Freddy Forrester, an old-time bachelor cop friend of his father's, something he'd been doing since he was a teenager; so Freddy didn't suspect that during the game Johnny hoped to learn something—and he did.

Organized crime was behind the Long Island heist, Freddy explained. "The young elite of the underworld have discovered it's a damn sight easier and more lucrative to rob an isolated mansion than to ambush a Brinks truck with armed guards, and police helicopters."

So where did he go from there? He was in the process of finding out, one step at a time.

Lost in thought, Johnny was startled when someone touched his shoulder. He turned abruptly. "Are you ready with your cross-examination?" A young, very pretty blonde with an anxious-to-please expression was standing there. Now why couldn't he have fallen in love with somebody who looked as pliant and pleasant as this young woman? Why was he always attracted by trouble and trauma?

"Cross-examination? Okay, you said it. Let's go."

He was thinking of writing about how exactly the huge amounts of money raised to fight AIDS were spent and whether anyone attending this kind of classy evening really gave a damn. The guests, as they were erroneously called, having coughed up a thousand dollars a ticket to get in the door, were dutifully wearing their little red ribbons, but how many of them had close ones suffering from the terrible disease and how often did they see them, help them, on a one-to-one basis?

He'd already got some quotable answers. If he ran across the girl in the two-faced dress again, he'd ask her the questions, too; then he could use the two-faced dress line. He'd probably use it anyway, whether he saw her again or not.

He followed the pretty blonde to the table where the main organizers of the DIFFA benefit were waiting for him. He'd get some facts and figures and then, he decided, he'd call it a night and give Dolores a surprise by getting home early.

Flash, flash, flash. Everywhere Ginny went photographers flashed away, their lenses focused not only on her front view, but the back view, too.

"This way, miss . . . look here . . . can we get that back view again . . ." With a dazzling smile she followed every command. Her dress was going to make it to the pages of *WWD*, she was sure of it . . . and Alex was there to see her triumph. What more could anyone ask for?

As she dutifully posed, there was a shout, and in seconds all the photographers had rushed to the other side of the room.

Why? Who was arriving?

Ginny thought she was going to be sick. It was Poppy Gan, and there was no question that Poppy was a spectacular standout in a white satin Lana Turner number, which, Ginny noted sourly, accentuated everything, including the incredible boobs Poppy had just confessed in a *People* magazine profile had been "tailored" in Los Angeles by the world-famous cosmetic surgeon Steven Hoefflin.

There wasn't anything Poppy wanted to hide about the way she looked, however manufactured. The same article credited Stephen Knoll, New York's leading hairdresser, as the one responsible for all the gold in her hair. Only her extraordinary brown-black slanted eyes were for real, Ginny had noted. They were courtesy of her Korean father.

Couldn't the paparazzi see the difference between class and brass? Tonight it couldn't be clearer what was the crux of Poppy's problem with fashion. Everything was out on display; whoever was making her clothes had left nothing to the imagination.

Men obviously loved it. Even Alex, who she thought would have more taste, kept his eyes fixed on Poppy's sultry glide through the room, followed by the inscrutable portly Buddha figure Ginny had seen at Mr. Chow's, the mysterious Svank, still followed by his group of thugs.

When the music began, Alex steered Ginny swiftly onto the floor. He was a great dancer, but he wasn't dancing around the room, he was dancing across it, in a straight line, headed toward Poppy's table.

"Where are we going?"

"You'll see. I want little miss goldilocks with the varoom figure to see your dress. I happen to know she's looking for a fashion makeover."

"I know. I know her," Ginny said sulkily.

Alex held her out at arm's length. "You know Poppy Gan?"

Ginny definitely didn't like his incredulous tone. "Yes, of course I do. I was going to do some things for her, but I got . . . got sidetracked."

"Hmrph! You can say that again."

"I got sidetracked," she repeated. It was a silly game they used to play, but Alex wasn't in the mood for games.

"Let's go and say hello."

Ginny felt her color rising. She was furious. Surely her sophisticated cousin couldn't be interested in anyone as obvious as Poppy?

"Why, for goodness' sake? You always say table-hopping is vulgar. I can't believe you of all people would want to meet a bimbo like Poppy."

Alex laughed the laugh she'd forgotten how much she missed. He pulled her tighter to him. "It isn't Ms. birdbrain I care about, honey-chile. It's you. The man she's with—"

"I know . . . I know . . ." Ginny snapped. "Mr. Skunk or Shrink is the most powerful industrialist et cetera, et cetera in the world. So what?"

Alex jerked her arms crossly. "Svank is the name. I want to get to know him; I want him to take a look at you, at what you're wearing. He could be your backer. I know him slightly. I want to know him better."

When the music stopped, Alex said, "All right, Ginny, it's time you paid for your supper. Whether you like it or not, we're going to pay a visit to your old friend."

She felt uneasy, barging in, pretending a relationship where none existed, but in Alex's tight grip, she had no alternative. She was being a fraud, she told herself. She wanted Poppy to see her dress, too, didn't she?

"Hello, Poppy." Shy, unsure. "I'd like you to meet my cousin, Alex Rossiter."

"Hi, there, Jenny! Howdy, Alex. Wow, Jenny, as usual you're wearing some piece of dress and how about that necklace!" Poppy, as warm and welcoming as she'd been at Mr. Chow's, rattled on; Alex, Ginny noticed, hardly looked at her. Instead he was paying a sickening, obsequious homage to Svank, as if the plump one was a deity or something. To make matters worse, Svank ignored them both, even when Poppy made vague introductions, getting her first name wrong, and not bothering to remember her last one.

Either Alex didn't know when he was being snubbed or, for some unfathomable reason, he didn't care. When he moved closer to the great man and started chatting him up, as if Svank had wanted to meet him all his life, Ginny longed for a hole to open up and swallow them both.

"I lost your number, Jenny. I really looove your clothes. Oh, boy, did you really make what you're wearing tonight? You are soooo clever." Poppy leaned seductively across the table, trying to evoke some response from Svank. "Pussy, isn't that the most gorgeous dress you've ever seen . . ." To her alarm Ginny saw one of Poppy's breasts pop out of her halter neck onto the table, then miraculously back in again as she straightened up. Svank's sphinxlike expression didn't change and he didn't utter a word.

Ginny tried to think of something to say. "Let's have lunch, Poppy."

"Yes, let's. D'you have a pen?"

"I do." Alex pushed pen and paper under Poppy's nose.

"Here's my number, Jenny, but don't call before noon," Poppy implored. "Then let's make a date."

Why on earth had she suggested to Alex they have a nightcap? Ginny was so tired, she couldn't keep her eyes open.

For the third time he said, "You won't forget to call Poppy, will you?"

It was one thing that he hadn't stopped singing her praises; it was quite another he hadn't stopped nagging her to get out of Gosman's and put together a business plan, "so you can set up shop for yourself."

"Build your friendship with Poppy Gan," Alex repeated one more time before he left. "I can introduce you to some entrepreneurs, but one word from Svank and all our—your—problems will be over forever."

Oh, yeah? Remembering Svank's sharp, cold eyes, Ginny wasn't so sure.

It was only when she woke up the next morning that she realized the diamond necklace had gone home with Alex. So it really had been on loan. For once Alex had been telling the truth.

Poppy was twenty-two minutes late for lunch. A record, she confided, usually she was much later. Although Ginny had called and asked for the date, Poppy had considerately asked one of her two "assistants" to book the table at Le Cirque, where, she told Ginny over the phone, "you have to be known to get the right table." Ginny sat slumped at it in her smoky-gray suede.

Except at Thanksgiving and Christmas, she never drank at lunch. Today, it was a necessity. She ordered a kir and drank it down so fast it might have been colored water. She was in despair. Her whole life had just been turned upside down. It seemed impossible to believe, but Gosman was closing his business.

She stared into space. The day had started so happily, a red-letter day when she was going to convince Poppy not only that she could turn her into a fashion plate, but also that as a designer with a future, she was someone Mr. Svank should back, in order to add more millions to his trillions.

She'd left the loft in the morning, all prepared with a business plan. She had sketches to show Poppy of the kind of clothes she should wear to impress the judges of the Best Dressed list—if that's what Svank still wanted for her. And she was wearing her own knockout suit, sure something momentous was going to happen.

It had happened all right.

At ten-thirty Gosman had come into her office and, flinging his arm around her shoulder, had walked her back over into his. When he shut the door, his face white and tired, Ginny's stomach had turned over. He didn't waste words. He was ill; he was tired; the business wasn't doing well. Unlike her daydream he wasn't leaving the business in her talented hands; he was closing it down. Finito.

"How can a business where everything is continually on sale be anything other than sick? Now, I'm sick, too."

"But what about your accounts? Neiman Marcus, DelAnn's . . ." She'd reeled off a list of powerhouse U.S. stores, the sales they'd projected for the year (ten million dollars), the women who adored his clothes, but he just sat slumped, shaking his head.

"Too late, too late, Ginny. I've filed for Chapter Seven. You're supposed to know about finance. You know what that means."

Yes, she did. Bankruptcy protection from the hungry creditors who'd start pounding on the door as soon as the news got out.

"I'll try to get you another job. It won't be easy, despite your talent. Retail sucks; too many manufacturers, too many clothes at too many different prices. Too much competition." He'd put his head down on the desk and moaned. "I'm sorry, Ginny. I'll give you six months' severance pay, which is more than anyone else will get."

Now waiting for Poppy, as time ticked by, sitting at the right table at Le Cirque (in the corner, sharp right from the main entrance), Ginny wanted to put her head down on the right tablecloth and weep, but of course she didn't.

She hadn't meant to tell Poppy.

"The world doesn't like losers; only winners."

"Smile and the world smiles with you; cry and you cry alone."

Where had those well-worn clichés of wisdom come from—Alex? Or her father? It didn't matter. Poppy only had to ask her, "How are you, Jenny?" for the truth to come pouring out.

"I'm afraid I'm in a state of shock. My boss—I work for Everard Gosman as his senior design assistant, he's closing the business. I've only just heard. I was going to start my own business—in fact, I intended . . ."

Was Poppy listening?

It was hard to tell, as a succession of Italian waiters received from Poppy the sort of greeting Ginny reserved for long-lost friends.

"Hel-lo, *Benito!* Kiss Kiss."

"Hel-lo, how are you, Mario? Long time, no . . ."

"Paolo, *ciao, ciao, bambino* . . ."

"Svank can help you," Poppy volunteered as the waiters took an intermission. For the third time since her arrival she opened up a gold compact with her initials PG large and bold in emeralds and critically reviewed her Stephen Knoll curls.

"He can?" Relief, as hot as the crunchy roll Ginny took from a busboy, rushed through her. "Really, you mean it?"

"I mean it. You help me, I help you."

Poppy looked bored with the subject. She changed it abruptly. "Don't you have anyone in your life? Love life, I mean? What about that cousin. You don't really mean he's your cousin, do you? Is that a blind or what? Are you and he—Sirio, how are you?" Poppy screamed in a tone a couple of notes higher and warmer than those awarded Benito, Mario and Paolo. "Sirio, you bad boy, where have you been? Meet my friend, Jenny . . ." Poppy smiled up into the eyes of the elegant Italian just arrived at their table. Ginny guessed he had to be the owner of the celebrated restaurant.

He kissed her hand. Ricardo used to kiss her hand all the time. There was, she decided, very little difference in the kisses. How could she have been so dumb?

"Ginny," she said loudly, "Ginny Walker."

Jenny, Ginny, who cared? Nobody, but she had to get through to Poppy somehow, to pin her down as she pinned her up. She was lightheaded. Of course, she was. She'd been drinking in the middle of the day.

"Truffles, we have delicious fresh truffles today . . . a little light fettuccine with truffles . . . a baby chicken perhaps, with a touch of madeira . . . portobello mushrooms grilled with just a trace of garlic . . ."

"Oh, you terrible fellahs, trying to make me fat . . ."

"No, no, no! No calories, I promise you, Miss Poppy."

Ginny fixed her well-rehearsed "happy-to-be-here" Sophie smile on her face as the game of ordering Poppy's noncaloric feast of the Gods was discussed with winks and smiles and more hand kissing as soothing as the Sargasso Sea.

"Lobster salad, please," was her contribution; she wasn't at all sure it got through, but her appetite was long gone anyway.

Sirio had hardly turned away when Poppy said, "Can you get me on this fucking Best Dressed list or not?"

Ginny gulped. Will the real Poppy Gan please stand up. She couldn't believe Poppy's language. Was that what happened after months, years of dealing with potentates like Svank?

"I can try." Ginny smiled wide, showing all her fascinating Elite-style crooked teeth. "Don't see why not."

"That's not good enough, Jenny. Oh, sorry—Ginny. Okay, okay, I've got it now. Ginny, Ginny, Ginny." Poppy paused as if waiting for approval. "When Svank says he wants something, he'd better get it or else. D'you follow me?" She laughed nervously. "He's used to getting what he wants, one, two, three."

Like somebody else I know, thought Ginny.

For the first time since her arrival Poppy looked at her directly. "Why aren't you a big success on your own, Ginny? Why d'you need to work for anyone? Your clothes are adorable."

The sweet innocent thing. This was the opening she'd been waiting for. Ginny plunged in with the story of her life, only slightly embroidered and not embroidered at all when it came to the urgent necessity of being seen out and about at all the places she read Poppy regularly attended.

"We can soon fix that," Poppy said, with another click of the compact. "The social whirl!" She sniffed. "That's no big deal." Her words came through clenched teeth as if she really meant it. "Svank likes parading me around like some kind of clotheshorse, but then it's nothing but 'Why didn't you do that?' 'Why didn't you wear that?' Believe me, I'd sooner be down in the Village hanging out . . . the social whirl, believe me, Jen—Ginny, it can be one big bore." As if to convince her, Poppy yawned, showing straight, perfectly white teeth. "No big deal," she repeated.

"Maybe not for you, but it's one route to *Women's Wear Daily* for me, for my clothes to be noticed, to be talked about, to get the backers I need to start up—"

"I told you, no problem, you can come along with me, and Svank will help. But you've got to help me, too. Can you get me on that fucking list or not?"

"Not just like that. Poppy, you've got to know threats from your Mr. Svank aren't going to get you anywhere either. Why he wants you on the list beats me. I'm not sure that it matters much anymore, but that's beside the point." Ginny warmed up. "You're gorgeous . . ." On hearing that, Poppy sat up tall and beamed as if she'd just become Miss America. ". . . but your dress sense is lousy." Poppy beamed on. Ginny swallowed hard. It had to come out. "You look too . . . too . . ."

She didn't have the heart to say it, but Poppy said it for her. "Flashy, loud. I know. Svank tells me so all the time, but that's where you come in. Your clothes are sexy without being . . . oh, I don't know."

By the time the fettuccine with truffles arrived, Ginny and Poppy had started on a bottle of white wine sent with Sirio's compliments, "Made from grapes grown near my family home in Florence."

As the wine went down, Poppy grew softer, confiding, "Svank wants me in *Vogue* because—don't tell anyone—he's buying Bloomingdale's or Bergdorf, I can't remember which, but it's one of those stores. I mean one of those stores belongs to the big, big group he's buying. So he wants me in every fucking fashion book as a fashion leader. Sorry, Jen—Ginny—but he scares me sometimes. If you can help, you'll never have to worry about a job again."

"Let's start right now."

Poppy squealed with delight when Ginny showed her the tape measure in her purse. By the time they left Le Cirque, nearer to three than the two Ginny had intended to be back on Seventh Avenue, she had taken Poppy's vital statistics in the ladies' room and her despair had diminished considerably.

She had a commission from Poppy to make her a dress—and not just any dress. It was for a very big night on her calendar, when Svank was to be honored at a dinner at the Waldorf-Astoria honoring leading citizens of New York.

Poppy had rummaged through her purse, looking for her date book, but it wasn't there. Instead, she found her checkbook and insisted on giving Ginny a check for five hundred dollars, "to get you started."

"Whatever happens about that ol' list, I promise I'll get you invited to the dinner," Poppy slurred with affection. "We'll walk in together and I'll tell the world you're my designer, 'cos by then you will be . . . and all those ol' retailers will drool and get their order books out."

One of Poppy's assistants called Ginny the next day with the date of the dinner, three weeks away. Thank God she had the assignment, because it was nothing but gloom and doom at Gosman's.

After that first Monday Everard hardly came into the office. There really wasn't much need. Ginny was mortified to see how quickly things started to collapse once the news got out.

She threw herself into designing the dress of all dresses for Poppy, usually the kind of challenge she thrived on, but so much was at stake, she kept changing her mind. On the one hand it had to be simple, to play down Poppy's top infrastructure, while emphasizing the leggy lengthiness of her torso. On the other hand, it had to be spectacular.

Alex, who knew all about it, didn't help, forever interfering, either on the phone or bursting in to see how she was getting on.

She was having dinner in Chinatown with Esme and Ted (they were now officially engaged) when the idea struck. She would design a Chinese red silk tuxedo for Poppy to wear on Svank's big night, a tailored, skintight to the body, high-necked Mao jacket, with skintight to the leg trousers, slit thigh-high at the sides.

At night she worked on the design, not giving a thought to what she would wear herself on the big night. During the day she went on job interviews, a few arranged by Gosman or Lee. There was nothing out there that she wanted, no design assistants needed, no creative "holes" gaping in the structures of any of the designers she admired.

She wasn't taking her out-of-work situation seriously—yet—because in her mind it was already day one after the big Waldorf night, with backing from Svank signed on the dotted line.

If she worried about anything it was having the time to look for premises, and, studying her address book, trying to decide whom out of all the talented people she now knew, she would try to hire once her name was on the door.

"Can I speak to Miss Gan, please?"

"Sorry, she's not available. Can I take a message?"

"Is this her answering service?"

"Yes, can I have your name and number, miss?"

"Ginny Walker. Please tell Ms. Gan to call me at 808-3592. I need her for a fitting for her . . . her dress. It's urgent."

"Can I speak to Ms. Gan, please?"

"She's not available. Can I take a message?"

"Can I speak to Betty Porritt, her assistant?"

"She's no longer working here."

"Can I speak to Ms. Gan's new assistant?"

"Hold on."

Ginny had started biting her nails again. She chewed on two while waiting.

"Sorry, no one's answering. Would you like to leave your name, a message?"

A week before the Waldorf dinner Ginny swallowed her pride and called Lee. "I've been trying to get hold of Poppy Gan for a fitting. I'm desperate. Do you have any idea where she might be?" It was a long shot, but Lee was a voracious student of trivia and squirreled away odd pieces of information.

"God, where did I hear she's gone?"

"Gone?" Ginny wanted to throw up.

"No, wait a minute. I saw her on TV recently, on *Entertainment Tonight*. Hang on, yes, now I remember. She was in L.A. attending the premiere of that Demi Moore fiasco. She looked like a floozy. Are you making her something, I hope?"

Ginny was blazing, but she controlled herself with, "Yes, I am, for a big dinner at the Waldorf next week, but the moron obviously doesn't understand I have to fit her. How on earth can I get in touch with her?"

To her fury Lee started to laugh. "Through Svank, my dear. I told you, he's the man to know."

"Thanks a lot." She slammed the phone down.

Forty-eight hours before the big night, Ginny worked out she'd made at least a dozen phone calls to Poppy without one response. How could Poppy be so thoughtless? How could she change from the con-fiding, warmhearted girl at Le Cirque, full of promises—"You help me, I'll help you"—to a remote stranger who didn't even return her calls? Depressed and nonplussed, Ginny stared at the red tuxedo suit hang-ing on her wardrobe door, waiting for its first fitting, let alone the final one.

The phone rang. Poppy? Low-wattage optimism spluttered out when she heard Alex's voice. "Something must have come up," was his way of cheering her up. "Don't for God's sake hold it against her."

"Don't hold it against her!" Even though he couldn't see her, it made Ginny feel better to wrench the red silk suit off the hanger and hurl it across the room. "If I ever see her again I'm going to show her just how much I hold it against her."

The day before the dinner, with still no word from Poppy, Ginny's depression turned into a white hot anger that tightened her mouth— and her backbone. She didn't deserve this.

No Poppy. No invitation. Okay. Fuck Poppy. Fuck fancy invitations. She would go to the dinner without either and she would wear the red silk tuxedo herself. If by any remarkable chance Poppy happened to be there, she would march up to her and publicly announce what she thought of her manners, her character, her zero chance of ever being well dressed, let alone best dressed.

What was one of Alex's famous dictums? "Aim high; get higher; even hired."

What had she got to lose? Nothing; and perhaps if she could get to Svank and show off what she knew was a brilliant piece of work, he might agree to discuss real business with her later. So she was whistling Dixie; there was no way she could stay home and do nothing on the evening when the leading citizens of New York were to be honored.

Ginny spent the day remodeling the suit to fit her willowy, noncurvaceous figure, well aware it would have suited Poppy better, but from a fashion point of view, it was still something to be proud of.

In Chronicles, the so-called gossip column of the *New York Times*, she read that the Waldorf dinner would start with cocktails at seven, dinner in the Grand Ballroom at eight. Twelve "leading citizens" were to be honored, including the "giant industrialist, known only by one name, Svank, who has already been so good to New York City in the short time he has been here."

Lee called in the afternoon to see if she'd heard from Poppy. "Nope, but it doesn't matter. I'm wearing the dress myself."

"What d'you mean?"

"I mean I'm going to the dinner in the most spectacular design you've ever seen."

"When?"

"Tonight."

"Alone? You mean that award dinner? Were you invited, too? I don't get it."

"No, I haven't been invited, but I'm going."

"You mean you're going to crash?" Lee sounded as if Ginny had told her she was about to go to the moon.

"Yep."

"You'll never get in. You'll be turned away, humiliated. Oh, Ginny, don't do it, don't crash. It isn't worth it. Keep the dress for another time, please! It's a seated dinner, for goodness' sake. Where d'you think you're going to sit? You'll hear from Poppy one of these days. Please, Ginny, you'll make a fool of yourself; you'll never get in."

"There are a thousand ways to get in. Don't worry so much, Lee. You sound like Sophie Formere. There are always no-shows at this kind of thing." Ginny couldn't believe how breezy and confident she sounded, but before Lee could scuttle her resolve, she put the phone down. It rang twice again, but she ignored it.

Between five-thirty and six-thirty she changed her mind a dozen times about going; put the suit on, took it off, put it on again; combed her hair severely back, backcombed it forward, adding a brilliant red ribbon.

When the phone rang at six fifty-five she rushed to answer it, sure it had to be Poppy, apologizing profusely, saying a ticket had been left at the door. Even hearing static on the line didn't prepare her for Ricardo's voice, warm and throbbing down the line. "Hel-lo, Gin-ny. *Come esta?*"

It was all too much. As if a demon had arrived in the room, she slammed the phone down, grabbed her bag, and without looking in the mirror again, rushed downstairs.

It was diving off the top board; it was facing all the Paul Robespiers, the Annie Jourdans of *Elle* magazine, the Katie Fords of the world rolled into one. She hailed a cab. It was bumper-to-bumper all the way uptown.

By the time she neared the hotel, she knew she couldn't go in without a drink. She went into the Waldorf's Lexington Avenue entrance where there was a bar, the Bull and Bear. With her eyes shut, she threw down a vodka martini.

Somehow it had gotten to be seven forty-five. It was now or never.

The escalator going up to the ballroom floor was packed with people, couples, men in black tie, women in every kind of dress, mini, micro, calf, long, half and half, not many trousers, and no one as chic as she. Despite the crowd, she had never felt more alone. There was a crush around a long table in the hall. Seat assignments? There was no reason for her to go there; she didn't have a seat.

Swept along on a perfumed tide, she concentrated on looking over shoulders, into space, as if looking for someone, a tardy escort, a lover, a husband. She tried to keep a half smile on her face, to show she really wasn't worried. She was ready with the words, if she were to be apprehended: "I am Poppy Gan's guest. She was supposed to meet me here with my ticket, but"—confiding laugh—"she's always late, you know. Please just show me to her table."

Nobody stopped her. Nobody was showing a ticket. All around her she heard, "What's our table number, darling?" "Thirty-six . . . eleven . . . can't remember . . . I think it's fifteen . . ."

The lights were going up and down in the foyer; a ringing gong began, summoning the pushing, shoving crowd, as thick as any encountered on the subway. Her story about the ticket Ms. Gan had left for her was trembling on her lips, but she was inside the ballroom before she knew it, with no one checking names or tickets.

The ballroom seemed much darker than the foyer, flickering for as far as she could see with tiny votive candles, surrounding soaring vases of arum lilies on every table. A crewcut in a tux was at the mike on stage, begging the crowd to behave, to find their seats, take their places and sit down so the evening could begin. He looked vaguely familiar, but she was too nervous to stare to see if he really was Tom Brokaw. She was inside, but now where should she go?

There was a spectacularly beautiful woman with the whitest skin she'd ever seen, staring at the stage. There was something familiar about her, too; perhaps she was a movie star, more likely a ballerina; that's what she looked like. For some ridiculous reason Ginny felt she'd met her, but couldn't remember where or when. Perhaps she'd seen her picture in the papers. The man beside her was trying in vain to attract her attention, but she ignored him. If only she could be with a man like that.

With a fast intake of breath, not far away Ginny spotted Poppy in the same Lana Turner white satin sheath she'd worn to the DIFFA evening. Her fear was replaced with fury. She didn't care what happened now. This was the moment for a major confrontation.

Grimly she pressed through the tightly packed throng. It was like a jungle, but she would fight her way through. "Mr. Livingstone, I presume." Justice would be done.

As the lights dimmed still further and she paused to get her bearings, a large couple barged by, literally knocking her off her feet into a chair. As the man turned briefly to apologize, Ginny waved her hand to absolve him of blame. She sat upright, as stiff as a poker, too terrified to move, staring at the stage without seeing anything. Now, Tom Brokaw—she was sure it was he—was banging on the podium for silence.

All around her a buzz buzz buzz of conversation continued. The lights went up a watt. She moved surreptitiously back in the chair and looked around. Now she couldn't see Poppy at all.

There were two other empty places at the table, one next to her. As a waiter started to pour wine, a man with a five o'clock shadow and a carnation in his buttonhole slid into the chair beside her.

"Arthur St—" As he held out his hand, his name was lost in a screech of laughter from the next table. Despite the threats and demands for silence still coming from the podium, to Ginny's amazement, no one took any notice. She began to relax a fraction, noting that opposite her was an older woman with a kind expression, and too much blue in her white hair. She was wearing, Ginny was sure, a Gosman copy of a feathery Lacroix. The realization made her want to sob like a homesick child. Instead, as the woman complimented her on her "stunning suit—whoseisit?" she heard herself say coolly, "Virginia Walker."

"Virginia Walker? Is that a British designer or someone from Hong Kong? It's so smart, I love it. Did you get it here?"

"Oh, thank you, well, yes, I did. No, it isn't British. It's mine. I mean I am Virginia Walker. I designed it myself. I am, well, actually I am a designer, Virginia Walker."

As Ginny stuttered on, there was a roll of drums, and for the first time she registered that there was a dais on the stage. With only a slight letup in the din, the New York citizens to be honored started to file in alphabetically as the man at the mike—too unsophisticated to be Tom Brokaw, Ginny decided—yelled out their names, including that of Quentin Peet. How her father would have loved to be here. She quickly blocked the thought of his disapproving face from her mind.

With ninety percent of her concentration on the other empty seat, wondering when the knell of doom would come with the missing couple's arrival at the table, Ginny was too nervous to look to see what her father's idol looked like in the flesh. At the table near the stage she could see white skin and her attentive escort applauding wildly. Of course, that was who she was, the beauty she'd seen at Doubles, the stunning woman Alex had told her was married to Peet's son, although she'd been busy in a dark corner with somebody else. Was she with her husband, Peet's son, tonight?

She forgot all about it as Svank's name was called and he strode in to take his place on the dais. Ginny only gave him a second's attention. Was she imagining things? Wasn't that Poppy calling out "hip hip hooray"? She strained her head over the packed ballroom, but couldn't tell where the cheer was coming from.

As the first course arrived at the table—something pale sitting on a tuft of lettuce—introductions were made. It didn't matter what was served; she was far too nervous to eat. The names all ran together in her head, Steve Bottomley, a banker, his wife, Lucille, who joined the Gosman-clad lady in praising Ginny's "boo-ti-ful trouser suit."

After ten minutes' chitchat with an advertising man on her left, the man who'd scooted into the chair on her right, Arthur-with-the-five-o'clock-shadow, said with a leer, "Who're you with, Ms. Virginia? You haven't been stood up, have you? Not a delicious lady like you?"

Ginny nervously giggled along with him. "Not a chance, alas. He's bound to get here sooner or later."

"Who?"

"You'll see . . ." By the time the main course arrived (as far as Ginny could see, a larger helping of the first bland offering, decorated with technicolored carrots and peas), her relief at having so far gone undetected as an interloper was tempered by having to deal with Arthur, who obviously thought he was a dreamboat who could get away with anything.

He told her that he was Arthur Stern, an extremely successful textile manufacturer, who'd been honored himself at the same event a couple of years before. Her wavering attention span straightened up when he told her he liked to diversify. "Guess what my latest venture is?"

"I can't imagine," she said coyly, wondering how to turn the conversation to her business aspirations.

"I'm the nation's leading manufacturer of teddy bears," he said with a wink.

She smiled weakly as he went on, "I like your point of view."

Startled, she began to ask, "Which point of—"

"This one." Openly ogling, he stroked her knee through the right-hand slit of her Chinese red silk trousers.

As she flinched, he removed his hand. "I'm interested in new businesses. As I told you, I like diversifying . . ."

"Into what?"

"How about from teddy bears to teddies," he smirked. "What could be more natural." Again his hand touched her thigh. "You're a new face in town, aren't you? Where's your business located?"

"I've . . . I've just begun. I'm looking for premises."

"This could be your lucky night. Come on now, come clean. Are you really waiting for someone? Who're you with? Who's coming to take you home?"

What could she say to keep him interested in her business and take his mind off her? "I'm a guest of . . ." In for a penny, in for a pound. "Mr. Svank."

"Hmmm. I'm not surprised. Well, it's your lucky night," he repeated.

There were shushes all around as the man at the mike introduced the evening's star mistress of ceremonies, Barbara Walters. The teddy bear manufacturer slung an arm around the back of her chair. She wanted to turn her back on him, but in another way, knew that his familiarity made her look as if she belonged at the table.

As the evening's business swung into action with everyone on the dais receiving an accolade and an award, once again Ginny felt her leg being stroked. She didn't know what to do. If she left for the ladies' room she'd never have the confidence to come back, and who knew if Mr. Teddy Bear with the evil leer wouldn't follow her. As she was wrestling with her next move, he whispered, "Why don't we split and go to your place to discuss a little teddy business?"

If only that was all he wanted to discuss. She could design teddies. She could design anything. What she didn't know was how to deal with men who had designs on her.

As she floundered, the lights went up, and like a gift from God she looked around to see Poppy approaching. She stood up and so did her dinner partner, placing a paw on her shoulder.

Although an hour ago Ginny had wanted only to tell Poppy what she thought of her poor manners, now she was longing for her help to extricate herself.

There had to be something in her expression that Poppy recognized only too well, Poppy who surely knew all about lecherous advances.

Without a trace of embarrassment, she said, "So there you are, Ginny. We've been looking all over for you. You're at the wrong table. We've been saving your place. Svank is joining us for coffee. He's dying to meet you."

CHAPTER FIVE

ONE SVANK PLAZA, NEW YORK CITY

The twenty-one tables were centered with three-foot moss-covered malachite candelabra, also entwined with mauve, yellow, and white exotic orchids. Beneath the napkins—mauve, yellow, and white to match, each one embroidered with the guest's name—small boxes nestled, wrapped in heavy white paper and sealed with a wax seal from Bulgari. They contained expensive, personalized gifts. The tablecloths were woven with silver thread and each chair was slipcovered in silver damask tied with heavy, silver-tasseled ropes.

It was hard to imagine a more wondrous sight, but the host, known for his singular sangfroid, with emphasis on the froid, and celebrated for his equally phlegmatic name, Svank, not only showed no pleasure, his jowly polished face was tight with rage.

"Where is she?" he hissed to the giant who rarely left his side. "Where is she?" he repeated, making the three words sound like a threat.

The giant's voice trembled. "The car went to collect her, boss, but Evie said she hadn't come back—"

"Come back from where?"

"Evie wasn't sure."

The usual impassive countenance was back in place, but Svank's measured tone was menacing. "We don't pay Evie not to be sure, do we? You know what to do about Evie. Now go find the girl, and I suggest you don't come back without her."

The giant, whose name, Hugo Humphrey, always caused titters behind his considerable back, muttered, "Yes, boss, yes Mr. Svank."

Hugo loped, head down, into the marble vestibule of the penthouse forty floors high over Central Park, commanding majestic views of Manhattan from all points of the compass. At the elevator bank, disguised with antique latticework domes, his cellular phone rang.

"Yep, yep, what is it?"

As he listened, his whole demeanor and posture changed. From whipped dog to fanged wolf, Hugo Humphrey straightened up, all six feet eight inches of him, and loped back to his master. An ingratiating smile cracked across his moon of a face. "It's okay, boss. She—" He hastily corrected himself as Svank scowled. "Ms. Poppy's on her way up—er—with the designer of her dress."

Only one finger tapping the ormolu surface of a commode gave any sign that Svank continued to be displeased, but his voice was quiet as he commanded, "Go see Evie. Show her how we cure amnesia."

When Hugo continued to hover nervously, Svank imperiously flicked him away with his hand. "Go. I don't need you for an hour."

As Humphrey disappeared into the elevator, Svank cursed himself for acting so out of character, for indulging an idiosyncrasy he rarely allowed himself. This evening, with the Rosa Brueckner matter decided and nothing too arduous clouding the U.S. business horizon, he had given in to sentimentality and deliberately arranged to arrive an hour before his guests. Why?

It had nothing to do with approving or disapproving arrangements that had been made, or with checking up on his people. He had other people to do that. In fact, he had specifically directed that the small army of assistants who were always on hand to supervise his rare social events would be gone before his arrival. And they had gone, after ensuring that the distinguished decorating maestro Robert Isabell and his team had literally left no leaf unturned, no bud out of place.

He took it for granted that he had the best that money—enormous money—could buy, not only superb food from his international chefs, but experienced food tasters, who "designed" delectable, memorable menus with every guest's religious or allergic rules taken into account. One was a food critic from a major newspaper who enjoyed augmenting his salary this way. Svank also took it for granted that his personal food taster would already be in the hotel-size professional kitchen, sampling every piece of food his palate would encounter.

So why was he so miserably alone in the splendor of his residence, one of many he maintained throughout the world? He had come early to enjoy, he'd thought, an hour alone with Poppy, savoring her and the sumptuous setting his money had wrought, sparing a moment or two to look back, although no one would know it, least of all Poppy Gan, comparing what he had now to what little he had had once.

Again he tapped his impeccably manicured finger irritably on the commode, waiting for Poppy's arrival. She had spoiled everything, the way women always spoiled everything. He had become a sentimental fool, which was dangerous, for why was he giving the party anyway?

He disliked society, and rarely socialized, invariably regarding people, however lofty their credentials or loaded their bank accounts, as wanting something from him. He was giving this party for Poppy, because it was her twenty-first birthday, the reason there were twenty-one of everything. But she obviously didn't appreciate it, and because of that she'd have to pay, as all the women in his life eventually had had to pay.

When the elevator doors opened, another giant preceded the two young women who slithered out, both visibly nervous.

"Pussy," Poppy cried. "Oh, Gaaawwwd, I hope you're not too mad at me, I know I'm just the tiniest bit late, but I was suddenly scared shitless you might not like my birthday outfit, so I had to find Ginny and bring her with me in case you wanted any last-minute alterations. You remember Ginny, don't you? She's made the most marvelous dress for—"

She stopped in mid sentence. There was something in Svank's eyes as he came up close to her, ignoring Ginny, who was carrying a garment bag and a small suitcase.

As Svank lifted his hand as if to slap Poppy across the face, Ginny shut her eyes. It all happened so quickly, she couldn't be sure if his movement turned into a blow or a fierce caress. Surely it had to be the latter?

When she opened her eyes, Poppy was standing motionless as Svank, without a word, walked into another room and carefully shut the door.

The painful silence was broken by the busy sound of television news coming from behind the closed door.

Suddenly, all business, Poppy said overly brightly, "Okay, Ginny, let's go to work. Follow me." She teetered on stiletto heels toward the heavily chintzed room Ginny knew she called her own.

Poppy was work, all right. She had been nothing but frustration and work since the Waldorf fiasco almost a month ago, when, remaining on the dais, Svank had not come to the table, so Ginny had yet to meet him properly.

Having tea with Ginny the next afternoon, Poppy had apologized again, explaining with a long face, "Svank rules the roost. I often don't know, I swear, Ginny, which country I'll be sleeping in at the end of a day. It's terrible."

She had shown Ginny the typed agenda she received from Svank's office every week, telling her where and when she was supposed to be on parade. "But often I go where this sheet tells me—to the office or the penthouse or the mansion—and he's not there. But then if I'm not where he expects me to be when he wants me, brrrrrhhh . . ." Poppy had shivered dramatically.

The birthday dress had been plotted that afternoon among the elaborate silver and gold tea urns of New York's Palace Hotel, with Ginny sketching out a design she thought of as schizophrenic, a dress with multiple personalities, finely tailored on the one hand—in midnight blue hammered satin—yet cut so "close to the bone," it followed every one of Poppy's stupendous curves, conveying major seduction without being revealing or playing any peekaboo.

Poppy had told her that at her birthday dinner there would be "a lotta top-drawer business people from Svank's businesses around the world," as well as what she called "a lotta New York glitterati," pronounced "glitteray." Without actually putting it into words, she'd conveyed that she was letting Ginny design something for this extra-special event to make up for the lost Waldorf opportunity. But disagreements had started almost at once, with Poppy insisting on a halter neck, "so I don't look too straitlaced."

Over several days Ginny had negotiated, trading flamboyance for fashion, Poppy's love affair with low necklines, frills and furbelows for streamlined elegance. She'd finally had to give in to the halter neck in exchange for abolishing the thigh-high slits Poppy angled for in the far from simple cut of the straight-as-a-Grecian-column skirt.

Instead of slits ("old fashioned," Ginny insisted), she had pleased Poppy, and herself, by setting a small bow tantalizingly on the lower back, at the point where the slow curve of Poppy's buttocks began. The size of the bow caused more cajoling and argument, not to mention the ripping and resewing of seams and darts.

Even a few minutes before arriving at the penthouse Poppy had been paranoid that Svank wouldn't like what she kept calling her new "schoolmarm" look.

"No schoolmarm ever looked like you, Poppy." Ginny had been saying the same thing in a dozen different ways since she began work on the dress, still remembering her earlier sense of despair that whatever Poppy wore, she would always be in danger of looking like a juvenile delinquent.

It was now seven-ten. The guests were coming at seven forty-five. After inspecting herself from every angle for a long, intense five minutes, Poppy was about to whirl away to show herself off to Svank when Ginny saw one of her false eyelashes hanging loose. That took another three minutes to fix, and Poppy fidgeted so much, Ginny wasn't sure it would last.

For one crazy, nostalgic second Ginny suddenly remembered Dallas and her precious box of Supreme Sables. She stared out at the Hudson River and the Jersey shore. Was she looking in the direction of Dallas, Texas? She thought so. She hadn't come as far as she'd expected. She straightened her shoulders. But at last she was on her way, wasn't she?

Not more than five minutes passed before Poppy was back, trying not to cry, stumbling toward the closet where, Ginny remembered from an earlier fitting, Poppy kept some of her clothes.

When Ginny saw Poppy's back view, she could have wept, too. Where the bow had perched so deliciously was now an ugly rent exposing Poppy's bare buttocks.

"He didn't like it?" Ginny stuttered, reddening at the absurdity of her question.

"No, no, no. That's not it," Poppy wailed. "He doesn't like me." She moaned as she rustled through a rack of clothes, finally taking out the white Lana Turner.

"Oh, please, Poppy, anything but that!"

Poppy took no notice. She continued to moan like a wounded animal. "You'd better go, Ginny. I don't want you to get blamed. It'll all blow over. It always does."

But Ginny was on her knees behind Poppy, assessing the damage.

"Stand still," she commanded sharply. She opened her small suitcase. It was packed with threads, ribbons, bows, fabric samples, cords—and artificial flowers. She found what she was looking for. A pale blue satin rose with satin leaves falling from a navy blue velvet stem.

"Stand still," she commanded again. "You'll wear that Lana Turner number over my dead body . . ."

Poppy flinched. "Don't joke, Ginny. You don't know what you're saying."

Ginny didn't hear her. She was too busy stitching fast, murmuring as she'd so often seen her mother do as she worked, singing a song under her breath. Ginny wasn't singing. "This is the dress you're going to wear tonight, Poppy," she intoned. "This is it . . . or else!"

That night, on Svank's stiff arm, Poppy and her satin rose (which didn't totally cover the tear in her dress) paraded themselves into the fashion headlines.

"Derrière Delight . . . On her twenty-first birthday Poppy Gan initiates a new and daring soirée idea," ran an item in Tuesday's *New York Times* fashion page, while "Birthday Buttocks" was the description used, with a picture of only that part of Poppy's torso on the front page of the *New York Post*. Mary Hart of TV's *Entertainment Tonight* used it, too, awarded the rare privilege of covering the celebrities as they arrived at "Model Poppy Gan's splashy birthday party given by New York's powerful new retailer."

Svank! Even reading his name made Ginny feel nauseated, but at least the ugly scene had had one good result. She would never again be jealous of Poppy. The entire episode had made her look at what Alex called the A-list social scene differently. Now she understood the price the Poppys of the world could pay to lead the life Ginny had viewed with such wistful envy. If Poppy had to put up with that kind of treatment from her monster of a sugar daddy, who knew what the other women she read about in the social columns endured, women far less attractive than Ms. Gan?

Poor Poppy. She'd traded her freedom for what? Unlimited pocket money, which could dry up at a second's notice; luxurious residences she could never call home; expensive clothes that could be ripped from her body if she displeased the monster paying for them.

Ginny Walker would never put up with that kind of behavior for one second, no sirree. Every time she thought about Svank's treatment of Poppy, not to mention his crude rudeness in ignoring her own existence, it stiffened her resolve to make it on her own.

She would play the monsters at their own game and take them for all she could until she found a way to be independent, to build and own a thriving business, for unlike Poppy she had something she loved more than herself: her work, her passion for designing.

"I'll never forget what you did," Poppy cried over the phone later that week. "Right from the first day we met, when you recommended me to Ford, you've always been such a friend."

Ginny gulped down her guilt, remembering her hypocrisy at Ford as Poppy wailed, "You're my only true friend."

Perhaps she really was, because since the birthday party she certainly wanted to do what she could to help her, although she didn't have much hope she could change anything or make Poppy see where Svank's domination was leading.

"You help me; I'll help you." It was time to put into motion the deal she'd made with Poppy at Le Cirque.

"What are you, er, up to this week, Poppy?" She didn't know how to proceed and stuttered, "Or rather, what are you supposed to be doing this week, so we can plan to see each other. Remember, you said I might be able to go with you to—"

"Wait a sec. Let me look at the agenda. Oh, where did I put it?" Ginny heard rustling sounds. She could well imagine the chaos. Poppy came back on the line sounding harassed. "I'm going to get Evie . . ." There was a pause. "No, Evie isn't here anymore. I'll get someone to call you with my itinerary in a minute."

"Could you ask her to give me a call every week or send it over?" Ginny held her breath, wondering if she'd gone too far, but no.

"Ab-so-lutely. And then between my dates we can work out when we can see each other." Poppy giggled. "I guess I'd better get me some more schoolmarms; the press seems to like 'em."

Between dates? Poppy was forgetting the purpose of the plan. Who did Poppy think she was talking to? And "schoolmarms," for heaven's sake!

"You promised I could go with you sometimes, to show off my clothes, remember?" She sounded sharp, but what had she got to lose?

"Sure, sure, Ginny. I remember. Love ya."

When Poppy hung up, Ginny went straight to her drawing board with a suit idea for Poppy in mind. As she sketched she told herself she was a new, much more sensible Ginny Walker, no longer inhibited about not belonging, or thinking that any of the rich-as-Croesus people, who, now she knew, often paid to go to a party, were any better than she was.

On the contrary. She'd gotten her feet wet at the Waldorf in the so-called social swim. Now she was more than ready to dive right in the deep end. She wasn't looking for a sugar daddy. No way. She was looking for a well-connected, well-heeled backer, male or female, someone who would look at her clothes and know he or she could make money, lots of money, by investing in Ms. Ginny Walker.

She told herself, if you want to be an actress, you go where the producers, the directors are: you move to Hollywood. If you want to be a fashion designer, you go to fashionable events attended by entrepreneurs, retail magnates, powerful manufacturers, and you stay put in New York, home of American fashion. If Poppy forgot to ask her, she'd repeat her Waldorf adventure, she'd crash again.

With Poppy's agenda and many major upcoming events listed in *Town and Country* every month she would be able to plan a proper campaign.

"How are you making out with Poppy and the best-dressed crusade?" Alex asked.

They were having supper on the eve of his return to Europe, where, he'd just told her, he was now "dedicated" to the business of buying and selling fine art.

Ginny hesitated. She decided she wouldn't tell him the ugly birthday party story—not yet, anyway. "Svank"—she couldn't help wrinkling her nose in distaste—"he wants her on the Best Dressed list just as she is now, with everything hanging out, but I'm persevering."

"Atta girl! I know you are. I saw the press coverage on that extraordinary birthday suit, if you'll excuse the expression. I was only sorry your name wasn't mentioned as the designer. Why not? When are you going to stop being so retiring and get some credit for all that hard work?"

Although so far Poppy had only asked her to a boring art exhibition—and then not turned up—she'd been true to her word about sending her agenda.

Ginny had already had two glasses of wine, so it was easy to tell him her news, to prove to her sophisticated cousin she wasn't retiring at all anymore, if indeed she'd ever been.

"My dear Alex, I'm just starting to show off my designs at some of the best parties in town."

"How so?"

"Sometimes with Poppy, sometimes without, I give the hosts the benefit of my unique solo fashion presentation." Ginny paused, she hoped provocatively. "Whether they've had the sense to invite me in the first place or not."

"You mean you crash?"

Ginny nodded. "You could call it that. I consider it doing the host a favor."

Alex's sanguine face slowly opened up with a beam of approval. "Atta girl," he said again.

Ginny suppressed the urge to giggle. Alex was such a chameleon. He always picked up the accents and words of those surrounding him. Now, she reckoned, he must be seeing a lot of Texans.

"I think that's smart, Ginny, providing you do it with a lot of class. I mean I hope you're being really choosey. You only go to—crash, that is—the parties that will do your business or you some good, right?" He tilted up her chin, the pointy chin that had, through his obstinacy, led her into the modeling agony. "Don't turn into a party junkie, will you, and start trying to crash the opening of an envelope."

Ginny laughed at the concerned look on his face. "No way. My time's too precious."

"Good. You're just as smart as I always thought you were. It's the best training in the world for your future in the Seventh Avenue jungle and I can help you, too." He stared at her reflectively. "If I don't have to leave tomorrow I may have time to tell you about some special parties coming up, parties that are not written about, receptions, fund-raisers in private homes, where the real money is." He sipped his wine, still studying her face. "I can take you myself and help you recognize who's who and who isn't, the influential ones, what they wear, that sort of thing, you know what I mean."

She wasn't sure she did, but she reveled in grabbing Alex's attention.

Before he dropped her off at the loft, he reiterated, "Don't overdo it. You have natural poise, a great fashion talent for looking good with just a couple of dollars, and I don't doubt that your father's conceit and your mother's manners will get you through most doors." He chucked her under the chin again. "Just remember, stay cool under fire and whatever you do, never lose your temper if cornered. It's a total giveaway."

Not long after Alex's departure, Ginny had reason to remember his parting words of advice.

At a reception honoring Philip Miller, the czar of the Saks group, she was already late, dropping her stole as she rushed up the stairs in an old Gosman she'd reworked with shimmering paillettes.

Retrieving it, she collided with someone rushing down. It was none other than the dreaded Mauve, the Gosman tailor.

"What are you doing here?" His eyes flicked over her dress. "In number 715, if I remember correctly?" He laughed, but from his expression Ginny could see his feelings about her hadn't changed.

"What a surprise," she said lamely. "I'll see you inside."

"Who're you with?"

She mumbled Poppy Gan's name as usual, although she very much doubted Poppy would turn up. "I'm late, see you."

When she reached the next floor she ducked inside the ladies' room. Seeing Mauve had shaken her up. She took several deep breaths to recover, peeping round the door to see if by any horrible chance he was lurking outside to waylay her. He wasn't there, but the curtains to the reception room were closed, and a large, official-looking woman blocked her path.

"Ticket, miss. The guest of honor's speaking. You can't go in now. You'll have to wait. What table number? Ticket, please."

She hadn't been faced with this since her debacle at the Calvin Klein show so long ago. Now she was unusually flustered because of her encounter with Mauve.

Be nice, Ginny. Be courteous. Whatever you do, Ginny, don't be haughty or lose your temper.

She dug her nails in her hand as she said with a small smile, "Oh, sorry, I've been in before. I just had to go to the ladies' room." She looked down at the floor shyly. "That time of the month, you know." Then, "I'm with Saks. If I don't hear the chairman's speech, I'll be in big trouble." She bit her lip and tried to smile. "Please," she repeated timidly, "I'm not far from the door. I promise I won't make any noise."

The woman put a finger to her mouth as if to say "sshssh," then moved the curtain slightly aside, allowing Ginny to slip in.

Regularly receiving Poppy's agenda (although, so far, no more invitations to accompany her), in the space of only a month Ginny discovered that what had been her liability as a wannabe model—her "facelessness," her lack of a distinct "look"—was a major asset when crashing.

Because of the way she dressed, because of her posture, she easily merged with the fashionable crowd; she looked vaguely familiar, she fitted in, so crashing wasn't anything like as difficult as she'd imagined it would be, particularly events and benefits held in major hotels or stores, where rarely was anyone at the actual door checking names or tickets. Instead, partygoers checked in at a desk or table often a room or corridor away for their table numbers or seat assignments.

At an Oscar de la Renta fashion show benefit, held at the Plaza Hotel, however, there was a forbidding guard at the entrance. Ginny tried the "I've already been in before" line, this time to no avail.

"Over there, miss." The guard pointed to a check-in table down the hall, where she noted a number of de la Renta-clad women clamoring for their seat assignments.

This was infuriating. She particularly wanted to see this show and be seen, hoping at the end, perhaps, even to meet the great man himself.

She'd made a point of knowing where all the ladies' rooms were in the major hotels—bolt holes in times of trouble—and she was on her way to one to plot her next move, when she saw waiters going in and out of a small door behind a screen. She quickly looked around to see she wasn't spotted, then darted behind the screen to follow them.

As she'd hoped, she found herself in a corridor leading to the hotel kitchen, where surely there would be another entrance, if not several, into the ballroom itself.

"Where are you going, miss?"

A preppy young man in horn-rimmed glasses and holding an intercom stood in front of her.

"To the fashion show, sir. I work at the hotel—in marketing. I'm looking for my boss." She sighed plaintively. "There's such a mob scene out there, this is a shortcut. I thought I'd use it."

"What's your name?"

"Ginny Walker."

She put her hand in her new tweed purse, which looked like a small muff, so the man wouldn't see it tremble.

His intercom beeped. He listened intently. "Okay, okay, on the double."

He looked her up and down suspiciously, then snapped, "You should have been told, Ms. Walker, no shortcuts today. You'll get in big trouble. Here—" He took her by the shoulder and hustled her between two huge soup urns. "This way and don't come back."

She found herself exactly where she wanted to be, inside the ballroom, beside the stage. Horn-rims was staring after her. She smiled and gave him an appreciative little wave, then rushed ahead, looking for her "boss." After a few minutes she looked back. Thankfully, he was gone, to deal with his "on the double" business.

She spent the next twenty minutes sauntering around the rows of little gilt chairs, being photographed in her new shiny "tweed" skirt (actually made from nine-dollars-a-yard oilcloth, printed with a tweed design, that she'd found in a local hardware store) and her "new" Harris tweed jacket, remodeled, after being purloined by her mother from her father's wardrobe. An act of revenge, Ginny was sure, as right after Labor Day her mother had once again pulled up stakes and followed her father to Miami, where he was "opening the first branch of the new Walker School."

Across the runway, in the front row, Ginny saw to her surprise the beautiful Dolores Relato Peet. She knew her name now, a name she might not be using for much longer, because in Suzy's column only the night before, she'd read a Suzy scoop: the Peets were getting "an amicable divorce." Whatever that meant.

Certainly, from the look of her today, it meant Dolores wasn't grieving. Animated, laughing, throwing her elegant head back so that a cloud of dark hair continually brushed her shoulders, Dolores appeared ecstatic.

How could a woman whose divorce had just been announced show off so soon in public her happiness, her relief? It was such a slap in the face to her about-to-be-ex-husband. Or perhaps that was what an "amicable divorce" was all about? Perhaps Mr. Peet junior, who she read from time to time in *Next!* magazine, was somewhere at this moment having an equally good time? Ginny felt hopelessly naive. What did she know? Only that Dolores was wearing a suit she'd give her all for, in broadtail, the delicate, incredibly expensive fur from baby lambs which looked and felt like silk.

With the Peets in and out of her mind, it was only when the de la Renta show was over (seen from a fourth-row seat marked "guest") that Ginny learned what hot water she could have been in.

When the lights went up came an announcement which stunned her: "Will everyone kindly remain in their seats until the First Lady has left the ballroom." Ginny hadn't even known that Hillary Clinton was in the packed audience. Thank goodness horn-rim's intercom had gone off. He must have been a Secret Service agent.

Dolores had been at the Waldorf and now at the Plaza. Ginny decided she had to be her lucky omen, for at both places she'd gotten away with murder.

Murder, it had to have been murder, Johnny thought, although the Los Angeles police still persisted in calling it a tragic accident.

Why didn't someone challenge the police? Why didn't someone remind the world that Rosemary Abbott had been risking her life for years, working as Rosa Brueckner for the Drug Enforcement Administration? Why didn't someone in the DEA admit the enemy had obviously decided they were tired of having her around?

Her husband, her parents—they were professionals, used to sudden death, but for Godsakes, this was their own beloved wife and daughter, who'd burned to a cinder in her own home. They couldn't have swallowed the electrical fault story? And yet ever since he'd first heard about Rosemary's gruesome death, there hadn't been one word about foul play, not even in *Time* magazine, which had broken her story back in '93.

Not much more than a year and a half had passed since that piece extolling her courage, yet now where had *Time* run the story of Rosa-Rosemary's death? In Milestones, the page that contained their mini-obituaries, where they'd gone along, no questions asked, with the official "accident" verdict and her official job description, "retired."

Johnny stared at the backs of the people sitting with bowed heads in the front pew, one almost bald, a gray-haired woman, a pepper-and-salt tousle-haired man.

They all knew Rosemary was no more "retired" than Clinton. She'd been on the front line right up to the day somebody had shut her in her basement and torched the place down.

Before flying to the Coast for the memorial service, Johnny had called Rosemary's husband, Ben Abbott, to try to arrange a meeting. He hadn't been able to reach him and her parents had been "unavailable," too.

Today, no matter what, at the buffet lunch for out-of-town mourners at her parents' house in Santa Monica, he intended to tell them all, husband, mother and father, that if they weren't prepared to make a lot of noise about the true facts behind Rosemary's death, he was going to, in his own column in *Next!* and at each and every TV opportunity that presented itself. There were more and more these days. Johnny shut his eyes, trying to concentrate on the eulogies.

He felt old, beaten. As if finding out that all his suspicions about Dolores were true hadn't been enough for one year. Even now he felt ill, knowing she'd been two-timing him with the same obscenely oil-rich, much-married man, not only all through their marriage, but even since his Albany days.

It was good riddance, there was no doubt about that. Her body had attracted him in a way no other woman's ever had, but even before he'd caught her in the act, the deadwood in her brain had been getting more and more in the way.

He'd had to live through his father saying "I told you so" in as many diabolically clever ways as he could think to say it, but he'd never have to hear it again. Never. He'd learned his lesson about women. He'd never make the same mistake.

Thank God, his father couldn't say the same thing about his job. His job had saved his sanity. His father would never admit it, but *Next!* was soaring in popularity and so was his much quoted and talked about "unpredictable" column.

There were dozens of photographs of Rosemary to be seen in her parents' comfortable home, as a gap-toothed, freckle-nosed kid, as a scrawny beanstalk of a teenager, as a radiant bride. How could they live with the knowledge they would never see their brilliant, courageous daughter again? But then, while she was alive, how could they have lived every day with the knowledge she was out there somewhere, putting her life on the line for her job?

Since their February meeting, Johnny had seen Rosemary only once more, in New York, following another well-publicized, multimillion-dollar heist in the summer from a heavily guarded Southampton estate.

On a tip from Freddy Forrester, Johnny had learned that if a bomb hadn't exploded, arousing the neighborhood, the robbery might not ever have been reported. There was some question as to who really owned the estate and Peter Licton, the alleged owner, disappeared two days after filing the stunning list of art treasures and jewelry missing.

One of Dolores's birdbrains had been to a couple of wild weekend parties at the estate, and Johnny, remembering Dolores's gossip, had passed along the names of some of the partygoers, believed to be involved with the Mafia. Was Licton a card-carrying member, too? It didn't make sense if the Mafia were behind the heist, as the FBI, the police, and the DEA seemed to think. There were too many similarities between the Southampton job and the Stimson Court Place robbery to ignore.

He'd immediately called Rosemary on the Coast, asking her to get in touch with him. He felt ashamed now, remembering how irked he'd been to discover she was already in New York.

He hadn't asked her why she hadn't let him know, but he'd felt peevish and probably had sounded it, too. She'd told him she'd been following up leads on Licton for some time and was now ready to prove he wasn't the charming investment banker people who'd enjoyed his hospitality believed him to be. He was the American- and British-educated Pietro Licone, a member of the Comorra organized crime family of Naples, heavily involved in the cocaine business in Europe.

So why would one group of criminals burglarize another? Gang warfare? Revenge?

Rosemary had told him it all figured. "Thievery has become an increasingly competitive business, because the most experienced thieves know the serious buyers are from the drug cartels, who have more money than some countries do. Pietro, I'm sure, was sent here last year to open a lucrative branch for the family . . . and blood brothers or not, the American Mafia finally decided it was time to discourage him."

It was a good story that nobody else had, but it was too early. More would come and hopefully, like Rosemary, with patience, one day when the time was right, he'd be able to expose and cripple some major players in the drug business himself.

She'd returned to Los Angeles without finding Licton—or Licone, as she was sure he really was. "He's probably back in Italy, trying to recover his ego," she said bitterly. "But he'll try again. Those kind of people never like to lose."

"Shall I keep in touch?" he'd asked like an eager rookie, inspired as he always was by her tirelessness in fighting for a better drug-free world.

"Oh, please, Johnny, please, but promise me you'll be careful," she'd replied. He had been careful; she hadn't been careful enough.

He saw Ben Abbott go into the garden into the sunshine. Following him, feeling the golden warmth on his face, Johnny thought of the wind and gray he'd just left behind in New York, an early announcement of the winter ahead.

Soon he'd be a free man. Perhaps he should base his column in California for a few months, getting to know these people, earning their trust as he'd earned Rosemary's? Above all, getting the real story behind her death. It wasn't because of the story either, although with what he already knew, it would surely be the kind of cover piece *Next!* wanted from him. No, he would write it to vindicate her death.

"Ben . . ." Johnny put out his hand. "John Peet. I've tried to reach you . . ."

He was startled to see the man's eyes full of tears. He felt his own begin to prick. "I'm . . . I'm so sorry, Ben."

Abbott's handshake was hard, almost brutal, as if he needed someone to stop him falling down.

"Thanks, John." The tears were gone and in the brilliant sunlight, Johnny saw that Abbott's eyes were as blue and as piercing as an acetylene torch.

"Can we talk?"

"What's there to talk about? I've got to go on with my life . . ."

"But it wasn't an accident, you know that. For two years they must have been planning—"

Ben Abbott interrupted him harshly. "Who's been planning? You're treading on dangerous ground, sonny. You don't know what you're talking about."

Johnny could feel himself flush. He was twenty-nine years old. Ben Abbott may be fifteen or twenty years his senior, but only his father had the right to call him sonny, and he didn't like it from him, either.

He controlled his anger. "Ben, don't you know I was in contact with Rosemary? About the Stimson Court Place robbery last Christmas, then the Licton job this summer and its link to organized crime, the Comorra family and Cali—"

The blue eyes flashed, then, "Stay away, sonny," Abbott snapped. "Stay away from my business. If that piece hadn't appeared in *Time* and then your fucking follow-up on Joan of Arc heroines," he spat on the ground, "Rosemary wouldn't have been burned alive; she'd be here right now, making you one of her fucking famous margaritas."

Joan of Arc. Johnny had used the phrase in his *Next!* piece. He hadn't connected Rosemary's death by fire with the piece until now. No wonder this man hated him. But he wasn't going to blame himself; he'd get nowhere that way. He wasn't going to be beaten down by anyone, not even a grief-crazed husband. "So you agree she was murdered and it's not too difficult to guess who did it," Johnny snapped back. "Why the hush-up? If you don't want to go after—"

Abbott grabbed Johnny's arm. It was as if he'd caught it in a vise. Beads of perspiration broke out on his forehead. He thought it was going to break.

"Listen to me, Peet, one word out of you in your fucking magazine and you're going to be found accidentally dead, too. Understand?"

Johnny didn't answer. He was in too much pain.

"We're serving lunch now, won't you come in, Mr. Peet, Ben?" Rosemary's mother was calling from the door.

His hold on Johnny hadn't relaxed, but to Johnny's amazement, he saw Abbott smile a warm, relaxed, perfectly normal smile. "Okay, May, we'll be right there."

"*Capito?*" he said to Johnny.

Johnny nodded, afraid he might be about to throw up.

Abbott gave the same warm smile to him. "Look, I know you're trying to help, but Rosemary died in a tragic accident. When I find out who was responsible for the faulty wiring, I'll let you know if I need any help, okay?"

"Okay." It wasn't, but it wouldn't help anyone, least of all him, to let Abbott think otherwise.

As they strolled toward the house, Ben caught his arm again, not viciously, but with it still throbbing from the last encounter, enough to make Johnny wince.

"I'll say this for the last time, Peet. Stay off our turf. It isn't a place for amateurs. If you really want to help what Rosemary and a helluva lot of others are trying to do, keep your word processor shut and your fucking mouth, too."

By day Ginny scoured the want ads, taking part-time jobs through a temp agency as a receptionist, a spritzer of scent at department stores (providing they weren't owned by Svank), a hotel operator, and, swallowing her pride, a hand model. It had to be her new self-confidence, she told herself, for her nails had never looked better. In the new year, when people started to want help with their income tax, she'd earn still more money, and this was the way she would keep her head above water until that elusive prince charming turned up, the one who was going to back her business.

If crashing hadn't produced him yet, she was far from giving up. She'd thought she'd found him after only three months of regular crashing, meeting a venture capitalist at a reception for the Council of American Fashion Designers at Lincoln Center.

For the first time since Ricardo, she'd worn her silver birdcage jacket with the inside-out seams, and this thin, tall version of the polished Svank had come over to introduce himself, because he was so impressed by what she was wearing. He was heaven-sent (she'd thought), that rare creature, a money man with such a finite knowledge of fashion, he'd been able to price her original design accurately, right down to its last silver button.

They'd had an animated discussion about the profit and loss situations of many well-known designers. He'd understood what had happened to Gosman. "No financial controls," he'd said.

As if she didn't know. Old man Gosman hadn't cared that she had a finance degree, had never been willing to listen to her about money, because "whatsaslipofagalikeyouknowboutbusiness?"

The venture capitalist had given her his card and she'd called to set up a meeting to discuss her financial needs. On the day of the meeting, she'd opened the paper to see his photograph above a story reporting his arrest for swindling thousands out of their life savings.

"Bad luck," was all Alex had to say when, calling from Europe, he'd listened to her sad story. And Alex was right. She had to look at it that way and concentrate on her good luck.

Lee Baker Davies, thinking that Poppy was taking her everywhere, was "thrilled" that at last Ginny was being noticed by the mainstream press. "I'm so proud of you, my protégée," she said fondly. "It won't be long before you're in business for yourself."

What was the point of disillusioning her? Ginny knew she'd be worried to death if she knew her "protégée" was crashing events. Instead, she told Lee the truth, that a number of affluent-looking women, admiring her clothes, had asked for and received her business card (Ginny Walker Fashion, dark gray letters on pearl gray vellum).

No one had called yet, but "they will eventually," said Lee. Ginny was sure they would, too, just as she was sure she'd run into Arthur Stern again, the man she'd sat next to at the Waldorf the night of her first crash, the man she'd dismissed too quickly as an obvious lecher.

If she'd only known then what she knew now from concentrating more on the business pages of *WWD* and the *New York Times* . . . that Stern, who'd jokingly passed himself off as a "teddy bear manufacturer," who might like to diversify into "teddies," was married to one of America's richest women (the daughter of the man who'd invented noninflammable children's clothing). Together they sought out and backed promising small fashion businesses. "Always on the lookout for talent," one headline had said. Now, she was on the lookout for Mr. Stern; one more chance was all she needed.

Svank was another matter entirely. She'd made no more attempts to meet the terrible tycoon, nor would she. Poppy hadn't volunteered to help anymore in that direction either. It was probably just as well. Her luck would change, if not tonight, next week, next month. It had to happen.

"Has Poppy Gan arrived yet?" (Poppy's incorrigible unpunctuality was a godsend to crashing, as was the fact she frequently didn't turn up at all.)

The girl at the door hastily looked down the list. "No, eh, you are . . . ?"

"Ginny Walker."

Cool, looking only slightly put-out, Ginny stared over the girl's shoulder. She was in the lobby of the great stone mansion on Fifth Avenue, home to New York's National Academy of Design.

"I don't suppose Mr. Svank is here yet, either, is he?"

As three or four people arrived behind Ginny, the girl, flustered, began, "I didn't think he was able to . . ."

"Schlesinger, Paterson . . ." More names were being given as Ginny casually picked up a program and walked toward the cloakroom with an "I'll wait for her upstairs."

She shed her coat and gave herself a quick once-over in the floor-to-ceiling mirror. She was wearing the Chinese red tuxedo top made for Poppy, then reconstructed to wear herself at the Waldorf. Now it shimmied over a new, darker red sarong skirt that she'd designed to be pinned together with a giant silver safety pin.

The name atop the invitation, Mrs. Theodore King—Nan, to her special coterie—was at the door of the upstairs drawing room. She was more striking and even thinner in real life, Ginny decided, wearing, she was sure, a svelte black velvet number from Valentino's latest collection.

Nan King described herself as "born with a couture spoon in my mouth," and no one appreciated fashion innovation more than she; any designer worth their sketchpad knew that.

In a split second Ginny, hoping the celebrated doyenne of fashion would realize she was looking at a new talent's work, decided to call attention to herself by approaching very, very slowly. It was worth taking the risk of being accused of false entry.

Alas, one of Mrs. K.'s nearest and dearest was apparently right behind Ginny, because after the quickest, most perfunctory smile of greeting, screams of "Daarrling" filled the air and Nan brushed her aside to move into an embrace. Disappointing, but at least she was in without any problems.

Ginny scanned the room. Darkly paneled, heavily marbled, it was already filled with men in black tie and mostly rail-thin women in long or short black. Like actors in a play they milled around, laughing, talking, smiling, sipping, gesticulating, all to show the constantly flashing cameras what a wonderful time they were having.

Ginny took a spritzer from a passing waiter and moved to a table beside an archway, where, apparently engrossed in the program, she positioned herself to show off her tuxedo jacket with its new skirt, a blaze of color in a sea of black. It didn't take long to catch the photographers' attention, one of the evening's objectives.

She was collecting a neat little portfolio of herself photographed in Ginny Walker designs, so far unidentified, but she wasn't discouraged. She had succeeded in her first ambition—to appear in *Women's Wear Daily* and, even better, the glossy monthly *W* version—with a three-inch picture on Suzy's page, carrying the flattering caption, "For once somebody young and slender enough to wear her negligee to dinner."

A few pictures of her standing next to Poppy had also appeared in the tabloids (alas, only once had Poppy been wearing one of the two evening dresses she'd so far made for her), but her pride and joy was the last entry, a large shot by Bill Cunningham, the brilliant *New York Times* fashion sleuth, who'd photographed her for a new trend page in Sunday's paper.

"Chic leather after dark" was the headline, which was incredible, considering he'd snapped her unawares, crossing Madison Avenue in the oldest piece of leather clothing she possessed, her ginger leather skirt, admittedly worn that night with a new faux suede vest.

She tried to concentrate on the program. It was confusing: Following the reception, pre-dinner sonatas would be played, arranged by Affiliate Artists, an organization that helped young musicians by introducing them to play in rich people's homes. Post-dinner, there was to be a concert given by—in case she was asked, Ginny mentally practiced pronouncing the name—the Bach-Gesellschaft, "a group originally founded to celebrate the three-hundredth anniversary of Bach's birth."

Did these elegant people really care about a composer's three-hundredth birthday? Ginny doubted it. She read on, getting more confused.

"The concert will be recorded for public broadcasting, a cultural event made possible by the generosity of . . ." Ginny could hardly believe what she was reading, none other than General Motors. What on earth did they have to do with Bach? It seemed they'd paid for everything, all to help launch their latest $55,000 roadster, "on display, outside on Fifth Avenue, at the end of the evening."

From Poppy's agenda, Ginny had chosen to crash this evening mainly because of Nan King's chairmanship. Because of her clothes sense, no socialite was photographed more, so it stood to reason Nan's guest list would also be eminently fashionable; ergo, she would be surrounded by women likely to be interested in Ginny Walker clothes.

She'd made a mistake, that was all there was to it. The people here had come to hear the music, see the new car and go home. At least the photographers had noticed her, so it wasn't a complete waste.

She looked around, hoping someone would smile at her or say "Hi" or "How are you." It happened occasionally, because someone thought they knew her, she reminded them of someone else, for which she supposed she had to thank the "anonymity" of her looks.

At the end of the room she saw the musicians enter. People were already rushing to grab what Ginny could see were far too few seats.

She made eye contact with a bearded man. Had she met him with Oz? No, that beard had been strictly redwoods; this one was Van Dyke. The bearded one came over and said, "Hi, how are you?"

"Hello, there. What a busy evening."

"I hope so—that's what we've been planning. Aren't you . . . ?"

"Ginny Walker." The more authoritatively she gave her name, the better she felt about herself.

"Oh, yes, one of Nan's fashion flock." He had a clipped way of speaking. Ginny couldn't be sure if he was mocking her or was merely clipped.

"Peter Arveson." He gave her his card. "Executive Vice President, Plomley Advertising."

They strolled together to stand behind the rows of now-filled little gold chairs. She tried to think of something to say. "Is General Motors one of your accounts?"

"No, I'm here as an extra man." Was he kidding? No sign of a smile, no sign of a laugh.

Her brain plotted away. An advertising man could be helpful, surely? As Mrs. K. hadn't exactly rolled over in admiration on seeing her red tuxedo, meeting Arveson was better than nothing.

They stood together in attentive silence throughout the sonatas, but at the end, in the sudden rush for the buffet Ginny found herself alone again.

That Poppy's agenda had stated "buffet supper" had been another reason Ginny had chosen this event to crash. She could stay for the duration of a "buffet supper," something not easily accomplished at a seated dinner, although, as she'd learned at the Waldorf, the more mammoth the event, the greater the likelihood of seats going unoccupied. At often a thousand dollars a ticket Ginny didn't understand it, but there was so much she still didn't get about New York.

Now, she deliberated about joining the crush or going home. The empty state of her fridge made her mind up. She joined the throng of beanpoles in black, wondering if any of them really did eat and if so, were they bulimic?"

Arveson was beside her again. "D'you want to join us?"

"I'd love to."

She sat between him and a merchant banker named Tony.

"How well d'you know the hostess?" Tony asked.

"Not that well."

"Well, then, *was bringt Sie denn hierher*? Are you a lover of all things Bach, *The Well-Tempered Clavier*?"

"Alas, no, although I'm looking forward to . . ." Ginny stopped. Not only had she forgotten how to pronounce the group's name, she'd forgotten what it was. "The concert," she finished weakly.

Tony roared with laughter. Arveson pursed his lips.

"Tell the truth, why is such a sexy thing like you at such a heavyweight evening? Are you hoping to win the Allante?"

Though it was obvious that she didn't know what the Allante was either, Ginny threw away caution. "No, I'm hoping to find someone with enough style to invest in my business."

"What kind of business?"

"I'm an important, undercapitalized fashion designer."

Tony hooted with laughter again. "How much are you looking for?"

She was weighing up whether to say fifty or a hundred thousand when Nan King came by. Ginny was impressed that all the men stood up. "Here, take my seat, Nan," they all more or less said in different ways.

"No, no, no," she replied, settling gracefully all the same into Tony's chair.

"You've done it again, Nan!"

"How much have you raised this time?"

"Ezra only came because of you, naughty Nan . . ."

"Is that Valentino's?" Ginny leaned forward, her question lost in a guffaw of laughter.

"When on earth is that buffet line going to get shorter?"

"Is that Joan Rivers over there?"

"The food's going to run out, I know it."

"I hear the Allante's going to be raffled? But where are the tickets? Have you driven it yet?" (So that solved the Allante mystery.)

"I'm sure that's Joan Rivers."

"Did you hear what she told Nancy Reagan? Johnny Peet ran the item last week. Whenever she thinks her house is dirty, she calls the Beverly Hills police to report a robbery and they come right over to dust for fingerprints . . ."

Ginny joined in the general laughter, but most of the time she sat silently, aware after a time that nobody was paying much attention to what anyone else was saying, because everyone talked at once.

Tony leaned over her chair and whispered, "Let's get out of here, now, okay, fashion princess?"

She looked at her watch with its Swatch strap, Chinese red to match her jacket. It wasn't even nine o'clock. The thought of all that Bach ahead made the idea attractive, and who knew if Tony the banker might not be interested in the fashion business. There was nothing doing with Arveson; since sitting down, he hadn't even glanced in her direction.

Outside on the sidewalk, guarded by a New York cop, was the Allante. By the curb was another gleaming vehicle, a plum-colored Mercedes with a plum-covered chauffeur at the wheel. "Climb aboard," said Tony. Then, "We'll do a few drop-ins, Frank. Head toward K and P."

He leaned back against burnished leather and yawned. "There are at least one hundred parties going on in this city right now, each one, I guarantee, more lively than the General Motors bullshit we've just left behind. Okay, Mademoiselle Chanel, the night's about to take a turn for the better."

To Ginny's surprise, they first stopped at Barneys department store on Madison Avenue. "What's going on?"

"I forget—some fashion celebration—supposed to be full of the really Beautiful People, no one over sweet sixteen."

She held his arm as he swaggered into a sea of sweltering bodies. There was a huge poster just inside, a blowup of the cover of the Italian men's magazine, *L'Uomo Vogue*, but she never did find out what the party was all about, because no sooner had they made it through to the cosmetic counters than Tony turned around and started to try to shove his way out again, muttering, "This is a no-go; place is full of no-shows."

Hardly, but she got the gist of what he was trying to say. She wasn't sorry. They didn't look like beautiful people to her either. It may have been an international fashion crowd, but they all looked as if they shopped at the Gap, rather than their host's establishment.

Tony slept on the way downtown. Ginny didn't mind. She was busy doing mental arithmetic in case the subject of capital came up. She didn't want to ask too little—or too much. She had to Be Prepared. Alex had always been right about that.

K and P turned out to be Kelley and Ping, the antithesis of the American Academy of Design, a beer and cold cuts kind of place. It was sweltering, too, from too many bodies squeezed into too little space, Rastafarians, long-hair-to-the-waist male musicians, male and female models, and on-the-way-up starlets.

"It's for *Huh*. I put some money in. I like to play a wild card or two," Tony murmured in her ear as they joined a group grooving in a corner.

"Huh?" There was surely only one way to say Huh? Out of the corner of her eye she saw Sandra Bullock and someone of indeterminate sex who'd shaved his or her head.

"Yep . . . it's a very cool new music magazine."

By midnight they'd dropped into Nell's, a party at an art gallery on Prince Street, and Barocco, which she loved because there were a couple of real stars on the premises—Tim Robbins and Susan Sarandon (was she pregnant again?). More important, there was food. She was consuming a kind of hot bean sprout patty with a glass of delicious white wine when she saw in the corner Dolores, her lucky omen.

Ginny crossed her fingers. Perhaps it meant Tony was going to back her. If he'd backed *Huh,* why not Her?

"Oopla, there's going to be a nasty little scene, I believe. Did you see who just arrived? Let's get out of here before the fur starts flying."

So far she hadn't seen Tony take a drink, but as he pulled her toward the door he downed a couple of glasses of champagne in two swigs. "Hi, Johnny," she heard him say as she went ahead into the street. "Your ex-missus is in there with Mr. Oilwell himself."

"Was that Johnny Peet?" she asked as she got in the car.

"None other. Good guy, Johnny. We knew each other at Princeton."

"I wish I'd known. I'd love to meet him. My father's crazy about his father. I wonder if I'd like his son . . ."

"You will never know, Mademoiselle Chanel. *Après le déluge, après* Dolores, he's sworn off women for good."

"A likely story."

Because Tony hadn't attempted to touch her, in or out of the car, she didn't think twice when, arriving at the loft, he asked to come up for a nightcap.

No sooner had she closed the door than he lunged, like a rapist, pushing her down on the floor and yanking away at her tuxedo jacket. She screamed so loudly he sat back on his heels, looking mildly surprised for a few seconds. It was enough time to unpin the safety pin in her sarong and stab him furiously in the arm.

His face slowly flushed a deep, unbecoming red. She said her prayers, knowing there was no one in the building at night, sure her end was about to come. Instead he stood up, bowed like a Japanese dignitary, and left.

Ginny quickly locked the door and went to the window. After what seemed an interminable time, she saw him come out and the Mercedes slowly drive away.

Two days later he called with profuse apologies. He called three more times before she relented and agreed to meet him—for dinner at La Grenouille, a restaurant she'd always wanted to visit.

She sat poker-faced, well into the second course, when Tony made a confession.

"I'm an alcoholic, Ginny. Even a sniff of the stuff turns me into an animal. Don't let me near it and we'll never have a problem."

She looked suspiciously at his glass. It was true, he'd ordered Perrier for himself, white wine for her.

"Okay, now let's talk about your business."

She started to, but it was hopeless. He interrupted, meandered around the subjects of his ex-wife, his ex-mistress and how greedy women could be when love was out the door. "Look at poor Johnny Peet . . ."

She didn't want to hear a word about poor Johnny Peet. It was time for poor Ginny Walker.

Except for an attempted foray under her skirt in the Mercedes going back to the loft, there were no more passes, and when Tony gave her his business card, Ginny decided it was all going to be worthwhile after all. "Best come to the office. As I told you, I do like to back the occasional wild card. Come up and we'll get into margins."

She called him three times to set up the meeting. Twice he was out of town, once "unavailable."

"Che sarà, sarà," she said with a sad smile, telling Esme the story over dim sum one rainy day in Chinatown.

Esme had her own troubles, seeking Ginny's advice on how to pin down an irresolute fiancé and set a wedding date sometime in '95.

"I know he loves me, but he's sooo busy," she moaned. "He just hasn't got time to sit down and work it all out with me."

"Too busy counting his millions." Ginny tried to laugh, but it wasn't funny. Despite Esme's many attempts to help, although Ted was always talking about how rich he was, Ginny had never been able to talk him into giving her a loan.

When Esme frowned, Ginny put her arm around her. "Cheer up. You said yourself Ted loves you. Men are lazy. Why don't you choose a date yourself, something you know won't screw up his itinerary. Are you friendly with his secretary?"

"Absolutely. I made sure of it."

"Well, then, collaborate with her. Find out what, if anything, he has planned for '95, then work the wedding date in somehow . . . I'm sure he just doesn't want to be bothered with the details."

Esme beamed. "You really think so? Oh, Ginny, that's a marvelous idea. Why didn't I think of that?"

"Because you're a shy shrinking violet, I don't think."

Esme smiled. "Okay, now let's plot something for you. Where shall we start?"

Ginny sighed. "I'm trying to keep my spirits up, Es, but my luck's getting worse, not better. Whenever an appointment seems to be leading somewhere, it ends in a race around the desk or some heavy trying to get me into bed."

"I'm not surprised, Ginny. You're looking gorgeous and so skinny."

Ginny was too proud to tell her best friend that she used what little money she had to spare to buy fabric, not food, that with the Gosman severance pay almost gone, along with the two thousand dollars Poppy had given her for the two dresses, she often relied on crashing to provide her main meal.

There was something else new about her crashing. She hadn't, as Alex had feared, turned into a crashing junkie. She was still selective, but she no longer crashed just to show off her clothes (or to eat). She'd grown to love crashing for other, more complex reasons.

She loved the rush of adrenaline it delivered as she mingled with the "in" crowd. She felt a sense of triumph, chatting up potential investors at night, the same people who promised but never returned her phone calls during the day. She was vaguely familiar to some of the security guards now and some PR party people, who acknowledged her with a smile or a wave.

In some convoluted way crashing had become her act of revenge to everyone who let her down, to the smooth strangers who wanted more, much more, than her designing talent, as a return on their investment.

Not that she'd dream of telling Esme she'd turned crashing into a major occupation. Esme thought it was a fun thing she did sometimes—rarely—on the spur of the moment. Ginny knew Esme didn't approve of that, either.

"I thought you were making clothes regularly for Poppy Gan?" Esme asked now.

"She talks about getting a 'real wardrobe,' but she's as impossible to pin down as ever."

"Well as soon as we—I—set the date," Esme started to giggle, "you're going to be too busy to do anything for Ms. Gan. I'll need you full-time to design my dress, my trousseau, the bridesmaids' dresses . . . yours, of course, and one for Ted's sister, Carol, and my cousin Sue Jane."

As they watched the rain turn into sleet outside the window on Mott Street, they ordered rice wine and more dim sum. Esme always made Ginny feel optimistic, and the feeling stayed with her until she got back to the loft.

It was really sleeting the evening she planned to crash a party at New York's Guggenheim Museum. She was already dressed in a lilac-colored diaphanous sheath made from delicate embroidered material Lee had brought back from a trip to India as an early birthday present. She was tired after helping Lee style a shoot that day. Should she go? Shouldn't she go? She started to play a game with herself. If the phone rang before seven P.M.—whoever it was—she'd go. If not, she'd put the dress away, give herself a bubble bath and go to bed early. But it wasn't the phone that rang; it was the intercom from the front door.

"Hello?"

"Ginny Walker?" She didn't recognize the accent.

"Yes."

"I'm Angus Tollmach, a friend of Alex. He called you, didn't he?"

"Nooo," she said slowly. "He didn't."

"Oh, shit . . . sorry, Ginny, but your cousin promised . . ."

Ginny decided as he knew Alex was her cousin, he was probably bona fide. "I'll let you in, but I'm actually on the way out."

"Oh, don't worry. I'm in a rush myself, but I've got something for you. If you could buzz me in and come down for it soon, I'll leave it just inside, okay?"

She was ashamed of her suspicions, but after Tony, she was wary of letting any strangers in. "Oh, please come up for a quick drink . . ." She pressed the front-door buzzer.

The phone started to ring. She looked at the time. It was well before seven. "Just a minute . . ."

It was Alex. "Alex, Angus is downstairs. Hold on." She put the phone down and hollered down the intercom. "Come on up, Angus. Alex is on the line."

"No, tell him I've done my bit. The package is in the hall."

Alex said excitedly, "Go down and get it, Ginny. I'll call back in five minutes."

She ran down the flights and retrieved a small box. She had only just opened it when Alex called again.

"Do you like it?"

"Like it! I adore it."

"It" was a gold bracelet, heavy with gold petals, decorated with, she supposed, sparkling rhinestones.

"It's entailed, Ginny darling."

"What on earth does that mean?"

"You can wear it as much as you like, but you can never own it. It has to be passed on to future generations."

"But I don't have any future . . ."

As usual Alex wasn't listening. "Half the good stuff you see on the dolly birds, including your friend Poppy, is entailed, although they never know it. I'll need to borrow it back sometime, but meanwhile take care of it for me. It will look great on your skinny arm. What are you up to?"

She looked at the time again. Six thirty-five. "I think I'm going to the Guggenheim Museum—to a reception and a dinner. Where are you?"

Alex cut right across her. "Wear it tonight with joy, Ginny dear. I have a feeling it's your lucky night."

"Where are you?"

"On my way back to New York." He sounded more serious than usual. "And Gin . . ."

"Yes?"

"You were right to be wary of Svank. Now I know him quite well. He's greedy, dangerous—"

"Oh, Alex. Do be careful." In a rush she told him the Poppy birthday story.

There was silence, then, "Don't worry, pigeon. If you have something he wants, he's still very much someone to know."

By the time she put the phone down it was ten past seven. It was now or never. Okay. Now.

The bracelet lit up her pale skin. She felt a surge of confidence. Perhaps tonight would be the night her luck changed.

There was that kooky girl, gate-crashing again, well, not so kooky, quite cute really. What trouble was she talking herself out of this time? Or, for once, perhaps into trouble.

Standing inside the garlanded circular entrance hall of the Guggenheim Museum, smoking a frowned-upon cigarette, Johnny Peet watched with cynical amusement as the skinny swan, draped in veils of lilac, at first coolly and then more heatedly argued with an overbearing dowager holding a list, obviously the keeper of the gate.

The more he observed, the more he remembered the girl, mainly because of her outlandish, extraordinary clothes and . . . what was the other reason? It came to him in a flash. She was the girl who'd worn what he'd described as "the two-faced dress" in one of his columns. In a way he couldn't begin to fathom, she was the girl who still in some way reminded him of Dolores. But what exactly was behind her modus operandi?

From the dowager's sour expression he saw the girl wasn't getting very far. There was something he glimpsed for a second on her face, a scared, lost look that struck a chord. There could be a story here.

Without thinking it through, Johnny strolled over. "I wondered where on earth you'd got to," he scowled as he approached. He tucked her arm through his (not surprised to feel it tremble). "You said you'd only be a second, but as usual . . ." he exchanged another scowl with the dowager, "as usual you're about to miss the first course. I'm ravenous, even if you aren't."

The girl shot him a furtive look that mingled astonishment with gratitude, but without missing a beat she smiled sweetly at the lady with the list. "I'm sorry to have been such a nuisance, but I did tell you I'd been in before. Sorry to have troubled you."

He couldn't help smiling himself. She really was a well-trained con artist, not making the mistake of turning into a prima donna and dressing the dowager down now that she'd been rescued.

"Oh, I didn't know she was with you, sir. She didn't say so."

"I can't think why!"

As they climbed up and around the soaring staircase, Johnny already regretted getting involved. There may be a story, but he had other stories on his mind.

"Thank you, Mr. . . . ." She obviously didn't have a clue who he was. For some reason that irritated him.

"I can't imagine why she was giving me such a hard time," she blithely chattered on. "I'd just gone downstairs to collect my wrap—it's a bit cool upstairs, and—"

"Where is it then?"

"Where's what?"

"Your wrap."

Her eyes were almost on a level with his. They were a strange greeny-brown color. She had very long lashes which looked like her own. Now she batted them a few times, and without a pause, went right on, "Well, I changed my mind. I didn't want to hide my dress. I decided to be . . . well, chilly for the sake of fashion." She laughed charmingly. "I'm Ginny Walker."

What chutzpah. He didn't respond or introduce himself as they reached the main room where the party was taking place. It didn't strike him as cool, although the air, sweet with the scent of a hundred thousand roses (as he'd been told several times already), made him feel lightheaded.

"Well, thank you," the girl said again. "I better go find . . ." She held out her hand.

He ignored it. "Watch them move." He pointed to all the grand dames milling about. "They never rub their noses, never move their hands to their faces or sip a drink at the wrong time. Their heads will rise on cue and the turkey necks will disappear."

She gave him the furtive look again, not sure where all this was leading.

"As one takes out her perfect little gold compact to powder her nose, so one by one will the others follow suit. Oh, the misery of all those lifted faces without the hands to match, because you can only lengthen a sleeve so far, right?"

There was an awkward silence as he waited for her to speak. "Well, yes, well, yes, you're right." Ginny turned as if to look for someone else to rescue her. He enjoyed her obvious discomfiture.

"Well, thank you, Mr. . . . I'd better be going." Now she looked wary. She was no doubt convinced, he thought with more amusement, that she'd been shanghaied by a madman.

"The reason for that little monologue is simple. It's leading up to an important question. Why, ma'am, do you want to be with these people? I've watched you before in similar situations. You're crashing this party, aren't you? You're what I would call a professional crasher. There's no one out there waiting for you, is there?" He waved a hand casually at the chattering crowd. "But why bother?"

She blushed, a pretty pink blush all the way from her collarbone to her forehead. He couldn't remember the last time he'd seen a woman blush. Trained to blush? An interesting thought, but then women could train themselves to do anything if it suited them. Perhaps this little episode wasn't going to be such a waste of time after all. Why would anyone, least of all a cute young woman, as this one appeared to be, want to put herself in such a potentially demeaning situation?

As she moved her hand to brush a stray piece of hair from her face, he noticed her bracelet. Spectacular. If she owned a bracelet like that, she could surely afford to attend this dinner and any others without crashing.

Despite the blush, there was no sign of embarrassment on Ginny's face. She stared at him loftily. "I'm sure I don't know what you mean. I'm a guest of Poppy Gan. I've just forgotten the number of her table."

"Poppy Gan isn't here. This isn't her crowd. That's new money, a downtown fast crowd. This is old money, slow, not half so much fun. I'll give you a thousand bucks to buy a real ticket for yourself if Poppy Gan's here. Try again." Johnny gave her an amused sardonic grin.

The blush was still on her face as for the next few minutes she obstinately clung to her Poppy Gan story, even throwing in the monstrous Svank's name. Johnny decided he'd had enough of her mental contortions. He pulled a crumpled sheet of paper out of his pocket and handed it to her.

"What's this?"

"A list of the table holders as of six o'clock tonight. So what's it all about, Ginny? I really want to know why you'd sooner be here than in a cozy little bar with pals of your own age."

She looked like a cornered deer. "Why . . . why do you have such an up-to-date list? How can you be so sure Poppy isn't here?"

Before he could speak, a languid blonde came up and placed a proprietary hand on his arm. "Hey, Johnny, so glad you finally made it. The Rockefellers are at your table. We're all waiting for you so the party can really begin." She smiled, showing perfect bonded teeth.

Johnny clapped a hand to his head. "Susan, did I tell you I was bringing a date? Ginny Walker, meet Susan Barker."

Susan flicked a glance in Ginny's direction, then averted her eyes quickly as if the sight was too painful. "No, you didn't, Johnny. That could be a problem."

Squirming, Ginny couldn't wait to make a getaway. "It doesn't matter, really. I can't stay long . . ."

"Neither can I," said Johnny. "I'm on deadline." He smiled at an increasingly flustered Susan, then taking Ginny's arm, said, "Let's pay our respects to the Rockefellers, and squeeze in for the first course." He grinned again. "We'll be out of your hair by the main course, Susan . . ."

"But Johnny . . . so many people are waiting to meet you . . . ," Susan wailed.

"I've met them, all of them," he said firmly. "I've got the story."

As he shepherded Ginny through the crowd Johnny was hailed and stopped time after time by people of all ages, most of whom seemed to adore him.

By the time they reached the table, Ginny's stomach was playing somersaults. It had nothing to do with Susan Barker's unmistakable disdain and cold fury. That was easy to put up with. No, as she'd stumbled along with this strange, sarcastic man, a lurking suspicion had begun to build.

As introductions were made, and she heard his name loud and clear, her worst fear was confirmed.

"Johnny Peet, pleased to meet you."

"Hi, Johnny, love your column. This is my wife, Sheila . . ."

"Glad to meet you."

"Mr. Peet, a pleasure to meet the mastermind behind . . . what's your magazine called?"

"*Next!*, dear. Don't mind my husband, Mr. Peet. He often forgets my name."

John Q. Peet!

She'd been rescued by Dolores's ex-husband, by John Q. Peet, who wrote the wickedly satirical column for *Next!* magazine.

No wonder he wanted her to answer his questions. No wonder he'd guessed she was a crasher. He was everywhere. He must have seen her before. Her cover was blown. He would turn her into a laughingstock in his column, by exposing her as a gate-crasher. Her fashion career was over before it began.

CHAPTER
SIX

11 WEST 77TH STREET, NEW YORK CITY

As often happened, Johnny's alarm went off when he was already awake, although he hadn't yet opened his eyes.

He lay still, trying to recover from a dream, more accurately a nightmare about his father. He didn't need a psychiatrist to explain it. He'd dreamed he'd let his father down in some terrible, tragic way. It had something to do with an envelope he'd been entrusted to deliver, but no matter how fast he ran down a never-ending street, chasing his father's shadow, he never managed to catch him.

It wasn't too different from real life. He'd been running and trying to catch up with his father for years. He was almost thirty now, but his father remained as far away and as remote as ever.

He shrugged on a robe and went into the handsome bathroom of his new apartment overlooking the Museum of Natural History. As he began to shave, his feeling of gloom and doom deepened. Again he knew why. He was lunching with his father in a few hours at the Century, the illustrious club for men of letters, and, following a feminist hullabaloo that had changed the club's bylaws, now for women, too.

He wasn't a member. Until recently he'd never given it any thought, although as Quentin Peet's son, he guessed he probably wouldn't have a hard time getting approved by the board.

Johnny nodded at his bleary, sleep-deprived reflection, agreeing with himself that he had never sought membership because he knew his father wouldn't think he'd earned it.

That was what the dream was all about. No matter that the "perceptive spin" of his ego-pricking pieces on society and people in the news in his *Next!* column were being talked about; that he now occasionally appeared on McNeill-Lehrer and Charlie Rose. His piece on the homeless woman, wrapped in sacking, lying on the pavement beneath a fancy costume in a Saks Fifth Avenue window, had brought that about. As far as his father was concerned he hadn't earned anything, period.

Yesterday a messenger had brought a clipping to his office from his father. It was a flattering item in Liz Smith's *New York Post* column that he'd already seen, praising his work. "Like father, like son," she'd written, reminding her readers that, "after all, the 'Q' in young Mr. Peet's name does stand for Quentin."

His father had attached a note, which told Johnny what today's lunch was going to be all about.

"Quidnunc, if you ask me," he'd written.

He didn't know the word but he'd expected the worst, and looking it up in Webster's, he'd been right.

"Quidnunc: what now?" he'd read, "an inquisitive, gossipy person; a busybody."

"I don't care," he'd told himself yesterday, tearing the note to shreds and hurling it across the room. Working for *Next!* may not be as significant a career step as running the Albany Bureau of the *New York Times* (where, his father still cuttingly reminded him, many of the men now in top jobs at the *Times* had first been sent), but it provided a forum for him to write about whatever he liked; injustices, perversities, anomalies, sometimes trivial ("The Art of Raising Money as a Form of Social Mountaineering"); sometimes consequential ("Who Runs This Place? A Look at the Battle Between New York's Mayor and New York's Governor"). So he hadn't cracked a big one à la Woodward and Bernstein, but he was building a name for himself, not only as a shrewd commentator, but as someone who stirred things up, sometimes for the better.

Yesterday, he'd thought bitterly how much he agreed with what a number of young reporters sneeringly called the old-time way of "access reporting." So his father knew the secretary of state, could get to him easily with one phone call, and then give his millions of readers around the world the inside story about U.S. decisions in the world's trouble spots, Bosnia, the Middle East, Africa, but did his father ever sit down and explain what bungling had led to the mess in the first place? Did he ever write about the suffering masses, about poor people—not only the ones thousands of miles away, but also those in New York, on his own doorstep?

No, Johnny had thought yesterday, burning over the quidnunc crack. His father was too busy being James Bond, not accepting that there was room in the world for another kind of reporting, the kind that was now bringing him kudos. If he had to have a role model, he supposed it would be Robin Hood.

That was yesterday.

Today he cared, waking up, longing as much as ever to receive the look of approving camaraderie he'd seen his father give brilliant young journalists such as Tom Friedman, who'd already earned a couple of Pulitzers as a foreign correspondent.

What was he going to do about it? There was no point telling his father that he wasn't a lightweight, that along with his column, he'd been working with a member of the DEA on a dangerous story to expose a link between two major New York robberies and the international drug trade, tying that in with Rosa Brueckner/Rosemary Abbott's horrific death by fire.

Would his father have been deterred by Ben Abbott's threat to stay off his turf?

Of course not, so what was the point of proving to his father still more that he didn't measure up, because he had been deterred. The Licton/Licone lead had turned into a dead end, and he'd filed the story away, not because he was trying to save his own skin, but because he did not know enough. Abbott had been right. Inadvertently he might risk the life of somebody else. Even now a chill went through him, remembering Abbott's Joan of Arc crack. It would haunt him forever.

He turned on the triple jets in the fancy shower he loved. How lucky he was, thanks to his mother, to be able to afford such a great pad. That was another thing. The old man had probably never forgiven him for inheriting his mother's money, because he'd been banking on inheriting it himself.

Although Quentin Peet was among the world's top-earning newsmen, for as long as Johnny could remember his father had always talked about being short of money. Why? What a story it would make for Next! Few people knew—and they'd never know it from him—that Quentin

Peet not only gambled with his life; he gambled on anything and every-thing—horses, baccarat, politics, baseball, football, even Scrabble. His father was an addict and it had made their family life, what there was of it, unadulterated hell.

Paying some of his inheritance out in alimony to get rid of Dolores fast hadn't helped the situation either. His mother would have ap-proved, he knew that. He had his freedom and a clear conscience. He could have left Dolores in the gutter, where his father thought she be-longed, but he'd behaved like a gentleman.

Johnny looked carefully through his wardrobe. That was another great thing about *Next!* He could wear what he liked to the office and it was often jeans, a sweater and a cord jacket. Not today though. It was a suit today, somber serge, the one he'd worn only a few times since his mother's funeral.

When he reached his office around ten, there was a FedEx envelope on his desk. He glanced at the sender's name and address before open-ing it. He often received information he hadn't asked for this way, from diligent or overanxious public relations companies trying to signal that this communiqué was too good to miss, hoping to ignite a story idea for his column. This "urgent" missive was from Fay Needham of Random House.

He opened the envelope with a sense of guilt. He knew what this was about and he'd definitely been negligent. More than a month must have passed since he'd received the first letter from Needham, a senior editor at the publishing house, asking if he'd be interested in writing a book for them, "a serious sociological look at a year spent 'inside' New York society."

"We want the ultimate insider's look; available to someone like yourself," her letter had begun. "Single, attractive, invited everywhere because of your eligibility, your humor, your family background, con-nections and, yes, of course, your column inches. From reading your col-umn, we feel you would bring to this study an unusually penetrating, unjaded and, we hope, witty perspective.

"Would you be interested in discussing this idea with us? Perhaps comparing 'now' with 'back then,' as well as comparing today's society in New York with that of other American cities, Washington, of course, Los Angeles, and any other city or cities you might suggest."

He'd been intrigued and called to say he'd give the idea some thought, but with Rosemary's death, it had completely slipped from his mind.

Obviously his silence hadn't hurt. Now they were suggesting an advance of two hundred thousand dollars for a hundred-and-fifty-thousand-word book, subject to agreement on his outline. It sounded pretty good to him. Did he have the discipline to add that load to his regular weekly thousand-word column?

He thought he did, and if he wrote a successful, good book, a soul-searching, truthful John O'Hara meets Tom Wolfe sort of book, wouldn't that be one way to redeem himself in his father's eyes?

Should he bring it up at lunch? He already knew the answer. No way, not until he'd written every one of the one hundred and fifty thousand words and the book was approved and at the printer's.

He pushed Needham's letter aside. He would meet with her group this week and then make a decision. He picked up the phone to retrieve his voice mail. There were eight messages, two of them, both agitated, from a Ginny Walker, asking him to call.

Ginny Walker? Oh, yes, the gate-crasher.

He'd stayed at the Guggenheim longer than he'd intended to, enjoying some fast repartee with a modern-art-loving young Rockefeller, and even taking to the floor for a brief body encounter with Ms. Walker (who, in his arms, surprisingly turned out to be nothing like as bony as he'd expected from her skinny silhouette).

As midnight struck, she had done a disappearing act. He'd been relieved. He'd acted too impetuously and once she knew exactly who he was, he'd wondered how he was going to cope with her jitters, which had shown up on the dance floor, when she'd started pleading with him not to write anything about her. He hadn't bothered to reply. If she thought she was about to be exposed as a gate-crasher, perhaps she'd think twice about doing it again. Then again, the reason behind her gate-crashing did interest him, but not that much.

Because he'd woken up so aware of his father's continuing depressing effect on his moods, Johnny decided to be magnanimous. He would put the young woman out of her misery and tell her she was not about to be skewered in *Next!* He dialed the number she'd left.

"Welcome to the world of Ginny Walker Fashion. We are either away from our drawing board or on the telephone, but your call is important to us. Please leave your name, date, time of call and a brief message if you wish and we will get back to you as soon as possible. Wait for the—"

The beep went off before she was able to get the word out. With all that blather no wonder her voice sounded so breathless and who, Johnny wondered idly, made up the "we" of Ginny Walker Fashion?

"This is John Peet returning your calls. I would like to talk to you. Leave word when you're actually going to be present, creating at your drawing board, so we don't play endless telephone tag."

When Ginny received the message around six, she panicked.

"I would like to talk to you" could only mean one thing; Peet intended to write about her in *Next!* He wanted to interrogate her about her crashing habits.

Why on earth had she called him and left her number after running away from the museum so successfully? Because she might be able to appeal to a sympathetic side she sensed John Q. Peet possessed.

Now she castigated herself for her stupidity. How did she know he had an iota of sympathy in him? So many successful people appeared sympathetic, even when they were aiming straight at the jugular.

She'd just spent seven straight hours on her feet, working like a maniac in the December rush at Bloomingdale's. Climbing the stairs to the loft, she'd more or less decided she didn't have the energy to go to a holiday party after a movie screening that night, even though, for once, Poppy had actually invited her.

Peet's message changed all that. There was no way she could stay home, biting her nails from anxiety, wondering what to do next.

Would Peet be at the party? What of it? This time she had a genuine invitation. Poppy had promised "a gala night, to celebrate the holidays at the Rainbow Room." There was a string attached, but Ginny hadn't cared, in fact had welcomed it. Poppy wanted Ginny to give her a fitting for a new dress there, on the spot.

It wasn't so unrealistic. Poppy had loved the concept—basically being wrapped as tight as a mummy in high-twist heavy georgette; had ordered the dress, and then played her usual hide-and-seek game when it came to being fitted.

Now Poppy wanted the dress pronto, in time for Christmas, and Ginny had figured she could transport the georgette to the dinner in a matching georgette bag and fit Poppy quickly in the nearest ladies' room.

Ginny listened to Peet's message again. He had a great voice, with the suggestion of a laugh buried in it. Perhaps she was right after all and he really was a sympathetic soul. Perhaps he didn't only view her as column fodder? Perhaps he fancied her? Perhaps he still liked brunettes.

She laughed at her own absurdity. After being married to Ms. Gorgeous, who was he going out with now? Somehow from somewhere she knew John Q. Peet hadn't taken long to recover from his "amicable divorce," that despite what Tony had told her about Johnny having "sworn off women for good," he was already earning a reputation as a "ladies' man."

If only Alex were back from Europe, he would tell her how to deal with the Peet situation.

She went over to the tall, narrow, art deco wardrobe she'd found for practically nothing in the flea market, where she now kept her "best" clothes. What should she wear to the Rainbow Room to cheer herself up? She sighed. Everything hanging there she knew too well. The red tuxedo top with sarong skirt, the silver suit with the birdcage jacket with inside-out seams, the lilac chiffon and the two Gosmans in expensive fabric that she'd renovated, the back-to-front "Dior" pumpkin-colored sateen (once described, she'd been told, in Peet's column as "the two-faced dress") and the "Yves St. Laurent" she'd covered in paillettes.

For all the clippings in her portfolio, not one of them had brought her any success. Each stood for an unhappy memory, a disappointment, a letdown, the story of her life so far. She longed to burn the lot, but it wasn't so easy to replenish her wardrobe now that she was no longer at Gosman's. There, forgotten, leftover fabric and unsuccessful numbers gathering dust in drawers and cupboards had turned 554 Seventh Avenue into her personal Aladdin's Cave.

She decided sometime during the week ahead, in time for Christmas, she would turn the sparkling "YSL" into a shorter flapper-style dress, replacing the paillettes with fringes she'd found in her own dusty cupboard.

She only wished she'd thought of it before, because what could be more suitable for movie-going than uncrushable fringes? What was the movie anyway? Perhaps she should go there first? Women didn't wear long dresses to watch a movie, did they? Was the dinner dance listed as black-tie? She rushed to find Poppy's agenda. The movie wasn't mentioned, only the post-screening party, which didn't mention black tie or any tie.

Holiday party or not, she decided to dress down, not up, in something that didn't crush. She went to her everyday closet and took out her oilskin bodysuit just back from the cleaner's. Uncrushed and fresh, she'd go straight to the party.

She didn't like the anxious look she saw in the mirror. She practiced her Eliza Doolittle expressions to relax her facial features. "How n-ice of you to l-et me c-ome . . ." She added a few strokes of kohl around the eyes, vivid coral lipstick, and Alex's "entailed" gold petal bracelet around her wrist, which did the best job of cheering her up.

Her heart beat fast as she approached Rockefeller Center. To think, only a few nights ago she'd been sitting and chatting so confidently with members of the family. In one way she hoped Peet might be at the Rainbow Room, so she could show him she knew a few people, too.

Her ears popped as the elevator rushed her and a dozen others up to the sixty-fifth floor. Emerging was like leaving reality behind, each step down the glass hallway taking her farther into fantasy. Through floor-to-ceiling windows New York City's lit-up skyline sparkled like a trillion diamonds.

In the vestibule outside the Rainbow Room was a long table manned by a row of perfectly coiffed and made-up young women. Ginny recognized one of them from Peggy Siegal's celebrated public relations company, specializing in movie and movie star events. She couldn't remember her name, but that was all right; the young woman couldn't remember hers, either.

"Hi," they said together.

Ginny smiled and waved, about to move on.

"Don't you want your table number?"

"I may not be listed. I'm with Poppy Gan."

"Oh, she's already here with Mr. Svank . . . she looks bootiful."

"I'm sure." Ginny's smile was pasted on tight. Did "bootiful" mean Lana Turner white satin? Surely not tonight. Even Poppy wouldn't trot that old number out to wear to the movies. Ginny clutched the georgette bag more closely to remind herself of the main reason she was there.

"Table sixteen, Ms. . . . "

"Ginny Walker," she breathed over her shoulder.

The Rainbow Room might have been designed for grand entrances. Ginny was ready, preparing herself to stand still for a few moments on the top step, head held high, before slowly, gracefully descending the sweeping stairs.

Out of nowhere came a sudden fear that Johnny Peet was staring at her, about to materialize out of the crowd with an "I-know-what-you're-up-to" look on his face. Because of this, instead of posing on the wide step for those few important seconds, Ginny rushed down as if her train was pulling out of the station.

"Where's table sixteen?" she asked another well-put-together young woman holding a floor plan. As she began to scan it, Ginny glanced at the ballroom floor. It was slowly revolving.

In shock, so sudden it was almost physically painful, she let out a little cry. Poppy was dancing cheek to cheek with . . . Ginny couldn't believe it . . . with Alex, her cousin.

At that second Alex looked right at her. He winked, then whirled Poppy around as if to demonstrate his ballroom dancing technique.

The girl with the floor plan was staring at her. "Are you all right?"

Ginny nodded. She was far from all right. Across the room, presumably at table sixteen, she could see the loathsome Svank, as expressionless as ever, his eyes never moving away from the laughing, dancing pair.

"Sixteen is over there . . ."

"Thank you." Ginny didn't follow the pointing hand. She felt so shaken she didn't know whether she was crawling or walking toward a huge panoramic window, which revealed in dazzling detail Manhattan's ruler-straight main thoroughfares. Ginny saw nothing. She sank down in a chair, thinking for the first time how incongruous the georgette bag looked with her oilskin bodysuit.

First, she had to admit it, she'd felt jealous, seeing Alex dancing so ecstatically with, she again had to admit, an extremely "bootiful" Poppy in a tight-fitting gray jersey sheath. Now, however, came a stronger emotion. Fear. Did Alex know what he was doing, dancing so intimately with Svank's woman? Was he aware Svank was watching every step they took? Didn't Alex remember the story she'd told him about the birthday dress?

Ginny shivered. She had no doubt that Svank would stop at nothing to blot Alex out of Poppy's life. Nothing.

"Ginny, darling," said Alex, "there you are in your slinky, oh-so-svelte cheetah suit. Well, fancy seeing you here . . ." She tried to pull away from him, as Alex led her onto the floor, but it was impossible without making a scene.

"Congratulations," he whispered. "Poppy is looking like a stunning nun. It won't be long before she's on the BDL."

"I didn't have anything to do with it," Ginny snapped angrily. "Why didn't you tell me you were back? Why didn't you tell me you were coming here with Poppy?"

"Ginny, m'dear, I told you before, I'm working occasionally for Svank. I am under the Big Man's command. I didn't know I was coming myself until yesterday. I arrived last night. Don't look so mad, Ginny, especially if you're . . . eh . . . crashing. You look as if you'd like to murder me. Don't call attention to yourself that way."

Again she tried to pull away, but Alex held her tightly to him.

"Don't talk to me like that," she hissed.

He ignored her anger, saying brightly, "This has to be fate. Remember I told you about the parties that never get in the papers? The ones held in private, very private homes? Well, I'd like to take you to a very important one on Friday, full of the fashionable people, potential backers, Ginny, m'dear. Are you free?"

Over Alex's shoulder Ginny could see Svank still looking at him. It wasn't a pleasant look. "Alex, do be careful . . ."

"What?" He swirled her around so he was facing table sixteen. "Oh, Mr. Svank—is that what you mean? Relax. He never shows what he's thinking, poor guy. He can be thinking the most wholesome thoughts and he still looks like a thug. I promise you, he's very interested in my welfare. He's just checking that I'm in good company."

"I didn't like the way he was staring at you when you were dancing cheek to cheek with Poppy."

Alex laughed. "So you noticed! You couldn't be more wrong, my Gin. Svank doesn't like to dance and Ms. Gan does. I was taking her pout away and doing him a favor. Now be a good girl and come and say hello to your benefactors. I see you're wearing my bracelet. Good. I want you to show it off."

Alex had gone too far. She pinched him hard.

"What was that for?" he asked.

"You know. Benefactors, my foot. They've done nothing for me."

"Patience, patience. Not yet they haven't, but they will."

The Rainbow Room wasn't a complete waste of time. Not at all. With giggles and sly looks at Svank, Poppy excused herself and followed Ginny to the ladies' room where, much to the amazement of the attendant, she slithered out of her gray jersey, showing she didn't believe in underwear, and Ginny began to wrap her in the georgette. The fitting took twenty minutes from start to finish.

Although Poppy pleaded with her to stay, Ginny knew she couldn't enjoy herself, let alone eat any of the post-movie supper, with Svank continuing to ignore her existence (although he'd stared steadily at the bracelet). After a quick glass of champagne, she made a fast exit.

The next day a messenger arrived at the loft with a check for five hundred dollars "on account" from Poppy. It came just in time to help pay the rent.

Her mother had called, leaving a message, asking if she'd come down to Florida for Christmas. It didn't make much sense. Not this year. It was only a one-day holiday to her and she already had a couple of invitations, including one from Esme she intended to accept for Christmas dinner. At a time when a lot of people wanted time off she could earn more money staying in town; and in the new year, with store sales, income tax forms to be prepared, and a plea from Lee that some big shoots were coming up, she might even be able to save something.

"I'd sooner come in February, when the weather's really miserable," she'd said. The truth was she didn't want to go then either, although she longed to see her mother. She felt nervous about leaving the city, so full of opportunities. This is where my future lies, she thought. By February, who knew what might happen.

She was working at Bloomingdale's every day that week, and reworking the YSL at night. She decided to leave a message for Johnny Peet at his office around seven-thirty A.M., when she was sure he wouldn't be there, to say that she was out of town but would definitely "be back at my drawing board" by the weekend. She just had to pray he wouldn't write anything in Next! without first talking to her.

Alex called her every evening, asking more or less the same questions.

"Has anyone called for me?"

"No, why?"

"Where are you keeping the gold bracelet?"

"Locked in my cupboard. Do you want it back?"

"No." He paused. "But don't wear it on Friday. Are you sure no one's left me a message or a note at your place?"

"I'm sure. Who are you expecting?"

"Oh, forget it." Then casually, "On second thought, why don't you give me the bracelet back on Friday. I'll give you another one for keeps, instead."

He sounded jumpy, irritable, showing none of the charm so much in evidence at the Rainbow Room.

Ginny wasn't surprised. If her cousin was now working for Svank, how could he be anything but jumpy and irritable, however much Svank "cared" for his welfare?

What a joke that was. Alex was deluding himself if he believed that.

By Friday the YSL was transformed, from long to short, as "flapper" as she could make it. She took out the one credit card she possessed, usually locked away out of temptation with the bracelet. To help show off what she still considered to be her best asset, her long, shapely legs, she used it to buy a pair of Fogal hose, exorbitant at thirty dollars, but exactly the right shade of pale plum to match her new fringes.

Alex was supposed to pick her up at six to take her to the party given by an enormously rich Venezuelan Madame de Perez de something at 834 Fifth Avenue, according to him one of the best addresses in New York.

"It's a fancy holiday thank-you party for donors and would-be donors to a new room or wing at the Metropolitan Museum," he told her. "This, believe me, will be helpful to you, but you must let me handle it. If I say something that surprises you, don't, for God's sake, contradict me, and if I ask you to do something, do it. It's for your sake. Trust me."

She'd heard it all before, but as usual she said, "Of course, I won't. Of course, I will."

At six Alex hadn't arrived, but at five past he phoned to say he'd meet her in the lobby of 834 in thirty minutes. "Don't forget the bracelet."

"I won't, but Alex, don't be late. Don't let me down. You've told me we're expected, we're invited. It's such a relief not to be crashing . . . there's no way I dare crash this . . . ," she wailed.

"Don't worry, pigeon."

And he was there, urbane in a dark gray suit and darker gray silk tie, giving her a quick hug as he slipped the bracelet into his pocket. He looked so distinguished, she was proud to be by his side as they walked into the most magnificent, sumptuous apartment she'd ever seen. Svank should take a look at this, Ginny thought. His apartment cried "money" loud and clear. This, softly lit, richly draped, gloriously furnished, clearly stated "taste."

For once Alex hadn't exaggerated. He was expected and so was she.

She was so full of pride, there was a lump in her throat, as he began to introduce her to some of the elegant people, the men sipping champagne, the women Perrier water. What a relief it was not to have to look over her shoulder, to move about without fear of being accused as an interloper.

As they mingled with the crowd, Alex relaxed her further with a typical running commentary. "See the aging hippie with the terrible wig—he's the king of duty-free, worth zillions. The little wan blonde isn't in the poorhouse either—she just tucked away another few million, after being widowed, poor thing, for the fourth time. Over there, the horsey one with the chin? She likes girls, little girls . . ." He appeared to know plenty about the apartment, too, pointing out two Rembrandts, several Francesco Guardis and some Old Masters Ginny had never heard of.

"It's like being in a museum."

"It is a museum. See that cabinet?"

Ginny nodded. How could anyone miss it. It was immense.

"It's one of a pair—cost about ten or twelve million—by Boulle. The other's in Versailles." He looked around. "I'd like to show you the dining room—in fact, I'd like to see it myself. I'm told the table's eight feet wide and once belonged to James II."

A wave of love for Alex flooded over her as he murmured, "Well, not now. Perhaps later. Smile, Ginny. Here comes the lady of the manor, the hostess."

A tall, reed-thin woman with a helmet of gleaming jet hair was approaching. From one quick glance Ginny decided she'd had one too many face-lifts, but it was easy not to dwell on her face. Just below the ruffled collar of her black grosgrain dress, she was wearing the largest, most spectacular dark blue sapphire and diamond brooch Ginny had ever seen, while on her ears were huge sapphire and diamond earrings to match.

"Alex Rossiter, I'm so glad you left your beloved Scotland to be here again. Of course, I keep up with your travels." She gave a throaty little laugh. "From my English cousins, who love you as you know."

There was a faint, charming accent. Was it Venezuelan? Who cared! What she was saying was much more interesting. Beloved Scotland. English cousins. Would she ever be able to fathom her exciting cousin? Ginny looked at him, not bothering to conceal her awe.

"Luisa, Madame Perez de Villeneva, I am indeed fortunate that my travel plans changed. Thank you so much for allowing me to bring my cousin. We see each other so rarely and as you know I am devoted to her. Virginia is a talented dress designer, just recently moved to New York."

Ginny hoped she didn't look startled at the sudden lengthening of her name. More important, she hoped her fringed dress was making an impact, but she doubted it. All the women here, including horse face and wan face, looked as if they lived and died in safe black couture.

Madame Luisa extended a pale white hand graced with yet another stunning gem. "Ah, yes," she purred. "I am delighted to meet you, Virginia. Your guardian has told me of your talent. I believe . . ." She flashed an alarming smile at Alex. " . . . I believe, am I right, Alex, you would like me to show your ward my collection of Balenciaga gowns?"

Guardian? Ward? Balenciaga? Ginny didn't know where to look, but she didn't need to look anywhere. Alex had taken over.

"Luisa, that would be so very kind. One day when you have the time, I am sure Virginia . . ."

"No, no, no," Madame P. de V. interrupted. "Tonight, later, after the speeches. If we don't do it tonight, who knows when I will have the time. That is the reason you were kind enough to come, no?"

Ginny wanted to giggle, seeing the way the impenetrable-looking woman softened as Alex put a caressing hand on her skinny arm.

Ginny smiled warmly. "Thank you very much. You are too kind."

When she moved on to greet other guests, Ginny couldn't stop laughing. "Alex, what on earth . . ."

"Trust me, remember!" He winked. "I'll explain later. Oh, Alejo, how good to see you. Please meet my niece, I am sorry, I mean my cousin, Virginia Walker . . ." and so the evening went on, with Ginny feeling more and more like a cosseted ward in the protective care of a powerful guardian, loving every moment of it, not wanting it ever to end.

And the Balenciagas were incredible. Madame de Perez de whatever insisted on Alex coming to see them, too, but Ginny was too over-whelmed to be aware at first that he wasn't spending much time in the staggering mirrored dressing room, where with a slight touch the walls opened to reveal row after row of extraordinary clothes, all color- and designer-coordinated.

"Here are the Balenciagas. Ah, Cristóbal, how missed you are! There will never be anyone like him again . . ."

Ginny ventured, "What about his pupil, Yves Saint Laurent?" But her hostess was gone, back into her palace of a bedroom where, from time to time, Ginny could hear Alex's voice boom, followed by Luisa's throaty laugh.

She forgot about time as she examined the great Spanish designer's work, so much so she jumped in alarm when Luisa put a hand on her shoulder and said, "My dear, your cousin is so sorry. He received a phone call. He didn't want to disturb your obvious enjoyment, but he suddenly had to leave. He is so thoughtful, he has ordered a car for you to take you home. He is really so sorry. He is going to call you tomorrow."

The Venezuelan lady could hardly know how used she was to Alex's erratic behavior. She was a big girl. She could find her own way home.

From Luisa's slight look of embarrassment Ginny was sure she was going to meet Alex later and why not? Alex was into jewelry and art; no wonder this kind of richly bejeweled dragon lady appealed to him.

Although Ginny knew there was little chance any of the women at 834 could become her customers, Alex had done wonders for her morale bringing her here. It was eight-fifteen, but there was still a big crowd in the drawing room. She stood alone, savoring one more time the atmos-phere of great wealth, taste, and beauty.

Someone tugged one of her fringes. She turned around with her most polite smile and froze. It was Johnny Peet.

"I have to hand it to you. This was a tough one to crash . . ."

"How dare you." Her voice shook. How could she have thought he had an ounce of sympathy or sensitivity?

"Come on. I'm not out to spoil your fun. I'm just amazed how you . . ."

At that moment Luisa reappeared. "Oh, I see you know Mr. Peet. How nice. I just wanted you to know, Virginia, your car will be here in fifteen minutes. I'm so glad you came. I do hope to see you again." Despite her words, there was a tone in her voice that declared the party was over.

It was like being given a present to see the surprised look on Peet's face, but he quickly recovered as Luisa moved away.

"Shall I kneel now to beg your forgiveness, or will you allow me to apologize more profusely over a drink?"

Ginny didn't know what to do. She was seething that Peet had automatically assumed she was uninvited, that she had no right being in such lofty surroundings, that she was there because she'd dared to crash. She wanted to show him how much he'd insulted her by telling him exactly what to do with his drink. On the other hand, perhaps this was the perfect opportunity to convince him she'd been telling the truth at the Guggenheim, to convince him he didn't have a story.

He was looking at her in a funny, quizzical way. A strange thought occurred to her. Perhaps he wasn't so much at ease with women after all? His wife, or rather ex-wife, had cheated on him for years. That must have been devastating. Perhaps he wasn't as confident as he appeared?

"Thank you," she said primly. "A drink would be delightful."

"And the rain in Spain falls mainly on the plain."

"What?"

"Never mind."

He gave the doorman twenty dollars to send Ginny's car away when it arrived, and in a chilly wind they walked a couple of blocks fast down Fifth Avenue into the Hotel Pierre.

They settled at a corner table in the bar, a good pianist playing Andrew Lloyd Webber in a soft, romantic way.

"What would you like? A glass of champagne?"

Out of nowhere Ginny remembered seeing Dolores Peet for the first time at Doubles, almost next door to where they were now. How impressed she'd been, sitting there with Alex, drinking piña coladas in the afternoon. What an innocent baby she'd been.

"A Perrier, please." To show her sophistication, she added, "with bitters."

She had to be in charge of the conversation if she was going to convince Johnny Peet there was nothing about her behavior that could possibly interest his readers. How should she begin? Chitchat?

"Marvelous apartment, Luisa's, isn't it?"

Johnny laughed. "Marvelous. How well do you know her?"

"Oh, not well." Ginny toyed with one of the fringes on her skirt. "She's a good friend of my cousin Alex—Alex Rossiter." She hesitated, wondering whether to say "from Scotland," but decided against it. "She'd heard about my business and wanted to meet me."

"Oh, yes, your business. Ginny Walker Fashion, right? Or is it Virginia Walker?"

He didn't miss a thing. Ginny took a deep breath. "My name is actually Virginia. I was named after my mother. She's always called Virginia and sometimes Alex—er—our, er, my mother's nephew—forgets and introduces me as Virginia, but I prefer Ginny. What do you like to be called? John or Johnny?"

"Johnny."

"Of course, the Q. in your byline stands for Quentin, right?"

"Yep."

"After your father . . ."

"Yep."

"Of course, I knew that. My father's one of his most fervent fans. He's been writing to him for years, xeroxing his columns, quoting from them in the lessons he sends out. He runs college correspondence courses."

"Really." This was pretty boring stuff. It was time to change the subject.

"So tell me about your business? What kind of fashion?"

"Oh, it's small, but it's developing nicely. Moderately priced, day, evening clothes, like that . . ."

"Like what you're wearing? It's . . . it's different, but very pretty."

"Thank you." There was that slight pink blush again. "Well, no, I mean I designed this, of course. I always wear my own clothes, but this would be too expensive to go in one of my lines . . ."

"How many lines d'you have? Or should I call them seasons?"

She was relaxing. "There's an old saying in the rag trade that there are five seasons, fall, winter, spring, summer, and slack." She paused and he obliged her with a laugh. "Now there are more, resort, holiday, pre-spring, pre-fall because stores demand a constant influx of new stuff. Of course, I can't possibly cover all that . . ."

He could see she really loved her work and was beginning to unwind.

Until a second round of drinks arrived, they went on chatting pleasantly, she describing a business that didn't exist, he describing a close relationship with his celebrated father that didn't exist.

As she talked, he studied her, an idea beginning to formulate. This strange wild card, Ginny Walker, had to view society from a uniquely jaundiced vantage point, if, as he suspected, she was no novice at crashing. She must have plenty of stories to tell, stories about behavior that could be useful when he went ahead with the book. He noted he was already thinking "when" as opposed to "if."

After the miserable no-win, tense lunch with his father, of course he'd decided to do it; he just hadn't admitted it to himself until that moment. He'd kick himself forever if he didn't take a stab at it.

It was time to get down to business. "Now explain to me why on earth you wanted to crash that party the other evening?"

"But I didn't." She was mortified that she couldn't stop a flicker of fear crossing her face.

"Come on, Ginny, I'm not going to bite. Remember that list I showed you, the guest list? Whatever you call yourself, Ginny, Virginia, Veronica, Venezuela, your name wasn't on it and I happen to know that group is very sticky about their guest list. They practically wanted it certified before they gave it to me. In any case, the reason I rescued you from that battleship was because I remembered seeing you being put through a similar hard time before, somewhere. What's up, Ginny? Why do you put yourself through the wringer like that? It's not good for your psyche, your soul. It surely can't be good for your business. People must know what you're up to and the word gets around."

There was a long, painful silence. Soul! Who was Johnny Peet to talk about souls? What could he, the quintessential insider, know about what happened to your soul when you were always on the outside?

Was it any use continuing to deny his accusations? Would he understand more if she also confessed she'd never yet been able to start her fashion business, because she'd been let down financially so many times? Her euphoria at being a welcome guest at 834 disappeared.

"Ginny." Johnny touched her hand. It was cold. "Ginny, I was going to leave you a message telling you not to worry. I know at the Museum you thought I rescued you because I wanted to use your vile crashing habit as material in my column. Perhaps initially the idea interested me, but not now. When you left that message, saying you'd be out of town until the weekend, I thought it would be more fun to tell you so in person and perhaps discuss a project where you might be of help to me."

"Help?" she repeated. He could see she didn't trust him.

He was right.

Once I admit I'm regularly into crashing, Ginny thought, I'm finished.

Johnny gave her the winsome smile Dolores always said was modeled on his father's. Perhaps it was. It was usually effective. "Yes, help. If I trust you with a secret, will you trust me with yours? I know there has to be a fascinating explanation for your crashing." Johnny looked at his watch and pretended to scowl. "You're making me ravenous again with all this talk. Let's stay here and have dinner. The food isn't bad and at least it's quiet."

Before she could answer, he beckoned a passing waiter. "We've decided to eat. We'd like a table for two in the back."

It was pointless to resist, and over dinner Johnny strongly reiterated that he had no interest in writing about her crashing in his column. "Zilch. There are lots of crashers out there, just as there's an army of place-card shufflers and people who use the names of people they don't know to get others to dinner. It's all part of the social con game. Boring!"

"What d'you mean? Ask people they don't know . . ."

Good. He'd captured her interest. It was the first time she'd responded since he opened his attack.

"Example: Mrs. Up and Coming wants to know Madame Already Arrived a whole lot better. She calls. She's giving a small dinner for Madame A.A.'s pals, the Very Socials. She would love her to come. If she accepts, she then calls the Very Socials and tells them the Already Arriveds are coming and wouldn't it be lovely if they came, too . . . and so on and so on."

"Don't these people ever talk to each other? To check things out?"

"You'd be surprised how many Already Arriveds are really Also Rans and love a free dinner when you get to know them. 'The penalty of success is to be bored by people who used to snub you'—one of the truest remarks ever made, by Nancy Astor, a remarkably feisty American-born English politician, as you probably know."

She didn't, but she nodded appreciatively as he went on, "The only reason I want to know why you want to be part of this nonsense is because I sense you aren't just another no-see-em."

"Now what d'you mean?"

"No-see-ems are what I call people who don't know they exist unless they see their names in print, in the gossip columns or their images on the idiot box."

"How weird."

"Well, I am weird. I thought you'd guessed that already. That's why we're going to get along as colleagues."

Colleagues? The word depressed her. It confirmed what she'd already guessed—that he had no interest in her as a woman.

What did he want? Anxious for the evening to end, Ginny decided to tell him the truth.

"For the past year I've been . . ." She stopped. She found she didn't want to use the "c" word to him. "I've been going to parties wearing my designs, getting photographed, meeting people who I hoped . . . I hoped through seeing my clothes, might help me find financial backing, enough to put my company on a firm foundation."

By the time coffee arrived, and because, Ginny supposed, John Q. Peet was so good at his job, using interview techniques she wasn't even aware of, she'd told him about her nomad childhood with the Walker School, run by a peripatetic father, who still thought he was Socrates, about the greatest influence in her life, her cousin Alex, and her subsequent disastrous venture into modeling, and about her on-again, off-again relationship with Poppy Gan (without mentioning the monster Svank), which had led her into taking Lee Baker Davies's advice literally, "to get out and about socially, so my designs can be seen."

"So I was wrong. Crashing helps rather than hurts your business?"

Was it time to tell all? Ginny sighed, not knowing how vulnerable and sad she looked.

"What business?" she said with a defeated shrug. "I don't know why I'm telling you everything now, but I don't think I've got much choice. You might as well know Ginny Walker Fashion doesn't exist . . ." she paused with a residue of defiance " . . . yet."

The more Ginny talked about her crashing experiences, the more pleased with himself Johnny became.

He'd struck pay dirt. Ginny was a natural observer of the cruelty alive and well in New York society. She saw through the hypocrisy, the hype, the hysteria. She could be invaluable as an undercover agent.

Although, luckily, she didn't realize it, despite her fashion designs, it was her . . . Johnny searched for the right word . . . her very unobtrusiveness that allowed her to crash so successfully eight times out of ten. It also helped her become so much part of the crowd that people gave things away, not realizing she was there.

There was no way he could explain this without hurting Ms. Walker's feelings; nevertheless, it was something he could turn into an incredible asset.

By the time Ginny finished telling him how many times the promises made of financial backing had ended in dead ends, if not in humiliating games of sexual hide-and-seek, they were alone in the restaurant, with the waiters clearly showing them they wanted to close up for the night.

"Where d'you live?"

"In Chelsea."

Downtown. That was a bore. He had to write tomorrow. "D'you mind if I put you in a cab?"

"Of course not." There was that sad, lost look again. Generally he avoided what he called wounded birds like the plague, but from what she'd told him and from what he'd already seen of her in action, he knew this Ginny Walker was no wounded bird.

Out on the sidewalk, when a cab came along he got in beside her. Immediately she tensed up.

He felt like laughing. She didn't have to worry about him, but women were funny. One minute they were afraid you'd make a pass; the next they were offended when you didn't. "Relax, Ginny. I'm already tied up with someone . . ." It was a useful line he'd been using to extricate himself if and when a woman came on strong, scarcely the case with Ginny.

They didn't speak much on the way downtown. When they reached her address, he was going to take the cab immediately back uptown, but again he did what he hadn't planned to do.

They stood awkwardly on the pavement. "I haven't told you my secret, don't you want to know?"

"It's late."

"A cup of coffee?"

"Only if you don't mind instant."

He wasn't surprised by the way she lived. Before hearing the story of her life, he'd guessed she might be living in a loft, spacious enough to double as a showroom for Ginny Walker Fashion.

He was strangely touched to see a small Christmas tree by the window, decorated with flowers, which on closer inspection he saw were cleverly made out of scraps of ribbon. On the drawing board, next to the tree, were some terrific sketches. Perhaps he could help Ms. Walker by showing them to Next!'s fashion editor.

On a side table was a photograph of a much younger Ginny, laughing up at a tall, dark, and handsome guy. He'd seen him before somewhere.

"Who's that?"

"Oh, that's Alex, my cousin."

Did the girl realize how often she referred to him? Johnny made a mental note to try to meet him sometime. Although he accepted the professional reason behind her crashing, he still felt there was more to it. Perhaps Alex could supply the answer.

Sipping coffee, Johnny told her about the book he'd been asked to write, "about New York society from my own, some would say, captious point of view, but don't misunderstand me. It's to be a serious book, a serious look . . ."

"How can I be of help?" Ginny interrupted, starting to laugh. "I can't even type. D'you want some illustrations?"

Johnny shook his head impatiently. "Remember Susan whatserface's look when I told her I'd brought a date?"

"How could I forget it?"

"What you've been telling me this evening, perhaps without even knowing it, is what I suspect but don't often have an opportunity to see for myself . . ."

She still looked puzzled.

"D'you want to hear a joke?"

He really was a weirdo. "Okay."

"I'll make it quick. A woman is talking on the phone about another woman. 'D'you know the two things I most dislike about her?' Answer: 'Her face.' "

It was her turn to oblige him with a laugh. "Okay. I get it. Society is two-faced"—she puckered her face into a cheeky grin—"like the dress I designed once, the one you called two-faced, remember? What else is new."

He laughed along with her good-naturedly. "What's new?" he repeated. "You are." He hoped she'd blush again, but she didn't.

"You mean despite your opinion of crashing, you still want me to go on doing it, so I can record what happens, as opposed to what happens when you walk through the door? Why should I? That's about as hypocritical as it gets."

"Not really. Think of it as carrying out a survey. Sometimes I'll send you to parties on my behalf, a bona fide invitation, a sort of alias Mr. Peet. Similar to what the *New York Times* food critic did—whatsername, Ruth Reichl, remember?"

Ginny shook her head. "What did she do?"

"She described what happened when she went to Le Cirque as a 'somebody' and then as a 'nobody.' There was quite a difference, although Le Cirque denies it to this day."

Visions of waiting for Poppy Gan, sitting at the right table, sharp right from Le Cirque's entrance, the day she heard Gosman was going to close, came to mind. How had she been treated? As a 'somebody' or a 'nobody'? That day, in shock, she wouldn't have been able to tell the difference. It seemed like another life ago. It was.

It was time John Q. Peet went home. It was too late for her to think straight anymore.

But Johnny was still talking. "I'll pay you for your reports and, by the way, for what you've told me tonight, too."

She looked frightened again and he hurriedly said, "Of course, your name will never be used and no one will know. It's just between us."

He could see she wanted him to go. She was standing by the rattan screen. When he got up to stand beside her, he was aware of her long lashes again and the fact they were almost eye to eye. Idly, he wondered if she always wore the same incredibly high heels that Dolores liked to totter about on.

Ginny could feel his breath on her forehead. She wanted so much to lean on him, to be close. She moved back. She must be tired. Johnny Peet of all people. Was she crazy?

"Well?"

"Let me think about it. I still don't quite get it. Why me?"

"I admire your spirit, the way you look at the New York goldfish bowl, and let's face it, you do view society from a unique position." He pulled on her fringed sleeve. "Look on the project as a fringe benefit."

And then he kissed her, a sweet, quick kiss on the mouth. He was as surprised as she was. He couldn't imagine what had prompted him to do it. Neither of them moved, not toward or away from each other.

Later Ginny wondered what would have happened if the phone hadn't started to ring.

"Who on earth can be calling you at this time of night?" Johnny sounded indignant.

She was wondering the same thing but, "How d'you know I'm not tied up, too?" she laughed.

By the time she reached the phone it had stopped, but he was already at the door, waving goodbye with a "You'll be hearing from me soon."

She didn't tell anybody about the book or the crisply worded letter of confidentiality she was asked to sign that came by messenger in a *Next!* magazine envelope later that week. There was a check for five hundred dollars in the envelope, too, and by signing the letter there was the promise of more checks to come.

It all seemed so simple. She would meet with Johnny Peet every other week or so and talk about her crashing activities, past, present and future (what events she planned to crash and why). Then occasionally she would act as his substitute without telling the host in advance that was to be the case. She was to note down everything she could remember, about the reception she received, the conversation around her, the objective of the evening, those who made the most impression, whether for good or bad reasons, and anything else she felt she should tell him.

Yes, it was simple, and it was flattering that he thought her observations would be useful, and exciting that she would have a chance to get to know him. She signed the agreement.

Esme called early that evening, full of happiness that she'd managed to talk Ted into a spring date for the wedding. Ginny couldn't resist telling her about meeting Johnny Peet.

Esme always came straight to the point. "Have you made love yet?"

Indignantly, "Of course not!"

"Why not? I haven't heard you sound so interested in a man since the Roman Romeo . . ."

"He was from Milan." Then, "In any case he's already tied up."

"What's tied can always be untied," said Esme. Ginny certainly knew that and so did Johnny Peet, didn't he?

"D'you want to bring him for Christmas dinner?"

"Gosh, no. It's all too soon. I wish I hadn't told you . . ."

She didn't mean it. She loved Esme and told her everything; well, almost everything. She was going to surprise her at Christmas with a modern cheongsam, made out of the heavy-twist georgette left over from Poppy's wraparound.

When she put the phone down she felt excited. Thank God she wasn't going to Florida. Thank God she was staying put in the city, ready for duty, all in the good cause of John Q. Peet's book on society. And then there was that kiss.

She told herself not to read anything into it, but it had been such a sweet, nonthreatening kiss. Surely, it meant he liked her, and like could turn into . . . who knew what? At least meeting him on a regular basis meant there would be opportunities for their relationship to develop.

"May I ask your name?"

Ginny was relaxed because she'd already been at the New Year fundraising party for PEN for close to forty minutes. Soaking up the atmosphere in the luxurious Sutton Square townhouse, she was sure she would be able to turn in an unusual report to Johnny on the hostesses, a different brand as far as she was concerned. A trio of excruciatingly earnest young women, who talked of imprisoned Chinese dissident poets Ginny had never heard of, they seemed more anxious to flaunt their intellectual capabilities than their husbands' money.

"Ginny Walker."

"From?"

The supercilious blonde accosting her looked about her age, Ginny decided. Her age, but rich, really rich in her black Chanel suit with discreet diamond and emerald pin and the kind of skin and teeth that looked as if they had been nurtured from the cradle by an army of experts.

She bared the perfect teeth now in a thin smile as she repeated, "From?"

Although Johnny hadn't sent her, without thinking Ginny said, "*Next!* magazine."

"Oh, I don't think so. No, no, no. Impossible," the blonde said.

"What's the problem, Felicity?"

"Someone from *Next!* magazine trying to crash. No way. No way. We would never invite anyone from that magazine again. Never. You must think we're out of our minds." Pincer fingers grabbed her arm, propelling her fast down the stairs and out into the street.

It all happened so quickly Ginny didn't have time to show any indignation.

"It's the first time I've ever been shown the door so dramatically and it was soooo embarrassing because I left my coat behind and had to keep knocking on the door, standing in the rain," she told Johnny the next day.

"Surely they gave it back to you?" Johnny sounded tetchy.

"Not until I was soaked." Ginny decided to be tetchy, too. She still had the gold-sprayed quill pen she'd been given on arrival at the party and pointed it at him now, accusingly. "The first time I crash a party for your benefit and not mine and look where it lands me—in the street. The minute I mentioned *Next!*, it was as if I'd said *Hustler* or *Penthouse*."

Johnny scowled. "You should never say you're from the magazine unless I've expressly told you to do so. I'm not surprised they hustled you out. *Next!* trashed a similar fund-raiser for PEN a few years back, given by a young woman who had the unforgivable temerity to be exceptionally beautiful, exceptionally gifted, with strong humanitarian instincts and, the final straw, married to an exceptionally rich young man. After the *Next!* piece PEN acted like a bunch of nitwits, quarreling among themselves about whether the rich and famous were up to the privileged job of raising money for poor, persecuted writers. As a result, today they're desperately short of funds."

As Johnny described the other PEN hostess Ginny felt a stab of . . . what? Jealousy? How stupid, but it sounded as if Johnny had known or did know this young, exceptionally beautiful, exceptionally gifted, ex-

ceptionally rich married woman. How many unmarried women like that
did he know and see? Who was the lucky one he was "tied up with"?

How would she know? The PEN crash was only the third she'd made
since signing the agreement before Christmas and this was their first
"business" meeting in the room he kept as an office on the floor below
his apartment.

As she reported on what had transpired in the first few weeks of
1995, Johnny was riffling through a filing cabinet. "Go on, go on. I'm
listening, but you've given me an idea. Good. Here it is." He was clutching a bunch of clippings. He sprawled across a weather-beaten old sofa.
"Listen to this."

So he hadn't been listening to her. He'd been reading his sought-
after clip. Okay, she was getting paid, wasn't she?

"How do you explain Arnold Scaasi to Galway Kinnell? How do you
explain Marty Raynes to Allen Ginsberg?" he read, with the same hint
of a laugh in his voice she'd detected at the Guggenheim.

"How do you?"

"This is the piece I told you about, the cynical job *Next!* did on one
of the better fund-raising days of PEN. I guess these people were on the
guest list. With what's happening to PEN's fortunes today, this will make
a good introduction. Thank you, Ginny, for jogging my memory." He
patted the sofa. "Come sit and resume your report."

She was attracted to him. Could he feel her body wanting a response
from his as she sat in the small space he'd allocated? To make matters
worse, he lazily flung an arm along the back of the sofa. "Good, good,"
he said from time to time as she read from her notes.

There was silence when she finished, then, "Money and power run
this town, Ginny."

"What about sex?"

"What about sex?"

His slow languid smile unnerved her. She knew she was blushing,
but he seemed to like it. "Pretty, such a pretty blush," he said, tracing its
progress from her collarbone to her brow. "Who taught you to blush like
that?"

"Taught me!"

This time it was his phone that rang.

"Yep, yep, of course I know her. Okay . . ." he looked at his watch.
"Okay. Thanks for telling me."

He switched on the small television positioned precariously in his bookcase. "You'll be interested in this, colleague."

" . . . and it appears the thieves got away with a ransom in jewelry and precious artifacts," ABC's Bill Beutel was saying, as first a picture of 834 Fifth Avenue appeared on the screen, followed by a picture of . . . Ginny put a hand to her mouth. It was Luisa dancing with an elegant man with hair as glossy and black as her own. In a voice-over Beutel continued, "Madame Perez de Villeneva, seen here with her estranged husband, was planning to leave New York this weekend for a business trip to Europe. It was only when her travel plans were advanced by a day that her personal maid discovered the robbery, the work, New York Detective Armitage confirmed, of a highly skillful professional gang."

Johnny switched the television off. He was tense.

"How terrible," Ginny said lamely.

Several minutes passed, then Johnny blinked, as if surprised to find her still there. He took a deep breath. "Yes, *pauvre* Luisa. This must be a big blow. I always told her not to travel with the family jewels. Funnily enough, I don't think she took 'em anyplace but New York. I heard her tell my father once she needed her jewels in New York to give her confidence." He talked hurriedly, not thinking much about what he was saying, wanting to get rid of her. "I must get over there to give her my condolences. I doubt she'll get them back."

"Why . . . why d'you say that?"

He looked at her guardedly. Another silence, then, "There's an international gang operating out there. They keep track of where the really important gems are, following them with the same dedication we give to watching our stocks. I've been studying some of these recent robberies, that's why I got the call. Okay, Ginny. That's all for the day. I've got to get to work."

As she caught the bus downtown, Luisa's array of sapphires and diamonds shone in Ginny's mind. She had to call Alex and tell him the terrible news. He'd be devastated. Where was he? In London. He'd told her last week he had to go back to London.

As soon as she reached the loft she looked for Alex's London number. It was a new one. She knew she'd written it down in her tiny kitchen. There it was. She couldn't remember the last time she'd called him. Probably when Ricardo left. She had to get the international operator because she couldn't remember the code for Great Britain. The phone rang and rang. She was about to hang up when a sleepy male voice answered.

"Could I speak to Alex Rossiter, please?"

"Who?"

"Alex Rossiter . . . Rossiter . . . I'm calling from the United States, from New York."

"You've got the wrong number, love. Sorry, no one of that name here."

"Is this London? 755-9443?"

"Yes, love, but Alex doesn't live here now and never has." She heard the receiver go down.

She found Alex's old number and called there, but the phone had been disconnected. It unnerved her. She felt strangely frightened; she didn't know why. She called a few friends she thought might know where he was, but they hadn't seen him in months. All the time she was putting off calling the one person who would probably know his whereabouts. Poppy Gan.

To Ginny's surprise, for the first time Poppy answered the phone herself. "Alex? Now where did he say he was going?" she drawled. "He had dinner with us only last weekend or was it the weekend before. No, we were in L.A. the weekend before . . ."

Ginny gritted her teeth to control herself. "It's really important, Poppy."

"Gee, I wish I could remember and I can't ask Pussy—he left last night on some mysterious business trip." She squealed. "That's where Alex is. He told me Alex was going to be his chaperone. Isn't that cute?"

"Where did they go?"

"Gee, that's the problem. I don't know, but it's far, far away . . . they took the new G 5 to someplace like Indochina or Polynesia or . . ."

"Indonesia?"

"That's it, but Pussy will be home Friday, he promised, so I'm sure Alex will be, too."

"In London?"

"No, New York, but don't ask me for his new number. I don't have it."

New York. New number. Indonesia. Svank and Alex had left only the night before for Indonesia. When had the robbery taken place? Ginny rubbed her eyes. What was getting into her? Now she felt really jittery. Should she call Aunt Lil, Alex's mother? No, she was ashamed she hadn't called her in months, although she'd heard she hadn't been well. Perhaps her mother might know something. Aunt Lil and her parents were regularly in touch.

It was nearing eight-thirty. Too late to call her mother without causing some ridiculous concern, and yet she felt she had to talk to someone who might know where Alex might be.

Unfortunately, her father answered. "What on earth is wrong, Ginny?"

"Nothing, Dad. Everything's great," she lied. What could she tell him to get him off the phone and get her mother on? What news, in his opinion, could justify a call at eight-thirty at night? There was only one thing she could think of.

"I wanted to tell Mother about the nice man I've just met . . ."

"That's very thoughtless of you, calling at this hour. You know how I feel about late night phone calls—"

"He's Quentin Peet's son." Silence. The next minute her mother had picked up.

"Are you all right, darling?"

"Yes, Mother. I called to tell you I've been seeing Quentin Peet's son, Johnny. I thought Dad would be bowled over by the sound of that name, but it didn't seem to impress him at all."

"No, dear. Your father went off Mr. Peet because he never answered his letters personally, however long and scholarly, just sent a printed acknowledgment." Her mother replied in the matter-of-fact voice she had long used when referring to her husband. "Are you all right?" her mother asked again.

"Yes, perfect." Ginny tried to sound casual. "I just wondered if by any chance you know where Alex might be?"

Her mother took so long to answer Ginny thought the connection was broken. "Hello, hello, are you still there?"

"Yes, dear. I don't know. Is there any special reason for asking?" Ginny knew her mother so well; she was covering something up.

"Is he in London? Do you have a number?"

"No, dear. I don't, but why do you want to know? Is something wrong?"

"No, no. Just some news I thought he'd be interested in knowing."

Ginny paused. "Is Aunt Lil any better?" Without waiting for the answer, she added, "I guess she'd have his most recent number, wouldn't she?"

Her mother snapped back quickly. "I don't want you worrying Lil. No, Ginny, she's far from better, but she doesn't want anyone to know, especially not her pride and joy of a son."

Often when her mother referred to Alex in her own sarcastic way, she'd soften her words with a laugh. Not this time.

"What's wrong with her?"

"They're not sure, but your Dad and I don't like the sound of it . . ." Their conversation meandered along, not going anywhere, except, Ginny felt on putting the phone down, to leave both of them feeling concerned about the other.

At ten o'clock she turned on Channel 5 to hear the local news. The lead story was still the robbery. Now they had interviews with the doorman and a friend of the personal maid, who'd been visiting and had seen a tall dark man watching the building when she left in the early evening. Finally the personal maid herself was shown, talking in broken English about the safe hidden so cleverly behind a wall in Madame's bathroom. "Apparently not cleverly enough," said the TV reporter. It all amounted to nothing.

Why did she feel so uneasy? What had the robbery got to do with her? Except Luisa had been so kind showing her the Balenciagas, while Alex and she had chatted in the bedroom . . . or had it been the bathroom?

Ginny lay down, but couldn't sleep. She got up to make some chamomile tea, and wandered about trying to think how she could get in touch with Alex sooner than later. She finally slept, dreaming of flying to a faraway place, but cold, not hot like Indonesia. She was still sleeping when a phone call from her mother woke her up.

"I'm sorry, Ginny. I know it's early, not quite seven. Your father's gone for his morning constitutional. You must tell me why you want to know where Alex is. Has he got you into some kind of trouble, too?"

Ginny was startled. "I don't know what you're talking about."

Her mother started to apologize. "I'm sorry, darling, but I know what an influence he's always been on you. I get worried now he's spending so much more time in New York."

"Why, Mother? There's something you're not telling me, I can sense it. What's up?"

"Well, I know you're so headstrong. If I say black, you'll say white. And I know you won't hear a word about Alex."

"What is it?" Ginny almost screamed into the phone.

The facts then came quickly. "He's been in trouble in Europe, Ginny, accused of being a fence or something. He got off, but I don't think he's heard the end of it. Now you've got to promise me, not a word of this to your Aunt Lil."

"Oh, Mother, of course not. Why didn't you tell me before? How do you know?"

"A horrible coincidence. One of your father's students coming back from London—he's luckily giving more private lessons now—"

"Yes, yes, yes . . . what happened?"

"He brought your father a Christmas present—a copy of Milton's *Paradise Lost* that he found in a London market called Portobello, like the mushroom. It was wrapped in newspaper and there was Alex's picture on the front page with the story." Her mother sighed. "He wasn't using his real name, called himself Angus O'Keeffe or something like that, but I recognized Alex, even with a mustache, staring out of the page as large as life."

Ginny swallowed hard. Angus. The name of the man who'd delivered the bracelet, which for some reason Alex hadn't wanted her to wear at the Villeneva party. She tried to laugh. "Perhaps he has an identical twin."

"Don't be silly, Ginny. This isn't anything to laugh about."

"Mama, you don't know it was Alex at all. A man named Angus, with a mustache! I'm surprised at you, jumping to conclusions about your own nephew."

"He's not my nephew; he's your father's."

"Mother, really!"

"I know it was Alex." There was a stubborn note in her mother's voice that Ginny knew meant there was nothing she could do to change her mind.

"Well, he was proved innocent, you said? That's enough for me."

"There were other charges pending," her mother said firmly. "The story said he'd skipped the country."

Angus O'Keeffe. Angus and Georgia O'Keeffe. It was the sort of name Alex might dream up. It was Alex who'd introduced her years ago to the great artist's work.

When her mother hung up, with another admonition not to tell Aunt Lil, Ginny was unable to go back to sleep, unable to go to work. Lee had asked her to help style a fashion shoot later that day, but Ginny knew she'd be all fingers and thumbs. She called Lee, pleading a migraine headache.

When the phone rang later that morning, she picked it up but no one was there, although she cried, "Is that you, Alex? Don't worry. Please answer, Alex, if you're there."

Just before lunch Lee called and begged her to come over to the studio in the afternoon. "I really need you. Can't you take a Tylenol Plus or something?"

It was a dreary day. Perhaps it would take her mind off things if she flung herself into the crazy world of fashion photography for a few hours. "Okay, I'll come," she said, although her head was now really beginning to pound.

As if to make her life more miserable, the old-fashioned toilet in the loft was making a nonstop trickling sound that was driving her mad. It had happened before.

With effort Ginny lifted off the heavy top of the toilet, intending to tinker inside. Thank goodness she carefully put the top down on the bathroom floor before peering inside or she most certainly would have dropped it to smash on the tiles. "Oh, my God." She reeled back.

Like some extraordinary piece of abstract art, a large black pearl necklace dangled from the ball cock, while at the bottom of the tank gleamed the magnificent sapphire and diamond earrings, the sapphire and diamond brooch and the large diamond ring she had last seen adorning Madame Perez de Villeneva at 834 Fifth.

1995

CHAPTER
SEVEN

The February morning was forcing its way into the bedroom through a broken slat in the shutters. Virginia Walker squeezed her eyes tightly together to try to block out the blinding light, but it was impossible.

Graham was always pontificating, "Every year millions of people flock to Florida to retire, as much for the joy of waking up every day to the brightest light in the nation, as for the warmth it represents." There was no joy in it for her.

Since their move to the wrong end of South Beach, Miami, for the first time in her life Virginia had begun to suffer from migraine headaches, the only ailment which had ever prevented her from turning up at work. Despite Graham ridiculing her reasoning, she was sure the brilliant, low-latitude light was responsible, for she never got migraines on sunless days. Luckily for the family budget, they happened quite frequently, despite the propaganda put out by Florida's tourist board.

Reluctantly Virginia opened her eyes. There was a tightness behind her right ear and the suspicion that if she moved too quickly nausea might develop, familiar migraine symptoms. Graham maintained she brought them on by thinking about her headaches too much. If only that were true.

Eight-ten A.M. Oh, no, she was late! The moment of panic was quickly followed by the grateful realization that it was Sunday.

She didn't need to turn to know that Graham was no longer in the other twin bed; and because the house was so silent, with no blaring of a religious service on television, she also knew with a sense of relief that he was no longer in the house. He would already be in church.

Early churchgoing was a new Graham habit, not only on Sundays, either, and as she showered, she wondered how many more "pupils" he might boast of having signed up on his return home.

For the first time it seemed Graham had landed in the right place at the right time to open a branch of the Walker School. There were a lot of retirees around with nothing much to do, and recently there had been a healthy response to his Socrates ad, offering one-on-one lessons on Western civilization for seventy dollars an hour.

Neither of them had known before their arrival that Florida was so much part of the country's Bible Belt. Although Graham denied it, Virginia was sure he hadn't had any idea how much that kind of environment would suit him. So much so that in his latest courses, Quentin Peet had been dumped as a source of knowledge and wisdom to be replaced by the Bible. It was typical of Graham that he'd written Peet one more "final" letter telling him so.

Propped up by the coffeepot was yesterday's *Miami Herald* with the Ann Landers column heavily circled with a marker pen. What was Graham about to commandeer for his own use now?

"Dear Ann Landers," she read, "When a woman wrote to ask how many times a wife should forgive a husband who cheats, you quoted the Bible—Matthew 18:21-22. Peter asks Jesus, 'How often should I forgive a brother who sins against me? Seven times?' Jesus replies, 'No. Seventy times seven.'

"Does that mean I should forgive this rat 490 times? If so, I've got to live through 470 more affairs. I don't think I'll make it. Any advice? signed, No Martyr."

Virginia stared out of the window at the solitary stunted palm tree marking the end of the scrubby patch which passed for their garden. The sky was cloudless, a perfect tropical blue. It already looked hot. She hoped Graham would be invited to take a glass of lemonade with the minister and his wife. She hoped he would be home late, very late, so she could enjoy a long call to Ginny without his frowning, disapproving presence as the expensive minutes ticked by.

She poured herself a cup of lukewarm coffee and resumed reading. "Dear N.M., You took me too literally. Every woman whose husband cheats should ask herself this question: 'Would my life be better or worse without him?' "

Virginia shook her head. That wasn't a very good answer, Ms. Landers. She was sure the only kind of cheating Graham didn't do was with another woman, but dealing with his other petty con games over the years, she'd asked herself "Would my life be better or worse without him" so many times, she knew it didn't resolve a thing. There were too many "ifs" and "buts" to take into account.

The tightness behind her ear was getting worse, but if she took a pill now she'd be a zombie for the rest of the day. She picked up the paper again, trying to figure out why Graham had marked it. "Dear Ann Landers, I'm the wife of a clergyman and—" Virginia screamed as a hand touched her shoulder.

She spun round in terror. "Sorry, Aunt V. The door was open . . ." Virginia stared in disbelief. There was her bad egg of a nephew Alex, who despite his rueful smile and placating outstretched hand, was standing before her as debonair and self-assured as ever.

"Alex, where . . . where on earth have you sprung from? This is a surprise. Really, you . . . you should have given me . . . us some warning." Not sure she'd even buttoned all the buttons on her housecoat, Virginia nervously turned away to check.

"I know I should. I meant to, but frankly I've just come in from the Far East, from Asia, and I'm a little discombobulated." Alex laughed in the easy way she knew so well. "My watch tells me the time, but I have no idea whether it's A.M. or P.M. Well, I do, but . . ." He touched her arm placatingly again. "I'm dying for a cup of your Cuban coffee, Aunt V. Where's the man of the house?"

"At church." She hadn't meant to tell him. She was seething with anger and stewing with anxiety at the same time.

Alex raised an incredulous eyebrow. From anyone else it would have seemed insulting, but then with a quick smile and a wink, he somehow conveyed his understanding of something which didn't need to be further explained. Not for the first time Virginia realized why Ginny was so under her cousin's influence. It was infuriating, but even she had to admit, there was something about Alex that was mesmerizing.

"I'll make some more coffee." She bustled around, now really praying Graham would stop over for that lemonade, not sure how to deal with Alex herself, but dreading the confrontation she knew would occur if Graham saw him.

"Have you heard from Ginny?" Alex didn't quite manage to hide the anxiety in his voice.

Virginia felt her heart pounding. All the fears Ginny's call of last week had triggered flooded back. There was something going on between them. According to the British press, Alex was a wanted man. It would be typical of Ginny to want to hide him. Who knew what trouble she might put herself in to protect her beloved Alex?

The tightness in her head was building, but she had to fight it to find out the truth, if Alex was capable of telling the truth.

Virginia faced him with a cup of steaming coffee in her hands. "Yes, I spoke to Ginny a few days ago. She's been looking for you urgently all over. Frankly, Alex, I want to know what's going on."

"Easy, Auntie, you look as if you want to scald me to death with that coffee." The easy banter was back as Alex took the cup from her. "I don't know what you mean—'something's going on.' I don't see Ginny anything like as much as I'd like to . . . I travel too much. I just wanted to know how she is, in case I miss her on the phone." He stopped, seeing Virginia's pursed lips. "What's biting you, Aunt V.? What did Ginny say when she called?"

"I told you. She's been looking for you urgently. I don't know why and I'll tell you right now, I wish she never gave you any thought, I wish you were right out of her life. She called the number you gave her in London and no one had heard of you there . . ."

When Alex shrugged as if it was nothing to do with him, Virginia lost her temper, blurting out, "Even your own mother doesn't know exactly where you live. When did you last speak to her? Do you realize how sick she's been?"

Alex stared at her coldly. "Sick?" he repeated. "Not yesterday when she'd just come back from her bridge game and not ten days ago when I called to see what color she wanted for the new car I'm buying her. Sick with what?"

Ashamed she'd broken her promise to her sister-in-law and not in the least mollified by Alex's reply, Virginia made a snap decision. She wouldn't get anywhere unless she told Alex straight out what she knew, what Graham and she both knew, and what she had told Ginny about her precious idol.

"Alex, Graham and I both know you've been in trouble with the law in Britain. You're on the run, aren't you?" Now she'd started, she couldn't stop. "We saw your picture in a British paper. Even though you used another name, and had a mustache, we easily saw it was you. Don't worry, we wouldn't dream of worrying your mother, but I told Ginny, because I don't want her getting into any trouble because of you. As far as we're concerned you've always stood for trouble. What are you doing here anyway after all this time? How could you arrive here from Asia?"

Even as she asked the question, she knew she was being stupid. What could she know about international air travel, moving as she did the cheapest way possible?

"You told Ginny what exactly?" There was a note in Alex's voice Virginia had never heard before, a note she'd never heard in anyone's voice. She pulled the housecoat around her and backed toward the kitchen counter. She had to be wrong, but Alex sounded menacing.

There was the hot coffeepot on the counter. She would pick it up as if she was going to pour some more coffee. She would hold it in front of her as a weapon—in case.

She was surprised how calm she sounded. "I told Ginny what we'd read, that you'd been charged in London in connection with a theft and got off; that there were other charges pending, but you'd skipped the country." She was unable to resist adding sarcastically, "Obviously, as I see with my own eyes."

"You don't see anything; you don't know anything; you never did," Alex sneered. "How could you arrive here from Asia?" he mimicked. "You've lived here for over a year and you still don't know Miami's one of the major international airports in the world." He looked around, not bothering to conceal his distaste for the shabby surroundings. "How much do you know about your precious little daughter? How d'you think she lives? Has she sent you any of her clippings, the ones where she's wearing some pretty fancy jewelry? Do you know anything"—Alex brought his face close to hers—"anything about the way your little princess lives now, the one you brought up so carefully to be Miss Prim and Proper Perfect?"

When she didn't reply, showing him with her sudden pallor and strained expression how his words hit home, he laughed, extracting the coffeepot from her in one easy move. "We don't want any accidents, do we Aunt V. You might burn yourself if you're not careful." He tilted the pot a fraction as he spoke, as if to pour a drop onto her housecoat, then, moving it quickly upright again, put it carefully down on the table.

She didn't know Alex anymore. Perhaps she had never known him. Both Graham and she had dismissed him as a lightweight, a ne'er-do-well, but harmless except for influencing Ginny too much with his racy way of life. Now she knew he wasn't harmless at all; he was a common criminal, whose winks and smiles no longer fooled her.

Thank God, he appeared to be leaving. He was at the back door, bathed in the brilliant morning light. Once more he said mockingly, "No, you don't know anything, Aunt V., and you shouldn't pass judgment until you know who and what you're dealing with." As suddenly as he'd arrived, he was gone.

Like a robot, Virginia washed up the cups and threw out the freshly brewed coffee. She put her hands to her ears, trying to blot out the sound of Alex's voice.

Was Ginny working with him? Virginia began to weep. She knew why. She was too frightened now to pick up the phone to call her daughter; too frightened she might learn that the fears she'd had for a long long time about Alex's power over Ginny were all about to be confirmed.

The jewels were still where she'd found them. She'd only unhooked the black pearl necklace from the ball cock to let it slide to join the other gems on the floor of the tank, so the toilet had stopped trickling.

Where else in the loft could the jewels be hidden? But for her migraine that made the sound of the trickling water intolerable, she would never have found them herself, for who would ever think of looking there? No one, except a member of "a highly skilled professional gang" —that was how the New York detective had described the robbers. Was Alex the ringleader or was someone leading her cousin around by the nose?

Svank. It had to be something to do with Svank, for what had Alex told her at the Rainbow Room? "I am under the big man's command." Svank had to be behind everything.

For the first twenty-four hours Ginny had been too ill, too terrified to move, locking her door, refusing to see anyone. She hadn't needed to act to convince Lee that she couldn't come to the studio to help style the shoot after all, that she had the mother and father of all migraines.

She'd sounded at death's door; she'd thought she might well be. The only effort had come from convincing Lee not to visit, because she wouldn't let her in however long and hard she rang the bell.

Lee probably thought she was suffering from another unrequited love affair. So let her think it. Ginny hadn't cared what Lee or anyone else thought; she hadn't cared about anything except solving the biggest problem of her life, a problem she couldn't share with anyone.

Not even Johnny. Especially not Johnny. It had been gratifying to hear how concerned he'd sounded when she'd called in sick. He had also sounded relieved, when she'd assured him she felt too poorly to receive any visitors.

Every time the phone rang Ginny rushed to answer it, certain it had to be Alex. How could he do this to her? How had he gotten himself into such a mess? She couldn't, just couldn't accept the logical conclusion—that Alex, her beloved cousin, counsel, best friend in all the world was a crook, and not just a petty crook either, for now she remembered with horror his "gifts."

The necklace he'd "borrowed" from Harry Winston, the one he'd fastened around her neck the night of the downtown DIFFA ball, the one she'd assumed was made of rhinestones, although they looked like diamonds. Where had the necklace come from? Whose diamonds had she been wearing so innocently? Then there was the mysterious "entailed" bracelet dropped off by his Scottish friend Angus—a name she would now never forget; the bracelet Alex told her not to wear to the Fifth Avenue party, the bracelet she'd given back. Why? Was it because it was too recognizable? Would Luisa have recognized it as belonging to someone she knew?

Why had he wanted it back? She hadn't given it much thought, so used was she to Alex giving and taking back, coming and going.

Exactly when had he told her he'd left the "Wall Street trenches for good" and was now "dedicated to buying and selling art, jewelry and objets"? It was soon after he'd gotten to know Svank. She was sure of it. Svank had to be responsible for Alex's and now her terrible predicament.

She talked herself into believing this at the end of one day, only to wake up at the beginning of the next with her mind churning with new hows, whys and wherefores. That Svank was involved seemed obvious, and yet, if so, with such valuable loot stashed in her loft why hadn't she heard from the monster himself or any of his henchmen? She shivered thinking of the biggest of them all, Hugo Humphrey.

Because Svank didn't know she had the jewels. Nobody would think of her loft as a hiding place for such valuables, let alone her toilet. And the reason Alex hadn't called? Because he was acting as he normally did, floating in and out of her life, in order to avoid attracting any attention to her. Obviously he never dreamed she'd find what he'd planted on her so soon, and he didn't know that by a curious twist of fate she also knew of his problems in England.

When the time was right Alex would turn up and explain everything. Please God, she prayed, let it be soon, for how long could she live with such a secret?

A murder on the West Side had knocked the East Side robbery off the local TV news, but rehashed and reexamined, it was still in the papers, although not on the front page. Perhaps Johnny would know something the papers weren't printing?

"Johnny?"

"Yep." He sounded preoccupied.

"Ginny."

His voice warmed up. "Ginny! I was going to call you today. You sound better. Ready to go to work?"

"Of course." She wasn't, but just hearing his voice made her long to see him, whether he knew anything or not.

"You don't sound too eager."

"Oh, I am. I am."

"Tomorrow's the opening night of the Cocteau revival with a splashy party afterwards at Tavern on the Green."

Ginny felt physically sick. How far removed from real life all that was. She heard Johnny shuffle through papers. She thought of the way his hair thinned at the back, although it curled up around the nape of his neck. In her weakened, low condition, it made her feel weaker.

"I've missed you, Ginny," he was saying. She didn't believe it but please, say it again, she prayed. He didn't hear her prayer. "How about coming over this afternoon, late, say about five-thirty. We'll go over the drill for tomorrow night. I'll explain to you a theater press-agent's nightmare."

She dressed carefully in what she'd come to regard as her "First Lady" tweeds, remembering her close encounter with the Secret Service at the Plaza Hotel. Esme had already given her a generous advance on all the dresses she was going to make for the wedding, so she took a cab over to Johnny on the Upper West Side.

Someone had left a copy of *Quest* on the seat, the glossy real estate magazine given away in tony apartment houses, which often carried coverage of parties.

On one of the pages was a picture of Johnny with his arm loosely around the waist of a very pretty, petite blonde. "Duane Dickens, the actress," said the caption. "A new squeeze of John Q. Peet, the columnist, at Mortimer's, celebrating the publication of *Green Ice: An Exposé of the Drug Business*, by his illustrious father, Quentin Peet."

Ginny felt like turning back. Why hadn't Johnny asked her to crash the Mortimer's book party? Why hadn't he even mentioned it? Was he ashamed of her meeting his father? Was this a new squeeze or an old squeeze? Was Duane Dickens the woman he was "tied up with"? For the first time since the robbery, her mind was focused on something other than the jewels and Alex.

When Johnny opened the door she couldn't hide her depression, although he didn't seem to notice it at first. Holding her away at arm's length he exclaimed, "Well you look better than ever."

She smiled stiffly. "Thank you."

"Oops! Have I done something wrong? I know. I didn't send you any grapes for the sick room. Okay. I'll make it up to you, partner. How about a glass of grapes, champagne style? This just arrived from"—he picked up a card—"from Elizabeth Taylor."

She shrugged her shoulders to show how unimpressed she was. She hated being addressed as partner, too. "No thank you, I don't like champagne."

"Perhaps you'd like this bottle better?" Laughing at the look on her face, Johnny tossed a small bottle of perfume onto her lap. Black Pearls by Elizabeth Taylor. "I have to confess, Ginny, I am not being pursued by the great star, but by the public relations department of the company putting out her new smell." When she didn't respond, he joined her on the sofa, his closeness as disturbing as ever. "Is something bothering you? You look upset."

She could feel tears pricking the back of her eyes. This was terrible. Once she started crying, she'd find it hard to stop. "No, nothing. I've changed my mind. I'll have a glass. Why not?"

Why not indeed?

There was an awkward silence. She tried to think of something to say before she asked the question burning in her mind. "I liked your piece on Rosemary," she said haltingly.

He looked startled, even shocked. "Rosemary?"

"Yes, the homeless woman whose story you've been following, once a college graduate. Isn't that her name? From Sacks to Saks . . . the one you first mentioned curled up beneath the Valentino window at Saks, the one wrapped up in a sack."

His face brightened. "Thank you, Ms. Ginny. I've been getting quite a reaction to those pieces. Her name *is* Rosemary, although I only mentioned it once. I usually call her Madame Saks. You're very observant . . . but I know that."

He got up and expertly opened the champagne with no more than a soft pop.

"Have you heard anything . . . anything more about Luisa's jewels . . . the Villeneva robbery? Did you see Luisa?" She hoped she didn't sound anxious. She didn't think so, although a small nerve throbbed in her throat.

"Luisa is devastated, although there's plenty more where they came from," Johnny said casually. "There doesn't seem to be anything new . . ."

There was, but Johnny wasn't about to tell Ms. Walker. He smiled, then said, "Didn't you tell me that cousin of yours introduced you to Luisa? What's his name, Alec?"

Was she blushing? She didn't know. More likely the blood had drained out of her face. "Alex," she corrected him.

"Alex what?"

"Alex Rossiter." Why was he mentioning Alex? The nerve throbbed again.

"Did you tell him what happened? I thought, since you say he's so smart, he might have some angles."

He suspects something, she thought, trying to smile as Johnny handed her a glass of champagne. "No, I haven't told him." She tried to sound indifferent. "He's traveling right now."

"Travels a lot, doesn't he? One of these days when he's in town, I'd like to meet him."

When Ginny didn't answer, Johnny ran his hand through his already unruly hair and to her consternation continued, "Something's not quite kosher about this robbery, Ginny."

Alarm bells went off. Johnny's attitude made her think he was holding out on her, or was she being paranoid? It wouldn't be surprising.

Tense, she waited for him to go on, but instead he clinked his glass against hers and now, all business, outlined what he had in mind for the following evening.

"I want you to stand outside the theater with the paparazzi and cover what they say and everyone says about the stars and wannabe stars arriving. Just before curtain up I want you to use this ticket." He handed her an envelope. "I was specific about where I wanted to sit . . ."

When she looked surprised, he added, "All part of the plan, partner. I don't usually care where I sit, although many columnists do, stomping out, saying they don't like their seats in order to get better ones. This time I made a point of asking for a certain row, so the press agent will notice I'm not sitting there."

"He won't like that." This week of all weeks. Ginny wasn't sure she was up to being publicly bawled out.

"It's a she. Of course she won't, but you can say I sent you."

"Then what?"

"You describe the reaction; who you're sitting with, who's behind, in front, et cetera, and how they behave toward you—in other words, a rundown of first-night priority seating, then you go over to Tavern on the Green for the first-night party in the Crystal Room . . ."

She was about to say, "I can't; I'm not up to it right now," when he went on, "Whatever happens, I'll be there soon after with all the credentials, and if it's fun we'll stay. If not . . ."

"What about Duane Dickens?" The question was out before she could stop it.

A strange look, half amused, half puzzled appeared. "Duane . . . who the Dickens . . . Dickens? Who's that?"

Ginny bit her lip. "Your new squeeze," she stuttered. "It's none of my business, sorry . . ."

"You're damned right it isn't." His arm was on the back of the sofa. He began playing with a piece of her hair. "It certainly isn't any of your business, little Ginny . . ." Then, almost absentmindedly, "I wonder why I always think of you as little? You're almost as tall as I am in your perennial stilts. Then I think of you as vulnerable, too, and you're about as vulnerable as a rhinoceros."

When she leaned forward to get away from his playful fingers he gently yanked her back. "In another life I reckon you could have been another Marguerite Higgins . . ."

"Who?"

"Oh, just another squeeze of mine. One of the most famous female war correspondents ever, who washed her undies in her tin helmet at the front line in World War II, as pretty as a picture, but as tough as nails. You are as tough as nails, aren't you, Ginny?"

He laughed, but he was looking at her in a searching, sweet way, as if he really wanted to know; and goddamn it, one of the tears escaped. Johnny pretended to pick it up on the tip of his finger to examine it. "I don't know if this has anything to do with Ms. Dickens, I seriously doubt it and I seriously hope not, but if it means anything at all, I think I met an aspiring actress of that name recently for the first time and I haven't seen her since."

He got up to pour some more champagne. "Okay?"

"Okay," Ginny said in a small voice. Then, "I saw your picture with her at a book party for your father."

"Oh, yes." Total uninterest.

"I'd love to meet your father sometime."

"Oh, yes," he repeated.

"Can I?"

Johnny frowned. "Don't push your luck, Ginny. There's absolutely no reason for you to meet my father, just as there's absolutely no reason for me to meet yours. Okay?"

"Okay." It wasn't, but what else could she say?

When Ginny left, Johnny went back to his Toshiba and reviewed the first chapter of The Book. Ginny's visit had upset him. He'd been looking forward to seeing her, had even thought he might take her out to one of his favorite places, Café des Artistes, for dinner, but all desire for more of her company evaporated when she'd come on strong about meeting his father.

The Duane Dickens mention had amused him, but it really wasn't funny. Thinking about it now, he wondered whether Ginny should continue, as he put it to himself, as "his secret agent."

There was something very appealing about her . . . her high energy, her faith in her fashion designing, her astonishing degree of chutzpah, not to mention her knockout legs and kooky face. He thought about her face a lot, more than he wanted to, more than he should . . . and that was why he questioned his judgment in working with her, seeing her so much. Perhaps it was because in some inexplicable way, Ginny Walker still reminded him of Dolores, and the last thing in the world he wanted was another entanglement.

He rubbed his nose reflectively, half smiling. All the same, Ginny was one of a kind, a mixture of wistfulness, little-girl wonderment and cheeky urchin.

Perhaps he should have taken her to Café des Artistes after all, if only to see those strange green-brown eyes light up in appreciation. When it came to behavior, Ginny was the antithesis of Dolores, who had never known how to say those two simple little words, let alone understand them. Ginny, on the other hand, not only said "thank you" all the time, but also obviously meant it.

On the screen Johnny stared at the opening paragraphs of his first chapter. He changed a word or two, moved a sentence around, then put it back as it was, added, subtracted. It was slow, but it was coming. How his father rattled off a book in less than a year, he would never know. That reminded him of what he'd read in his morning *Times*.

It was just as well he hadn't taken Ginny to dinner. The President had just announced a new drug czar and it was important he watch *Nightline* tonight, where he'd read his father was joining a panel to discuss (with Ted Koppel's usual impeccable timing) the war on drugs and the pros and cons of drug legalization.

He ordered Chinese takeout and settled down to work until the eleven o'clock news. He got on so well, he didn't notice the time until it was just past eleven-thirty.

"Oh, shit." He quickly switched on the television. Tom Constantine, one-time cop, now chief of the Drug Enforcement Administration, was speaking. "I ran the organized crime force in New York from seventy-four to seventy-eight and, as you know, Ted, Quentin"—Constantine's steely glance flicked from Ted Koppel to Quentin Peet—"we had some big successes against the Mafia back then. I probably don't have to remind pros like you, but the public should understand that dealing with those old-style families, the Genoveses, the Joe Bonanos, was like dealing with elementary-school kids compared to the people we're up against today, drug lords like the Rodrigues brothers in Cali, Colombia, for instance. Those guys have been earning seven to eight billion dollars a year, unchecked, unsanctioned for years, and they've used that kind of wealth to build an incredibly sophisticated empire of intimidation and influence."

Johnny was cynically amused, even pleased, to see that Constantine was not easily interrupted, even by a seasoned TV pro like his father, who was trying, he guessed, to get in as many mentions as he could about his latest book. Every time his father tried to butt in, Constantine calmly carried on, explaining, with facts and figures, why legalization would worsen, not lessen, crime and addiction.

Siding with the DEA boss on the anti-legalization issue (against two other heavyweights on the program, William Buckley and the *New York Times's* Anthony Lewis), Peet's moment finally came.

"In my new book, *Green Ice*, I explain how for years the Cali guys have adopted the attitude that the drug trade is really no different from any other commodity business," he said sternly. "One side of the organization moves the commodity; the other side collects the proceeds, pays the producers, processors, shippers, and returns the net to the home office. A single U.S.-based branch office or, to use the correct language, 'cell' of the Cali cartel, may take in twenty million dollars a month. There are dozens of cells in New York alone. Now other organized crime gangs, domestic and from other parts of the world, want some of that action. And how does the Cali Cartel describe that? 'Competition, to be expected, just like in any other business' . . . except unlike 'any other business,' they move immediately to snuff it out with violence. That's at the root of all the increased crime."

Johnny grimaced. He knew that already.

How long had his father been paying attention to big-time drug trading? Ever since his days in Albany? That would make it . . . at least four years. It didn't seem possible. No wonder his father's book was so revealing, but not revealing enough. Johnny had scoured it, searching for clues, leads that would help him understand which faction in the drug underworld might be connected to Rosemary's death, the Villeneva robbery, or the Licton-Licone bust. If his father knew, he wasn't telling, not in this book anyway, although he'd used other deaths, other bombings, other major crimes to illustrate how drugs were today so often to blame.

Did his father know he'd asked his old cop pal, Freddy Forrester, about the Peter Licton/Pietro Licone robbery? Probably, although he'd never mentioned it.

Johnny wouldn't make the mistake of going to Freddy or any of his father's old friends again. He hoped he wouldn't need to. He'd begun to develop his own information network, starting with an acquaintance at Princeton, Matt Fisher, who'd become a friend in New York and who was now with the FBI.

Through tenacious sniffing around, Johnny had learned that the FBI was now involved in both Long Island heists and the Villeneva robbery, where apparently a fingerprint had been found.

"At the National Crime Information Center in Washington, D.C.," Matt told him, "the FBI operates a computerized system containing the world's largest database on known criminals. If the print can't be identified there, it won't be anywhere."

If Matt could only help him get to the FBI on the West Coast, to find out what prints, if any, had been found among the ashes at Rosemary's house. Johnny sighed. He was out of his depth, but something still urged him not to give up, to do as Rosemary had once told him to do, keep his eyes and ears open and "put the pieces together, one by one, until the jigsaw begins to make sense."

He hadn't been paying enough attention. What was Constantine saying now? Johnny turned up the volume.

"Puerto Rico's beginning to resemble New York. There's at least a hundred different illegal drug operations there now, and with the island's two hundred miles of coastline it's—"

"I often wonder why it took Cali so long to use it as a major drug corridor into the United States," Peet said, sailing in unperturbably. "What do they say? With no Customs to worry about, Thursday in San Juan, Friday in South Dakota."

Constantine scowled as Peet added, "Now it's the number-two route after Miami, with about eighty-four tons of cocaine and high-purity heroin coming in a year. You've opened another DEA office in Puerto Rico, right, Tom?"

"Right," Constantine said in clipped tones. "Puerto Rico now has a serious crime situation, a forty-percent increase since 1991 with transporters often paid in narcotics instead of dough." He shook his head ruefully. "There's a different kind of wrought ironwork decorating the entrances to San Juan homes today and there's razor wire at the back door."

A few blocks away from Johnny's apartment, in his penthouse towering over Central Park, Svank, sitting perfectly still, watched the same program.

The phone rang. Svank picked it up, listened intently, grunted and without saying a word, replaced the receiver. He looked again at the screen, where Constantine was reiterating his commitment to the drug war. He yawned and switched it off.

Beside him was a copy of *Green Ice.* Although one of his little-known forms of relaxation was reading nonfiction (particularly the lives of self-made, tyrannical rulers), he didn't usually waste time on subjects he knew more about than the authors, but Peet's book fascinated him. Peet didn't exaggerate; he knew a lot. There was a great deal he didn't know, but that wouldn't stop the book's success. He knew that Peet's name on the cover meant instant sales.

In the next couple of months, Svank recollected, he would have an opportunity to tell Peet so. He smiled at his own private joke.

Svank had recently given a million dollars to the New York Public Library, toward a new reading room. As a major donor, he had been invited to something called the Literary Lions dinner.

At a million dollars, it was an expensive ticket, but he'd been told by those advising him on charitable donations that it was an important occasion and could only add to his social clout to be seen there.

Peet was one of the Literary Lions to be honored—there were eighteen illustrious writers in all—and during *Nightline,* Svank decided it would amuse him to meet some of these men of letters.

He opened Peet's book at random. " . . . there's a hitch. U.S. law requires banks to send the Internal Revenue Service extensive information identifying anyone who deposits $10,000 and up in cash. Since the Colombians cannot risk being fingered by the IRS, they need the help of a third party with legitimate-sounding reason to churn huge amounts of money through the banking system."

There was a discreet tap on the door. Svank pressed a small button on his chair and the door opened. "He's at Miami airport, boss," said Hugo. "Do you want him back in New York? He's waiting for instructions."

"Let him wait." The door closed.

It would be a long wait. Although his reputation had certainly been earned as the cool mastermind behind some brilliant jobs over the past couple of years, Alex Rossiter was showing an increasing greediness, recklessness, which Svank knew from a lifetime of dealing with both big and small crooks could lead to ruin for everyone.

He didn't mind that Alex had come close to disaster a few times before working for him. Those who thought nothing could touch them were the ones to avoid.

No, it was always the same problem, whatever the sex. Greed. Despite the fact that Alex was well rewarded, very well rewarded for the big jobs that provided collateral when he'd needed it for start-up operations, in Ireland, for instance, Alex still wanted more. He'd agreed at the beginning of their arrangement that, providing there was no conflict of interest, and no involvement on his part, Alex could continue to carry out a few of his own operations, but this latest heist had definitely been one too many.

Who needed the extra headache?

Alex had assured him it had been a piece of cake, a totally smooth operation. But the family involved was too well known, too powerful, with friends who could interfere with his own business.

Alex had to be curbed, taught the hard way that some things were best left alone—like the Villeneva jewels.

As Svank remembered something from the program he'd just watched, he smiled for the second time that day. Puerto Rico. Yes, Puerto Rico was the perfect place for Alex to be taught a lesson.

"Are you all right?" Esme had asked.

"Is something bothering you?" Johnny had said.

To add a final insult to outrageous injury, Ginny had picked up the phone during the terrible weeks following her discovery of the jewels to hear Ricardo's voice with an opening line of *"Va bene?"*

It was all too much. Not that Ricardo affected her anymore. It was embarrassing to remember how swept off her feet she'd been by such an obvious, aging lothario, who'd needed his ego massaged (among other things) by a naive young girl who'd believed every one of his well-worn lines (so romantic, delivered in his broken English), who'd rushed into his arms and bed after receiving bunches of the least expensive flower.

It was worse remembering how much time she'd wasted, recovering from being dumped by such a corny Romeo. *Va bene* indeed!

"*Bene, bene, bene,*" she trilled, exiting off the line with little courtesy.

She thought she was doing very well, acting like a normal human being while, in her bathroom, like a sinister shadow enveloping every aspect of her life, lay a stash of stolen goods that could send her away to Sing Sing or wherever they sent accomplices, willing or unwilling, to a major crime.

She thought she was putting on the greatest act of her life, one that far exceeded her performances as a gate-crasher.

And yet, while she and Esme were out shopping for her wedding shoes, Esme kept asking her the "Are you all right?" question.

She longed to break down and tell her how very "un-all right" she was. She longed to break down period, but she couldn't. It wasn't her style and it would immediately attract suspicion, so she shrugged and pretended that her big problem was to stop falling in love with Johnny, because he was "already tied up" and had clearly shown her he regarded her as a friend and nothing more.

She didn't have to pretend very hard. She did have to guard against falling in love with the wrong man again. And yet, compared to extricating herself from the giant hole Alex had put her in, everything else was insignificant.

"It's early days yet, Ginny. Look how long it's taken me to make an honest man out of Ted," teased Esme.

Comparing someone like Johnny to pompous, boring Ted was laughable, but she was far too fond of Esme to point it out.

With Esme's enthusiastic approval, Ginny had bought a lightweight buttery velvet for her wedding dress in a delectable silvery kind of pink. Pink was Esme's favorite color and she'd been adamant that she wanted her three bridesmaids, Ginny, her cousin Sue Jane and Ted's sister Carol, in pink, also—not the same shade, of course, but in complementary tones. It hadn't been easy, but Ginny had found a special crepe, which draped like a dream in tones ranging from deep fuschia to rose to blush. She'd suggested the blush for herself, knowing of the three she had the least figure faults, "if you can call a stick a figure."

To move the subject away from Johnny, Ginny said, "It seems so funny looking for pink shoes for a bride and not white. You know, when

I found the pink velvet for your dress, I kept thinking it was for the bridesmaids, not you."

It was the wrong thing to say. It only made Esme more worried, if not a little angry. "Ginny, now I know there's something really wrong with your marbles. That's the second time you've said that today, yet you've known from the beginning my parents will only come to the wedding if it's traditional in Chinatown. White is for funerals in China, remember? Red is for joy. How many times do I have to tell you, for goodness' sake?"

"Sorry, Esme," Ginny said lamely.

"Can I speak to Ms. Gan?"

"Who wants her?"

"Ginny Walker." (With all his money, why couldn't Svank employ a secretary who knew how to answer a phone?)

There was a long wait, then, "Ginny, darrling . . ." For a second Poppy's exuberant greeting took Ginny back to the waiters' serenade at their Le Cirque lunch. And she'd thought she had problems then! "I know what you're calling about, that di-vine wrap dress is ready. I can't wait to wear it. Perhaps to the Library do."

Ginny felt terrible. She'd forgotten all about the georgette number. It showed how mentally deranged she'd become. She couldn't even re-member where she'd put it. "Sorry, Poppy, it's taken so long. I've been swamped." She didn't sound very credible. She cleared her throat. "You'll have it this week, I promise." She hesitated, but she had to ask, "Do you have time for another fitting?"

"Oh, no," Poppy wailed. "Just send it over and I'll see how it looks."

"Okay, okay." She would agree to anything to move on fast to the real reason for her call. "Have you h . . . heard from . . . Svank? I guess he must be back by now?"

"Oh, sure." Poppy sounded so uninterested, Ginny wasn't sure she'd understood.

"He's back? With Alex?"

"He's back all right." Poppy was yawning.

What was going on? A breakup? A falling out? Who cared. It was only Alex she was interested in.

"And Alex?"

"I don't know about Alex, hon. I haven't seen him, but then I've

hardly seen Svank. I gotta message telling me to go over to the apartment, but after waiting for hours and hours and hours he never turned
up."

So that was it. Although Poppy kept everyone waiting, she hated to
wait for anyone herself. In Svank's case she had no alternative. "But you
did see him?" Ginny persevered nervously.

"Oh, sure. He turned up in the middle of the night, just like a sweet
dream, I don't think. That's why I'm soooo tired. Svank doesn't care. He
always does it, till he gets used to a different time zone." Poppy yawned
loudly into the phone, then repeated, "I don't know about Alex, hon."
Obviously expecting the question, she added, "I can't find his number,
but when I do, I'll get someone to call you, but be a doll and send over
the dress."

When Ginny hung up, for the second time she called information
for Alex's number, but there was no Alex Rossiter listed or unlisted, no
A. Rossiter or A. P. (as in Peter) Rossiter in any of New York's five bor-
oughs, although Ginny hardly expected to find him outside Manhattan.
Without much hope she tried Angus O'Keeffe. Nothing for that name
either.

She started looking for the georgette dress. There it was, still rolled
up in the bag she'd made to transport it to the post-movie party. She
shook it out. It was remarkably unwrinkled. She couldn't do anything
about it today. In a few minutes, Esme and the bridesmaids were coming
for fittings.

As she stared at Poppy's dress, she remembered Alex's excuse at the
Rainbow Room for not telling her he was back in New York. "I'm under
the big man's command." She shivered, full of premonition that something else was about to happen.

But what else could happen? She imagined the toilet overflowing
while the girls were there; they'd try to fix it, find the jewels and . . .
She was seriously considering fishing the jewels out of the tank and hiding them under her bed, when her mother called.

Her quavering voice was so low Ginny had to strain to hear her.

"Mom, you sound sick? What's wrong?"

"I can't talk for very long. I've had this migraine for days, can't seem
to shake it, but I've been wanting to call, had to wait for the right moment. Your father's been here all the time, with a stomach upset or
something. I thought he'd never leave the house—"

"Oh, poor Mama. I can just imagine. But aren't your migraine pills helping?"

"A bit, not much." Ginny heard her mother take a deep breath. Here came the purpose of the call. "I'm very concerned about you, Ginny."

"Why, for heaven's sake?"

Silence, another deep breath. "Alex was here—"

"What!" To Ginny's dismay the intercom buzzed. "Hang on, Mother. I've got to talk to you." She raced to pick up the internal phone. It was Esme with her cousin, Sue Jane. "Just a second, Esme, I'm on the phone." She buzzed them into the hall, out of the chilly day. It would take a few minutes for them to climb the stairs.

"Mother, where on earth is he?" Ginny cried urgently. "I still haven't heard a word and it's really vital, vital, I speak to him."

To Ginny's horror she heard her mother crying. "What on earth's wrong?" Suddenly everything came clear. Alex was ill, that was the reason she hadn't heard, perhaps very ill. She had visions of him covered from head to foot in bandages. "Is Alex sick? Has . . . has he been in an accident?"

Her question seemed enough to dry her mother's tears. "Sick," she snorted angrily. "Yes, sick in the head, but as far as I'm concerned not, alas, sick enough. Ginny, I told you about the story in the British press? Are you involved in any way with that?"

Ginny could hear Esme and her cousin laughing as they climbed the last flight of stairs. What was her mother getting at? "Involved? I don't know what you mean."

In a rush of words Virginia Walker told her about Alex's Sunday morning visit. "I was very angry. I told him we all knew he was on the run—"

"You told him I knew?"

"Yes, I did. I also told him I wish he would stop bothering you, that I wanted him out of your life . . ." Her mother was sobbing again, but Ginny was too furious to care.

"Go on," she said coldly. The doorbell rang, but she ignored it.

"He said we didn't know anything about your life anymore. He implied that somehow you were involved with him . . . in these . . . jewel robberies. Are you, Ginny? I haven't slept a wink since. Ginny, if you are in any way—"

Strong color flooded across Ginny's face. She said fiercely, "I don't know what you're trying to say. I can't believe what I'm hearing, what you're trying to insinuate. I don't believe Alex could or would ever—"

The doorbell rang again and Esme called out, "We're here, Ginny. Let us in. It's freezing."

"Mother, I've got to go. Esme's here for the wedding fittings. In any case I'm so upset I don't think I'll make any sense. I'm horrified you would ever suggest Alex would involve me that way, but I've got to go. I'll call you back." As she spoke she realized that Alex *had* involved her, and that her mother hadn't answered the all-important question, "Do you know where Alex is?" She sounded desperate, but she didn't care. "After what you've just said, it's more important than ever I speak to him. I've got to clear this up."

"I don't know and I don't care. The sooner the police find him the better."

"You don't mean that." Ginny's voice shook with emotion. "I refuse to believe you could really mean that." Esme started knocking on the door. "This is terrible, but I have to go. I'll call you back as soon as Esme leaves—"

"No, no, no. Your father doesn't know anything about this. He doesn't even know Alex was here. I'll call you back. Just stay away from him, I beg you. He's not who you think he is. He's a . . . a monster." Click. Her mother hung up.

The afternoon passed in a blur. She was on automatic pilot, snipping, pinning, tucking, first Esme in the toile, a muslin pattern, identical in every detail to what the final wedding dress would be, right down to the tiny hand-stitched flowers that, in organza, would surround the neck and wrists of the sumptuous, flowing gown.

She joined in the giggles about the future bride going to the altar in a see-through paper bathrobe (which was what the toile looked like); she marked every alteration with a tiny red thread, telling Esme (who wanted every detail explained), "This helps keep the design in perspective, in the same way a site line does on a construction job."

When bridesmaid number three—Carol—arrived, Ginny had to explain the reason for the paper dress all over again. "All couture dresses start first with a paper toile like this, to avoid handling the expensive material more than necessary."

She worked fast, answered all questions, laughed and joked, but her mother's words banged in her brain like a hammer. Her mother wasn't a fool, by any means. She didn't exaggerate either, so somehow Alex had given her the impression that she was involved in his ill-gotten gains. Every so often, thinking about Alex's inexplicable behavior, Ginny had to excuse herself and go to the bathroom, afraid she was going to be sick. She felt sicker still when she looked at the toilet.

"How many more fittings, Gin?" Esme asked.

The wedding was about six weeks away. Apart from the wedding dress, and the empire-style bridesmaids' dresses, there was also the red and gold brocade Esme would change into after the ceremony for the sixteen-course celebration banquet in Chinatown's Silver Palace.

"Two, three, not more," Ginny promised.

As she fitted Sue Jane in the fuschia, perfect for her Asian coloring, and ash-blonde Carol in the rose, she tried to recapture the excitement she'd felt on discovering the crepe and planning who should wear which pink, but it was like working with sackcloth and ashes.

By the time she finished fitting Esme in the banquet dress ("as important as the wedding dress, because the banquet is a vital part of the joyous day"), it was getting dark.

"You're a genius, Gin." Esme hugged her, ecstatic.

Ginny smiled wanly. She felt she must look worn out; but, despite her presentiment and misery over her mother's call, she knew all the dresses were going to work.

"I'm happy, Esme," was all she could think of to say.

The intercom buzzed as she spoke. She tensed up. Alex. It had to be Alex. How could she get rid of the girls, pronto?

But it wasn't Alex. It was a delivery from Asia-Pacific Pearl, a nearby Chinese restaurant. As a surprise Esme had ordered up a feast for them all. "A fitting celebration," she wisecracked, opening up her huge Prada carryall and taking out a magnum of pink champagne.

"You must bring Johnny to the wedding," Esme cried, as the last crispy noodle was consumed with the last drop of wine.

Ginny knew she was blushing again. It was so typically sweet of Esme to ask. "I'd love to, but let's see what happens."

When the girls finally left, the clouds descended. If only her life were really as it had appeared to be during the afternoon and early evening, full of innocent jokes, teasing, girl talk, preparing for the happiest day in a girl's life, her best friend's life. If only—but instead she was swamped in this sinister fog with nothing to be optimistic about, with her own mother believing she could be a fence, if not a thief.

Tears welled up. Esme had this rosy picture of Johnny and herself at the wedding; she would throw her bouquet to Ginny and Johnny would suddenly realize she was the one for him.

But it wasn't going to happen. Johnny had made it abundantly clear that he had no personal interest in her, that there was "no reason" for her to meet his father, just as there was "no reason" for him to meet hers. She was his "partner," his "observer," and a good one, as he'd been at pains to tell her following the ghastly Cocteau evening.

How she'd hated every moment of it, a stupid grin pasted on her face, putting up with a lambasting from the press agent at the theater, who'd blamed her for Johnny's nonappearance. Then barred from entering the Crystal Room, noting down every insult and every incident, on agonizing tenterhooks until Mr. *Next!* magazine Peet deigned to arrive, when, one, two, three in sickeningly speedy fashion, she'd become so very persona grata, waltzing in on his arm.

She hated herself, but she was aching for that arm right now. So much so that when the phone rang, she had no thought of her poor mother who'd promised to call back, and picked it up expecting to hear Johnny's voice. It wasn't Johnny or her mother. It was Lee Baker Davies.

"How are you, m'dear? I know it's late, but I just saw a seductive little picture of you in the latest *Vogue*. At least, I think it was you—a back view, but I'd recognize that behind of yours anywhere, draped if I'm not mistaken in that Indian material I gave you last year?"

Ginny had cut down on her magazine subscriptions and, except when she remembered to ask Esme, rarely saw *Vogue* nowadays. "What was the occasion?"

"I can't remember exactly. Some fashionable gathering. D'you want to have dinner tomorrow night? I'll bring the book with me. It's ages since I saw you, birdy."

Ginny was about to say no. These days every time she left the loft—day or night, whether for a few minutes or a few hours—she returned panic-stricken that somebody would be waiting for her there, either the police or Svank's Hugo or Svank himself or . . . she didn't know who, but some threatening presence.

She probably should stay home to work on the wedding dresses or finish Poppy's, but she didn't want Lee to think she didn't want to see her. Perhaps the best thing was to make dates again and go out regularly to try to overcome her fears.

If Johnny called with plans, it wouldn't hurt for him to hear she was already busy.

"Why not?"

"Great, great. What d'you feel like, Italian or Chinese?"

She didn't feel like eating ever again. How could she breathe, let alone eat, when her own mother thought she could be a jewel thief? She was being stupid. "Italian?"

"Okeydokey. Toscana on Lex between Sixty-third and Sixty-fourth. Eight-thirty tomorrow night?"

"Eight-thirty, great."

Lee had never seen her "tweeds" and it was the warmest outfit she had, so Ginny wore it again, beneath a coat with a fur collar "on loan" from her mother.

"You still look a bit peaky," Lee said. "Good, here's the wine." As the waiter poured out two generous glasses, she moved closer to Ginny. "How's it going?"

"Nowhere." Ginny tried to laugh, without success. "I'm busy—with Esme's wedding, the usual long-drawn-out commission from Poppy, and a few other jobs." She wasn't about to tell Lee about her assignment from Johnny. She wasn't about to tell anyone about that.

"Poppy certainly looks a little more soignée in the pictures I've seen lately. I thought you had to be hanging in there." Ginny decided not to comment. By now she was well used to the way Lee used conversation as bait, hoping to land a fat piece of gossip.

There was silence, then, "I may know of a job for you," Lee said with a catlike grin. "I was just on the Coast for a few days on an SOS job, styling a Max Factor campaign. Oh, yes, by the way, recommended by an old flame of yours. He asked me whatever happened to—"

"Baby Jane." Ginny looked around the pretty, brick-walled restaurant, not bothering to hide her uninterest.

"What? Oh, yeah." Lee sailed on. "Oz, remember Oz? He was supposed to do the campaign, but he got sick, then Herb Ritts was supposed to do it and he couldn't and then . . ."

"Lee . . ."

"What?"

"Could you get to the job?"

"Oh, yeah, well, it's all involved with this ad agency on the Coast. The stylist never turned up and Oz recommended me and that's how I met Becky Corey, who designed these terrific clothes for the campaign and—"

"Never heard of her," Ginny said sourly. (And I certainly don't care to, she added mentally.)

Lee spent the next twenty minutes explaining how much Becky Corey had reminded her of Ginny. Every so often she patted her cheek, stroked her arm and even squeezed her knee once or twice. Ginny didn't object; in fact, feeling particularly unloved and starved for affection, she almost welcomed Lee's demonstrations. Almost.

"You have much more talent; you're much more inspired, but in many ways Becky's story could be yours," Lee said emphatically. "I mean she missed three mortgage payments to keep her company alive; she went hungry; she tried everything, then word started to get around and JC Penney went crazy over her sheaths, but said she had to install an on-line order system, which there was no way she could afford. With no collateral, no track record, she couldn't get a loan from her neighborhood bank. Boy, did I think of you when she told me that . . ."

Ginny buried her nose in the large menu, but true to form Lee went right on. "She finally found a manufacturer in Burbank willing to handle her first season of production on credit—all she had to pay in interest was her entire profit margin . . ."

"Lee, I'm starving." To her surprise Ginny found she actually was. "Can we order or is the end of this happy-ever-after story nearly in sight? And what's this got to do with my new job?"

"Wait a minute. Be a good girl." Lee refilled her glass, although she hadn't taken more than a few sips. "Becky then had to resort to factoring—she sold twenty-five hundred pieces, but all her profit had to stay with the factoring company."

Ginny began to tap her fork on the table. Was Baker Davies in love with this woman or something? Her stylist friend looked more butch than ever, with a haircut which seen from both back and front defied gender identification. Lee went on talking. "The last straw, a venture-capital investment fell through. Becky used all the cash within reach, from her husband's income . . ."

Husband! Ginny longed to shoot Becky Corey dead, there and then.

With a husband, at least she had emotional support and someone to help keep a roof over her head.

"... her mother's nest egg, loans from friends ..."

"Bang bang you're dead, Becky Corey," Ginny said childishly.

Lee was not deterred. "Everything went into her overhead. She was two thousand dollars in arrears with the IRS, but she was still in business. With her pieces flying out of the place, her profits were still with the factoring company. Then ..." Lee paused dramatically. "Then her neighborhood bank was swallowed up by a big bank." Another dramatic pause. "Three years after practically laughing her out of the place, thanks to a new program for women borrowers, the new bank owners finally agreed to finance Becky ... and now"—Lee swallowed down more wine and speeded up—"her business after one year is in such great shape, the Sterns want to invest so she can expand and she's looking for a number one—"

"Wait a minute. What did you say? The Sterns want to invest? Any relation to Arthur Stern?"

"Yes, yes, yes ... Arthur Stern married to the dreadful Muriel, who never saw an illness she didn't like."

"What are you talking about, Lee?"

Lee tossed her head impatiently. "Everyone knows Madame Muriel is a chronic hypochondriac who hates to go out, always terrified of catching something. That's why she lets the equally dreadful Arthur off the leash from time to time. Their home is like something out of a sci-fi comic, with major dust-busting vents in the ceilings where other people that rich have chandeliers...."

Ginny burned. Why hadn't Becky Corey sat next to Stern and spurned him at the Waldorf? Why had it had to be her? Why was she always in the wrong place at the wrong time? Where had she gone so wrong?

"I told her I knew the best there is, Ginny Walker of New York ..."

"The best what?" Ginny asked listlessly.

Lee looked exasperated. "I repeat, she's looking for the best design assistant. I told her I know the best there is, Ginny Walker of New York."

"You mean she's moving to New York?"

"Of course not. Well, not yet, not until the Sterns really get involved. You would have to move to L.A. I still have to check out her credentials, but I'd say her business is on solid ground and if the Sterns are serious, the sky's the limit." Lee gave Ginny her usual once-over. "I think the West Coast would suit you. It might even give you back that look you used to have . . . as if something wonderful was about to happen in the next twenty minutes. Where did that look go? I miss it."

It was all too much to bear. Incensed, Ginny cried, "You and your looks! That's all you ever think about. I'm the girl without a look, remember?"

Lee was hurt. "You don't have to get so excited. Is there any interest or not?" she asked huffily.

California. A new life. Lots of Stern money. Away from crashing, away from deceit, away from the loft with its sinister secret. For a few seconds, it was so tempting, so uplifting, but, of course, it was impossible.

How could she go anywhere until Alex freed her from her crushing burden? And then there was Johnny. Somehow, for no reason that made any sense, the thought of leaving New York and Johnny was impossible, too. At least for the moment it was.

Lee still looked hurt. To make amends for her outburst, Ginny put out her hand. "Sorry, Lee. I probably shouldn't have come tonight. I'm in a foul mood. Forgive?"

Lee never wasted time on recriminations or sulking. She shook Ginny's hand as vigorously as if they'd just concluded a deal. "This is made for you, Ginny. I know I'm right, just as I was right about Gosman."

"How is he? I'd love to see him."

"Oh, he's okay, living with some old croc-skinned widow down in Fort Lauderdale . . . don't give him another thought. So let's see, when can I get you two designing dames together?"

"Not so fast, Lee. I am interested, but right now, it would be impossible, I'm so tied up."

"Nonsense," Lee boomed. "Who with? Don't tell me Rossano Brazzi has reappeared from Milano?"

Ginny shook her head crossly. "If you're referring to Ricardo, you're miles out of date. I closed that door well over a year ago."

"So where's the tie-up? Or rather, who is he?"

"No one. I mean I just can't move like that, one, two, three. I gave up that life when I moved out of the family nest."

The waiter came and they ordered tuna carpaccio, followed by pasta with sun-dried tomatoes and crabmeat. As they ate, Lee continually tried to persuade Ginny to think about starting over in California.

To change the subject, Ginny finally said, "Did you bring the magazine, *Vogue?*"

"Oh, yes." Lee fiddled inside her backpack hanging from the chair. "That's your behind, right?"

"Right." Her back view, one among three or four others, had been chosen to illustrate a one-page fashion story on the new way to wear "seven veils." Without bothering to read the caption she recognized the scene immediately. The Guggenheim Museum. It was the night she met Johnny for the first time. As if she needed to be reminded, half of his back view was in the picture, too.

"So you're out and about?"

Ginny nodded. "Just as you advised me, remember, Lee? All those shiny events you said I had to go to in order to be a success? Well, I'm out there, all right . . ."

"How?" Lee's eyes narrowed. "You're not crashing, are you? I remember you had that crazy idea once. I hope I dissuaded you."

Ginny didn't answer, just shook her head smiling, but she must have given something away because Lee was still looking at her suspiciously. "Who's the guy in the picture, the one you're holding hands with?"

Ginny snatched the magazine back to look at the picture again. Oh, shit. She was holding Johnny's hand or rather he was holding hers. It must have been just before he propelled her through the crowd to his table where the young Rockefellers were waiting to meet him. "Oh, some journalist . . ."

"John Q. Peet," Lee crowed, reading the tiny caption. "So he's the new attraction. I don't blame you . . ."

Careful, Ginny told herself. Don't get mad and don't be coy. She finished her glass of wine before speaking. "Oh, we're good pals. Like you, he knows everyone. Sometimes when he's covering an event he'll take me along or we run into one another if I'm out with Poppy. He's going to show my sketches to his fashion editor—you know, at *Next!* magazine. He's really a good friend."

"Have you met his father?" There was an unusual note of awe in Lee's voice.

"No, but I will soon . . ."

"Oh, are you going to that Library dinner?"

Library dinner. Why did that ring a bell? Poppy. "Perhaps I can wear it to the Library do," Poppy had said only yesterday.

"Life's strange," Lee said. "Remember how mad you got that night at Mr. Chow's when I started to give you the list of Must Events to Attend? The opening of the Costume Institute at the Met, the Literary Lions Dinner at the New York Public Library . . . You were such a little nose-in-the-air snob in those days or at least you pretended to be . . ."

"I had a lot to learn. I hope I've grown up some." Ginny felt ashamed. Lee had always been such a wonderful friend and tonight she'd treated her unforgivably. She leaned over and gave Lee a quick peck on the cheek. "The Literary Lions Dinner . . . yes, absolutely right. Quentin Peet's one of the Lions this year, isn't he? When is that, I've forgotten?"

It was irritating to see Lee flash her catlike grin again. She probably guessed Ginny was playing her game and not so well, trying to hook some information she didn't have.

"I'm not sure. Sometime in May, I think. Ask Johnny Peet. He'll know." Lee paused, then looked at her anxiously. "Do watch out, honey chile, won't you? I hear he bites."

"I don't believe it," Ginny said.

"You don't believe what?"

It was early on Sunday evening. Johnny had taken her to watch the New York Rangers play ice hockey against the Florida Panthers at Madison Square Garden and they'd run through pouring rain to grab a cab to Johnny's home office, where he wanted to go over the next week's agenda.

"People say you bite," she said.

"What people?" He was rubbing his hair dry. Little wet tendrils stuck to his forehead. He looked like a kid. He looked adorable.

"Oh, journalists, writers I know."

She was in a reckless, challenging mood, because the afternoon had been so wonderful, because Johnny was undoubtedly becoming more re-laxed with her, teasing her, showing her with his quick grins, playful touches and in a myriad little fond ways that he liked working with her and having her around.

He came over to the well-worn sofa, where she was sitting with her notebook, ready to take notes.

He began to rub her hair dry vigorously.

"Stop! Don't! You're messing up my twenty-dollar haircut," she squealed.

He stopped as if in shock. "What did you say? Twenty dollars? Is that what you pay for that kooky-looking head of hair?"

He was smiling, but she wasn't amused. "Thanks for the compliment," she said sharply. "I happen to like this look." She wasn't about to tell him she kept a list of top salons, mentioned in *Vogue*, where, after hours, trainees cut and styled hair for next to nothing.

"And so do I, Ms. Ginny . . . and so do I." He brushed her hair back with a strong hand, holding the back of her head, smiling, looking at her intently. "Twenty dollars?" he repeated.

She felt weak as he held her, but managed to say, "Why . . . why are you staring at me like that? Yes, twenty dollars if you must know."

"I'm trying to understand something . . . something I've never told you."

"What?"

His hand was still there. Her body stirred as if to say, don't go away . . . bring me closer . . . closer . . . can't you tell how much I want you?

He didn't react, just stared, then said, "I think it's the hair, the way it curls so perfectly around your perfect head and also the way you always stand so tall, such perfect posture . . ."

She groaned inwardly. Sexually aroused as she was, she found herself thinking about another man in her life; remembering to stand tall, to think about her posture, was so inextricably linked with Alex.

"So?"

Johnny took his hand away abruptly. "Don't take it as too much of a compliment, but sometimes, although you really look nothing alike and, thank God, *are* nothing alike, you remind me of Dolores, my ex-wife, who, if my memory's correct, wouldn't dream of paying less than a couple of hundred bucks for a haircut not so very different from yours. Not different at all, in fact . . ."

Ginny was stunned. Dolores the Beautiful?

"That's crazy," she said. "I've seen her and I am going to take it as a compliment because she's probably one of the most beautiful women I've ever seen . . ."

"Outside maybe; inside as ugly as sin." He was snarling. "When did you see her? You never told me that before."

"I didn't think it was important. Oh, I don't know. Around. At fashion shows, parties . . ."

"Crash, crash, crash . . . all part of your modus operandi, right? To see and be seen by the beautiful people."

The change in his voice, harsh, sarcastic, was so unexpected, tears filled her eyes, even as she snapped, "Now I believe it . . . you do bite . . . you're horrible . . ."

He slung a casual arm around her shoulders. "I'm sorry, Ginny. I'm really sorry. Perhaps I do bite, perhaps I do, but I don't want to bite you, ever . . ." He pulled her head onto his shoulder. He softly began to talk, his voice, sometimes as he turned, muffled in her hair.

"I guess I didn't know how to be a husband. My father certainly didn't. He was always away, getting the story, beating the other guys to it." He sighed, long and heavy. "A hero, not a husband." He talked about his parents' empty marriage, and his own, "doomed from the start."

Once he started, he didn't seem to want to stop. "I obviously should never have gotten married. They were both against it . . . my father, my mother . . . looking back, I think that made me even more determined to go ahead, although the writing was on the wall almost from the beginning. I didn't want to see. I wanted to believe her, just as I guess my mother always wanted to believe whatever my father told her . . ."

Ginny shut her eyes to hide the longing growing for him, the bittersweet longing that was getting her nowhere.

She opened them when he chucked her under the chin. "Why am I telling you all this? Why am I wasting your time and mine?"

As suddenly as that first night in the loft, he turned her face to his and gave her the same sweet, quick kiss on the mouth. This time no phone rang to stop the magic, but, she supposed, some inner voice warned him to go no farther, because almost immediately he jumped up with a rueful smile.

"Getting late, Ginny. I don't know what came over me. We have work to do, n'est-ce pas?"

It was later, during that Sunday evening, that Ginny showed Johnny some sketches she'd made of the facial expressions she frequently encountered when crashing (disdain, shock, disbelief, snobbishness, fury). He liked them so much, he decided he might use them in the book.

From then on, when he "booked" her (his word), either to crash something or go in his place, or, best of all, accompany him to an event, he often asked her to bring a sketchbook along. He still called her "partner" and "colleague" and "super spy," but he also called her "skinny swan" and "kooky head" and "twenty-dollar baby" and showed her more and more he hadn't forgotten she was a woman. No more kisses, but no signs of being "tied up," either.

With the jewels stashed in the same unsavory place in her toilet, it all added up to the high-wire tension of her life. There had been no word from Alex and no news of him, either—not from her mother, from Poppy or, thank God, from the police.

It was hard to say she'd grown used to living each day as if it was her last before captivity, but that was the reality. Thank God, she was busy, busier than she'd been since her Gosman days, working and reporting for Johnny at least twice a week and designing and making clothes for the fast-approaching wedding.

Several outfits for Esme's trousseau had been added to the original order, plus a couple from guests who'd heard from the bride-to-be about Ginny's "genius."

As the big day drew near Ginny set the alarm for six and worked till midnight, sometimes even forgetting for a few hours the secret she was hiding. At last, everything was finished.

The wedding ceremony in the Transfiguration Church on Mott Street was so moving—and Esme in her silver-pink velvet gown so serene and joyful—Ginny's waterproof mascara wasn't up to coping with her continually moist eyes.

As she cleaned up in the cloakroom of the Silver Palace in Chinatown, she tried to suppress her excitement. Any moment now Johnny would be arriving. Because of a deadline, he hadn't been able to make the church ceremony, but of the banquet he'd said, "I wouldn't miss it for all the tea in China."

And as she emerged, there he was, holding out his hands, saying with the voice that had the laugh buried in it, "Hi there, gorgeous. I haven't missed any of the fifteen thousand courses, have I?"

What had Lee said about her over dinner that night? That she used to look as if something wonderful was going to happen in the next twenty minutes? She may have lost the look, but for the first time in weeks, Ginny felt an unexpected surge of optimism, as if life was about to change for the better. It was irrational; there was no reason for it, except for the unmistakable look of admiration on Johnny's face.

The reception was jammed. Taking Johnny's hand, Ginny pushed through the crowd to introduce him with pride to the other bridesmaids—Sue Jane, with her boyfriend, Ping, who looked like a Chinese Robb Sinclair with an earring in his left ear, and Carol, who Ginny had decided at the first fitting was just as predictable and stiff as her brother Ted.

As they stood laughing and drinking, there was a loud clanging of gongs. The guests began to clap and cheer, dividing without direction into two seas of people to make way for the bride, exotic now in the red and gold brocade, on the arm of an obviously embarrassed groom.

Behind them came Ted's parents, ramrod straight, his father in a tuxedo, his mother in an elaborate tiered evening gown with a small train. Ginny felt disloyal, but she couldn't help thinking back to Dallas and a certain Robespier creation, which hadn't flattered that wearer either. Ginny scolded herself. Just because she hadn't been asked to design anything for Ted's mother. She told herself she was glad she hadn't been asked. It was hard for Caucasians to equal Oriental elegance anyway, particularly in the splendor of the Silver Palace, and particularly when Esme's parents and the procession of her relatives who followed were now all in full Chinese ceremonial regalia.

"Aren't they breathtaking?" Ginny sighed.

"You are," Johnny responded, bending to kiss her hand.

She was cocooned in pleasure as the night of celebration went on. She sat next to Johnny, thighs touching, at a closely packed table with Sue Jane, Ping, and four more of Esme's relations.

The restaurant was festooned with balloons and swagged from ceiling to floor with brilliant crimson and silver drapes. On every table were dark red velvety roses, tied with matching velvet ribbons in elaborate silver cups, arranged by Perriwater, a new florist-find of Esme's.

Ginny inhaled the exquisite aroma of the roses, joined in the laughter and the merriment as one delicious course followed another and Chinese musicians delivered what to Ginny's ears was a cacophony of strange sounds. Every so often the music stopped as someone grabbed the microphone to make a speech or a toast—some hilarious, others just hokey—but who cared, everyone was having a wonderful time.

When a downtown group Esme had told Ginny was "really hot" began to play, Johnny pulled her onto the dance floor to dance cheek to cheek, body-to-body close. She wished she could hold the moment forever; she had never been happier.

There was only one jarring note. "Excuse me," said a familiar voice. Oz's weird, pale face appeared over Johnny's shoulder. What on earth was he doing here? Then she remembered. Way back she'd met Oz through Esme's introduction.

What nerve, he was trying to cut in. She couldn't believe it.

"No, Oz," she said angrily, trying to hold on to Johnny.

To her added fury, Johnny stepped back with a graceful little bow, laughing as he said, "Come on, Ginny. I can't have you all to myself all the time."

"Loosen up, Ginny," said Oz as he tried to steer her around the floor. "Why are you treating me like some ogre? Why do you never return my calls? Who exactly do you think you are anyway? Do you know how successful I am now? Loosen up, for God's sake. After all I did for you!"

She was as stiff as a board. She knew it and she wanted Oz to know this was the way she would always be with him. She prayed the music would stop and to her relief it did, almost immediately. She rushed away, leaving the photographer red-faced, in the middle of the floor.

"Who's that? An old boyfriend? He looks as if he could kill you," said Johnny, still amused. "Can't say I blame him. You were pretty rough."

In the excitement of the cake cutting, with more speeches and toasts, she soon forgot about Oz; and then came the precious moment when Esme looked around for her and tossed the wedding bouquet almost into her lap.

"You look like a little girl," Johnny said, as she buried her nose in the sweet-smelling flowers. He was smiling at her in the way he'd smiled the first night he took her home from the Pierre, the way he'd smiled as he'd studied her face so intently on West Seventy-seventh Street.

The bridal pair left the restaurant in a hailstorm of rice, and as the party wound down, Ginny knew she'd drunk too much rice wine, too much Chateau Lafite-Rothschild, too much champagne, too much of everything. It had to be the reason she told Johnny as they waited for a cab, "I never, never, never want to go home again."

He had a solution. "Come back to my place."

It seemed the most natural thing to do. And it wasn't to the office part of "his place" either, but up to the tenth floor, where she saw for the first time the apartment where he lived as opposed to worked.

Darkly paneled, richly draped, paintings softly lit, bookcases overflowing with books, and photographs in silver frames on polished wood tables, the apartment had an understated grandeur that stopped Ginny in the doorway. "Wow," she said, trying to think of the right words. "This looks . . . rich."

"What did you expect? That I live in a hovel?"

As she stood unsteadily, examining a small, elegant bronze, Johnny came up behind her and started to kiss the nape of her neck. "Oh, Johnny."

If she'd ever thought she was in love with Ricardo, this was the moment of truth. There was no comparison. Her feelings for Johnny ran deep, too deep. As much as her body was ablaze, she tried to hold back, knowing that while she'd already made a commitment, Johnny had not.

Turning to face him, she said hopelessly again, "Oh, Johnny."

"Oh, Ginny, darling little giant of a girl." There were no more quick, sweet kisses. He was kissing her as if he'd been longing to kiss her for months, their mouths, tongues at first meeting softly, then fiercely, crazily, the fever building, tenderness going fast.

The blush crepe bridesmaid dress was only half unzipped before she was out of it, the lamp throwing rosy shadows over her pale skin, her tiny breasts with such delicate nipples. "Ginny . . ." He groaned. "Ginnnnny. . . ." It was the last word spoken as they discovered each other.

She heard a clock chime one, two, wondering for a panic-filled second where she was. Johnny opened his eyes at the same time, stroked her hair, lifted her up from the living room floor, carrying her across his shoulder, into his bedroom, as light and spare and modern as the living room was dark and cluttered and antique.

He lay her down on the white bed as carefully as if she were a piece of porcelain. He clicked on the light and straddled her thighs, looking down, inspecting her. "Taking inventory," he called it later. Their breathing quickened; the steep, sweet climb began again.

When next she heard the chimes, there were five, and he was smiling down at her. "Hello, sleepyhead."

She was too full of happiness to speak, frightened that any word would be the wrong word. He shifted his arm to wrap it more firmly around her. "Ginny, Ginny, Ginny . . . what am I going to do about you?"

"You don't have to do anything," she whispered. "Talk to me . . . tell me about you . . ."

It had been painful to listen to him talk about his life that Sunday evening of several weeks back, when she'd yearned so much for him, feeling so close and yet so far. Now, as he whispered about his sense of failure, of never measuring up to his Goliath of a father, it was the most natural thing in the world to murmur comfort, to nuzzle her face against his, to sweet-kiss his neck, his chin, his shoulder.

"When I was a kid of five or six I added to family history the day Dad won his first Pulitzer. 'I'm tired of your awards, Daddy,' was apparently my response to the news. I'm told he thought it was very funny, but somehow I doubt it. Pulitzer, Polk, Overseas Press Club . . . there have always been so many, all related as far as I'm concerned to moments of painful growing up."

Johnny felt her shiver, pulled the coverlet up, drew her closer. He went on dreamily, "I can still remember the yellow telegram on the white tablecloth in the thatched cottage in Wiltshire, England, where he'd put Mother and me while he covered Europe. I can still remember how nervous my mother looked as she opened the telegram, although it was addressed to him, announcing yet another triumph. As usual he wasn't home, but he'd promised he'd make it for my birthday, my eleventh, and I rode my bike to meet him with the news at the train station, but also as usual he never turned up, and riding back I was so angry I fell off and broke my arm."

His chest heaved in an almost silent sigh. "Another time, I forget when, we were living in Cairo and my mother waited and waited for him to arrive and a huge wooden plaque, his most recent award, came home instead. It was the first time I ever saw her lose her cool. She was so angry she threw it out the window . . . I spent my youth acting as a buffer between my parents, Ginny . . . between my long-suffering mother, who won the prize for long-distance sulking over the phone, and my celebrated usually absent father . . ." His voice trailed off, his face almost on her breast, he was falling asleep and so was she.

Brilliant shards of light hurt her eyes. It was morning. She could hear water running, smell coffee brewing. Johnny. She caressed the word in her mind. Her Johnny.

He poked his head around the door, his hair wet, close to his head, a few tendrils curling up. He looked young, happy, relaxed. "Good, you're awake. Thank God, it's Sunday. I'm going down the block to get some bagels. Okay? If you behave I might even spring for some carrot juice."

While he was gone Ginny showered and looked in his closet for something to wear to breakfast. A pale gray heavy knit sweater appealed to her, but it was too rough on the skin. She settled for one of his denim shirts, leaving the top buttons undone, not at all sorry, because of her height, it barely covered her behind.

Exploring the roomy, beautiful apartment, she padded around into a large, brightly lit kitchen where, below a television mounted on the wall, Johnny had already set the breakfast table with cutlery, glasses and coffee mugs. Through a swinging door was a small formal dining area, with round, dark green, almost black malachite table and high-backed, elegant blackwood chairs; concealed by a handsome Japanese screen, the dining area led directly into the living room.

The peach-colored drapes were still drawn, the soft lamps still lit on the polished tables. Ginny wrapped her arms around herself, shutting her eyes, savoring the memory of the night before.

On an antique desk in the corner she saw a large silver-framed photograph. Although she'd never studied his face, she knew it had to be Quentin Peet. There was a slight resemblance to Johnny, but there was also something formidable in this face, or was it better described as a look of leadership that Johnny didn't have?

On the desk a couple of invitations spilled out of opened envelopes. Ginny picked them up idly. One was to a private screening of a new movie, followed by supper at Le Madri. The other looked like a slim book of heavy cream-colored paper with a red-ink sketch of a noble lion on the cover. Was this the Literary Lions invitation? She opened it excitedly.

"A Literary Evening at the Library honoring literary friends of the Research Libraries of the New York Public Library," she read. On the next page, side by side, were two lists of names, one under the heading "The Lions," the other under "The Patrons," both columns in alphabetical order. Ginny casually scanned the list of Lions, finding, as she'd expected, Quentin Peet's name.

She grimaced as she found a name she was not expecting on the patrons' list—none other than the dreaded Svank. No wonder Poppy wanted a new dress for the "library do."

Just reading Svank's name was enough to bring the black pit of fear and despair back, along with the now unavoidable knowledge that Alex was using her, involving her in something that could only end in disaster.

Should she confide in Johnny? No, it was too soon, or was it? After the events of the past few hours she could trust him, couldn't she? Trust him to look after her, yes, but he would have to tell the police. And perhaps he'd even feel this was the story he'd been looking for, the big one to put him on the map, a story that would surely lead to Svank and who knew what else?

Nothing had changed. There was nothing she could do—yet—until she heard from Alex. She would give him another month, she told herself. By then she would have met Johnny's father at the Library do, as Poppy called it. There was no one in the world who had more influence than Quentin Peet, no one who knew more about tracking somebody down and solving problems. She would pretend she'd only just found the jewels and tell both father and son without mentioning Alex's name. They would know what to do. Yes, that was the answer. She would give Alex one more month. If he hadn't come to her rescue by then, the Peets would. A rush of relief came just from making this decision.

She heard the door open. The invitation still in her hand, she turned to greet Johnny, glowing with love, waving it as she said, "I can't wait for this event, Johnny, darling. I'll design something special to look like a literary heroine to meet your famous father."

Before she finished the sentence, she knew she should never have said it. Johnny scowled and walked past her into the dining area and on into the kitchen. Before she reached him, he'd switched on the television and was pouring himself a cup of coffee, the brown paper bag he'd been carrying, thrown down on the counter.

"What's wrong, Johnny?"

At first she didn't think he was going to answer. Tim Russert's voice on *Meet the Press* filled the kitchen. Then, "Ginny, I told you once before not to push your luck. After all I mistakenly told you no more than a few hours ago, I'm surprised you keep on pushing it."

It was impossible to reconcile this tight-lipped stranger with the sweet, loving man who, his arms wrapped around her, had confided in her some of his childhood memories.

Ginny stared at him uncomprehending. It wasn't as if his father and he were sworn enemies or never saw each other or talked on the telephone. That wasn't the case. He'd told her so in a dozen different ways.

"My father told me at lunch . . ." she'd heard him say; or "I've got to rush, meeting my old man . . ." And how many times had she read: "John Q. Peet, the columnist, seen here attending one of the many book parties given to celebrate the latest book by his illustrious father, et cetera, et cetera . . ."

"What's going on, Johnny? I don't get it," she said angrily.

Silent, he kept on sipping his coffee, staring at the TV.

This was crazy. She wasn't going to accept the drawbridge going up. She tried to put her arms around him, but he hunched away. "Don't you understand, Ginny, I keep my private life separate—totally separate—from my father. I made that promise to myself when my marriage broke up. I'm never going to give him the opportunity to say 'I told you so' again."

She knew she was flushing, for all she knew from her bare behind to her eyebrows. "Thanks a lot. Has it crossed your mind your father might approve of me? Might think I'm a worthy . . ."

"Don't say another word," Johnny yelled.

The invitation was still in her hand. Ginny smacked it down on the kitchen table. "So you're not going to take me to meet your father?"

"Absolutely not."

"You're sick," she screamed.

"Maybe so. I call it self-preservation." As suddenly as she'd triggered his black mood, it was gone. He stood up, pinning her to the wall, his hands tight beneath her naked bottom. "Be patient, Ginny. I know this situation better than you, wouldn't you agree."

"No, I would not. You're—" His mouth stopped her. She tried to wrest herself out of his arms, but as he began to caress her body, kiss her mouth, her neck, her anger disappeared fast. She was too much in love with him not to respond. As he opened the rest of the buttons on the shirt and his mouth reached her nipples, they began to slither down the wall, wanting each other so much that neither noticed the cold of the tiled floor.

She didn't refer to the invitation again or certainly to his father. Johnny tried to make amends when he said sometime during the long, lazy, delirious Sunday, "There are some interesting things coming up, Ginny, things we'll go to together, maybe even a short trip—and others you'll go to alone, things we'll plan a strategy for—to cover for the book."

"Yes, Johnny," she said sweetly.

There was one thing she would be planning a strategy for, strictly for herself. The big night at the library. If Johnny was not willing to take her, she would have to take herself—as surely she was experienced enough to do.

She had to meet his father sooner than later, and the Literary Lions evening would be the perfect opportunity. She would prove to Johnny there would be no reason for the great Quentin Peet to say "I told you so" about the folly of their relationship.

Equally important, if by then she still had the jewels in her possession, with no word from Alex, she would put her new plan into action. She would "discover" the jewels as if for the first time, and cry to both Peet senior and junior for help.

If everything went as well as she hoped, the library "do" could be the last crash of her life.

It would certainly be the most important.

CHAPTER EIGHT

Coulda, Woulda, Shoulda was the name of a new play opening soon in a neighborhood theater on West Twenty-second. Ads for it were everywhere. Pasted on trees, poles, and stuck on graffiti-covered walls, they exclaimed the play was about "the sick insane world of gambling"; but every time Ginny saw the title, she thought the same thing: How perfectly it summed up her relationship with Johnny.

As she said dolefully to Esme on the phone, "You're back from your honeymoon. I'm back where I started with Johnny."

At least that's how she felt most days, dwelling with despair (as opposed to regret) on what she thought of as "the wedding weekend," torturing herself with the knowledge that despite all the warning signals, she'd ended up as just another notch on Johnny's well-notched belt.

To begin with, after he'd dropped her back at the loft that Sunday night, it had taken four painfully slow, count-the-minutes days before she'd heard from him again, and when he'd called, every molecule of her had strained to hear a different, intimate note in his voice. Yet he hadn't sounded different at all.

Friendly, warm, casual, "Hi, Ginny, when can we get together to go over some things? I'd like to book you for . . ." Same voice, the same kind of words, "booking" her, as opposed to asking her for a date—or, as she told Esme in her best Tallulah Bankhead voice, "asking for my hand in marriage."

She didn't tell Esme that the first time she saw him after the weekend, miserable wretch that she was, when he'd opened the door (to his office on West Seventy-seventh, not his home upstairs), she'd dived straight into his arms, although they'd scarcely been outstretched. Had there been a fierce new look of love (she told herself she'd have even settled for lust) on his face?

Frankly, no, although she'd had scant time to do a study. While they were still standing awkwardly together in the doorway, Quentin Peet himself had phoned, announcing he was back in town unexpectedly, and suggesting a quick drink.

Johnny hadn't blinked, let alone hesitated or even made much of an apology to her. He'd literally dropped everything, including her, to rush right over to the Century where, as he'd said with a mock bow, "The eagle has landed."

Since then, they'd hardly seen each other, although with increasing reluctance, she'd acted as his stand-in at some events, delivering her notes over quick coffees in midtown cafés near his *Next!* office, because he said he was too busy to do it any other way.

Was he trying to avoid meeting her anywhere where they could be alone? Was he fighting an ardent love for her, or at the very least, an attraction he feared could grow into something stronger? If so, he appeared to be winning the battle, she thought; and she moped.

On a brilliant, sunny, bird-singing spring day, he phoned to say he had to go out of town for a few days on a special assignment for the magazine.

"Nothing to do with the column. Something I've been following for the past few weeks, which might turn into the kind of story I've been looking for."

She wasn't comforted by the fact he'd taken the trouble to tell her. His voice had lost the laugh. He sounded distant, distracted.

"Where are you going?"

"San Juan."

San Juan. The name hit her like a shower of ice water. Hadn't Dolores, the Latina bombshell Quentin Peet had so thoroughly disapproved of, hailed from San Juan? No, no, no, of course not. Dolores was Bolivian.

"Something I've been following for the past few weeks," he'd said. Or did he mean "someone"? Ginny immediately thought of someone just like Dolores, a voluptuous beauty in an itsy-bitsy bikini, exotic, hot-blooded, hiding her passion beneath a lily-white skin, sheltered on a golden beach by a giant parasol. Or perhaps, now that Johnny professed to hate his ex-wife so much, he was into deeply tanned Latinas?

San Juan? Bolivia? What difference did it make? Both places were full of scorching women. "I'll miss you," he was saying. "Sorry we haven't seen much of each other. I'll call as soon as I get back, probably in about a week."

How she managed to stop asking, "Can I come with you?" she didn't know.

There was a painful pause. She dug her again half-bitten nails into her palm, not yet giving up, praying he might still say, "Oh, what the hell, why don't you come, too," but he didn't.

She'd hardly put the phone down before she started waiting for his return. She tried to stop thinking the worst—that he might be taking somebody to the golden beaches with him (the somebody he'd once said he was "tied up" with?) . . . tried to stop thinking of who might be waiting for him down there . . . tried to stop thinking, period.

But everywhere she went she was reminded of Johnny. *Coulda, Woulda, Shoulda* taunted her as she went to get her shoes soled, while in her mailbox came a leaflet announcing *Women Acting Up*, "A dark comedy soon arriving on West 17th Street, which explores friends and family through bedtime prayers, dark secrets and lies . . ." She needed every prayer she could get for the dark and dirty secret she was still being forced to live with.

The day after Johnny's departure, locking the loft door in the afternoon, shuddering with every move, Ginny took the gems out of the toilet to give them a shower. None seemed any the worse for their watery incarceration. On hitting the light, they emitted the same spectacular flashes of fire in her pathetic little bathroom as they had at 834 Fifth. When she returned them to their hiding place, her hands were shaking so much, she had to go out to the nearest bar and drink a brandy and soda.

Slumped in a corner of the bar, she reflected that all of February, March, and half of April had gone by since she'd first discovered the jewels. She started to count. Seventy-four days! She could hardly believe she'd managed to live through one day, let alone seventy-four, but then so much had happened in her life, so much—meaning Johnny— had happened.

"You need cheering up," Esme insisted. On returning home from the bar, with Johnny only gone for twenty-four hours, Ginny had called her best friend to admit she'd fallen into a deep, dark depression.

Esme had an antidote. "A wonderful new flea market I've just heard about, loaded with incredible fabric bargains."

Ginny had to laugh. "Es, you certainly know the right buttons to push."

Esme picked Ginny up early the next morning, hoping to have breakfast or at least coffee at the loft before they set out. Not for the first time Ginny had forgotten to restock her kitchen, so instead on the way across town they stopped off at a café not too far from Gosman's old factory.

Over cappuccino, with all the poise of an experienced married woman, Esme asked, "D'you think you and Johnny have any kind of a future?"

Ginny sighed. Esme could always be relied upon to aim straight for the solar plexus, no matter how much one tried to deflect her. Except when it came to Ted, with whom, perhaps from some innate sense of insecurity, Esme usually took a circuitous route.

"A future? Sure," Ginny lied. "If I want one." She tossed her head optimistically. "I just have to become as indispensable to Johnny as I once was to Everard Gosman—in a totally different way, of course."

"Of course," said Esme, pouting, showing she didn't believe a word of it. "If he'll let you." Ginny couldn't remember Esme ever irritating her more.

"He'll let me, you'll see."

"Well, you should always have some food in the house, Ginny. You know the old saying . . . the way to a man's heart is through—"

"Esme, shut up!" They glowered at each other and hardly spoke until, after being at the flea market for about thirty minutes, Ginny stumbled across a stunning find, a wide brocade border, heavily embroidered with fat gold bumblebees and laurel leaves, tacked onto the skirt of a decrepit, badly sagging sofa.

"Just look at this, Es." In her enthusiasm, she forgot how maddening Esme had been. "I must have it."

"That! Surely you're not that hard up. It will cost a fortune to repair and who knows where it's been."

"Not the sofa, dopey. The skirt, the border. Look at that embroidery, that work. It's special. How much?" Ginny asked a shriveled little woman who appeared to be the owner.

"Hundred and fifty."

"No way!" screeched Esme. They started to walk away.

"Okay, okay. What's your offer, miss?"

Ginny bent down to examine the gold stitching more closely. It really was amazing. She lifted up the skirt. Good. It would be a cinch to remove. She had to have it. She would get it cleaned, then use it to border a magnificent velvet cloak, the Napoleonic kind, in which to sweep up—and down—a staircase, the kind in which to make a grand entrance.

She knew just where to get a bolt of exactly the right color velvet, burnished copper chestnut, against which the fat gold bees would glisten even in the dark.

"Well, miss?"

"I only want the border."

"Well, then, but that's the beauty of it, isn't it, then. That's what makes it different . . ."

"You can say that again." Ginny blinked hard, startled by sudden tears as she thought of Alex. Whenever she used that expression with him, he would smile his wonderful sardonic smile and repeat whatever he'd just said. "Fifty dollars . . ." she offered.

"Oh, don't waste my time, miss."

It started to rain. "Oh, do come on, Ginny," Esme moaned.

"Sixty."

Esme saw a passing taxi. "Taxi!" she cried. It sped by, but the sofa owner saw she was about to lose her customer.

"Seventy-five. That's final." She put a dirty hand out.

Ginny hadn't planned to spend anything like seventy-five dollars in the flea market, but she knew nothing like this border would come her way again. "Okay, if I can take it now." Much to Esme's disapproval Ginny paid by check and, with the help of the woman's sharp knife, stripped the border carefully away.

When she got back to the loft, Johnny had called. "It's rainy and gray and as hot and humid as hell here. Where are you, Ginny Walker, Inc. Get back to your drawing board at once."

He didn't leave a number, and to take her mind off his absence

Ginny went out to the wholesaler to buy the velvet. She started work on the cloak as soon as she returned.

As usual, she'd acted on impulse, and okay, so now she had to admit it: She was making the cloak for the Literary Lions dinner only two weeks away. Once she'd spotted the imperial bees, she'd immediately thought of making a cloak, the kind of protective armor she would need to bolster her courage on the night of the Lions.

Designing a cloak, rather than a dress, to wear to such an important event was peculiar, she knew that; putting the horse before the cart, but that was the kind of designer she was. She got carried away when a piece of fabric "said something," and generally it lived up to her expectations.

She held the velvet against her skin, in love with its deep rich color. She had an idea. The copper chestnut would enhance the color of a dress she already owned. Not just any dress. The only one endowed with ecstatically happy memories, her "blushing" bridesmaid's dress.

Excited, she took the dress out of the art deco wardrobe and carried it with the velvet to the window. She was right. It enriched and showed off the blush dramatically. She would have to change the dress's shape—drastically—it was far too *jeune fille*. She already knew what she had to do, but she would work on the cloak first.

Preparing the paper pattern, she thought about Esme's tactless question and her reaction to it. If Johnny wasn't "tied up" with anyone, and despite her insecurity, she couldn't really believe after their weekend together he was, there was nothing to stand in the way of a future together.

Except his father.

She daydreamed, staring into space. She would set out to prove to the formidable Quentin Peet what a thoughtful, caring, home-loving, nurturing, undemanding, thrifty daughter-in-law she could be. Or, if he was looking for something else, what a money-producing, street-savvy, articulate, dazzling hostess; in other words, the perfect woman for Johnny.

In any case she *had* to meet the great man in order to ask for his help with the jewels. Her mind was made up about that. She'd set a deadline as far as Alex was concerned and nothing was going to lessen her determination.

Despite the fact Poppy still referred to it as a "do," Ginny knew from Lee that there was a grandeur, a special sense of importance about the

Literary Lions dinner, presided over by Mrs. Vincent Astor, the Chairman Emeritus of the New York Public Library, and the city's most revered citizen.

Perhaps this was one time when arriving early could be to her advantage. On the other hand, crashing early was always a more difficult proposition.

It depended on the weather. Rain would be helpful, with a lot going on in the cloakroom area. On the other hand, she didn't want her wonderful cloak to get wet.

What was the best time to arrive? It was an impossible question to answer. There was no "best time" for crashers in a city like New York, where unpunctuality was the rule rather than the exception, and "fashionably late" could mean anything from fifteen to sixty or more minutes later than the stated time.

Other people's lateness had helped her crash in the past, when she'd attached herself to the tail end of a late crowd, rolling in with them like an unexpected giant wave, engulfing any checkers left at the point of entry. Should she try the same approach for the Lions dinner?

She was too tired to think about it anymore; too tired to go on working. She packed up the velvet and went to bed, but she couldn't sleep. She took a sleeping pill and dreamed she was surfing with Alex through the mighty halls of the library. As the waves grew bigger, Alex effortlessly sailed across them, leaving her farther and farther behind. She couldn't stay up much longer, but Alex obviously didn't care. "Alex! Help! Alex!" She woke up screaming, on the floor.

No wonder she'd dreamed Alex didn't care. She hadn't heard one word from her thieving cousin, while night and day the gems glittered like evil reptiles in her toilet tank.

As she lay tossing and turning, she remembered the decision she'd come to in Johnny's apartment: She would give Alex one more month to redeem himself and rescue her, and not a second more.

She got up, agitated, and went into the kitchen where the 1995 fashion calendar Lee had sent over in March was hanging beside the stove. Ringed in red was the April "wedding weekend." By the time the Literary Lions dinner arrived, the month would just about be up.

Ginny started pacing around the loft. If she hadn't heard from Alex by then, whether she succeeded in crashing and meeting the mighty Peet or not, she would go ahead with her plan and put on the greatest act of her life: She would pretend to Johnny that she had discovered the jewels for the first time.

Having made this decision, she again felt a sense of enormous relief, just as she had in Johnny's apartment, and slept like a baby until almost eight o'clock.

She was at the sewing machine, finishing Poppy's georgette dress so that she could give her full attention to the cloak, when the doorbell rang.

"Yes?"

"Delivery."

Her heart thumped in her chest. From Angus? From Alex? Oh, please God let it be a word, any word from Alex about collecting, not delivering.

"Who is it?"

There was a long agonizing pause, then an irritated voice said, "Grace's Marketplace. Is this, eh, Ginny Walker?"

"Yes, but I haven't ordered anything."

"Well, somebody has. It's paid for. D'you want me to leave it or not?"

"Wait there." She was sure it was a trick or maybe a message from Alex buried in a basket of fruit. Half praying, half dreading what she'd find, Ginny rushed downstairs to discover Esme had sent her a food parcel with crackers, cheeses, herbal tea, and three different kinds of coffee "for when Johnny comes home." Darling Esme.

There had always been people in his life who said he aped his father. Even his mother had accused him of it at some time or another, and Dolores had never stopped.

Johnny thought of both women now as he cut his chin with the straight-edged George Trumper razor he'd bought years ago in London. The kind his father always used, although Johnny had never seen so much as a scratch on the old man's face.

He scowled at the blood as it spurted into the basin. Actually, he rarely cut himself. He couldn't blame his father; he could probably blame Ginny Walker. In fact, he did blame Ginny Walker.

Whoever wrote "I've Got You Under My Skin" sure knew what he was writing about. He'd got Ms. Walker under his skin all right, and he didn't like it one little bit. He didn't want to fall in love again; therefore he wasn't in love—certainly not with a giraffe-legged, kooky, crazy girl with such a major personality flaw that she spent half her time going where she wasn't wanted. He corrected himself: where she wasn't expected.

The phone rang, but as had happened before, when he picked it up there was no one there. Very James Bondish; but then this drug business could have come straight out of Ian Fleming's imagination, it was so bizarre—and brutal. Johnny shivered. He'd always suspected he didn't have his old man's guts. Now he knew he didn't.

It was ironic. He'd received the tip in the first place only because of a mix-up: Trager, one of the FBI contacts he'd made through his Princeton pal, Matt Fisher, had dropped it thinking Johnny was working with the elder Peet.

It hadn't been much of a tip, more of an eye-opener, which should have been obvious. It had recently been announced that Limpo Delchetto, one of the most famous, fearless—some said foolhardy—journalists based in South America, had won the Pulitzer Prize for the *Miami Herald* with his series exposing close business connections between prominent South American industrialists and the biggest drug czar in Cali.

"You and your dad better get busy," Trager had said casually. "Delchetto's walked away with the big one this year and I hear he's moved to Puerto Rico, working on the Venezuelan Villeneva drug connection . . ."

Puerto Rico! Of course! The hottest new playing field for the drug business. Why hadn't he thought of that before. Johnny had immediately called for a transcript of the "war on drugs" *Nightline* he'd watched back in February, reading and remembering, still with some embarrassment, how smoothly his father had interrupted Tom Constantine, the new chief of the Drug Enforcement Administration, and Constantine's scowl as QP had sailed right on.

"I often wonder why it took Cali so long to use it as a major drug corridor into the United States," Johnny read. "What do they say? With no Customs to worry about, Thursday in San Juan, Friday in South Dakota. Now it's the number two route after Miami, with about eighty-four tons of cocaine and high-purity heroin coming in a year . . ."

When Johnny had finished the transcript, he'd made a few phone calls, including one to Detective Armitage, still working on the Villeneva heist, and one to Alfredo Relato, an influential, well-connected cousin of Dolores in San Juan, a man he'd always liked and the only member of her family who'd taken the trouble to tell him how sorry he was over their breakup. "Marrying you was the only wise thing she ever did," he'd written.

With Delchetto's clips from the *Miami Herald*, the Pulitzer Prize announcement, the transcript and his own notes he'd gone into Steiner's office, who hadn't needed any persuading to fund his trip.

Steiner came into Johnny's mind now. He grimaced as he tried to stem the blood flow. His boss had thought that at last he was going to follow in his father's footsteps—something he'd always hoped for and never bothered to hide. Well, Steiner was going to be disappointed, that was all there was to it. The lead to the Villeneva jewel heist and, more important, its connection to the drug world was as dead as the dodo, as dead as Limpo Delchetto apparently was.

God, how his father would laugh, for instead of feeling aggressive and determined not to give up, Johnny's major emotion was immense relief that there didn't seem much point in hanging around. He could return home without showing how lily-livered he'd discovered himself to be when surrounded by real danger.

He'd lived with fear since his arrival, when he'd learned from Alfredo that although it had not yet been announced, Limpo Delchetto had disappeared.

"At eleven o'clock he left La Mallorquina in Old San Juan, saying he wanted an early night, but he never reached home and he hasn't been seen since." Alfredo had sighed. "Life is cheap here these days and getting cheaper."

Searching for clues, an agent in the San Juan DEA office told Johnny casually, "He's probably been pulverized in an auto wrecker's yard." The agent's eyes had reminded Johnny of Ben Abbott's. Cool, piercing, revealing nothing, not even distaste, as the agent added, "It's the method the Cali drug family most favors to dispose of interlopers."

Was this another warning to stay away? In his head Johnny could hear Rosemary say, "Put the pieces together, one by one, until the jigsaw begins to make sense." With his luck, he'd end up in the wrecker's yard before he found any pieces to put together.

He filed a story about Delchetto, "missing in action," capturing, he thought, the newly sinister atmosphere in San Juan, "the number two drug route into the United States."

When he'd returned to his hotel room on the third day of getting nowhere, he'd been sure someone had been looking through his things . . . and wanted him to know it. There had been a broken penknife in the bathroom, which the maid swore she knew nothing about; and his alarm clock had been missing, until he found it, stopped, under his pillow, at twelve o'clock.

High noon or midnight? The hour of Delchetto's death?

He'd toughed it out, wondering every day if his own famous, fearless (but apparently never foolhardy) father would care if, in pursuit of a story to expose a necessary truth, he disappeared off the face of the earth? Would QP expect his son to aspire to his own impossibly high standards, and imperil his life for his work?

Yes to both. His father would care, well, certainly publicly. Johnny could imagine him proclaiming, "I'll stop at nothing to bring those responsible for my son's death (ditto disappearance) to justice." And dear old Dad really would stop at nothing, yet would manage to stay alive and probably earn next year's Pulitzer for his trouble.

Would Ginny care? God damn it, he'd had an erection just thinking about her. Yes, she would care. Dear naive Ginny. She actually thought she could impress his father once they met or at least make him look on her with favor. Johnny could write the scenario.

"What does Ms. Walker do for a living, Johnny?"

"She's a very talented dress designer."

"For whom?"

"For herself—her own label. She just hasn't made it yet, but she will. And, oh yes, in her spare time she gate-crashes—eh—for me. She's getting material for a book I'm writing on today's society, its values—or lack of them."

"Gate-crashing. How unusual. And you pay her? How dignified." The famous Peet eyebrows would do their elevating act and that would be the end of Ginny.

The cut on his chin still spewed blood.

He couldn't even stand the sight of a cut made by his own shaky hand, so what made him think he could act the hero? And why should he? To try to prove something to a father who'd shown for years he didn't think he was capable of anything?

Four knocks sounded on the door. It would be Alfredo, but he couldn't join him until his chin dried up. He looked and felt a mess, but it didn't matter anymore. He was quitting, getting out before Cali declared him an enemy.

"I'm on the phone long-distance," he called through the door. "I've decided to leave today on the afternoon flight. I'll meet you in the lobby around noon to say goodbye."

But it wasn't to be. At noon Alfredo told Johnny that the governor, embarrassed and mortified by Delchetto's disappearance, had sanctioned a surprise attack by the National Guard on a San Juan housing project, thought to be the headquarters of a major drug supplier. If Johnny wanted to see some action, they could follow behind. Johnny, ashamed of his lack of fire-in-the-belly, agreed.

It didn't produce any of the answers he was looking for, but it took three more days of surveillance to penetrate and break up what turned out to be a more sophisticated drug distribution center than anyone had understood.

It wasn't the story he'd come down to Puerto Rico to break, but Steiner had been happy with his first piece and now he had another one—about the one-of-a-kind governor, who, to fight the gigantic drug invasion of his island, was willing to go out on a limb against the civil libertarians and install the National Guard inside the housing project, for as long as it took to declare it drug-free.

The piece almost wrote itself. It touched on another issue Johnny felt fervently about: how "civil liberties" could be interpreted to the detriment of society. He'd been writing about this on and off since he'd landed at Next! He'd written about the damage done by civil libertarians back home who were sticklers for following the civil liberties movement and laws of the sixties; die-hard types who railed against the concept of taking those too mentally sick to take care of themselves off the street, back into hospitals or institutions. People like the homeless "Madame Sacks of Saks" he'd made famous in his column.

"The other Rosemary," as he sometimes thought of the homeless woman, had been a teacher in an Indianapolis suburb. Introduced to "recreational drugs" when hot-tub parties were all the rage, she had had a love affair with a pusher, drifted into addiction and lost her job, her husband, her family. When he'd first looked into Rosemary's story, she'd already been living on New York pavements for almost a year, screaming awake and asleep, slowly drowning in her own sickness.

It wasn't too much of a leap to compare the courage of the Puerto

Rican governor with the courage of a New York mayor, who despite an enormous hue and cry decided that the meaning of the law had to be changed. That instead of narrowly reading the law as "no one can be removed from the streets who is not in imminent danger to himself or others," one could read it more broadly to mean "in danger of harming themselves in the reasonably foreseeable future." Rosemary had been one of those taken away for treatment, cursing every inch of the way.

He felt a surge of satisfaction as he typed the last word. It was good. He hadn't solved the Villeneva story, but this piece had heart, lots of heart, linking the streets of San Juan with the streets of New York, and describing the ordinary people who got caught up in the life of the streets and who got lost there.

"You write so well," Ginny had once said to him. "What do you want to do . . . to write . . ." Ginny, wonderful supportive Ginny.

He'd talked to her more or less every day he'd been away, and reluctantly had come to the conclusion that absence could definitely make the heart grow even fonder. What had the mighty La Rochefoucauld said? *Absence diminishes mediocre passions and increases great ones, as the wind blows out candles and fans fires.* One day he might even pass that piece of information on to Ginny. One day. Perhaps.

She hadn't mentioned meeting his father again; hadn't even hinted, let alone nagged him about the Literary Lions dinner, which was now only a few days away. She had obviously forgotten all about it.

He decided to give her a surprise. He would call and book her for the evening, make up some occasion or other, then arrive early at the loft and announce he was taking her to the library after all. Would he introduce her to QP? Perhaps, perhaps not. It all depended on the old man's mood, which he could sense from a mile away.

It would be a perfect coming-home present. For her and for him, too. He couldn't wait to see her face.

Johnny had called to say he was coming home and wanted to book her on Tuesday night to stand in for him at some American Cancer fund-raiser.

What nerve!

Ginny had never felt so humiliated, so angry, listening to his oh-so-confident voice, "booking" her, assuming that although he'd been away for over two weeks, she wouldn't have any other plans or worse, that she'd cancel them as soon as she received orders from Mr. *Next!* Magazine.

She'd never doubted he'd be home later than the first week of May. He wasn't coming home because he missed her. As his week away had stretched into two weeks and then a day more, she'd told herself that no matter what, Johnny Peet would not miss his father's big night at the library, and of course, she'd been right.

Nothing had changed; she was still Cinderella without the magic slipper; he hadn't invited her to the library. He'd called to "book" her to take his place at an event, which he'd suddenly found conflicted with the Literary Lions dinner. Well, he was in for a big surprise. It was time Mr. *Next!* learned he could no longer take her for granted. He would be at the library dinner honoring his father—and so would she.

In her imagination she saw Johnny watch her arrive, sweeping up the grand library steps on Fifth Avenue. He would be stunned at first, perhaps a little angry, but finally he would be so impressed by how she looked, her magnificent cloak, her panache, her bravery, he would offer her his arm and together they would go to meet his father. It was a wonderful daydream and whenever she felt downcast, nervous, she brought it out until her spirits lifted.

She'd been working nonstop since Johnny's departure, helping Lee style a couple of shoots, spritzing perfume at Bloomingdale's, even swallowing her deep dislike of the runway to fill in for a sick house model to help a friend of Sophie Formere's.

With all this part-time work, it had been difficult to get all the clothes finished, hers and Poppy's. Night after night she'd worked into the early morning, until Poppy's georgette wraparound number had been delivered and her own cloak and dress needed only last-minute touches.

Poppy had called almost immediately with rave reviews.

"Are you definitely wearing it to the library?" Ginny asked. She was depending on Poppy's presence to help her crash.

"Right now I am." Poppy had been laughing, but she'd also sounded slightly hysterical.

"Good, so I'll see you there . . ."

"Oh, *wunderbar*. Are you going with Alex?"

Ginny had gulped. "Have you seen him?" For weeks she'd tried to avoid pumping Poppy for information in case she told Svank and he became suspicious.

"Nooo, but I thought I heard Svank saying something about meeting him this week."

"Oh, when?" There was no point in trying to show she didn't care. Her whole future depended on seeing Alex and getting everything sorted out once and for all.

Poppy had been as maddening as ever, ignoring her question, self-absorbed, cooing what once-upon-a-long-time-ago Ginny would have longed to hear. "Ginny, you are sooo talented. I'd like a black version of the georgette. Can you do it without a fitting? You know how I loooathe fittings."

At least it had given Ginny the perfect opportunity to lock Poppy into turning up at the library. "Yes, if I can see how it drapes, moves on you. I'll study it when we meet for the Literary Lions."

"Goody, goody. I'll send you a check tomorrow."

Poppy had been true to her word and it more than helped defray the cost of the velvet for the cloak, the embroidered border, and new copper patent stiletto sandals Ginny hadn't been able to resist, spotting them in a theatrical shop in Soho.

She was sure the cloak was the most majestic, stylish piece of clothing she had ever designed. She was also very happy with the way the bridesmaid dress—or what remained of it—had turned out. Minus the sleeves, with a radically deepened décolletage (held up with shoestring silk straps) it looked like a totally new gown, seductive in its shapeliness, impressive in its formality. Luckily, she'd over-ordered on the crepe, so managed to make two new side panels to flow out from the waist as she walked, increasing the dress's overall "presence."

After Johnny called to "book" her, she'd rushed out to pick up a copy of *Next!*, hoping to learn what he'd been writing about in Puerto Rico, hoping to see if he revealed the mysterious "something I've been following for months." His byline was on the cover, which showed a photo of a man she'd never heard of, Limpo Delchetto, with the cover line, "Pulitzer Prize Winner 'Missing in Action.' "

So Johnny had his cover story. To her surprise, it was mostly about drug trafficking, a very different beat for him.

She marveled at his use of language, his knowledge. Johnny knew so much of the world. She sighed, thinking of her poor father and his endless posturing and striving to be known as a man of letters.

In *Next!*'s movie column she saw that Abel Gance's movie,

Napoleon, was showing in the Village and the next day she went alone to see if there was anything Napoleonic that she could still add to her ensemble. Not really, although one ballroom scene impressed her, where people were dancing with red ribbons tied around their necks to show that someone in the family had had his head cut off.

Back at the loft she decided to have a dress rehearsal, deliberating whether or not to add a red ribbon to her own neck. During the last dreadful two and a half months, since discovering the jewelry, she'd often felt her own head was someplace else; in case Quentin Peet knew its historical significance, she decided against it.

The phone rang soon after she climbed wearily into bed.

"I'm back. I'm home, Ginny. Did I disturb your beauty sleep?"

What time was it? She groped for the light switch as she huskily said, "No, no, of course not."

It was not the middle of the night. It was only ten thirty-five.

"Can I come over now?" Johnny sounded keyed up, like an excited schoolboy.

Ginny sat up in bed, trying to wake up. She looked around the loft. It was a terrible mess, with bits of velvet and blush bridesmaid all over the floor. If the loft looked a mess, she knew she looked worse. Her long pause must have been too off-putting, because before she could answer, Johnny said accusingly, "I think I did wake you up. Go back to sleep. I've got a ton of things to catch up on here anyway."

As she began to say, "No, it's okay, really . . ." he said in a softer, sweeter voice, "Can't wait to see you. Be ready about six tomorrow. Wear one of your spectacular long dresses. I'll come over with all the details and tell you who and what to look for." He laughed boyishly. "Ready to go back to work?"

Now wide awake, she fumed, trying to think of a suitable cutting reply. He couldn't wait to see her? So what was he doing all the hours in the day before six o'clock tomorrow evening, when he obviously thought he could just drop in for a quick smooch, deliver her marching orders and then be on his merry way in time for the grand library event?

Should she tell him to go to hell now or let him turn up on her doorstep and find no one at home? She couldn't think fast enough. "I don't know," she said lamely. "Possibly."

"Are you okay?"

"Of course, I'm okay," she said crossly. "You just startled me." Without thinking she blurted out, "I was going to a dinner party tomorrow night . . ."

"Where?"

How dare he question her after being away for fifteen whole days. Who did he think he was? Coolly, "Oh, a friend of Ted and Esme's . . ."

"Male?"

When she didn't answer, he went on in the same sweet, soft voice. "I've got a surprise for you, Ginny. Can't you make it tomorrow, for me, at six, please?"

She sighed, a deliberate, subordinate-reporting-for-duty sigh of resignation. "Okay, okay, I'll try to change my plans. Long dress, six o'clock, American Cancer, right?"

"Right. Until then, Ms. Ginny. I can't wait, but you're worth waiting for."

So he'd bought her a surprise in Puerto Rico. She wished he hadn't. She'd had enough surprises to last a lifetime. Now she was so awake, she wondered how she'd ever get back to sleep. She deliberated about calling him back to ask him to come over after all, but she worried she might not be able to lie about her plans face-to-face with him.

The phone rang three times between six-thirty and eight the next morning, but every time Ginny picked it up there was no one there, not even any heavy breathing.

It was so unsettling, and in the bright light of day she knew there was no way she could see Johnny at six, no way she could pretend to be going one place and turn up at another, no way she could see him at all that day and still be able to go through with her crash plan.

She'd already given herself the day off to relax, to wash and set her hair and perhaps give herself a face mask. She was just out of the shower when Esme called to see if she'd like to come over "for tea or catch a movie this afternoon?" Esme sounded bored. "Ted's at a meeting in Toronto, and won't be back till about eight or nine . . ."

Darling Esme—here was Ginny's solution.

"I'd love to, but I can't do a movie. I have to go out early this evening. I was thinking of calling you. I'd love to come over to change at your place and get some help with my hair . . . I want you to see how your bridesmaid dress looks now. I need your vote of approval." She did, too, or at least some reassurance that she'd never looked better. With

Esme's endless curiosity about her life, Ginny was sure she wouldn't be able to resist the opportunity to find out the latest episode.

"Oh, I'd love you to come over. Is Johnny back?"

"He's back."

"So you're meeting him later? Where are you going? Somewhere suitably romantic, I hope?"

Ginny hesitated, murmuring, "Uptown somewhere . . . I'll tell you all about it when we meet."

Before she left the loft just before four, with her total ensemble, cloak, dress, evening sandals and purse, in a voluminous old Gosman garment bag, Ginny decided she couldn't let Johnny arrive all the way downtown and find no one home. At least she would cover herself by leaving a message. She prayed she'd get his answering service. She did.

"I'm really sorry, Johnny, but I couldn't get out of my date. It's such a bore. I hope you'll understand, but you didn't give me enough notice. See you soon. Tomorrow? Miss you." She knew her voice was wobbly, but it was the best she could do.

On the way to Esme, Ginny decided to tell her best friend the truth, to confess she was crashing because Johnny, for some paranoid reason, didn't want her to meet his illustrious father.

When Esme opened the door with a big grin, bursting with excitement about her imminent "reunion" with Johnny, Ginny couldn't get the real, unflattering facts out.

"Is Johnny picking you up here? I hope so."

"No, he's . . . eh . . . he's on deadline. I'm meeting him there."

"Where?"

Ginny sighed. There was no chance Esme wouldn't demand to know all the where-why-and-how details. She'd mentioned she was going somewhere uptown, but she'd just have to hope Esme hadn't caught it.

"The New York Public Library," she said defensively. "There's an important dinner there tonight, something called the Literary Lions, where Johnny's father's going to be honored."

"Oh, my! How glamorous." Esme squealed with pleasure when Ginny showed her the cloak. "My, my, my, there's that border from that godawful sofa. Who would believe it! It's sumptuous, ravishing. You've really outdone yourself this time. Ginny, you're just a genius, there's no other word for it."

When Ginny took out the renovated bridesmaid dress, Esme was far more restrained, and from her lack of comments, let alone compliments, Ginny realized the changes didn't meet with Esme's approval. She could have kicked herself for her insensitivity. Obviously, Esme was upset; obviously she'd wanted Ginny to preserve the bridesmaid dress just as it was, even if she could never wear it again.

"Sorry, Esme. I can see from the look on your face I should never have altered a stitch, but when I saw the velvet for the cloak I knew the blush color would go so perfectly with it. I hope you're not too mad at me?"

"No, I'm not mad, Ginny, just a bit shocked. I . . . I only wish you'd started from scratch and made a new dress . . ."

It didn't take long for Esme to forgive and forget and soon they were shrieking with laughter—Ginny didn't even know what about. She was light-headed with a mixture of fear and elation, apprehension and anticipation.

By the time she was ready (Esme helped, first coiling her hair into a sophisticated chignon, then making up her eyes, and finally insisting Ginny borrow her deep gold Lancôme lipstick), it was after six and it had begun to spit with rain.

When the phone rang Ginny tensed, sure it was Johnny trying to track her down, but it wasn't. It was Ted's company chauffeur telling Esme the boss's arrival time at the airport.

Looking out of the window, receiver in hand, Esme turned to Ginny. "You can't get that divine cloak wet—or your dress either. You must take Ted's car. He won't need it until later this evening. He's not arriving until eight forty-five at La Guardia. What time d'you need to be at the library?"

With such a heaven-sent offer, Ginny saw that the best time to arrive was being decided for her. "Seven-thirty?" she suggested. Her heart thumped beneath the soft crepe.

"Does that give you enough time to pick my husband up?" Esme said into the phone. Ginny could see from the look of pride on Esme's face she loved saying "my husband." Who wouldn't?

"Okay. Why don't you come over now. To the New York Public Library on Fifth Avenue. Yes, fine." Esme put the phone down. "He's just filling up with gas. He'll be here in about twenty minutes."

*   *   *

The rain had decided only to spit and not to pour as Ted's Mercedes pulled up at the fine stone staircase leading to the library's main entrance on Fifth Avenue.

Strange, there was no canopy outside, no red carpet and nobody climbing the steps. Aware that the chauffeur obviously couldn't wait to be on the way to the airport, Ginny thanked him politely, and pulling the cloak around her, began her ascent.

Now her nerves were giving her trouble. She thought she might easily be sweating away all Esme's eye expertise. She began to feel faint. It looked as if the giant doors were shut tight. Had she made a mistake about the date? She couldn't have. There had been a few references in the papers to the Literary Lions dinner since the day she'd first opened the invitation on Johnny's desk. The date was etched in her brain.

She stopped after climbing the first flight. Was someone calling her name? At first she was too nervous to look around, but when it came again, "Ginny . . . Ginny Walker, is that you?" she turned, remembering for some unknown reason Alex's advice about the importance of good posture.

She froze. It was Oz, the wily wizard of Oz bounding up the steps toward her, a camera bag slung over the shoulder of his tux. "Whew," he blew a long low whistle. "Do you look gorgeous or do you look gorgeous, Miss Ginny." He was the last person in the world she expected or, certainly, wanted to see. She gave him a feeble smile.

"And where are you going, so dressed to kill?" Luckily he didn't give her a chance to reply. "Looking like a heroine, it must surely be the Literary Lions dinner? But you're going the wrong way, m'darling. The invitation says enter on Forty-second Street, cocktails in the Celeste Bartos Forum, remember? May I escort you?"

She remembered only too well her behavior to Oz at Esme's wedding. She didn't deserve any courtesy from him. Why was he being so charming? Whatever his reason, she was already unnerved by choosing the wrong entrance and she realized Oz could be a valuable lifeline if, God forbid, she needed one.

"Oz, how lucky you saw me. I wasn't thinking. My car dropped me here . . . How stupid of me. Of course, I should be around the corner . . ." She gave him her most vivid smile, and tucked her arm in his.

"Who are you meeting? That magazine guy, Peet? Can't he ever pick you up?" Now, his tone wasn't so friendly.

"Maybe." She tried to sound coquettish. "Maybe not."

"Oh, so you're a woman of mystery tonight. Well, perhaps by the time the evening ends, you'll tell me why you've never returned my calls and why you were so fucking cold at Esme's wedding?"

"Perhaps," she said, determined to keep the same light, flirtatious tone. "Perhaps not."

As they reached the portico on Forty-second Street the rain started up again. Now there were plenty of people arriving in various styles of evening dress, scuttling to get inside, where there was already a line for the cloakroom.

"Give me that doozy of a cloak. I've never seen anything so gorgeous."

Ginny hated to take it off. Photographers were approaching. She twirled around once or twice as their flashes went off, before reluctantly unfastening the clasp.

"I hope you're not wearing anything underneath," said Oz. He looked at her closely. "Are you feeling all right? You look pale, very pale in fact. Here"—he pointed to a bench—"why don't you go sit while I check this."

"No, no, I prefer to stand. I'm all right."

Had she given anything away? Did Oz suspect something, because he winked as together they joined the line for the cloakroom, saying in the suggestive voice she hated, "I'm honored to escort you, slinky Gin. This is turning out to be fun after all."

He put his arm around her waist and squeezed her with the lecherous grin she remembered so well. Oz was making her more, not less, jittery. What if Johnny came in and saw her with someone he already thought was an old beau?

To make matters worse, Oz tightened his grip. "I'm only here because I'm being paid a bundle to do something special, shooting these so-called Literary Lions for *Hello*, you know, the hot European magazine."

She didn't, but who cared, as long as Oz could sweep her into the lions' den with him, smoothly, quickly before Johnny might see them together. "Please God, please God," she prayed under her breath, "let me get in without a problem."

"If this turns out to be as big a yawn as I think it might be, how about you and I cutting loose after I've taken what I need?" Oz's arm was still wrapped tightly around her waist as they reached the counter and he handed over her precious cloak of armor.

"Why not? Let's see." As soon as she was through the barricade she would have to get rid of him, fast. Before Oz had a chance, she took the cloakroom ticket from the attendant and put it in her tiny purse.

They were part of the elegant, laughing, talking crowd approaching a long table, covered with dozens and dozens of small envelopes, all inscribed in perfect, expensive calligraphy, with the guests' names. They were lined up in alphabetical order, obviously holding the table assignments.

With a giddy sense of relief Ginny realized that this special-invitation-only occasion, despite the high cost of tickets to benefit the library, was still being handled like a private party. There was no forbidding guardian at the gate with a master list checking names. It was taken for granted everyone arriving was an expected, welcome guest.

She let out a small sigh. With luck, she wasn't going to need to use Oz as an entry pass, for although a number of eager, earnest ladies were behind the table—library staff, Ginny supposed—trying to help everyone find his envelope, most people were just picking them up themselves.

On the right was a small separate table marked "Press." As Oz went toward it, Ginny quickly joined the crowd and, without looking at the name, picked up an envelope from the far end, where she expected the W's to be. She put it in her purse.

"Cocktails this way . . ." someone called. Later, if necessary, she would find a way to return the envelope, but right now she had to get to the cocktail party fast—for her the most important part of the evening.

Oz was still at the press table. Quickly, Ginny followed the crowd, just managing to squeeze into a packed elevator before the doors closed.

She was in. It had been easy, but she felt ill with the strain. She longed to find a ladies' room to regain her composure, but didn't want to get lost.

She had no idea where she was going. She'd once worked at the library as a volunteer during *Vogue*'s Centennial Celebration there, hoping to catch the eye of a *Vogue* fashion editor, but there had been fat chance of that. Down in the bowels of the giant building, she'd been a gofer in every sense of the word, going to and fro, fetching and delivering, at the mercy and direction of a lowly assistant in the promotions department. It had been a nightmare.

There was a roar. She was nearing the cocktail arena, the lions' den, already full of literary lions. Who was who? As she stood at the entrance, she didn't have a clue, except that around the necks of a few guests she saw not a red Napoleonic ribbon but a large bronze medallion.

In one corner of the huge, already crowded room Ginny saw a familiar back with unruly hair, curling up at the nape. Johnny. He was part of a small, attentive audience—the word *audience* came immediately to her mind—surrounding the only literary lion who mattered as far as she was concerned, Johnny's father, Quentin Peet.

Ginny took a deep breath. It was now or never. This is what she'd come for.

As she attempted to cut through the shoulder-to-shoulder crowd, someone grabbed her arm. Sure it was Oz and not wanting to antagonize him, Ginny turned with a flirtatious smile to excuse herself for a few minutes, but it wasn't Oz.

It was the man she'd so hoped to meet again one day, the man she'd sat next to at the Waldorf, the savior of designer Becky Corey and dozens like her, Arthur Stern, seeker of new talent, according to Lee Baker Davies, and married to the richest hypochondriac in America.

"Hello there, how goes the designing? Long time no see." Stern put out his hand. "Arthur Stern, and you are . . . ?"

"Ginny Walker." She wanted to die. How could she have such bad luck to run into Stern on this night of all nights.

"Well, Ms. Ginny, you're looking pretty good. As I remember you're a friend of that luscious piece of ass, Poppy Gan. Haven't seen her yet tonight, although Mr. High and Mighty Svank has put in an appearance. Is that who . . ." As more people poured in, they were jostled and Stern turned angrily as the glass of wine he was holding spilled over. "Watch where you're going."

She didn't know what to do. She was torn between not letting one more second pass before showing Johnny she was there and joining the circle around his father, or not missing another opportunity to make an indelible impression on Stern now, which would lead to a business appointment later.

As Ginny hesitated, still watching Johnny, he turned to indicate something to his father and saw her.

He stared in astonishment, tightening his mouth the way she knew he did when he was really angry. He turned back to his father for a second, appeared to be excusing himself, and started across the room toward her.

"Oh, excuse me, Mr. Stern. I'll be back, but I must give a message to . . ." She didn't even finish, but started to push her way toward Johnny. It wasn't easy, and as usual he was continually waylaid as he tried to cut through, but finally in the middle of the maelstrom they met. In her stiletto heels, they were eye to eye.

"Well, this is a surprise." Cold, curt voice.

"Johnny, please don't be mad. It isn't what you think. This isn't an ordinary cr—" He put his hand lightly over her mouth.

"Don't say the word in these exalted halls. It doesn't belong here and neither do you. I can't imagine how you got in, but it doesn't matter because I don't care. You're a very silly girl, Ginny, very silly. Why d'you think I asked you so specially to be home at six this evening?"

"Johnny, how are you? So glad you got back in time. I told your father . . . where is he anyway?" A thickset warrior of a man with a mane of dark silver hair and a medallion gleaming on his stiff white shirt appeared beside them.

"Oh, hi, Norman. Dad's been looking for you. Ginny Walker—meet Norman Mailer."

It could have been the Pope. She didn't care. Johnny was furious, upset, that was all she cared about.

"Excuse me, Ginny, I'll be back." Johnny began to lead the distinguished author over to where his father was holding court.

"Can I come, too?"

Without turning, Johnny shook his head. She took no notice, doggedly following him, until another hand clutched her arm. This time it was Oz, a hostile Oz, who demanded, "Why didn't you wait for me? What was the big hurry? Who are you with, anyway? It doesn't look as if your loverboy is taking much care of you."

"Oh, Oz, don't be jealous." She couldn't risk his drawing attention to herself or, worse, making a scene.

As she tried to calm him down, over his shoulder she saw Johnny ferrying people to and from his father. It sickened her. Johnny was acting like an aide-de-camp, an errand boy, a gofer, but what could he have meant when he said, "why d'you think I asked you to be at home at six o'clock"?

She had to get to Quentin Peet, but how could she get rid of Oz?

"Which room are you in for dinner?" Oz asked.

She'd forgotten about the envelope in her purse. She didn't dare take it out with Oz there. "I'm not sure . . ."

To her relief Oz wasn't listening. "Don't worry," he said. "I have to check with Lili Root where some of my Lions are sitting. I'll get your table from her and catch up with you later. Hey, hold that look, you look cute." He raised his camera. "Stay like that."

So relieved he was going, Ginny posed as he took a few shots. Then he went off in search of the seating plan. Ginny started to cross the room. The circle of Peet admirers had disappeared, for good reason. Quentin Peet was no longer there; neither was Johnny.

"Delivered your message?" As Stern asked the question, a gong echoed through the room. He didn't wait for her answer. "That's only the first bell . . . it will be a good twenty minutes before people start going in to dinner. Where're you sitting?"

There was nothing for it, but to open the sealed envelope. "Berg Collection, Table Fourteen."

"My bad luck," Stern said. She was partly disappointed, partly relieved, because she had no idea whose envelope she was holding.

"Mine, too." What a disaster the evening was turning out to be, but perhaps she could spend at least some of the twenty minutes he'd mentioned, arranging another appointment with him later. "Have we time to talk now?"

"Absolutely, Madame Designer. But not here." He had a point. The noise was deafening, but there was also that leer she didn't like, the one she remembered from the Waldorf.

Don't overreact, she told herself. Remember Becky Corey and all the other Coreys the Sterns have helped. All of them must have had to deal with Arthur Stern's flirting at one time or another. Now it's your chance. Perhaps she could show him her extraordinary cloak.

"I tell you what," he was saying, "let's go for a few minutes in the direction of the main reading room. There's a quiet spot where you can tell me about yourself, then I'll steer you to the Berg Collection . . ."

As he escorted her out, Ginny looked around anxiously again for

Johnny or his father. If she'd seen either of them she'd have changed her mind about accompanying Stern, but they were nowhere to be seen.

To her alarm Stern steered her into the elevator. As the doors closed he boasted, "I wish I could show you the rare fifteenth-century manuscript my family has just donated to the library . . . but I can't. It's under lock and key, where I'd like to put you, pretty one."

Ignore it, Ginny told herself, and any other innuendo. As for the rare manuscript, it was more likely to be from his wife's family than from his.

She still smiled as sweetly as she could and he took her arm as the elevator stopped and they emerged in a lofty, badly lit hall.

"Where are we?"

"On the way, on the way. Don't worry, I know where I'm going." He stumbled and Ginny realized for the first time that Stern was loaded.

"So, Madame Designer, did you make that pretty dress you're wearing, or should I say not wearing?"

"My name's Ginny Walker, Mr. Stern. Yes, I did . . . it's from my latest collection and I'd love to show you . . ." She paused as he ran his hand over her bare shoulder, threading his fingers through one of the silk straps.

As they took a few steps, Ginny became acclimated to the dim light, and saw to her relief they were not alone. At the far end of the long hall two men seemed to be arguing, one man tall, slim, dark, gesticulating wildly to the other who was much shorter, his face hidden in shadow.

There was something familiar about the tall man, something terribly familiar about the way he moved, his posture . . . it couldn't possibly be and yet . . . Ginny forgot about Stern, forgot about everything. "Alex?" She thought she was shouting, but the name came out in a nervous whisper. She tried again, louder but not much, "Alex, is that you?" She started forward, her breath coming in gasps.

"Not so fast, young lady." Stern used the silk strap to pull her back, then pushed her so violently into an alcove that she knocked her head sharply against the stone wall. As the strap snapped, Stern's knee pinioned her to the wall, and he became wild, ripping open her décolletage, covering her mouth with his, his hands everywhere. She didn't stand a chance. He was as strong as an ox and he didn't waste any time, unzipping his fly, yanking the blush dress farther down her body.

Dazed, in shock, unable to scream, Ginny was almost down on the floor, when there was a violent crash. Stern sprang back, releasing his hold. As she let out a piercing scream, it was joined by another from somebody else and both she and Stern turned to see the two men fiercely fighting. A gunshot echoed through the hall. In disbelief she and Stern watched as the two men grappled over the balustrade and one man pushed the other over, to smash on the floor below.

It all happened in seconds. Ginny saw the tall, slim man run and disappear from view. Clutching her torn silk dress around her, she struggled to her feet, sure Stern was still about to rape her; but he, disheveled, his trousers agape, seemed befuddled, leaning against the balustrade to stare down below.

Ginny quickly looked down, too. A guard appeared, then another, followed by a small group in evening dress. People started to scream. There were yells for help. Both guards looked up to the upper floor.

Fast, she had to get away fast. Ginny ran to the end of the hall, tripping over her torn dress, tearing it more. Any minute she expected Alex to appear. There was blood on the floor. She started to retch, but fear gave her a manic energy.

Where had he gone . . . the tall, slim man who moved like Alex? Her question was easily answered. There was a narrow door, slightly open, otherwise she wouldn't have seen it, set flush with the wall. Shivering, Ginny opened it farther to see an iron stairwell, fire-exit steps. Far below she could hear somebody clambering down.

"Alex!" This time her cry came out loud, clear.

The scurrying stopped. Was someone looking up at her? The murderer. Who was it? The cousin she had adored or a dangerous stranger? He could be one and the same person. She knew her face was clearly illuminated by a single bulb just inside the doorway, but below, the face that could see hers was obscured in shadow.

She heard a door creak open, then slam shut. Whoever it was had gone. Something familiar she'd just now seen in the shadows tugged at her memory. What was it? She was too hysterical to think straight.

She hesitated, half in, half out of the doorway, as the whole hall was flooded with light. Arthur Stern was where she'd left him, slumped against the wall, wiping his mouth free of her lipstick.

To her horror he straightened up, and started to stagger toward her. "Come back here, Madame Designer," he yelled. "Come back, you little slut . . ."

As he approached the end of the hall, he stopped. She saw him bend down. He picked up a gun, the gun which had fired the shot. Was he going to threaten her with it now?

Terrified, she stepped inside the doorway and shut the door behind her. Immediately the light went out. She ran her hand over the door. There was a latch. She fastened it. She would wait inside—for hours if she had to—until she was sure Stern had gone, but even as she cowered in the dark, she heard voices, Arthur Stern's loudest of all, angry, accusing.

She had to get away before anyone found her and asked her to explain what had happened. How could she explain? Who would believe that Arthur Stern, such a pillar of American society, and married to one of the richest women in the country, had attempted to rape her? No one would believe her. How could she explain what she was doing in a darkened corridor with a married man anyway? She couldn't explain it to herself. Above all, how could she make Johnny understand, Johnny who already was ashamed of her? Whatever danger awaited her below was preferable to public exposure now.

Footsteps were getting closer. There was no alternative. She had to go down the stairwell in the dark. She slipped off her stiletto sandals and, clinging to the wall, began her descent, the rough iron grating of the stairs cutting through her hose. With every step she expected to hear the door above being broken down, to be hauled back and publicly humiliated, but she didn't stop until she reached the bottom. She caught her breath. Silence.

She groped until she found the door that had creaked and slammed to signal the murderer's getaway. But had he gotten away or was he waiting there to deal with her, the one person he knew had witnessed his crime? Here came the creak as she carefully opened the door, holding on to it so it didn't slam.

Where was she? In the basement of the giant old building, where once upon an innocent time she'd fetched and carried for *Vogue*'s centennial party. A solitary dim lightbulb hung in the corridor stretching ahead. Was anyone waiting for her in the shadows?

"I regret to inform you that a tragic accident has occurred. One of our guests has been found dead, apparently as a result of a fall from an upper floor."

Johnny was looking at his father as the president of the library was making the shocking announcement. Even listening to such awful news, Johnny noted with irritation that his father, who had joined the table only a few moments before, didn't seem at all surprised. It would be just like the old man to know what had happened before, if not as soon as, the president. To his increasing uneasiness he saw his father whisper in a flirtatious way to the stylish woman on his left, one of the younger members of the library's board of trustees.

"Because of the unusual circumstances," the president continued, "I regret to inform you that we will have to curtail service of the dinner, and the after-dinner entertainment has, also regrettably, had to be canceled."

What the hell was going on? How could anyone fall to their death at the library? Had someone dived over the balustrade to commit suicide? Johnny tried to catch his father's eye, without success. He was too busy gulping down the salmon in front of him as if he was never going to be fed again.

"I have to ask you all to remain seated. I will be able to make another announcement shortly."

The president left the room and everybody began to speak at once. Johnny leaned across the table. "What's going on, Dad?"

"Perhaps a great story for your gossip column, Johnny, important man falls from balcony and breaks his neck." Quentin Peet rolled his eyes in such an exaggerated way, other guests shook their heads, trying not to laugh.

He put up a hand, his face now grave. Everyone, including a fuming Johnny, waited on his words. "In fact, a tragedy has occurred. I was told about it just seconds before I joined you. I'm afraid we're not talking about an accident here. It seems a murder has taken place . . . a murder of a most distinguished man."

"Good evening, sir, I'm Detective Petersh, this is Detective Reever, Manhattan Homicide. We'd like to ask you a few questions."

"I've already answered enough goddamn questions. I want to go home." From a chair in the library's Trustees Room, mutinous, belligerent, his breath belching alcohol fumes, his clothing still untidily buttoned, Arthur Stern growled at the two new arrivals.

Forty-five minutes had passed since two security guards had found first the bloodied corpse and then a befuddled, apparently drunk Arthur Stern, unaccountably on the third floor, from where it appeared the victim had been pushed to his death. As the guards told the first police officer on the scene, Stern had behaved in a threatening manner when they tried to find out what he was doing there.

When the president of the library was summoned, he hastily identified Stern as a generous benefactor, and took the responsibility of moving him to the greater comfort of the Trustees Room to await further instructions.

The two detectives, who'd dealt with hundreds of "D'you-know-who-I-am" blustering Stern types in the course of their lengthy careers, politely and firmly went through what Stern had admitted to the police officer.

"You say you went before dinner to the third floor, because you were looking for somewhere quiet, somewhere away from the party, where you could discuss some business with a new young designer . . ."

Stern, staring down at the floor, nodded.

"You chose that particular floor because you knew you would be undisturbed there. You are well acquainted with the area, because of the rare manuscript your family recently donated to the library. Is that correct?" Petersh sounded pleasant, respectful.

Stern looked up, stopped glowering, and pompously said, "That is correct."

"The problem is you can't remember the young woman's name?"

"Why the hell should I remember every bit of skirt who thinks she's gonna be the next Donna Karan. I see dozens and dozens of 'em a week. This girl was wearing something interesting. I'd met her before. She'd been after me to invest. I was bored . . . she kept bothering me . . . throwing herself at me . . . you know . . . I thought I'd give her a few minutes." Stern gave the detectives a sly look to see if they understood what he was insinuating.

Petersh's manner remained pleasant, respectful. "When you were discussing business, you both became aware of an altercation, a disagreement going on at the end of the hall?"

"Yes, yes," Stern said eagerly. "Two men were fighting, shouting, God knows what about."

"Can you describe the men?"

"No, the hall was pretty dark. One was tall. Oh, I don't know. They were at the end—well, you know what one of 'em looks like now." Stern tried a sick grin. There was no response. "Who was he, anyway?"

"Confirmation of identification has not yet been made. What happened next?"

"Well, this young chick got nervous . . . wait a minute." He frowned. "I seem to remember she called out something . . . she seemed to know one of them . . . no, scratch that. I don't remember. Anyway, suddenly a gun went off and the next thing we know one guy is pushing the other over the rails."

"What did you do?"

"There was nothing I could do. I looked down and saw the body crash on the floor. The other guy disappeared—"

"And the girl?"

"The girl?" Stern repeated listlessly.

"Yes, the girl, Mr. Stern, the young designer, where did she go?"

"I don't know. She disappeared, too."

"What did she look like?"

"Dark . . . she was dark . . . skinny. No boobs." Again he shot a sly look at Petersh. "Tall and skinny, not my type."

"And you don't remember her name?"

"No, it's damned stupid, but it's just slipped my memory."

"I think we can help you with that. Here's a list of all the guests attending tonight's dinner to remind you."

Stern snatched the list from the detective's hand. "This is an insult to intelligence. How can I go through all these bloody names. It'll take me to doomsday. I've got a sick wife at home."

"Would you like to call her?"

"No, I wouldn't like to call her," Stern snarled. "And wake her up? And have to listen to her complaints of selfishness for the rest of the week?" He fell silent, running his finger down the list from A to Z. "The name's not here," he said finally.

"Not there or you can't remember?"

There was a long pause. "The name's not on the list. I'd remember it if I saw it, wouldn't I?" He looked at the list again. "Either it's not there or I can't remember."

"I understand from the security guards that when they first saw you on the third floor, Mr. Stern, you were attempting to fasten your fly. Were you making out with somebody's wife or girlfriend, Mr. Stern? Did her boyfriend or husband catch you? Did you have to fight for your life?" The respectful note had disappeared from Petersh's voice.

"How dare you! I'll get you fired for this . . . this insolence, you cretin. I've had enough. I'm going home but I warn you I'm going to file a complaint through my lawyer in the morning. You haven't heard the end of this." Stern stood up glaring, pushing the chair away so violently that it rocked back on its legs and banged against the desk.

The two detectives also stood up. "I'm afraid that isn't going to be possible, Mr. Stern. There's a lot to be cleared up here. We are going to have to ask you to accompany us for more questioning."

Stern paled and wilted. "Why? What can I tell you you don't already know? This is terrible. I must call my lawyer at once."

"Certainly, Mr. Stern. I want to advise you of your rights. You have the right to remain silent and to refuse to answer questions. Anything that you do say tonight may be used against you later in a court of law, do you understand that?"

Stern closed his eyes. The detective went on, "You have the right to consult with an attorney before you answer our questions and to have an attorney present during this questioning as well as in the future. Do you understand that?"

Some of his bluster came back. "Damn right I do. Where's that phone?"

Where was she? Johnny's stomach was in knots as he searched for Ginny among the hushed crowd lined up in the Celeste Bartos Forum. His father had already been allowed to leave, but along with most of the other guests, he was still waiting while a couple of police officers checked everyone's names against the invitation list.

He could feel sweat forming on his upper lip as he gave his name. If he looked guilty, he sure as hell felt it. About Ginny. He'd treated her terribly. When his father told him who the victim was, he'd felt worse, terrified that in some way Ginny may have been involved, because she made clothes for the flashy blonde, but he was being ridiculous. They had a suspect, a surprising suspect, and as soon as he knew Ginny was safe and sound at home, without any urging from his father, thank you very much, he would be on his way downtown to get on the case.

At last, he was out in the fresh air. There was a cab. Should he take it and call in on Ginny first? The thought of arriving and not finding her there was too depressing. On the corner there was a phone in working order.

She answered on the third ring.

"Ginny, thank God you're there. When did you get home? D'you know what happened? Are you okay?" He sounded like a schoolkid, one word tripping over another, but he didn't care. She was safe, that was all that mattered.

"Noooo, what happened? I've been home about an hour." She sounded nervous. No wonder, with his frantic inquiries.

"Svank, your friend the industrialist, was shot, pushed over the library balcony, smashed—"

"What! My God!" It was worse than she could have possibly imagined. "Is he de—?"

"Dead as the dodo, either before or after the two hundred pounds of him smashed all over the library floor. Now I know you're okay, I'm going down to the precinct. They've taken Muriel Stern's husband there for questioning. What a night!"

Ginny thought she was going to be sick. "Muriel Stern," she repeated.

"Yes, she's the fainting billionairess, the only one with a bodyguard who's also a cardiac specialist. Her husband's a jerk, but according to Dad"—he made a face as he spoke—"he had a major falling-out with Svank some time ago and is well known to have loathed him . . ."

Silence. Ginny was shaking so much, she almost dropped the phone.

"Are you still there, you silly little Ginny?" Johnny's voice was tender. He'd forgiven her for her stupidity—for now.

"Did . . . the . . . did the dinner go on? Did your father have a good time?"

"And did you enjoy the play, Mrs. Lincoln?" Johnny shook his head, laughing. What a crazy, kooky girl. "You can imagine how I felt about you when the police were counting heads. I was relieved like hell that you weren't there, but worried to death where you'd got to. Promise me you'll stay away from crashing for a while."

"Don't worry." Couldn't he sense her terror through the phone? "Johnny, I think I've got a problem."

Anxiety made him snap. "What?"

"I left my cloak at the library . . . a very special one-of-a-kind cloak I made hoping to impress you and your—"

"Oh, God, Ginny, I don't believe it. How could you do a thing like that? Of course, no one will claim it—"

She started to cry.

"Don't, Ginny, don't. We'll work it out. Did anyone see you arriving in it?"

"Yes, Oz, the photographer, remember the guy who cut in at the wedding?"

"The one you were so charming to? Well, that's a big help. It certainly means the end of your days as a crasher, but after tonight that's not too bad a fate. I just can't think how you could have left it behind. How you—" He saw a cab across the street. "Look, I've got to go but I'll keep you posted. Go to sleep. I'll come by in the morning . . ."

"With the surprise?"

"Surprise?" He frowned, then remembered he'd told her he had a surprise for her, his plan to take her to the Literary Lions event as a bona fide guest. "No, Ginny," he said. "You blew that."

"What d'you mean?"

"Why d'you think I wanted you all dressed up and waiting for me at six o'clock this evening? Figure it out for yourself." He quietly put the phone down.

She stared into space. He'd planned to take her to the library after all. If only she'd known; if only he'd let her know.

The loft seemed ominously silent and empty. Svank. She couldn't believe it. Svank dead. Had Poppy been there? She hadn't seen her, although she remembered Stern saying he'd seen "Mr. High and Mighty."

She walked backwards and forwards, backwards and forwards across the loft, a horrible realization coming to her. Other than Stern himself, only two people knew he had nothing to do with the murder. She, Ginny Walker, the invisible guest, the crasher—and the real murderer.

Alex. Had it really been Alex in the hallway, fighting with Svank, pushing him over the balustrade to his death? Now she was really going to be sick. She rushed to the bathroom, vomiting.

Afterwards, she stared at the toilet. She lifted the lid of the cistern. The Villeneva jewels were no longer there.

CHAPTER NINE

1A BEEKMAN PLACE, NEW YORK CITY

Muriel Stern, all one hundred and seventy-four pounds of her, was in a terrible rage. To those who really knew her—and few did—it showed in the way she continually puckered up her face as if about to cry (although no one had ever recorded seeing a tear escape from Muriel).

It showed in the increasing speed and noise of her huffing and puffing as she walked, still in her bathrobe, backward and forward, tapping every piece of furniture she encountered, throughout her twenty-two room, L-shaped, hermetically sealed apartment.

The apartment had one of the most spectacular views of the East River, but more important as far as Muriel was concerned, it was situated more or less midway between two of New York's leading medical establishments, New York Hospital to the north and New York University's Tisch Hospital to the south.

Leroy Samson, senior partner of Samson, Kaunitz, Farquahar and Stern (no relation), knew Muriel as well as anyone, including her husband; certainly well enough to know that until Muriel stopped moving and slumped into one of her specially designed orthopedic chairs, he would do best to remain silent while his very important client digested the information he had given her over the telephone at seven A.M., less than half an hour ago that morning.

As her lawyer, executor of her will, unofficial financial advisor and official legal advisor to her family's far-flung conglomerate of fashion and textile businesses, Leroy Samson knew how to remain so silent and still that he would be almost invisible to Muriel, and so he remained for the next fifteen or so minutes.

He was also totally relaxed, an unusual condition for those in Muriel's presence, and a major asset in dealing with her.

Despite the seriousness of the circumstances, Samson even made a little bet with himself that as agitated as Muriel appeared to be, she was probably timing her perambulations, in order that they could substitute for the daily twenty-minute cardiovascular treadmill walk she continually complained about, but faithfully carried out in her private gym each morning.

He made another bet, which he had no doubt he would win. It concerned the first words out of her mouth to him, which would not be a greeting, but a familiar wail.

Sure enough, upon her collapsing into the chair came what he had anticipated: "Leroy, what have I done to deserve this?"

Right on cue Samson leapt up and began to stroke Muriel's shoulder as she reclined, body shuddering, eyes closed, saying soothingly as he stroked, "Nothing, my dear, absolutely nothing, but you must not work yourself up so much; you must think of yourself, the company. It is obviously a preposterous mistake, which will be corrected as soon as possible."

Because of Muriel's well-known "precarious health," Samson knew that she and Arthur Stern slept in separate rooms at opposite ends of the vast apartment. He also knew that Muriel kept to a regular bedtime of ten-thirty—except on very special occasions (invitations to the White House, for instance).

It was for both those reasons he'd decided not to wake her the night before when he'd first been wakened himself to learn of her husband's arrest. She wouldn't know Arthur hadn't come home till their also well-advertised regular-as-clockwork eight A.M. breakfast. Tossing and turning during an almost sleepless night, he'd correctly guessed the morning would come soon enough.

With her eyes still closed, but her voice firm and authoritative, Muriel asked, "Have you called Morgenthau? What did he say?"

It was typical of the woman that she expected him to have already contacted the New York district attorney. Other people, whoever they were, could be called at any hour of the day or night. Only Muriel's "do-not-disturb" edict could not be violated. Because the district attorney and his talented Pulitzer prize-winning wife had also dined with the Sterns, Samson knew Muriel would take it absolutely for granted that the D.A. would get busy on her husband's behalf and move to dismiss the charges.

"I'm sure he's well aware of the facts," Samson began in the same soothing voice. "I gave a very clear message to Matthew Mossop—"

"Who's he?"

Samson hesitated, knowing he'd made a mistake. It was no use fudging a title with Muriel. She was like a dog with a bone over details. "He's a good man, chief of the trial division and in close touch with the D.A."

Muriel opened her eyes, fixing them on the lawyer. "Trial," she repeated incredulously as if hearing the word for the first time. "Then if you've explained who Arthur is, and who he is married to, why isn't Arthur here, home with me now? How dare they stop him coming home? Where did you say he was?"

He was well used to Muriel's playing dumb. It never paid to let her get away with it. He had told her over the phone where her husband was and she never forgot a thing. Now was the time to tell her what was in store.

"As you will recall from our conversation this morning, Arthur was held"—he paused, rephrasing the sentence so as not to make another mistake—"was asked to spend the night for further questioning at the midtown south precinct. He has to appear at eleven o'clock before Judge Imiouse and—"

"Isn't that the greedy Greek appointed by Giuliani, the one who used to work for you, and so for us?"

Samson inwardly sighed. "His second or third cousin, I believe. Arthur will, of course, plead not guilty and I am confident—"

Muriel let out a short, shrill scream. "I can't believe the words I'm hearing under my own roof about my own husband. Trial! Not guilty! Of course, Arthur isn't guilty. He's too gutless to swat a fly." Again her face puckered up. "Of course, it would have to be the loathsome Svank who finally bit the dust. Arthur and he never got on and, you know"— she glared at Samson as if it was his fault—"Arthur was fool enough to let everyone know it . . . said Svank insulted him, then typically cut off his nose to save his face and wouldn't supply one of Svank's chains until I got wind of it."

Again she glared at Samson. "At least, thank God, we won't have to put up with reading anymore about Svank climbing to the peaks of whatever trash passes for New York society nowadays. He was shot, you say, then was pushed over the library balcony? Did they find a gun on Arthur? Of course not." She tossed her head in disgust.

Samson hesitated. There was no need at this point to tell Muriel Arthur had actually been found holding the gun. "The papers say it was the fall that killed Svank. No one is talking about a gun at this point."

Muriel moaned and shut her eyes again. "Oh, my God, the papers. Of course, it's in the papers . . . thank God we took the company private again and I don't have to worry about the stock. Is . . . was Arthur mentioned?"

He nodded soberly. There was no way he was going to tell her about the cluster of reporters and TV cameras from New York 1 and other channels already camped outside on Beekman Place. Luckily his driver, an ex-New York cop, had spotted them as they turned the corner, so he'd come into the apartment house the little-known back way he'd used before when plotting a secret business deal. It wouldn't take long for the media vultures to find it, but it wasn't necessary to tell her and so add to her agitation—yet.

Muriel was suddenly all business. "Now I'm fully awake after the rudest awakening in history, let's review the facts. Arthur was in the wrong place at the wrong time, giving advice, he says, to a new fashion designer when he witnessed two men fighting, one of whom fell to his death—Svank. The name of this young designer escapes him, and there appears to be no such person present at the library willing to corroborate his story. I'm not surprised the police don't buy it, but it's probably true."

Muriel gave Samson the smile he liked to see the least. "Why else would he be on a deserted floor, so far away from the party, giving advice I'm sure to a young, probably blonde bimbo who wouldn't know a pattern from a paper bag. Perhaps a night enjoying the hospitality of the New York police precinct isn't such a bad idea for Arthur after all. It may have even done him some good. We both know Arthur can be a fool. It's got him into trouble before, but nothing like this."

She crossed her arms the way she did in the boardroom before delivering a question to which she expected the answer she wanted to hear. "So what comes next?"

Samson was ready. "I've already asked Caulter—William Caulter—to represent Arthur at the arraignment this morning. He's the best defense lawyer there is. There's no question in my mind that Arthur will be released on bail, and Caulter and I will see that this terrible situation is resolved and brought to a speedy conclusion, with Arthur's reputation as an outstanding member of the community untarnished and—"

"Spare me the sanctimonious slop." Muriel spat the words out.

Although he didn't show it, Samson was furious. Despite his lack of experience in a criminal court, he felt he had every justification for saying what he had just said. He meant every word, for it was ludicrous to think of a man like Stern committing a murder, or indeed, even getting into a physical fight. Muriel was right. Arthur was gutless.

Once the facts were presented and evaluated in the cool light of day, the not guilty plea entered and bail set, he was confident Caulter with his pack of ex-FBI guys would speedily make mincemeat of the prosecution's circumstantial case and he'd happily help the Sterns sue the city for millions for so quickly making an arrest.

All the same, when he'd called Caulter after seeing Arthur the night before, Caulter hadn't taken the matter lightly. He'd made it perfectly clear then, and again around five-thirty that morning, that the climate for the D.A. to pursue a case involving a "big shot" was dangerously ripe, because of recent accusations in the media of "light sentences" when "money talks."

The gun Arthur was holding, which, it turned out, belonged to Svank, was a major problem; and as Caulter had explained convincingly, the police would never have arrested someone like Arthur unless they felt they had enough evidence for the D.A.'s office. That was the reason the D.A.'s "riding desk"—the all-night mobile unit—had been contacted the night before, and a young assistant D.A. dispatched to question Arthur further.

Arthur's rude stonewalling and sticking to the designer story had only firmed up their decision to go ahead.

In Caulter's opinion the D.A.'s office would proceed quickly with a prima facie case because of the identity of the victim, Svank, one of the country's biggest industrialists.

"There'll be plenty of pressure to get a quick conviction on this one," Caulter had said languidly as the new day finally dawned. Hearing Samson sigh, he'd added quickly, "Don't worry, Sam, it won't fly."

Now Muriel was growling, "It all depends what kind of bail they want. Perhaps letting Arthur stew may finally teach him a lesson he'll never forget."

Samson couldn't believe what he was hearing. He knew Muriel was a tyrannical despot, a formidable businesswoman, but talking about allowing her husband to "stew" when accused of murder! It was inconceivable.

He wasn't going to put up with it. "This isn't a matter of letting Arthur stew for a misdemeanor, Muriel," he said sharply. "Murder is a serious accusation. Of course, we know Arthur didn't do it, isn't capable of any such thing, but we can't let him 'stew,' as you put it. We have to fight with everything in our power—"

Muriel cut across him. "What do they base their case on?"

"A prima facie case, one based on adequate evidence to establish a fact or raise a presumption of fact until refuted. We have to get it thrown out before an indictment, and never let up for one second to show how weak their case is . . . ."

Now was the moment to tell Muriel what—he agreed with Caulter—she had to do. Although he felt more repulsed by her than at any other time in their long relationship, Samson forced himself to stroke her still-shaking shoulder for a few more minutes before looking at her directly and saying, "It will help, Muriel dear, if you show your support for Arthur and, of course, your total belief in his innocence, as soon as possible. First, I want to release a statement from you." He unfolded a single sheet of paper from his inside pocket and put it on the table beside her. "Here is a draft I prepared this morning."

She glared at him without moving, but he wasn't deterred. "Caulter and I agree it is vitally important you be seen with Arthur, giving him your full support." He used a childish habit and crossed his fingers before continuing. "As soon as Arthur is released on bail—"

There was another short, shrill scream. "You want to kill me, too! Doesn't Caulter know—"

"He knows about your condition, Muriel," Samson snapped. "We have two suggestions. I can bring Arthur to my office following the preliminary hearing, where you can be reunited and appear together at a brief—very brief—press conference, or you can be seen welcoming Arthur home here—in the lobby on his return."

When Muriel looked at him first with shock, then with loathing,

Samson held up his hand, repeating, "Caulter and I think it is extremely important for your support to be highly visible. In other words, let me say your absence—and silence—would be noted, commented upon, and construed as wishing to distance yourself from the accused, whereas a loving, supportive wife seen accompanying her husband with dignity and confidence through this terrible ordeal, certain of his total exoneration, can only be valuable for everyone concerned . . ." He paused effectively. "Including Stern Fashion and Textiles, Incorporated."

There was an embarrassingly long silence, as Samson expected there would be. Muriel looked around, searching for something. Without a word Samson brought her walking stick to her. She took more long minutes to get out of the chair, only to proceed to another one facing out over the East River. Finally, she said coldly, "You know my health situation—I don't want to put myself at risk, but I suppose I must accept your advice that it could look"—another long pause—"suspicious if I'm not anywhere to be seen."

Another silence. "The board—the building—would never permit such a circus . . . 'welcoming Arthur home on his return,' " she mimicked sarcastically.

"You're the chairman of the building's board," Samson said quietly, as if she needed reminding how often the board had been putty in her hands. In any case he knew exactly what she would choose to do. For all her protestations about going anywhere, he knew Muriel loved being the center of attention, providing she was in situations she could control.

Sure enough, she now acted as if the decision were already made. She would meet Arthur at his office for a brief, strictly controlled press conference. "Of course, David will have to go with me . . . have you called him?"

David Sorenson was, at the moment, her favorite cardiologist.

"Yes, I took the liberty of informing him this morning." Irritated by the charade that was dragging on for too long, Samson couldn't resist adding, "He thought I might call. He heard about it all on television last night—there was a news flash after *Nightline*."

She ignored him, looking at her watch, then pressing the bell on the arm of the chair. A maid appeared instantly. (Samson often wondered if one was detailed to hover outside any closed door, for once summoned, servants always immediately responded.)

"Tell Absley to arrange to pick up Dr. Sorenson and bring him here no later than eleven o'clock." Muriel looked over to the piece of paper on the table. "Let me look at that statement."

She took several minutes to peruse it, but he had no fears she'd hold up its release. From a lifetime of preparing documents for Stern, Inc., first under the direction of Muriel's elder brother (now deceased) and then Muriel, Samson knew exactly the language to use.

Muriel nodded her approval as she handed the statement back. "Now help me back to my room. I must get some rest." She pressed the bell again and when the maid opened the door, announced, "I'll wear the gray pinstripe."

Slowly she got to her feet. "If I went to the arraignment, would I be able to see Arthur before he goes before the judge?"

Samson inwardly shuddered, thinking of the squalor and turmoil of the criminal court at 100 Centre Street, swarming with hookers and pushers and pimps, the dregs of society, a place likely to give anyone a heart attack, let alone someone like Muriel. "That would not be wise, and in any case the answer is probably no."

"Make sure the oxygen is in the trunk," was Muriel's last command as she made a slow exit out of the drawing room. "This is just the kind of day when I'm going to need it."

Quentin Peet entered the Woolworth Building at 233 Broadway as if he owned it. He was a man in a hurry today, with an agenda that would have defeated most mortals, but there was nothing harried about his movements. He still had time to cast an approving eye at the intricate mosaics of the soaring vaulted ceiling as well as to give a brief nod of recognition to the men on duty at the information desk. They were both ex-cops, pleased to be acknowledged by the celebrated journalist, who was revered in their world for his contribution to fighting crime.

It wasn't surprising they were ex-cops. One only had to look at the directory on the wall to see that the building was full of police-associated organizations, from the CEA, the Captains' Endowment Association, to the SBA, Sergeants' Benevolent Association, to the SOC, Superior Officers Council.

What most people didn't know was what went on in the giant building's underground. Reached by a subterranean tunnel with many tunnel tributaries of its own was "Harry's at the Woolworth," a restaurant that was the literal watering hole for anybody who was anybody in law enforcement.

It was in Harry's restaurant, in dark corners and alcoves, that favors were exchanged, IOUs granted and honored between high-ranking members of the police department, the D.A.'s office, the FBI, and the CIA.

Some said more police business was conducted there than at One Police Plaza; and not for nothing had it been renamed long ago by its habitués "Corregidor," reminding many World War II veterans of the fortress of tunnels carved out of the island rock in the Philippines.

Peet was one of the few journalists, if not the only one, who didn't quickly empty the huge U-shaped bar on his arrival, and he was proud of the distinction. The press wasn't wanted here and there was no attempt to conceal it. If Peet wasn't welcomed with open arms, at least he was treated like everyone else, with studied indifference, everyone minding their own business, usually business of a very special kind.

While gratified that among this tough crowd he was known as a man who would always keep his mouth shut, he was sure he'd earned the privilege to witness who was trading with whom, adding two and two together to sum up a situation accurately after a lifetime spent on the front line.

As he moved into the room he waved to the police C.O./O.M.A, Commanding Officer of the Office of Management and Analysis, in a huddle with a deputy from the mayor's office; smiled, but shook his head "no" at a Special Agent from the Federal Bureau who, leaning at the bar, indicated he'd like to buy him a drink. He moved purposefully past the main dining room, where other tunnels burrowed their way to other smaller dining areas.

On the way he made eye contact with the man he'd arranged to meet, Patrick O'Neill, who with his crow-black sleek hair, olive skin and dapper, tight-fitting, but well-tailored suits looked more like the quintessential Latin lover than "just a poor Irish lad who got lucky," as he often referred to himself.

Nobody could remember if or when O'Neill had been poor, but to his detractors—and there were many—he'd certainly been lucky. As the recently named Commanding Officer of the Major Case Squad, part of the Special Investigation Division at Police Headquarters, O'Neill was resented for treading on other people's turf and, worse, getting better results. In that division there was plenty of turf to tread on, from the Special Fraud Squad to the Joint Robbery Task Force, the Safe, Loft and Truck Squad, not to mention the Missing Persons Squad.

For Peet there couldn't be a more valuable contact in the NYPD. Over the years each had seen the other score and bypass those so busy worrying about their egos, they'd missed some obvious professional chances to move ahead.

One reason they'd got on so well for so long was the way they conducted business. Neither man expected the other to volunteer much, if any, major information. The main object of every meeting was to receive either confirmation or rejection of information one or the other already possessed. Rarely was it greeted with a shrug of the shoulders "don't-know." Their meetings invariably saved them an inordinate amount of what they valued most—time—precluding false trails, setups and booby traps.

Once O'Neill joined Peet in an alcove far away from the main crowd, a waiter came by to place the usual tub of cheese and crackers on the table. Both men ordered a beer.

Cutting a chunk of cheese, with no conversational preamble, Peet began, "Pat, m'boy, I gather the Villeneva jewels haven't surfaced yet, and the theft remains on the unsolved list."

"Yep," said O'Neill, plunging a knife into the cheese tub to get his own piece.

"And it still looks like the work of the new guy on the team?"

"Yep."

"But so far no sign of the jewels being used for collateral?"

O'Neill shook his head. "Not sure that particular heist fitted the big picture."

"Could Stern in any shape or form fit the big picture?"

O'Neill rolled his eyes as he took a huge bite of cheese.

"A man can have more than one kind of enemy," Peet said softly.

"Damn right, particularly an ice skater like Svank. Pity."

O'Neill didn't need to explain himself. Peet knew Svank had been skating on thin ice, yet he'd been so cunning, so incredibly skillful, even as pieces of the labyrinthine puzzle of his criminal activities had slowly been fitting into place, he'd managed to distance himself from the underworld it was now believed he'd totally controlled. With his death he'd escaped forever from paying the penalty and public disgrace O'Neill and others had sought for him for so long.

"Pity indeed," Peet repeated, then, "Stern was arraigned this morning, out on a couple of million bail, right?"

"Right—after an almost successful plea to dismiss and file a new document."

"Unbelievable. With his fingers, not only his fingerprints on the trigger, he's lucky to get bail. Caulter's the best and Stern's not talking, on his advice. I hear Caulter might try for manslaughter. It wasn't the gun that killed Svank, right? It was the fall?"

"Where d'you hear that?" O'Neill smiled, knowing he'd never get a straight answer.

"Oh, around and about. It was a fight, Svank pulled a gun, it went off accidentally, a freak shot or something. The bullet ricocheted off the floor into his foot; in the struggle he lost his balance and Stern's push at the wrong moment pushed him over the edge . . . or rather, somebody's push."

When O'Neill didn't answer, Peet sipped his beer reflectively. "I hear the assistant D.A.'s are wetting their pants to get this one . . ."

"That's the fault of people like you, Big Q," O'Neill said with his lopsided grin. "If you didn't show 'em how it's done with your multimillion dollar book and movie deals and your name in the gossip columns with beautiful dames, they wouldn't have such big ideas about life after Centre Court."

Peet grimaced as he knew he was expected to. "I wish! That's a lot of bullshit. But I don't think Stern did it, although it's just possible. In any case Caulter's guys will work like crazy to delay the indictment on lack of evidence. They'll probably help lead you straight to the slippery light-fingered guy, the one from London we know that Svank loved to hate."

"We'll be watching."

"So will I." Peet took another sip of his beer. "It's catching, this collateral business. As I think you may know, Angel Face Maniero confessed in court last week he'd not only stolen the loot from Padua Cathedral, but Vivarini's *Madonna and Child* from the Ducal Palace in Venice. Can you believe it? To use both as plea-bargaining chips, he admitted, should he ever be arrested; claimed he made a deal with the head of the Italian Art Squad. Bad timing for them . . . they'd just announced the successful recovery of some other invaluable stuff from Rome. Now everyone wonders what they had to promise the thieves to get it back."

"Yep, works of art and big jewels have become the currency du jour, particularly in the drug trade. Once they've found their way to professional art handlers, we know they're being traded all over the place—at a discount—in every kind of criminal deal, for counterfeit notes, loans, for anything they can raise, but more and more for shipments of drugs or the setting up of new drug distributors."

"Glad the DEA's got Constantine. Operation Dinero seems to be working—"

"No thanks to Svank."

"Didn't the DEA guys stumble into a haul in Atlanta recently? A Picasso, a Rubens and some other masterpiece being traded for cash for cocaine?"

O'Neill nodded somberly.

"It doesn't sound like the kind of thing Stern would be involved in, but you never know. Always the least one you'd suspect. Remember that asshole Delchetto? Who would have thought after all he'd written that he was actually being paid off by Cali, but he got too greedy." Peet looked at O'Neill intently for his reaction.

"That hasn't been proved. I think Delchetto was a good guy who made a fatal slip."

"That's not what I hear from the DEA." Peet paused, then added casually, "from Ben Abbott . . ."

O'Neill didn't react and there was silence as both men drank their beer, then, "That reminds me," O'Neill said hesitantly, never sure exactly of the relationship between father and son, "I hear Johnny is following in his old man's footsteps at last."

"What d'you mean?"

To O'Neill's surprise and embarrassment, he saw something he'd never seen before on the old warrior's face, an angry red flush.

"I thought you'd know. Didn't you see his cover piece on Delchetto?"

"No, I only got back a day or so ago . . . in time for the library fiasco, and we obviously didn't have time to catch up that night. What's he been up to?"

Although Peet was doing his best to conceal it, O'Neill could see he was disturbed.

He sighed. "Johnny was in Puerto Rico for the magazine when Delchetto got taken out. Seems he's been working with the Art Loss Register, collecting quite a dossier on stolen goods. He was following a lead linking the Villeneva job to the drug trade operating down there, but the trail went cold with Delchetto's disappearance."

"For the magazine! But he's a muck peddler, a gossip columnist. What the hell was—"

"One of the DEA boys told me he was on special assignment. I didn't see the story myself, but I hear it was right on target," O'Neill added defensively.

As Peet drummed his fingers on the table, looking stony-faced, O'Neill cursed himself for opening his mouth. It was ironic, for although his old friend had complained in the past about Johnny not getting anywhere, and wasting his time on superficial rubbish, he obviously didn't want him anywhere near his turf. He could hardly believe he'd actually live to see the day when Quentin Peet, the high-and-mighty, much-decorated journalist, showed he had an Achilles' heel. It was unfortunate it seemed to be his one and only son.

"He never told me. I guess the boy was out to impress me. I had no idea . . . but then I don't keep in touch with him as much as I obviously should. He never told me," Peet repeated, looking at O'Neill ruefully. "Frankly, Pat, the thought of Johnny even putting a toe in that filthy sewer worries me more than I ever realized it would. Glad you told me. You say the trail went cold?"

Although he'd recovered his composure, there was still something in Peet's demeanor and tone of voice that worried O'Neill. He hoped he hadn't opened up a can of worms for Johnny, but it was too late to tell Peet to forget it.

"The trail went cold, so he obviously concentrated on Delchetto's disappearance, which is what his cover story was about."

Peet shook his head. "I'm certainly not going to help him get back on the trail. I'll have to think of a way to get him to forget about cover stories."

"And back to trash? That doesn't sound like you. What about all that stuff I seem to remember you wanted to instill in Johnny? About having the greatest respect for anyone willing to risk their own life for principle, honor, justice, et cetera?"

"Principle be damned. I guess my paternal instinct has kicked in at last."

"Too late, QP, much too late."

"We'll see about that."

Again O'Neill felt uneasy seeing the look on Peet's face. It was time to bring their meeting to an end. He beckoned the waiter for the check, saying, "Well, keep in touch if you hear before I do what Caulter's guys turn up."

As the check arrived Peet grabbed it. "I will. I'm sure they'll lead us—you," he corrected himself, "to the collateral thief. The way Muriel Stern's money works, it may not take so long."

"MYSTERY WOMAN'S CLOAK."
"WHO WORE THIS CLOAK AT THE MURDER SCENE?"

Esme had just arrived at the loft in the late afternoon with the *Daily News* and the *New York Post*. Tense, she watched Ginny read both front-page stories. The *Post* had a glimpse of her back view, just before she'd taken the cloak off in the line for the cloakroom, but that was all it was, a glimpse. Lucky for her, they'd been more interested in the perpetual party-goer Blaine Trump, who, it was noted in the caption, had been standing behind her.

The *News* went one better. They had a similar view of her back, but in an inset ran a close-up of the Napoleonic gold laurel leaf collar. On page three they had another shot of what they called the "artful" embroidered imperial bees on the hem. Thinking for a second of the source of the embroidery—the decrepit sofa from the flea market—Ginny suppressed a hysterical laugh. If they only knew how artful.

"What's going on, Ginny? How did you leave your cloak behind? Why on earth haven't you told anyone it belongs to you?" Esme's face was creased in wrinkles of worry.

Ginny wasn't surprised. She hadn't returned one of Esme's three phone calls, although she'd been sitting by the phone waiting, praying to hear from Alex—or Johnny.

She should have known Esme wouldn't give up. She'd arrived downstairs, saying through the intercom, "I know you're there, Ginny. I just know you're in some kind of trouble and I'm not leaving until you let me in."

Now Ginny was glad she had. She'd been talking to herself for hours and it hadn't gotten her anywhere near a solution. She was bursting to tell someone that, of course, Arthur Stern had nothing to do with Svank's death, but how could she talk without implicating herself, announcing to the world—and the real murderer—who the mystery woman was. That is, if the murderer needed to be told.

Did he? If the real killer was who she thought he was, he didn't need to be told about the mystery woman—he even had the key to her loft.

After Johnny's call she hadn't slept at all, returning again and again to the tormenting thought that the shadowy man in the hallway and at the bottom of the stairwell had been Alex. Her mother's words kept coming back to haunt her. "He's not who you think he is. He's a monster."

Suddenly Esme's look of concern and the sweet tone of her voice were too much to bear. Ginny put her face in her hands and wept.

"Oh, Gin, please don't, there, there. I can help. Don't keep it to yourself. What can I do? Can Ted do anything? Is it something to do with Johnny?" Esme fluttered around, trying to hug her as Ginny got up, sat down, then got up again. Once more Ginny had a hysterical impulse to laugh, thinking how ludicrous they must look, with Esme so short and she so tall.

"Don't you realize, by not claiming the cloak, you're likely to get implicated in this terrible murder business?" Esme was saying earnestly. "Who would have dreamed something like this could happen to Poppy's sugar daddy?"

It was enough to stop her tears. "He was no sugar daddy," Ginny snapped. "He was a tyrant, a devil."

"Oh, Gin," Esme sighed. "I know you're keeping something from me. If you can't tell me everything, at least tell me something to stop us both going crazy. You know I'll never tell. I never have, have I? If you rushed off and left your cloak behind at the library because you had a fight with Johnny, perhaps I can think of something to bring him to his senses."

Dear Esme. If only she was concealing a lovesick problem with Johnny. If only she was living a normal life like Esme and most of her friends. If only, instead of trying to crash her way to success during the last couple of years, she'd concentrated on settling down, getting married to a nine-to-five guy, having children, living in the suburbs, worried only about getting fat and saving enough to send the kids to college.

But she wasn't like anyone she knew. For months she'd lived like a felon, terrified that someone might discover Alex's cache of jewels, and now things were much worse. Svank had been murdered the same night she'd discovered the jewels had been removed—definite proof that Alex had returned to town. To settle a score with Svank? To recoup his investment?

Esme little knew how well she was putting it, except she was already up to her ears in this "terrible murder business."

In the tiny kitchen, as she made some coffee, Esme repeated, "Why don't you just go and claim your cloak, then you can tell the papers you designed it and get a lot of publicity and—"

The shrill ring of the phone made both girls jump. Ginny could feel her face flushing scarlet. If it were Alex, what could she do? There was nowhere in the loft to have a private conversation. On the fourth ring, the answering machine picked up.

As soon as Ginny heard Johnny's voice, she grabbed the receiver, forgetting that because she'd let the machine answer, everything Johnny said would be broadcast into the room. It was too bad that Esme would hear every word, but there was nothing she could do.

"Oh, Johnny, where are you? I've been so worried."

"Why, babe? There's nothing to worry about. I had to fly down to Washington. I never had a chance to ask you if you read my *Next!* piece or tell you anything about what I'm working on, but the trail's hot again because of, believe it or not, old man Svank's demise." His voice softened. "But how are you doing, baby doll? Did you get your cloak back? I hear it's been confiscated by the police . . ."

"No, Johnny," she moaned. "And it's all over the tabloids today . . . who's the mystery owner, that sort of thing."

She heard him tell someone to wait, that he'd be there in a second. She wanted to cry, no, no, no, Johnny. I need you. If you can't be here, at least stay on the line for a while, I'm so terribly alone, but when he came back on, all she said was, "Johnny, I'm nervous. Will you be in Washington long?"

"I may have to go back to Puerto Rico. As soon as I know I'll call you or I'll be on your doorstep. What were you saying about the papers?"

She read the headlines to him and some of the copy, relieved that when the message time was up, Esme could no longer hear what Johnny was saying, especially as he was becoming exasperated.

"For God's sake, Ginny, what is there to be so mysterious about? Call 'em up and go get your damned cloak back," he said sharply. "If the papers like your cloak so much, this could be the exposure you've been waiting for. Surely you can easily convince the cops you didn't even know a murder had taken place . . . I still can't fathom why you left the damned thing behind in the first place."

Without thinking, although Esme was there, Ginny cried, "Because I was scared—I thought the police would find out I'd crashed the party." She heard Esme gasp. It was too bad, but she had more to lose now than Esme's respect. "Once I admit why I left the cloak behind, the papers will go to town . . . the world will know."

"So what! Here's your opportunity. Use it to explain to the press why you crash—to get exposure, recognition for your designs. You can go into the brush-offs, the promises which never produce anything except passes from Seventh Avenue lechers . . ."

Ginny shivered. If only he was with her. It would be so easy to confess about Stern, to tell him everything, to crawl into his arms for protection, but again he broke off to speak to someone else. "Okay, okay, I'm coming." Then, "Ginny, I've got to go, but I promise I'll see you one way or another before I leave—if I leave. I'll come by to hold your hand and give you courage to face the music."

Before she could answer, he put the phone down. She had never felt so bereft, and Esme's look of shocked disbelief didn't help.

"Oh, Ginny, I can't believe you crashed the library. I thought . . . you made me think you were going with Johnny. Why, Ginny, why?"

"Because I thought he wouldn't take me, that's why." She was sick of pretending. "Because I wanted to meet his saintly father, who disapproves of him because of his gossip column, his choice of women, his expensive divorce, everything. I wanted a chance to meet the almighty Quentin Peet to start proving I'm the kind of person Johnny needs."

"How?" Esme made a face.

"God knows what I was thinking. I had it all planned out. I was a fool . . . and now I know Johnny was planning to take me after all. He wanted to give me a surprise.

"And that's not all . . . I . . . I met Arthur Stern there." Ginny started to sob again. "Lee Baker Davies, you know my friend from *Bazaar*. She told me Stern had just set someone up in business, some California designer who'd run out of money, who Stern rescued, someone, Lee said, with nothing like my kind of ideas . . . Stern Fashions . . . you know . . . with his wife he runs this powerful fashion conglomerate. I'd met him once before and blown it. This seemed too good to be true and—"

"Stern? You mean the man the police took—" Esme stopped short, looking stunned.

"Yes, Stern, Arthur Stern," Ginny sobbed.

Her handkerchief sodden, she got up to look for a tissue, rubbing her eyes with the only one left in the box. "He . . . he wanted to talk to me about my designs, but because it was so noisy, he took me to this place where he said we'd be able to talk in private. He . . . tried . . . he very nearly raped me." She could hear her voice high, hysterical; she was losing control.

Esme knelt beside her, cradling her, rocking her backwards and forwards. "Oh, poor Ginny, darling Ginny, how terrible. How absolutely terrible. But what happened? Did Svank try to rescue you?"

"No, no, no—"

Ginny stopped. In seconds she would be telling Esme everything, including her nightmare that it had been Alex she'd seen fighting with the man she now knew had been Svank.

"Go on," Esme said softly. "I understand everything, Ginny, honest I do. Go on . . ."

She thought quickly. "I had to fight for my life. I got away through an exit Stern didn't know about . . . I left him there. I don't know what happened after that. All I know was I had to escape . . . I ran all the way home. Look . . ." She slipped off her mules. "See, my feet are still cut up. Oh, Esme, don't you understand, that's why I can't claim my cloak. I can't tell the world what a fool I was to go with a man like Stern to a dark, deserted floor. I can't let Johnny know what I was prepared to do for my stupid, ugly, useless ambition."

As she spoke, she wanted to die. It was true. Johnny could never know. If he ever found out, he'd be convinced forever she was nothing but a tramp.

Esme confirmed it. "No, I suppose you can't." She shuddered dramatically. "To think you were with the murderer just before it happened.

I can't bear to think of what might have happened to you if you hadn't escaped."

When Ginny didn't answer, Esme said slowly, "It may have to come out, Ginny. It's all part of the evidence, pointing to the violent kind of man Stern is. Perhaps you should speak to a lawyer—one of Ted's cousins—perhaps he could help."

Cousin! If only Ginny had never had a cousin.

Ashamed she was allowing Esme to believe Stern was guilty, Ginny cried again, "No! I don't know why I told you, but I had to tell someone."

"What about your own cousin, Alex, the cousin you love so much? Can't he advise you what to do?"

Was Esme reading her mind?

"You always say he knows what to do about everything," Esme continued. "Can't you tell Alex what you've just told me?" There was often a suspicion of sarcasm in Esme's voice when she mentioned Alex's name, but not today.

Sure that her stricken expression must be giving Esme some idea of the fear her words conjured up, with a big effort, Ginny smiled weakly. "Oh, Alex and I don't see each other much anymore. He's got more important things to do than visit his unemployed relatives."

Esme was looking at her searchingly. Did she suspect something, or was Ginny, as usual, being paranoid?

Ginny suddenly desperately wanted to be alone. "I don't feel too good, Es," she said. It was true. "I think I'll take a sleeping pill and try to get some sleep. This whole business has really shaken me up."

"I bet it has. Can't I do anything?"

It took another twenty minutes before she could persuade Esme that all she really wanted was to be left alone to get some rest. "You won't tell anyone, will you? Especially not Ted?" Ginny pleaded as Esme still hovered in the doorway.

"Cross my heart and hope to die, but do think about seeing a lawyer. I'll come by tomorrow or perhaps it would be better if you tried to act normally? Why don't you let me take you out to lunch? We could meet at Mortimer's."

"Let's talk in the morning."

When Esme finally left, Ginny had a warm bath and tried to think what she would be doing if, as Esme put it, she acted normally. One thing, for sure. She would have called Poppy by now to offer her condolences, comfort, something.

With a jolt she again realized she hadn't seen Poppy at the library, although, for once, she'd been sure Poppy would be there, wearing the georgette wraparound she liked so much, because she wanted a version in black "without a fitting, Ginny darling."

Ginny frowned. It was strange. Despite the crowd, Poppy was always such a standout, but right up until the fateful moment when the first gong had rung for dinner and she'd made the sickening mistake of agreeing to go "somewhere quiet" with Stern, there had been no sign of Poppy Gan. She'd been so intent on breaking through the maelstrom to meet Quentin Peet, could she have missed her? Surely not, but then something else had been on her mind. What was it? A cold wave of terror went through her. Oz. She'd been intent on giving Oz the slip, too.

Ginny sank back on the bed. How could she have forgotten Oz, the man she'd already offended publicly at Esme's wedding, the man who'd admired her cloak and taken it to the cloakroom, who'd said he would meet her at her table, hoping they could get together later?

Why hadn't she heard from him? Had he already gone to the police, the press? Would she read all about herself in the next day's papers?

Calm down, Ginny. Act normal, Ginny. For all you know Oz is off in some far-flung place on assignment or too busy in the studio to read the papers or to think about you or your cloak.

She picked up the phone to call Poppy.

An answering service picked up. "Who's calling?"

"An old friend . . ."

"I'm afraid Ms. Gan isn't here at the moment. What's your name and number?"

Quickly Ginny hung up. She went over to her sewing machine, determined to pull herself together. There was a yard of poplin on top. For the new dart she'd been experimenting with, a dart curved like a crescent moon, a dart she intended to place in strategic places on a form-fitting dress, to increase body consciousness.

She sat down, trying to concentrate, trying to summon up her usual enthusiasm that could turn a piece of material into high fashion.

After a few tries, she gave up. Perhaps in the morning. Perhaps next month or next year. It was time for the sleeping pill.

When she woke up it was cold and dark and just after midnight. Oh, Johnny, where are you when I need you so badly?

She threw on a sweater and walked the route she'd run so feverishly only the night before, this time to the late-night newspaper stand, where she bought first editions of the morning papers.

They were all full of the arraignment of Arthur Stern in connection with Svank's death. There was a picture of Stern looking browbeaten beside a mountain of a woman, his wife Muriel. She was glowering at him, although she was quoted as saying her husband had her unswerving support and the city would live to rue the day they'd "tried to frame my Arthur."

Described in the *News* as "the bulldog billionaire," Svank was now pictured in all the papers, several times with glamorous women, including two ex-wives Ginny wondered if Poppy had ever known about.

In the *Post* there was a picture of Svank with Poppy. "In happier days," wrote the *Post*. Oh, yeah, thought Ginny. Poppy was wearing the dress which had garnered such enormous press coverage with its "derrière siren skirt," the skirt she'd saved after Svank had tried to rip it apart.

Even the august *New York Times* devoted a good chunk of space to the story, reporting that "Svank, one of the library's biggest donors, had been the honored guest of the library's president that night."

Nowhere in any of the reports did it mention that Svank had brought Poppy to the dinner—or anyone else for that matter. Finally she found the sentence she was looking for. "A close friend of Svank's, the model Poppy Gan, has been questioned by the police, although she did not attend the dinner because she was out of town at the time."

Stranger and stranger. Ginny closed her eyes wearily, remembering Poppy's often-repeated explanation for not keeping her promise to include her at various events. "I never know where I'm going to end up. I get the week's agenda, but that doesn't mean I'm always invited. He's gotta lotta business, you know."

Did he fall or was he pushed? On the *Times* Op-Ed page a famous defense attorney gave a case history of another sensational death, explaining the finer points of the law and how, if Stern's defense lawyer could prove it was not premeditated, a manslaughter charge, Murder 3, could lead to the accused's release after a comparatively short sentence.

Guilt overwhelmed Ginny. She had to go to Caulter and tell him everything, that Stern should not have been accused of anything, except attempted rape. Even as she thought about it, she visualized the look on Johnny's face when the facts came out.

She quickly flipped the pages over. To her amazement, anger, and frustration, on the Style page a sizable fashion box was devoted to the "new chic swagger of a cloak."

Here was the golden chance she'd longed all her life to achieve, and she couldn't claim an inch of credit.

In the morning she called Esme to say she couldn't lunch; she'd forgotten she had a long-standing date to help Lee with a fashion shoot out on Long Island.

Ginny was dreading that Lee would want to gossip about Arthur Stern, but luckily the clothes came late, the model had a rash, and Lee had too much to contend with to talk about anything except the job in hand.

When Ginny arrived back in the loft, she saw on the local TV news that a camera crew had been combing New York City streets to capture every cloak-wearing woman in sight. In less than forty-eight hours cloak wearing had become a major trend.

Another sleepless night, and worse was to come. Esme brought *Women's Wear Daily* to lunch the next day. It carried a spread on the most fashionable cloaks in town, with Barneys offering an almost exact replica of the Mystery Woman's Napoleonic version, "in fabric," a store spokesman pontificated, "similar to that used in Napoleon's campaign tents."

"You've got to do something," Esme said fiercely. "Other designers are stealing your ideas, claiming them as their own, while you're cowering in terror, all because you don't want Johnny to know you nearly lost it to the murderer at the library—"

"That's not the reason."

"Well, what is it, then? Stern's out on bail, living in high luxury with his old battle-ax of a wife, who's bound to know what he gets up to when he's off the leash, and you're as usual the one who's suffering. It's not right, Ginny. How about me telling Johnny what happened?"

"Are you out of your mind? If you even mention doing such a thing again, Esme, I'll never forgive you."

Where was Alex? Where was he hiding? Was he still in the country? Round and round her mind went, over the same ground. Once she would never have believed Alex could be a thief. Now she accepted the fact, horrifying though it was. But a killer? No, she couldn't, just couldn't accept that the cousin she'd so looked up to, respected and adored, would deliberately take another man's life, even if it was the loathsome Svank.

She remembered Alex telling her he'd been wrong; she'd been right. Svank was—how had he described him? "A greedy, dangerous fiend." But Alex had gone on working for the fiend. "He's still someone very much to know if you have something he wants."

Someone had had something Svank wanted—badly enough to fight over it. If it hadn't been Alex in the hallway, who could it have been? It was someone who knew that she and only she could prove Arthur Stern had never laid a finger on Svank. Someone who right this second could be thinking she and only she could identify him as the real killer, someone who wouldn't hesitate to eliminate her—once he found out who she was. Why wasn't Stern using her as an alibi? Had he been too drunk to remember?

As she went back over the same old ground, increasingly the evidence pointed to Alex. He must have seen her face illuminated by the lightbulb on the stairwell. He must have guessed she was the mystery woman in the cloak, because he was one of the few people in the world who knew about her crashing. Because she hadn't come forward to exonerate Stern, he must think she was still willing to protect him and, determined not to give her any more agony, he'd taken the jewels and escaped.

She prayed she'd got it right, that Alex, at last, was thinking of her. She prayed, for the good of Alex's soul, that Svank's death had been an accident, despite the gunshot she'd heard.

The papers obviously weren't getting all the facts, because although a gun had been mentioned, Svank's gun, the coroner's report had given as cause of death a fatal crushing of the skull. Would she ever be able to forget the sound of body, bone, matter hitting that marble floor? Never.

Alone in the loft, she thought she heard someone trying her front door. "Alex, is that you?"

She told herself she wasn't afraid, but again her mother's words came back. "He isn't who you think he is . . . he's a monster . . ."

It wasn't the front door. It was a latch on the shutter outside the window, blown loose by the wind.

Esme had stuck *WWD* in her shoulder bag. It was as if she wanted her to brood, hoping perhaps she'd suddenly call the trade paper and give them the scoop of the year.

"Hi, I'm Ginny Walker, the Mystery Woman. I left my cloak behind, running away from Arthur Stern. He wasn't busy killing Svank; he was busy trying to rape me." Gimme a break, Esme.

All the same, rereading the Barneys story the next day Ginny decided that never knowing what the next hour might bring, she'd go to see for herself exactly what Barneys uptown store's replica of her cloak in "Napoleonic tenting" was all about.

As she was leaving, Johnny called. She'd never heard him sound so pleased with himself. "What's up? Have you won the lottery?"

"Better still. I'm on the verge of a big story. Don't think I'll have to go back down to San Juan. I probably have enough."

"Are you coming home?"

"Soon, babe. Soon. I'll let you know. What's with the cloak?" Her silence sent him into a series of "tut tut tuts." Then, "I'll deal with you, young lady, when I get back," he said. "By Sunday at the latest."

Despite a resolution to save as much as she could for the rainy day she was sure was now imminent, when she saw a cab slowly cruising by she hailed it. She'd use the subway to get back.

The jerking, stopping, starting and bumping over Manhattan's many potholes was just what she needed to sharpen all her senses. These days with so little sleep, half the time she was going through life like a sleepwalker. She craved sleep; she longed for oblivion to escape from the pain of her thoughts. She stared out at the graffiti-laden walls, the barricaded shuttered buildings, that seemed to have taken over the city all the way up to the mid-Forties.

As the neighborhood improved, the traffic got worse. Seeing the meter she knew she should get out and walk, but it was beginning to rain, and she hadn't thought to bring her umbrella; she didn't want to arrive at Barneys a sodden mess.

In the middle of a gridlock on Madison Avenue at Fifty-fifth Street Ginny's stomach did a somersault. Crossing the road on the far side, weaving in and out of cars and trucks, walking as fast as they could, were, surely, Poppy, wearing huge dark glasses with . . . Ginny took a deep breath, blinking her eyes to make sure she wasn't hallucinating . . . with Alex.

She didn't hesitate. She jumped out just as the traffic began to move. There was a hideous screeching of brakes as a FedEx truck had to slam on everything to avoid her. "What the fuck . . . where d'you think you're going?" She could hear people cursing her, yelling, the taxi driver bellowing, but nothing and no one was going to stop her.

By the time Ginny reached the other side of Madison, negotiating construction on the corner, Poppy and Alex were out of sight.

She ran down East Fifty-fifth, panting, into the St. Regis Hotel. No sign of them. She ran to Fifth Avenue, looking left, right, left. Nowhere to be seen. She crossed over to the West Side, into the Peninsula Hotel, the lobby packed with a crowd of Japanese businessmen. No Poppy; no Alex.

Had her feverish brain conjured them up? Had she imagined seeing them? Was she finally going crazy as Esme had predicted?

No, the largest dark glasses in the world couldn't hide the identity of Poppy Gan, with her mop of blonde curls and seductive glide of a walk. But Poppy with Alex? Together. Going somewhere with a look of purpose? Looking as if they belonged together. What did it all mean? Did Poppy know about the jewels? Were they in her jewel box now? Or in her toilet?

Depressed, shaking with nerves, Ginny slowly retraced her steps, looking one more time in the St. Regis in the famous King Cole bar. There was no sign of such a standout pair.

The taxi driver, illegally parked on Madison, was blocking the passenger door with his bulk. He shook his fist, yelling, "What are you, some kind of fuckin' nut, trying to get me busted and yourself killed. You're not getting back in my cab, lady. You oughta be locked up somewhere. Gimme the fare—" He snatched the twenty-dollar bill she proffered and drove away.

Little did the driver know how much she wished she could be locked up somewhere, safe, sound, away from the rapists, the Poppys of the world and the double-crossing cousins.

It was one of the most depressing days she'd ever spent, and she'd been through enough of them in her short life. The Barneys Napoleonic cloak was, she was told by an airy salesgirl, "Just eighteen-fifty and running out of the store—there are only two left in stock."

She tried it on. It didn't have any of the grandeur—or gracefulness—of her design, let alone any embroidered gold bumblebees. She couldn't resist saying, "It makes me look like a tent, which isn't surprising considering the origin of the fabric." The salesgirl raised a superior eyebrow, swept the cloak off her back as if she shouldn't have bothered to waste her time, and strode away.

As she was all the way uptown, Ginny decided she might as well see if there were any other cloaks on sale. She didn't doubt that there would be, knowing how fast some of the more enterprising Seventh Avenue manufacturers could churn hot fashions out.

They were there all right, in several Madison Avenue boutiques, in every kind of material from stuffed sofa brocade to—perish the thought—diaphanous curtain sheer in Victoria's Secret.

She wandered in and out of stores, frequently standing still on street corners, looking up and down, still praying for a sighting of Poppy and Alex. But it didn't happen.

She called it a day at Saks, where every window on Fifth showed a cloak along with their seasonal evening looks, but even the Saks variety, one with a luscious roll collar of satin, didn't measure up to hers. It didn't make her feel any better. It was the first time she realized she missed her cloak. She wanted it back, but not for the price she'd have to pay.

As if fate wasn't teaching her enough of a lesson, as she descended by escalator she saw a sign in sunny yellow that made her want to throw up, there and then.

Monday through Wednesday
Personal Appearance on Three at Four.
Come to Tea with Becky Corey,
The hot new designer of
Corey's California Casuals.

Becky Corey. An escape route. For a few desperate minutes she contemplated calling Lee and asking her to set up a meeting to see if Ms. Lucky Corey still needed a number one assistant, but the feeling passed. Running away wouldn't solve anything. Her past would soon catch up with her. She was a prisoner of fate, destined to press her nose against store windows forever, if not destined to be locked up one day, just as the taxi driver said.

On the way home, she passed one of her favorite hunting grounds for ideas, an Army and Navy surplus store. Hanging outside was a long, lean epauletted khaki jacket. I need cheering up, she told herself. At twenty-six dollars it was a steal.

When she let herself into the loft, she felt more jittery than she'd felt since first discovering the jewels. So much so she even rushed to lift the top off the toilet to see if Alex—or Angus—or any of his accomplices—had paid another visit for safekeeping purposes. Nothing, and no messages on the machine either.

It was only five o'clock. During the shoot on Long Island, Ginny had promised Lee she'd drop into the first show of her artist friend, Marilyn Binez, in the Village.

She didn't really want to go. There were too many unhappy memories linked to Marilyn, the plump girl who'd wanted to trade one of her paintings for Ginny's suit with inside-out seams, the one she'd designed for somebody tall and skinny, like herself, not overweight and short like Marilyn . . . the artist, who, as Lee had pointed out with a mischievous nudge, she'd met the same night she'd met Ricardo.

"I'll be there," she'd told Lee, part of her determination to "act normal." Now she didn't think her nerves were up to it. To calm herself down Ginny went to her drawing board. She would design another kind of cloak, more Anna Karenina than Napoleon, tragic as opposed to tyrannical, oppressed as opposed to opulent.

She went through the ideas pinned to her pegboard—a clip about a Yohji Yamamoto coat, "all asymmetrical angles, uneven layers and sculptural seams, that looks like a cross between something Flash Gordon and a Bruegel peasant would wear"; a fashion report from Clairol, which she couldn't remember saving and now wondered why she had. Probably the color story they were pushing, equating fashion's new passion for technicolor oranges and fuschias with a return to funky hair color.

Fashions for the young and restless caught her eye. She was young and restless all right. She went back to the bathroom, staring at her pale image devoid of makeup, aching suddenly with the memory of the bright young thing who, an eon ago, had been directed by Alex to "start experimenting with looks."

Her hair was too long. If she went to Marilyn's show she had to do something about her hair. She pulled it straight up and secured it on top with an elastic band, then started to braid it from front to back the way the models had worn theirs at the Yamamoto show. It was like knitting or sewing—better because she didn't have to think about it. As she braided the last few tufts, it took a minute for her to realize the phone was ringing.

Probably Esme calling with another bright idea about a full confession. She waited for the beep. There was a pause. Something made her pick the phone up quickly before the caller hung up.

"Hello . . ." She sounded the way she wanted to sound, as if she'd just rushed in after a heavy day's work.

"Hello, little cheetah."

She was so overwhelmed, she couldn't speak.

"Are you there?"

It was Alex, speaking unusually softly.

"I can't believe it . . . I can't believe it," she gasped. And it was unbelievable, most of all because she couldn't think of what to say, first, last and all the dozens of other things in between.

"I know what you must have thought of me . . . I know how hard it's been for you, but . . ." To her horror, Alex sounded as if he was struggling not to break down.

"My mother's dying, did you know that, Ginny?"

"Oh, Alex . . . no, I didn't know . . . oh, my God." Now it was obvious he was choking back sobs. She started to cry herself, familiar feelings of love, fear, and anxiety for his well-being, pent-up for so long, sweeping away for the moment her anger and suspicion.

"I've been in hell, Ginny. I'm still in hell. I can't even go to the West Coast to see her, not until . . . until . . ."

Until what? There was no time to waste. She had to know the answer to the most vital question she would ever ask him. "Were you at the library?" she cried. "Were you with Svank at the library?"

There was a pause; then, to her amazement, when Alex spoke it was in the smooth, "just-between-us" tone she'd heard for years. "I can explain everything," he said. It didn't wash anymore.

"That's not good enough. I must know now. Svank . . . did you . . . did you . . ." She couldn't bring herself to say "kill Svank." She didn't need to.

"For God's sake, Ginny, how could you think that of me. I despised the old monster; he made my life a misery for the past few months, but murder . . ." He sounded shocked. He sounded as if he was telling the truth, but without seeing him, face-to-face, eyeball-to-eyeball, she just didn't know.

"Did you come to pick up . . . did you come to the loft that night, to pick up the jewels?"

"You don't sound like my sweet little Ginny anymore. What's happened to you, Gin?"

"You happened," she screamed into the phone. "You used me; you know how much I loved you, trusted you; you took me for a sucker; I was—probably still am—a sucker." Another question soared through her grief. "I saw you with Poppy today. What have you got to do with Poppy? Is she hiding your loot now?"

He answered quickly. "Yes, I saw Poppy today." Now his voice was serious, full of foreboding as he went on, "I want to take you into my confidence, Ginny, but there's too much at stake. Why did you ever, ever in your right mind think that I could be responsible for Svank's death?"

"Because I was there, goddammit. I saw everything." She paused dramatically. "I thought I saw you—" She heard his swift intake of breath. She took a gamble. "I'm the mystery woman behind the cloak."

Again there was that sound of gulped breath, of panic and shock at the end of the phone. "Ginny, Ginny, listen to me carefully. Your life could be in great danger. Who else knows you saw the murder?"

"Arthur Stern . . ." She was surprised how calm she felt, even if she was signing her own death warrant. "And the murderer."

"And you thought it was me?"

"Wasn't it?"

"No, Ginny, you did not see me." He seemed to be waiting for her to answer. Was he expecting her to apologize? When she remained silent, he said, "Ginny, you are in a dangerous situation. I promise you I'm going to get you out of it. We'll meet over the weekend."

"Where?"

"I'll call you, I promise . . . or if that's not possible, Poppy will call and tell you where we'll meet."

"Poppy!" She was stung, as full of the same old irrational jealousy as ever. "What on earth has she got to do with it? Why are you involving her?"

"Because she's very important to me right now. Have faith, Ginny.

We'll meet this weekend for sure, I promise. Meanwhile, don't let in any strangers."

He hung up. She sat, frozen with fear, for the first time wishing she'd covered the one big window in the loft with curtains to shut out the cloudy sky.

"Don't let in any strangers." What did Alex mean by that? Could she trust him? Had he been telling her the truth about his mother or had he been playing on her sympathy? There was one way to find out; to make that long-overdue phone call to her Aunt Lil.

A strange female voice answered on the second ring. "May I speak to Mrs. Rossiter?"

"Who's calling?"

"Her niece, Ginny Walker, from New York. I've just . . . just spoken to Alex, her son."

"One minute, please."

One minute, two minutes. The wait seemed interminable. Ginny was about to hang up and dial again when another strange voice came on the line.

"I'm afraid Mrs. Rossiter's not up to taking any calls today. Did you say you have a message from Alex?"

"Not exactly. Who am I speaking to?"

"Nurse Dobson, the day nurse."

Ginny's throat went dry. Day nurse. That suggested another nurse for night. Round-the-clock nursing for a very sick woman.

"Is there anything I can send my aunt?" she whispered. "Does she need anything?"

"Oh, no, miss," Nurse Dobson replied briskly. "Her son doesn't let her want for anything, except, of course, she'd love to see him. Is he back?"

Back from where? Nurse Dobson seemed to know more than most people about Alex's movements, which wasn't surprising.

"No," Ginny replied quickly. There was no use getting her aunt's hopes up. "He . . . he called me from overseas. I didn't realize my aunt—"

"Yes, I'm afraid she has taken a bad turn. If you hear from Mr. Rossiter before I do, please tell him to come as soon as possible."

When the phone went down, Ginny sat staring into space. Alex had told the truth. His mother was dying and yet he couldn't go to her bedside until . . . until . . . what? The jewels were disposed of? The murder was solved?

She dragged herself to the drawing board, trying to stop thinking about Alex, but it was hopeless. Only when she saw him face-to-face would she know. Would he really arrive on the weekend?

The phone was ringing again. She rushed to answer it, praying it was another call from Alex, but it was Lee, saying she'd called for a car and could come by to pick her up if she liked.

Yes, she would like. She had to get out of the loft, away from tapping shutters, frightening shadows on the wall, and the telephone.

Her new hairstyle was a success and so was the khaki jacket she'd picked up that day. She wore it with jeans. Many people were in jeans, but "no one wears them better than you, Ginny," said Lee approvingly. "I swear your legs look as if they start under your armpits."

For some reason she was the hit of the evening. It was bizarre. She'd never felt less sure of herself, or her looks. She hardly spoke, but, she supposed, thanks to the usual endless supply of jug wine at the art gallery, she laughed a lot and received two, if not three, invitations to go on to dinner after the opening, one from a good-looking Indian, who told her he was a psychiatrist. Perhaps a shrink was just what she needed, but "acting normal" couldn't extend to a date with a stranger. Oh, Johnny, please hurry back.

By the time Lee gave her a lift home, in a car packed with a rowdy, happy group, her jitters had subsided.

There was a large envelope pushed under the front door. It had her name on it, but perhaps because of the wine, the warm fuzz of camaraderie she'd just left behind, she didn't give it much thought, not even opening it right away. She tossed it on the bed while she went around the loft switching on lamps.

The answering machine was blinking and she pushed the message button on to hear Johnny's voice, still bursting with confidence. "Where are you, Ginny-o-will-of-the-wisp? No more crashing, I hope. Miss you. See you soon."

He cares about me. He really does care about me. She hugged the thought to herself. I mustn't give him any reason to change his mind. I'll wear the same jacket when he comes back. I'll fill the loft with flowers and food, I'll— She saw the envelope on the bed and ripped it open.

Inside were the pictures Oz had taken of her in her renovated blush bridesmaid dress, the pictures she'd posed for at the library, surrounded by other guests.

Clipped to them was a note from Oz and the newspaper story with the headline, "Who Wore This Cloak at the Murder Scene?"

"Time to talk, Ginny," he'd written. "Time to get together real soon."

CHAPTER
TEN

935 PENNSYLVANIA AVENUE N.W., WASHINGTON, D.C.

On his way out of the Hoover Building, the ugly sprawling home of the Federal Bureau of Investigation on Pennsylvania Avenue, Johnny realized he hadn't checked his answering machine at the office in more than twenty-four hours.

There was one unoccupied phone booth in the lobby and he grabbed it. He'd already dealt with the first two messages from a *Next!* copy editor; accounting was querying something on his Puerto Rico expense account; a Sister Cochrane had called for the second time, "some news about the homeless woman you wrote so inspiringly about." He scribbled down her number on the back of the pass he was supposed to give up when he left the building.

The last message came from an unfamiliar, high-pitched female voice, on behalf of a once very familiar name.

"Hello, Dr. David Sorenson is trying to reach you. Will you please return Dr. Sorenson's call before one o'clock today, Monday, May eighth, when he can be reached in his office, 212-555-0008, or this evening, after seven, at his New York apartment, 212-555-8543."

Two years ago Johnny had known all Sorenson's numbers by heart, including his number on Long Island, his car, and his beeper. Not anymore. Now, because the secretary rattled them off so quickly, he had to redial to hear the message again.

It was nearly noon. Johnny dialed the office number and was put through immediately. "Hello, Doc, long time no speak."

"Hello, Johnny. It's good of you to call back so quickly. I really appreciate it. Well, young fellah, it certainly has been too long, much too long. You have no idea how often I've thought of looking you up, but there it is, that's New York life for you. I read you though, from time to time. Sounds like life's pretty good. Enjoying yourself? You ought to be." David Sorenson's warm, confident voice, which gave away his Canadian upbringing only in the way he pronounced his o's, sent an unexpected shiver down Johnny's spine.

It was unfair, but just hearing Sorenson took him right back to the long, last weeks of his mother's life, triggering memories he'd thought he'd laid to rest. They were painful memories—of trying to track his father down somewhere halfway round the world, and then having to persuade him that he wasn't crying wolf as had happened once before, that his mother really was dying this time.

At first it had only been embarrassing to have to admit to Sorenson that his father didn't believe him, that Johnny needed him as the physician on the case to back him up and spell out how critical Catherine Peet's condition was.

He wondered briefly whether the doctor still remembered the phone calls during the last touch-and-go weekend, when, after finally reaching Quentin Peet, Sorenson had handed him the phone with a sad shake of his head, in order for him to hear for himself his intoxicated father dismissing Sorenson's warnings as "the exaggerated posturing of a publicity-seeking quack."

As usual his father had still arrived with impeccable timing—two days before the final goodbye—but his continued, inexplicably arrogant behavior during those dark hours had helped consolidate the warm, trusting relationship that had developed between doctor and son during Catherine Peet's long illness. It was only later that Johnny understood Sorenson had assumed a kind of surrogate father role, one he hadn't known how much he needed. Lonely and frightened, Johnny had been the only family member to witness his mother's life slipping away.

It was a relationship he'd hoped—and expected—would grow into an enduring friendship, but after his mother's death neither had sought out the other. A pity. God knew he had far too few real friends he could count on and trust, but the doctor was right. New York wasn't a place to nurture friendship. Few allowed themselves any time for that old-fashioned pasttime; few allowed themselves time for anything except work—and sex.

One thing was sure. Sorenson wasn't calling him belatedly now to develop their friendship. "What's up, doc? What can I do for you?"

"I'd prefer not to discuss it over the phone, Johnny. Could we meet later today, say a drink about five-thirty, six?"

"Sorry, I'm in Washington right now. Shall I give you a ring when I'm back in town?"

"Yes, yes, that would be fine."

"Can you give me a clue what it's about?"

He remembered Sorenson never liked to procrastinate. "I'm Muriel Stern's cardiologist. The family's getting a bad rap over this terrible Svank business. I'm sure you've read all about it?"

Johnny blew out a silent whistle. Hallelujah. Sorenson was Muriel Stern's doctor. It was too good to be true. He was about to hit pay dirt. "Yes, of course, I've read about it. How can I help?"

"Well, that's what I'd like to discuss with you. Muriel—Mrs. Stern—feels the right sort of article in the press could be valuable at this moment." Sorenson hesitated. "Shall I say, could possibly defuse the volatile situation, which is definitely deleterious to her health. She's naturally sought my advice about this. I told her I knew you. Well, the rest I would prefer to talk to you about when we meet. Unfortunately her husband has gotten himself involved in a very sorry state of affairs."

That was the understatement of the year, but Johnny also then remembered how Sorenson was often given to British understatement. He made up his mind. This was an opportunity too good to miss. He would leave Washington a day earlier than he'd planned.

"I understand. Let's tentatively say a drink around six-thirty tomorrow. I should be back by then. Your place?" Sorenson kept a small pied-à-terre near New York Hospital, getting back to his main home on the North Shore of Long Island only a couple of times a week, if then.

"Wonderful, Johnny. My place, you remember it." Sorenson's voice showed obvious relief. "Don't call, unless you have to cancel. Just come."

When Johnny put the phone down he was jubilant. What an incredible piece of luck—or as his father would probably put it, providence. If he was going to be able to place the Sterns anywhere in the byzantine world ruled over by Svank, he had to get to know them. Sorenson was going to open the door.

From what Johnny had ferreted out for his *Next!* column, byzantine was the perfect word to describe the structure, spirit, complexity and deviousness of Svank's empire; and from what he'd read during the past week it appeared there was already considerable evidence to pinpoint Svank as the mastermind behind a worldwide network of criminal activities.

Both Jim Hoagland of the *Washington Post* and Bill Safire in the *New York Times* had devoted their columns to "Svank, the mystery man," both men attempting to strip away the mystery.

According to Safire, "The colossus was killed just in time to avoid prosecution." Using his justified reputation of hotshot wordsmith, Safire had gone on to stipulate that for that piece of information he could, "in all fairness," use "hypostasis" as opposed to "hypothesis." All the same, Johnny hadn't been able to get anyone at the Hoover Building or at the CIA to go on record to confirm it.

He'd begun to develop a good relationship with Trager, and later that Monday they met for a drink at the Willard, one of the oldest and most elegant hotels in the capital, only a stone's throw from the White House.

Trager didn't say a word as Johnny began to spell out some of the accusations in Safire's column. "Money laundering, international thefts, major drug operations, Svank was involved in all of it, right?"

When Trager didn't answer, Johnny went on unperturbed. "It appears to me all his underworld stuff was so intertwined with legitimate businesses, held under a multitude of names, it will take months, if not years to untangle, right?"

"Same again, Johnny?" was all Trager would say as he beckoned the bartender, but then he winked and nodded.

The next morning Johnny woke up with a startling realization: He no longer wanted to be the one to do the untangling, didn't want to spend what could easily be the best years of his life in the bloody playground reserved for drug traffickers, swindlers, and murderers.

He'd spent the last few days locked in with the files of big-time fugitives, looking for links to Svank.

He'd listed their crimes—all so similar—fraud, conspiracy, racketeering, and again and again murder and torture.

He'd left the Hoover Building feeling dirty; he didn't want to crawl back into the dirt again.

Johnny stretched. For the first time in his life, for a reason he couldn't yet fathom, he was one hundred percent sure he was over trying to earn his father's approval. It was a giddy, even frightening sensation.

He reached over to phone Sorenson, to tell him he'd come by for a drink some other time because he didn't think he could be of much help to the Sterns. The line was busy and by the time he'd finished shaving, fast, smooth, cut-free, he'd decided, what the hell. He'd listen to what Sorenson had to say and perhaps it would be something for his column. His new sense of himself didn't mean giving up the column. Of course not, well, at least not yet.

In the early afternoon as he went to National Airport to catch the shuttle back to New York, he figured if he could get proof of the Sterns' involvement with Svank's dirty work, at least it would be a nice bone to throw to Steiner, but that was enough.

If he got another cover story out of it, that would be good, too, but he wasn't thinking to use it as leverage to a better job anymore—on a magazine his father would respect, like *Time*, or a paper like the *Wall Street Journal*, or perhaps even in television. No way. He felt good about *Next!* In fact, he loved writing his *Next!* column. The call from Sister Cochrane came to mind. What was that all about? His most recent piece on the homeless woman and civil liberties, as practiced in Puerto Rico and New York? He'd call her as soon as he could.

Again, the realization swept over him with a euphoric flush. He wasn't working to please or impress his father anymore. He was working to please himself. He'd crossed a personal Rubicon.

He called Ginny from the airport before he left. Her answering machine picked up, which was a bore. He left a message, telling her he was on his way back to the city and hoped to see her sometime soon. He didn't want to be distracted until he knew what the Stern deal was all about, so he didn't tell her about his meeting with Sorenson. He'd call her again when it was over.

It was cloudless all the way to New York. Cloudless, the way he hoped his life could be from now on. He started to hum "Blue Skies," shutting his eyes, thinking about Ginny's kooky smile.

He was still humming as the plane began to descend over New Jersey. One day in the not too distant future, surely even the great QP would have to slow down. Would he write his memoirs? Probably not yet. *Green Ice* had been such a success, he was probably even now getting fidgety, looking for another subject, another mountain to climb, a new adventure to get in and out of to write about in another best-selling book.

A wonderful, heady thought occurred to him. If through the Sterns he managed to get some new material, with leads on the Svank case that just asked to be followed up, what a great moment it would be for him to be able to hand everything over to his father. "Here, Dad. Here's my file on the Svank case," he would say. "It's all yours to use as you see fit, no strings attached."

It would be the perfect way to prove he was a free man at last.

The weekend had come and gone without Alex and without Johnny. Ginny's emotions had been on a roller coaster, diving down to depression, soaring with indignation and red-hot anger, stalling with fear over Oz's pictures.

On Saturday, waking up early, she'd gone back to the sewing machine to perfect her new arched dart. By ten o'clock, restless and nervous, she'd had to get out, and strolling aimlessly had lucked out at an arty bookstore, losing herself for an hour or two in a tome on the work of Mariano Fortuny, whose velvet cloaks and pleated Grecian gowns from the twenties, she knew, now fetched thousands of dollars at auction.

She'd spent so long making notes, learning about his secrets—"It is thought he used to cake cloth in clay and egg white and bake it to create some of his opulent fabric effects"—she'd begun to get dirty looks from the salesclerks. She hadn't had enough money with her to buy the book. She hadn't enough money, period. At two hundred dollars it would be a reckless extravagance at this perilous time in her life, but on the other hand, it could be looked upon as an investment. She'd left with a promise to return with her credit card, regretting it as soon as she got back to the loft to find no one had called, nothing had changed.

On Sunday, trying to bury her misery, she'd gone over to a new restaurant bar in the Bowery to meet up with the same crowd she'd met at Marilyn's opening, including, it turned out, the Indian psychiatrist. He'd asked for her phone number and told her to call him what sounded like "Chili." His soft, purrlike voice and gentle kindness were as soothing as a warm bath, particularly after drinking several glasses of California chardonnay. All the same she was relieved to discover she had a good excuse for refusing, when he wanted to take her home. His motorbike was outside, he'd said with a flash of white teeth in his dark, handsome face. "Sorry, not this time," she'd said sweetly, pointing out she was wearing her inflexible "tweed" skirt. "And I can't ride sidesaddle. I'll get seasick."

Before "Chili" knew what he was up against, Lee, who never liked to see Ginny getting embroiled with a man, had whisked her away in her usual Big Apple sedan.

At last there had been a message from Alex on her machine. He'd called at 9:05. Not much of a message. "Really sorry we couldn't get together this weekend. I've had a small problem to deal with . . ."

Black pearls, she'd thought bitterly, or diamond and sapphire earrings? Or would they be considered a big problem, as opposed to a small one?

"By Wednesday, I'll call you by Wednesday to see what suits you best," he'd said in a voice she hardly recognized, quiet, sad, lost.

She'd played the message back twice, each time hearing more suffering in his voice. Of course, he was suffering with his mother so ill, so far away. Why couldn't he go to the West Coast to be with her? "I'm in hell," he'd said the week before. More likely in hiding. From the police? From avengers of Svank's death? Whoever he was hiding from must surely now know of their relationship? Otherwise he could hide out with her.

Ginny agonized over what she could do to save her cousin from more grief. He may have brought everything on himself, but she couldn't let him down now.

The more she thought about it, the more she remembered the Alex of other years, always being there for her when she was growing up, coming to her rescue during childhood dramas, buoying up her hopes, teaching her how to live. Now he needed her. She couldn't turn away, not with his mother, Aunt Lil, at death's door.

On Tuesday morning, as Johnny was waking up to his new vision of himself, Ginny found more pictures from Oz in her mailbox. This time he included a copy of her old contact sheet and shots Ginny had no idea he'd taken of her at Esme's wedding in the blush bridesmaid dress, pre-renovation. Her heart beat fast; also in the envelope was a full-length shot of her in the cloak, looking forlorn as she used the wrong entrance and climbed the steps of the New York Public Library.

When the phone rang around ten, she knew it would be Oz.

"What do you want?" She tried to keep her voice calm, unthreatening, and unthreatened. "Why send me those pictures?"

"You've always liked being a woman of mystery, haven't you, Ginny? When I came back to town over the weekend I wasn't surprised to learn you were still playing games, but they're quite serious games now, aren't they? I must say you fooled me, and I can't understand what you're playing at even now."

When she remained silent he snapped, "You owe me and a lot of people some explanations, don't you? Are you getting a kick, some kind of weirdo feeling of power outa all this mystery woman stuff?"

Her mind raced, trying to think of a way to placate him without seeing him, to end the conversation without his feeling snubbed or rejected. Even as she played for time, she knew she was doomed to failure.

"Come over to the studio, tonight, about seven. I'd like to try some new shots of you, mystery woman. Then we'll go out and have dinner or something equally interesting."

"I'm not sure I can, Oz. I'm—"

"You can darling, believe me you can. Be here, no later than seven." He didn't add "or else." His tone of voice said it for him.

It was blackmail, but she had no alternative. If she didn't see him, didn't attempt to explain why she'd gone home without him that night, quite apart from explaining, as she had to Esme, why she hadn't claimed the Napoleonic nothing-but-trouble cloak, who knew what he would do to ruin her? She had to make peace; she had to make nice; she had to act as if she was about to fall under his spell and be seduced without letting him lay a finger on her.

She was thankful she had such a busy, chaotic day ahead. She wouldn't have much time to think about her problems, finding props for Lee, who as usual was working on the November issue in May, having to shoot winter scenes, although the sun was beginning to put in an appearance outside.

Ginny wasn't so thankful when she raced home to find she'd missed two important calls, one from Johnny at 2:15 from National Airport, on his way back to New York; one from Alex at 3:40 from—who knew where. Neither message gave her any pleasure. Johnny would see her sometime soon, thank you very much. Alex didn't even deliver that much information. "Alex here. I'll call back later."

It was no use relying on anyone except herself.

For the dreaded evening ahead she changed into the khaki military jacket, this time with a thin black cotton turtleneck and black leggings. She also wore a bra. For her, wearing a bra was like wearing armor. It would act as a reminder that with Oz she always had to be on guard.

She hadn't been back to his studio in nearly two years and as she approached Canal Street, her old lack of self-esteem threatened to surface. She shook her head to chase the feeling away. She was a different person, forced by circumstance to live without dreams, aware of who she was now—and who she was never going to be.

Would the eardrum-bursting racket of Heavy D still engulf her as she climbed the five flights to Sodom and Gomorrah?

Would the studio door still be wide open to the world? Or, in keeping with the confrontation she was sure was about to take place, would it be closed tight, so that she would have to knock humbly for admission, the way it had been the night the gorgeous Jamaican girl had been curled up on the doorstep, the night she'd almost succumbed to Oz, swept off her feet with too much wine and self-pity?

When she turned the corner to arrive at what she remembered as a decrepit, run-down entrance, she thought for a minute she'd come to the wrong address. It was almost impossible to believe that the modern structure she was now looking at was the building housing Oz's studio. She went back to the corner to check the street sign. It was the right street, the correct address, but it looked as if it had been through the most exacting car wash or dry-cleaning experience and then some.

She couldn't remember whether there had ever been windows in the building—in those days she hadn't exactly been paying attention to the architecture—but if there had been windows, they were all gone now, to be replaced by a smooth, soaring sepia stone facade, punctuated only at street level by an immense pair of stainless steel double doors with no apparent handle or doorbell.

She had to look hard to find the doorbell, which together with an intercom, also in stainless steel, was set into the left-hand wall.

It was immensely discreet. Ginny pressed, there were two beeps, and a robotic voice said, "Name please." She gave her name. There was no response, but in seconds the massive doors slid apart to reveal a long, stark-white hallway from which a jet-black staircase coiled upwards like a snake with no visible means of support.

There was no raucous Heavy D. In a strange way it was worse; there was no sound at all. Chilling. As she was about to start the long climb up, she heard a soft swish and another stainless steel door in the snow-white hall slid open. She couldn't believe it. An elevator.

Oz obviously had arrived. With no other tenants or names listed anywhere, could this mean he'd arrived to the extent he now owned the building? The whole place shrieked money, tons of money. Was there no justice in the world?

Ginny stepped nervously inside the elevator. It was totally mirrored, the floor, the walls, the ceiling. It made her think of another photographer, recently deceased, who was reputed to have had a small mirror attached to the sole of his shoe, for furtive glimpses up a woman's skirt. She looked down at the floor. She could clearly see a tiny wool thread hanging from the crotch of her leggings. She shivered. It was too creepy.

Which floor? There were no apparent buttons to push. She didn't need to know. The elevator quickly swished upwards, a blue light signaling each floor until she reached the top. The doors opened immediately onto what she supposed had once been the old studio. Now it looked like a penthouse from *Architectural Digest* with a sweep of floor so luminous and gleaming it could have been made of porcelain. It was easy to see why: beams of silver-hued light shone down onto it from a skylight in the domed ceiling.

She could imagine how the new faces, those desperate model wanna-bes, felt as they were precipitated without warning into a sudden, unexpected audition, having to cross what seemed like an acre of floor to the sumptuous sitting room, a few steps down.

There, Buddha-like, Oz sat cross-legged on a low, lush chrome silk-covered divan.

It was so calculated, so pretentious, so over-the-top in its orchestration, Ginny had to fight not to burst into hysterical giggles. Cut it out, Ginny. Show Oz how impressed you are. Don't lose everything before you've even begun.

At the far end of the transformed studio, chiffon sheers gently billowed against floor-to-ceiling windows, the result, Ginny supposed, of a well-positioned but invisible wind machine. She could still see dimly the high cranes of New York Harbor, but the view was all that remained the same.

Oz patted the fat cushion beside him. It was then Ginny smelled the thick sweet scent of pot and saw he was smoking.

"So there you are, mystery woman, and exactly on time. D'you like what you see? D'you realize what you missed?"

What was he trying to imply? That she'd missed the boat as a model? That if she'd only persevered, with his brilliant photography she would have finally made it? What a lot of bullshit. He didn't know what he was talking about and he didn't care. Facts had nothing to do with the world he inhabited, but Ginny sank down beside him, smiling, nodding, hoping her teeth could still be described as fascinating.

"You see that resin table over there? It cost ten thousand bucks and almost as much to bring here from Istanbul. Come with me." She'd only just sat down, but Oz pulled her up by her shoulders, and although she showed no sign of resisting, he pushed her roughly over to the back of the loft, where she remembered so long ago she'd timidly joined a gaggle of gorgeous models, advertising men, and Lee Baker Davies helping themselves to a still-life wonder of a buffet supper.

Now a series of curved lacquer screens stood in the buffet's place. They hid another staircase with frosted glass treads, which led down into what looked like a dark pit of iniquity.

"How . . . how . . . decadent." She'd meant to say decorative, but the true way to describe the scene slipped out.

Oz smiled as if she'd given him a present. "I thought you'd appreciate it. It was Peregalli's idea to put the bedrooms down there and open up this floor to get there. He usually doesn't take on small jobs, but this whole area of New York reminded him in a strange way of Milan." Oz swiveled her around to face him. "You know who Peregalli is, I take it?"

Oz was so intent on showing off, he didn't notice or probably care that she shrugged, because she hadn't the slightest idea. "He's created what he calls a series of metaphysical rooms down there . . . in extinct volcano lava colors, with wonderful images of past civilizations, chains, slaves, pain and pleasure . . ." Oz sounded as if he'd memorized everything he was saying from an overwritten catalogue. "Shall we explore now—or later?" He still had her shoulders in a tight grip, but at least it was only her shoulders.

She knew she should be alarmed, perhaps even terrified at what Oz had in mind. Instead she felt sorry for all the little damsels in distress he must have introduced to his "metaphysical" rooms, chaining them to one of his cold lava-colored floors, rather than . . . Ginny blinked away the memory of collapsing onto the deep pile of Johnny's sitting-room carpet.

The phone rang. Oz frowned. "Shit, but I better answer it. I'm expecting a call from Steve—Spielberg," he said over his shoulder. There was a clue in all of this. More than anything, for some inexplicable reason, Oz wanted to impress her. It was probably the same old reason as before. She was one of the few who'd gotten away and he still couldn't stand it, being the kind of guy who never gave up until he scored, when his fascination would be over instantly, one, two, three.

So what was she to do? Flatter him to death, over and over again, to defuse his hostility and make him think she was weakening—or would weaken eventually.

Ginny went to sit on the divan, waiting to drown him in compliments on his return. It would be easy. The interior space of the loft had been brilliantly redesigned. Ginny had to give Peregilli, or whatever his name was, credit for that. Softly curving walls concealed lighting that created alcoves from shadows while highlighting certain pieces of unusual furniture; it was a masterpiece of imagery.

From where she was sitting, she couldn't even see where Oz went to pick up the phone, although she could hear his sharp staccato laugh from time to time.

"This is the most fabulous place I've ever seen, Oz," she breathed as he plonked down beside her. "Do you own the whole enchilada? It's incredible; such taste; such vision; you're a genius."

Had she gone too far? No.

"You've never thought so before," he smirked.

"I was a dumb broad. Forgive?" She gave him her most radiant teeth-filled smile. To her horror he lunged over on top of her, the sickly smell of his breath making her dizzy. "Don't you want an explanation? Don't you want to talk?" she cried.

To her surprise and relief he rolled back. Perhaps he was too much on the stuff to do anything. "Of course, I want to talk." He corrected himself. "I want you to talk, to explain why you hate my guts."

"I don't, I never did." There was a vacant look in his eyes. Ginny thought fast. If she could get him high over dinner, there was a chance the whole evening could go by without a major tussle and she'd do what she could to convince him she thought he was the greatest photographer ever to get behind a lens.

Time was all she needed; time to stall Oz; to keep him from blabbing to the police until her meeting with Alex, when she would decide once and for all whether her cousin was a stupid, easily led fool who'd lost his way, or whether he was a cold-blooded murderer. If Alex kept his word—and at least he'd tried to reach her to make a date—then in no more than forty-eight hours, giving Alex enough time to escape, she should be able to tell her side of the story in order to get Stern released.

"You promised me dinner." Again Ginny gave Oz a big smile.

"Right, right." Oz ran his hand over her legging-covered knee up to her thigh. "The Tribeca Grill and then back here for brandy and coffee and a touch of the metaphysical for the mystery girl."

It was so easy. She didn't have to explain anything. She kept waiting for the other shoe to drop, but over dinner all Oz wanted to do was talk about himself, his success, his new house in Malibu, his endless supply of women, and his new interest in submission. Ginny kept her eye on the time, wondering if Johnny or Alex had called again, wondering with trepidation if either of them would be waiting on her doorstep.

It was still only nine-thirty when, without Oz's seeming to know or care what was happening, she hailed a cab outside the restaurant and gave the driver her address. Before she could stop him, Oz jumped in beside her, falling asleep on her shoulder. With little traffic, the cab soon arrived at the loft.

She intended to send Oz home in the same cab, but unfortunately he woke up as soon as it stopped and handed the driver a twenty-dollar bill.

"What are we doing here?" he slurred. "I thought you were coming back to my place. Are you up to your usual tricks, mystery woman? Okay, we can start here." He started to rattle the door handle to her building. "Give me a brandy upstairs."

There was no way that was going to happen. "Tomorrow," she cooed. "I promise I'll come to see your fabulous den of delights tomorrow."

"Is that second-rate reporter Peet waiting for you upstairs? Is that the problem?"

"I haven't got anyone, Oz, upstairs, downstairs, anywhere. I promise I really want to see everything, but hey, you fell asleep on me. I don't think you're up to being a tour guide tonight." To Ginny's relief she saw another cab cruising by. "Taxi!" It scooted to a stop and Oz, only feebly protesting, let her push him inside. She didn't wait to see the cab drive off. She rushed inside and double-locked the door. As soon as she got upstairs she would leave on Oz's answering machine a provocative message of something to look forward to. Despite what he thought, she wasn't very good at playing games, but this one she would play as if her life depended on it, because in a way it did.

It hadn't started well. In fact, with Sorenson's inability to beat around any bush for any period of time, it could not have been worse.

He'd hardly finished pouring out Johnny's scotch and soda before he'd given the game away with a wry grimace.

It wasn't the little Peet the Sterns wanted to talk to; it wasn't the pipsqueak Peet they hoped would write the redeeming piece in *Next!* magazine, which would lead to their salvation. Good God, no. Through Sorenson's acquaintanceship with the son, the Sterns hoped he would be able to get them to the father.

Johnny congratulated himself on not losing his cool. His self-control had nothing to do with his recently acquired confident frame of mind, all much too new to help him. He couldn't stop flushing as Sorenson rushed the truth out. At the same time, Johnny knew that his newly noncompetitive self *was* helping him to con the doctor with feigned willingness to help.

"Well, I can understand that." Johnny surprised himself with the level of sympathy he heard in his voice. "Of course, it makes perfect sense the Sterns would like to talk to my father, but why haven't they approached him directly?"

"Their lawyer is dead against it and I'm not sure he's wrong, but Muriel—Mrs. Stern—she's not an easy woman to deny. She believes in following her own instincts, and I must say she's often been right." Sorenson looked uncomfortable. "She doesn't know your father at all, but when she learned how much I think of you, she came up with the idea that you might be amenable to acting as some kind of go-between . . . in a strictly confidential way, of course."

Johnny plunged right in. "From what I've heard about Muriel Stern, I'm not surprised. She appears to be a remarkable woman, but Dr. Sorenson—"

"Oh, David, please. We may not see each other, but I feel as if we're old friends . . ."

"Well, then, David, you may remember my father isn't the easiest of men. I'd be happy . . ." Johnny paused for effect. "I think I'd have no trouble getting my father to meet them, but I could give no guarantee as to what position he might take. For that reason, er, David, I feel it's essential I meet the Sterns first, to find out what their expectations are . . ."

Johnny hoped he looked modest as he added, "I've grown more accustomed to assessing people's motivations, their feelings. I can be more helpful if I hear directly from the Sterns what they are trying to accomplish in meeting my father. After all"—seeing Sorenson was in a quandary, again he paused for effect—"what can I say to my father if I don't know what the Sterns want from him?"

Johnny was secretly amazed at how little Sorenson appeared to remember after all, especially about the relationship between his father and himself. If the doctor had remembered, he would have known there was no way Johnny would ever think of approaching QP on the Sterns' behalf. But if Sorenson didn't remember what made him tick, he thought he could still sum up Sorenson pretty well.

To Johnny's relief the doctor now acted exactly as he'd hoped and expected him to.

"There isn't much time to lose, Johnny, but I have to agree, what you say makes sense to me. Let me call Muriel right away and see if she agrees. Can I say, subject to the proper understanding, you are willing to ask your father to meet with them?"

Johnny nodded in what he hoped was a solemn, significant way. "Yes, I am."

When Sorenson reappeared in a few minutes he looked relieved. Johnny reckoned Muriel must have been nagging him into the ground ever since the hapless Arthur had been released into her formidable custody the week before.

"They're just about to sit down for dinner . . ." Sorenson waved his hands about apologetically. "They're very time-oriented people, always eat early, seven-fifteen dinner. Can you go over there for about fifteen minutes tonight, at, say, eight forty-five?"

Johnny nodded. "Yes, I can do that."

There was another grimace as Sorenson asked, "For an off-the-record meeting?"

Whatever that was supposed to mean. Again Sorenson received Johnny's significant nod. "Will you be there?"

The doctor sighed. "I suppose so. I have to run a couple of tests anyway. . . ."

Johnny sensed he would rather be a thousand miles away—or at least out at his Glen Cove house where, Johnny remembered, Sorenson liked nothing better than sitting with his adored golden Labradors beside him as he watched an opera video with his dull wife, who rarely came to the city. He couldn't blame Sorenson for his reluctance; but he'd also heard that although Muriel Stern was an overbearing, demanding boss, client, and, more than likely patient, too, at least she paid handsomely for the privilege.

He gulped down the whiskey. "I won't get in your hair any longer. I'll meet you there. What's the address?"

"No, no, no, I'll pick you up." Sorenson wanted to make sure he'd turn up. Well, that was understandable, too.

A short while later, when they arrived at the Sterns' apartment house, Johnny felt self-conscious, expecting to see an ink-stained wretch or two and some members of the paparazzi still hovering outside; but no, the wind was too chilly tonight and the story too slow for anyone to be about.

At exactly 8:45 Sorenson and he were announced. After a few minutes, they were allowed upstairs. A gray-faced man in gray livery to match waited at an open door, admitting them into a large marble foyer, which in size, beige tones, and lack of individuality could easily have been compared to the entrance hall of any small, uninspired Manhattan hotel—except for the glistening view of the East River clearly evident through a floor-to-ceiling picture window.

Ignoring Johnny, the servant said quietly, "Dr. Sorenson, Mrs. Stern isn't feeling too well. Would you come this way, please?"

When Johnny turned to follow, gray face put up a barricading hand. "Please wait here, sir."

Again David Sorenson shot Johnny his wry there's-nothing-I-can-do-about-it expression. Johnny indicated he really didn't care and for the next ten minutes alternately admired the view and shuddered at the huge bowls of artificial flowers on two ormolu hall tables.

He'd decided to explore and peep inside one of the doors off the hall, when a maid appeared. "This way please."

He was shown into a small room with shamrock-embossed dark green wallpaper. It reminded him of a wallpaper he'd once lived with in a country he now couldn't remember.

There was a sound of angry voices in the hall. It sounded as if the maid was unsuccessfully trying to keep somebody out. The door burst open.

"Oh!" Arthur Stern stood awkwardly in the doorway. "Wait a minute . . . wait a minute . . . this isn't Quentin Peet. Who are you?"

Didn't this couple ever speak to each other?

Johnny knew he stiffened up as he replied as warmly as he could, "I'm Quentin Peet's son, John Q. Peet."

"That's not who I'm expecting. Where's your father?" Stern staggered as he went across the room to sink into an armchair. It was obvious from his slurred syllables the man was half intoxicated, if not more so.

"What are you doing here?" The tone was unmistakably insulting. "Don't tell me my sainted wife got her Peets mixed up? The story I've got to tell isn't for amateurs, son. My story is big, big enough for the almighty to hear, big enough, crissakes, for the blessed Big Q himself to cover."

Johnny had to stifle a strong urge to give Stern a punch in the jaw. What the hell was he doing here, wasting his time, helping Sorenson play nursemaid? He wasn't going to learn anything from this sick excuse for a human being. Where was the brains of the family, Muriel Stern? Was he being set up?

To Johnny's disgust Stern started to blubber. "D'you know what hell on earth it is, young Peet, to be watched night and day, for the cops to know what time I pee, to live with this piece of police shit around your ankle?" Stern lifted his leg and Johnny saw he was wearing an electronic monitor. "D'you know what hell it is to be locked up with a woman who wishes you'd never been born?" He lurched over to a drinks tray in the corner and poured himself a large vodka.

"Women . . . they're the root of all evil. If it wasn't for a woman, you know, I wouldn't be . . . ." He gulped down his drink as if he were dying of thirst. "This evil little temptress, this so-called designer with the face of an angel and the body of a kid . . . she's the reason I'm in this fucking mess." Stern stopped sniffling, leering as he went on, "You're young— you're probably used to these beanstalk model types, who only know how to come if they're getting a fuck on the sly . . ." Stern wagged his finger at Johnny. "The kinkier the better, the more public the better . . . this one . . . this one," he growled, "she was trying to unzip my fly when . . . when Svank got what was coming to him."

Stern realized his listener was not reacting—was sitting stone-faced as he rolled out the lurid details. "I tell you, Peet, it wasn't worth it. No fuck's worth what I've been through the last few days—"

"Arthur! What are you doing here?"

Johnny didn't need to turn to know that the formidable Muriel Stern had entered the room. He jumped to his feet as Arthur Stern cowered back in the chair, trying to hide his glass behind him. Muriel Stern stood, glaring at her husband, leaning heavily on an ebony stick. There was no sign of Sorenson.

Although there was nothing in the world that could make him feel sorry for somebody like Arthur Stern, Johnny could understand anybody quaking under Muriel's unsparing gaze.

"I told you I would speak to Mr. Peet on your behalf." She turned to look just as coldly at Johnny. "I hope Arthur has not been wasting your time, Mr. Peet. He has a colorful way of describing the circumstances which have led to his wrongful arrest. This has not helped him—us. Do please sit down."

To Johnny's relief Sorenson appeared behind her, but he wasn't going to be of much help. "Johnny, I see there's no need for me to make any formal introductions." The doctor looked pale, worn out. "If you will forgive me, Muriel, I think I'm going to head out to the Island after all. I am reassured by your blood pressure and the other tests. I'll come to see you again on Friday—unless you need me before."

"Not much good if I do. Why you want to spend valuable time commuting back and forth I don't know. It's not as if you have any land! The helicopter can't even get in there to bring you back when I need you."

Sorenson had obviously heard it all before. He blinked his eyes in the semblance of a friendly wink, squeezed her hand, and said again, "First thing Friday then. Thank you, Johnny. I know Mrs. Stern can rely on you."

"David." The pronunciation of Sorenson's first name was an order. "David, I can think much more clearly if Arthur isn't here, drooling all over the furniture. Can't you give him a shot or something to stop him drinking?"

Arthur Stern stood up with effort. "All right, Muriel. I know when I'm not wanted . . ."

Johnny couldn't remember witnessing such a disagreeable scene between two people, let alone a husband and wife. He looked down at the floor, embarrassed to see Arthur start to walk unsteadily across the room, where Sorenson took his arm and helped him out.

After they left there was a long silence which Johnny was determined not to break. Here was the opportunity he'd been looking for, the chance to grill the only brains in the family, to see if he could find even the slightest link between the Sterns' celebrated fortune and the murky underground world of Svank; yet a dark cloud had settled in his mind. It didn't go away as Muriel Stern began to speak.

"I am appreciative of your offer to introduce your illustrious father to us, Mr. Peet. He is recognized by millions for his ability to bring about justice. I hope David, eh, Doctor Sorenson, has told you how I believe if only your father will write about the true facts in this case, Arthur, my husband, will be extricated from the sorry mess he is in. I am anxious for this to happen before this farce of an indictment takes place. Lawyers! Don't talk to me about lawyers."

She spoke as if she were presiding over a board meeting of Stern Fashion and Textiles, chomping at the bit to get her point of view across. Although she paused, obviously waiting for Johnny to agree with her, he stayed silent, fearing that what he was about to hear might make him sick to his stomach.

"For some reason I cannot fathom, Mr. Peet, my husband's legal advisors have told him not to repeat what I am now going to tell you. I believe it is a major mistake. My husband was in the wrong place at the wrong time, but as you can see for yourself there is no way he could commit a murder." She laughed. It was not a pleasant sound. "He had had his business differences with Svank, but if anyone took the trouble to look into that, it would soon be confirmed they had been resolved to everyone's satisfaction."

Muriel closed her eyes and sighed deeply. "No, the unpalatable fact is, at the time of the murder my husband was on the third floor of the library, when he should have been on the first floor. He was there, hoping for—er—privacy, advising a young, unknown, would-be fashion designer . . ." She pursed her lips in revulsion. "He uses the word 'advises' in a loose fashion; I have no doubt they were engaged in some sort of sexual encounter. This is not the first time Mr. Stern has abused my trust. In this instance . . ."

Johnny was no longer listening. He didn't need to. With the ugly details supplied by Stern, everything was becoming all too clear.

"A young, unknown, would-be fashion designer."

Ginny and Stern. Even as part of his mind refuted the shocking scenario, another part accepted that it all made terrible sense. Ginny's playing around with Stern at the time of the murder explained why she hadn't so far claimed the precious cloak she'd left behind, because it also explained the greater mystery: why she'd left it behind in the first place. She'd been fleeing from the scene of the crime . . . from Stern . . . from getting involved . . . from receiving the full spotlight of attention at the worst possible time on her modus operandi of crashing and flirting and— he still tried to block the thought, but it came right back—yes, if necessary, fucking her way to so-called success.

Muriel Stern was still giving her orders. Her words came and went as a kind of echo in his head " . . . If you ask me the lawyers haven't even attempted to find her. It's as if they don't believe she exists . . . Whose side are they on anyway . . . One word from your father and I know the search will be on for this wretched whore . . . but let me clarify what I mean."

He had to get out of this stifling apartment, out into the fresh air, before he threw up. He jumped up clumsily, knowing he must look wild. He didn't care about tracing a link between Svank and the Sterns anymore; he didn't care about anything. He'd been made a fool of; he'd been betrayed.

"I'm sorry, Mrs. Stern. I'm sorry, but I've got to go."

"But, but, Mr. Peet—"

He rushed out of the claustrophobic little room, out of the apartment, ignoring the shout to come back from the gray-suited manservant following him out the door. He was not aware until he hit the street that he'd been holding his breath, as he used to do as a child, witnessing emotional scenes between his parents.

He didn't know where he was going. He had to have a drink. He went into a bar on First Avenue and, head in hands, stared at his miserable reflection in the bar mirror. Ginny and Stern. Ginny and Stern. He kept shaking his head. Was it really possible his Ginny, his own little crasher, could go off with an obvious lecher like Stern to a deserted part of the library, just asking for trouble?

The answer had to be it was possible. The fact that Ginny had had the temerity—at the time he'd even half admiringly labeled it as guts— to crash the library dinner in the first place showed she was capable of anything. Even sex with Stern to get backing for her business? No, no, no, surely he couldn't be such a bad judge of someone.

Thinking of Stern putting a finger on Ginny made him nauseous. He had to hear it from her, face-to-face, but he was too angry to listen right now. He wanted to strangle her just as much as he'd wanted to knock Stern down.

He left the bar and started to walk slowly downtown in the direction of Ginny's loft. He welcomed the stinging air on his face, the wind howling up from the river, whipping away at his clothes.

Why should he care so much? He'd made no commitment. It was none of his business, but on the contrary, it was very much his business now. An old movie title came into his head: *License to Kill.* By encouraging Ginny for the sake of his book, and, God forbid, by paying her for the information, he'd given her license to crash.

He was the one who'd put a respectable spin on her crashing, filling her head with the noble idea that she was providing him with a sociological survey of contemporary mores and values. He'd stopped admonishing her and instead he'd showed her how much he loved hearing about her exploits, but how much had she left out? Was there no limit to what she was prepared to do for her business, for kicks?

He groaned as he walked. It was getting late, but he didn't want to give up walking and hail a cab. He wanted to put his body through the extra exertion, pushing against the cold wind, feeling his hands turn to ice in his jacket pockets.

Again and again during the nearly ninety minutes it took to walk to Madison Square Park, he remembered Stern's sick expression as he gave his account of the assignation . . . "the kinkier the better . . . the kind of girl who can only come when it's out in public." His footsteps quickened. He'd never really trusted Dolores, but Ginny . . . until he looked in her eyes and heard for himself it was true, he couldn't believe it. If it was true, he would never trust a woman again.

There was something else that gnawed at him. Ginny had to know Stern's life was in jeopardy.

If she had been with him that night, could she really be so heartless, so incredibly self-absorbed that in order to cover up her own crashing exploits she hadn't come forward to confirm Stern's alibi and so exonerate him?

It was inconceivable. As Johnny neared the loft he asked himself what or whom was Ginny covering up? Did she know something about Svank's death—or someone connected to it? Someone like Poppy? But Poppy had a cast-iron alibi of her own. Something nagged at him, but he couldn't think what it was.

As he rang the bell he thought he had his anger under control, until he heard her voice, shaky, breathless, nervous. Yes, definitely nervous. She was covering up something, or was it someone? He tried to sound lighthearted. "It's me, Ginny. Back from the front."

"Oh, Johnny, how wonderful. I hoped you'd come, but I wasn't sure. How wonderful! Oh, Johnny." There was no pretense in that welcome.

She was waiting for him at the top of the stairs, leaning over the banister as he climbed the last flight. She looked like a kid all right, with her hair in funny little braids, wearing a long primrose-colored nightshirt. "Oh, Johnny." She tried to wrap herself around him. She sensed his withdrawal. "What's wrong? My God, you're like ice. Is it still that cold out? I can't believe it. Quickly, come inside."

He was shivering, but he wasn't sure it was from the cold. He couldn't stop until she'd made some coffee and draped a blanket around his shoulders. He leaned back, carefully studying her face as he told her a little about what he had recently discovered about "your friend Poppy's beau."

Was it his imagination that she paled as he dropped a few lines he'd rehearsed on the walk over? "I know from you that Svank was no pussycat, but he was no law-abiding citizen either. It's lucky Poppy's seen the end of him. It looks as if he died just in time to avoid going inside for a long, long time. The shit's about to hit the fan."

Ginny's mouth was set in a tight line. Was she surprised? It was hard to say. He went on grimly, "Svank was done in by his own greed. It was contagious. By never delegating enough he signed his own death warrant. Someone wasn't satisfied with his share." He swallowed the last sip of coffee.

"Let me get you some more—"

"No, I don't need any more goddam coffee."

He pulled her down beside him, roughly turning her face to look at his. "D'you remember our old friend Luisa? The Villeneva jewel heist?" A flash of fear crossed Ginny's face. She began to tremble. He tightened his grip on her arm. He didn't care if he bruised her. He wanted to hurt her as she'd hurt him. "I'm on the case, Ginny. There's already proof that in some way that particular jewel robbery led straight back to Svank. Big-time jewel thefts, big-time art thefts—Svank had devised a unique way of using them—as collateral, for his real line of dirty work, drug-dealing involving zillions of dollars. The retail shops, the manufacturing plants, the legit trades—all window dressing, m'dear, for what Mr. Svank was really all about."

"Why are you staring at me? Why are you looking at me like that?" she cried. "You're hurting my arm, Johnny. Why are you telling me all this? What has it got to do with me?"

He'd had enough. He jumped off the bed, pulling her with him, shaking her like a rag doll. "Because we both know, don't we, that Arthur Stern didn't kill Svank? You know because you know the real killer, don't you, Ginny? You were with Stern, weren't you? You witnessed the murder because you were the young designer dallying with Stern at exactly the place and exactly the time when it took place, weren't you, Ginny?"

As his voice rose in anger, his heart sank. He'd been fooling himself. He hoped he'd see in her eyes her own fury at being accused, her stunned disbelief that he could think such a thing; but there was no fury there, no disbelief.

She didn't attempt to lie. She sagged in his arms, looked beaten, heavy with defeat. "Yes, Johnny," she whispered. "But it's not what you think—"

He let her go so quickly she tumbled back on the bed. He paced backward and forward, running a hand through his hair. Now he wished he'd never come. He didn't want to know the truth if it meant Ginny had betrayed him. It was too painful to deal with.

"Johnny . . ." The tears were coming now, noiseless tears in a steady stream down her cheeks. Fighting for breath, in fits and starts she told him about meeting Stern once before, and walking out on him, not knowing how much he could help her until Lee Baker Davies told her the story about the Sterns rescuing a California designer.

He slumped down in a chair. He didn't want to listen, but he was too tired to leave.

"He . . . he seemed interested in my dress at the library. I thought I'd show him the cloak, too, if I could only get him to the cloakroom before dinner. He was boasting . . . wanted to show off this medieval manuscript he'd given to the library. Oh, Johnny, I know I was a fool, but I hoped—"

"Ginny, I know what you hoped," he interrupted coldly. "What happened?"

"I knew I was taking a risk, but I thought I could handle it. He'd had too much to drink . . . I didn't think there'd be a problem." She was beginning to sound hysterical. "I was so unhappy, making you mad, not meeting your father, not getting anywhere, I thought at least I could make an impression on—"

"You made an impression all right. What happened?"

She shuddered. "He . . . he tried to rape me. He . . . he . . . might have succeeded if we hadn't heard a shot. We saw these two men fighting at the end of the hall. We saw everything."

"Everything? You saw who the two men were?"

She didn't even hesitate. At this, the darkest time of Alex's life, until she heard what he had to say, even now she couldn't give him away. "No, no, no . . . the hall was too dark. It was impossible to see who they were." She shut her eyes, trying to blot the tall, shadowy figure out of her mind.

"Oh, Johnny, please believe me. I don't know what you've been told, but that's what happened. Can you understand now why I haven't claimed the cloak? Why I haven't gone to the police? It's so . . . so degrading. If the story gets in the papers, I'll never live it down."

"What about Stern? He's about to be indicted for Svank's death, for manslaughter, if not murder two. What about him?"

"Every day I tell myself the police will find the real killer today . . . and Stern will be released—"

"You can't let another day pass, Ginny, you know that."

She covered her face with her hands, her thin shoulders shaking in the old-fashioned nightshirt. She looked so helpless, so fragile. Despite himself his anger and suspicion began to evaporate. It was replaced by tenderness and remorse, for not looking after her, for not protecting her from nightmares like Stern and Svank.

He let the silence settle in. He longed to dry her tears, to gather her up and hold her close for the rest of his life, but he did nothing. He was scared at the depth of his feelings. He wanted to think it through.

They were so alike, hiding their vulnerability beneath such tough "in your face" exteriors; both leading such unreal lives, he either the guest in other people's palaces, or the host with an expense account; she pinning her hopes and talent on bluffing her way into a society that measured merit on the amount of media coverage.

"Johnny . . ." There was the sweetest, most beseeching look he'd ever seen on a woman's face. It said everything he wanted to hear. She loved him; she needed him; she trusted him. He was in love with her; he didn't want to be, but he had to acknowledge it to himself, if not to her.

He switched off the light, threw off the blanket and his clothes. "Ginny, I believe you," he whispered. As their bodies made contact, they began to make love. It was impossible to stop.

Later, much later, neither thought they would be able to sleep; yet they were both sleeping deeply when the phone rang just before dawn.

"Hello?"

"Who's sleeping in my bed?" There was a high, maniacal laugh.

Ginny was so sleepy she didn't know if she was dreaming. "What did you say?" There was a click. Johnny groaned in his sleep. It must have been a bad dream. She snuggled up against his back and didn't wake up until his hands and mouth began to caress her once again.

It was eight o'clock. A cool light emphasized some of the shabbiness in the loft. Where was Johnny? She could hear him moving around the place, getting dressed. She hoped he didn't notice the peeling paint, the threadbare spot in the Indian carpet.

She stared at a damp patch on the ceiling. Did he love her? She longed to ask him . . . longed even more for him to ask her to be . . . well, the impossible . . . a proposal, a formal, legal, "Will you be my wedded wife?" She was crazy. Instead, Johnny called out from the kitchen to ask if she had any cereal.

She did. Somewhere. Thanks to Esme's good advice.

She showered while he made breakfast. It was Mr. and Mrs. Average America getting ready to face a working day until Johnny, facing her over the kitchen table, cupped her face in his hands and said, "Ginny, you've got to go to the police today. You can't put it off any longer. Stern's a nightmare, but you can't live with the knowledge you're letting an innocent man take the rap for somebody else."

She nodded, trying to stop the tears from falling again.

"I've got to check into the office, but I'll come back in an hour or so to take you to the precinct. We'll face this together. Okay?"

She nodded again, too full of remorse and fear to speak.

Johnny was getting ready to go. She couldn't bear it.

At the door he said, "Don't worry. I'll have a lawyer on hand to call, in case you need one, but I don't think you will. You can't be prosecuted at this stage for withholding evidence, but you must tell them everything, just as you told me. And Ginny, look your best, wear your latest design. You have to be prepared for a lot of press. You have nothing to worry about. You're an innocent party, so take what you can from this ugly episode and learn from it." He shook his head angrily. "I should never have encouraged you in your crashing. I must have been out of my mind . . ."

She tried to kiss him, but he moved his head away. "The whole thing's disgraceful. It's going to be hard for anyone to understand how a sweet young thing like you could go off with a guy like Stern, but I understand . . . at least I think I do. I'm ashamed of you for doing it, but I have to say this could be the opportunity you've wanted for years. Now you can take credit for that wretched cloak that you say is the talk of the town."

"Have you forgiven me?"

"I think so." He tugged at her braids. "I will if you get rid of these."

"Do you—"

"Do I what?" He was smiling now in the usual, crinkly-eyed Johnny way as if things were normal and she wasn't about to be sent to jail.

"Oh, nothing."

"Do I love you?"

He held her so close, she could feel his body stirring. In a second they'd be back in bed. She hoped so, but no, it wasn't going to happen this morning. Too much had to be cleared up first.

"How deep is the ocean, how high is the sky? D'you know that song, Ginny?"

"I know it."

"Then you know the answer to your question."

He ran down the stairs whistling. He felt like a different man from the suspicious, angry one who'd arrived the night before. He'd forgotten his suspicions. He had every reason to whistle. Once his frightened, foolish young Ginny told the police the truth, they could concentrate on finding the real killer; and he, John Q. Peet, was sure it would turn out to be someone in Svank's own hierarchy.

As Johnny opened the heavy downstairs door, someone was watching, waiting across the street. It was Oz, huddled in a doorway, way down after a drug high and consumed with rage and jealousy.

So he'd been right all along. Ginny Walker was the two-timing bitch he'd always suspected. She'd given him the slip the night before, as she always had; not because she was the Miss Goody Two-shoes she pretended to be, but because she knew she had this second-rate hack waiting upstairs to fuck her all night.

It was time for revenge. The whore was about to learn what happened when you mess with Oz Tabori.

Johnny had been gone about ninety minutes when the intercom buzzed. "Ms. Ginny Walker?"

"Yes."

"Detective Petersh and Detective Reever, we have reason to believe you have information pertaining to—" She held the phone away from her ear. The loft swung crazily from side to side. She held on to the kitchen cabinet. Johnny had betrayed her? Johnny had gone straight to the police? If she had to spend the rest of her life in jail, what did it matter? All her hopes and dreams were smashed.

"Are you there? Can we come in?"

"Yes, yes. Please come up. Top floor."

She wasn't wearing any makeup, but she'd brushed out her braids and was already dressed in the copper-colored velvet tunic she'd been able to squeeze out from the leftover cloak material, by cutting it on the bias à la Milan's Alberta Ferretti.

Johnny had told her to wear her latest design, she thought bitterly. Until today, she'd never been able to wear it. It had been hidden at the back of the cupboard. When Johnny told her to be prepared for the press after she made her full confession, she'd decided that wearing the copper velvet tunic was one way to prove she was the designer of the celebrated copper-colored cloak.

She was surprised by her composure, offering the detectives coffee (they declined), anxious to get the horror over with.

"I'm sorry you had to come here. I was on my way to see you this morning."

Although it was the truth, she knew how feeble and farfetched it sounded. Without much prompting she told the detectives in a low monotone the entire story of her decision to crash the event, making the special cloak for the occasion, arriving at the library at the wrong entrance, meeting Oz and being escorted by him to the right one. She even told them about picking up a card from the W section and not realizing until much later that she'd picked up Barbara Walters's seating assignment.

She didn't spare herself, knowing how cheap and calculating her whole modus operandi of crashing sounded. The detectives were expressionless, and she showed no emotion until she began to describe what happened when Stern and she arrived on the upper floor.

She bit her lip, aware she was going to break down.

"Was this the first New York party you crashed?" It was Reever, the older detective, asking a question for the first time. He smiled as he spoke; he looked kinder than Petersh.

"No, sir."

"Are you usually so successful?"

An ashamed, affirmative nod.

"Was there a specific reason for you wanting to crash this particular event?" Petersh's voice was much sharper, more suggestive of major wrongdoing. She could sense he despised her. She didn't blame him.

There was nothing to be gained by mentioning Johnny's name or, certainly, that of Quentin Peet.

"No. I've always crashed because I . . ." She couldn't think of how to put it into words. Her voice broke as it came out, " . . . because I want to get publicity for my clothes . . . to be photographed . . . to find a backer."

The detectives exchanged glances.

"But you went to such elaborate lengths for this occasion . . . the expensive cloak . . ." Petersh looked disdainfully around the loft. He didn't need to add, Why spend the money on that when there's so much to do here? "Did you go in the hopes of meeting Mr. Svank?" His tone was cutting.

"No, no, of course not. I already knew Svank . . . at least . . ." She felt she'd made a mistake. "I've designed, made clothes for a friend of his, Poppy Gan."

"How well did you know the deceased?"

"I shouldn't have said I knew him. I mean over the years I saw a lot of him . . ." Ginny waved her hands about helplessly. "Whenever I was with Poppy . . . he didn't really know me."

Her head ached as they grilled her for what seemed like hours. They wanted dates, times, and places where she'd actually seen Svank; they wanted to know who was with him and what had been said. They asked her the same questions over and over again, particularly about Stern and what she saw on the third floor.

"Let's go through it one more time, Ms. Walker. You saw two men apparently fighting at the end of the hall. Neither of them was Mr. Stern? You did not witness Mr. Stern fighting with anyone?"

"No, I've already told you, Stern was with me. If it hadn't been for the gunshot he would have raped me—"

Petersh cut across harshly. "You saw the victim pushed over the balcony; you saw a tall shadowy figure running away. What else can you remember about this tall shadowy figure?"

"I told you. It was too dark and after the . . . the accident, the murder, he disappeared—"

"Down the hidden stairwell, you say? The same fire escape exit you say you used to get away?"

She sighed. How many more times did she have to repeat the story of her own escape? Neither detective looked as if they believed her.

"Why did you follow this tall shadowy figure? Did you recognize him, know him?"

"Of course not, of course I didn't know him," she said hastily. "I was scared . . . terrified . . . I didn't know what to do, but I guess I had to be more scared of Stern, of what he would do to me if I didn't get away."

They were asking her to describe once again the tall shadowy figure when, to her horror, she heard the intercom buzz.

Alex. "I'll call you Wednesday to see what suits you best," he'd said. It was Wednesday. Oh, God, please don't let it be Alex. The detectives saw her tense up.

"That's your intercom," said Reever.

"Yes, I know." She sat, frozen, unable to move.

"Aren't you going to answer it?"

On leaden legs she went into the little kitchen.

"Ginny."

Johnny. How could he have the gall? "The detectives are here already," she said icily. "You could have spared yourself a trip. They came as soon as you called them."

"What the hell are you talking about? Let me in at once."

"No."

"I'll just keep my finger on the buzzer until you do. You silly woman, you don't think I went to the police without you, do you?"

By the time Johnny climbed the last flight of stairs, the detectives were standing up, looking as if they were ready to go.

"We'd like you to come with us to tell your story to the district attorney."

"Am I under arrest?"

"Nope . . ." Ginny could have sworn Petersh mouthed, "not yet." He looked angry, hot, and bothered.

The atmosphere changed for the better when Johnny came in, smiling, shaking hands. "I'm John Q. Peet, *Next!* magazine, a friend of Ms. Walker's." Although Ginny glared at him, he came over to her and put his arm casually around her waist. "She was coming to see you officers this morning. You beat her to it. I only heard last night about the whole sorry mess she got herself into. I've been in Washington on a story. She wanted to go to the police, but was too afraid . . ." He grimaced in his most charming, self-deprecating way. "I'm afraid I was the reason she crashed the library dinner the other night . . . it was an innocent adventure which ended very badly, nothing more than that."

"I'm sure it can all be cleared up, Mr. Peet. We'd like Ms. Walker to make a statement now to the D.A.'s office."

"Does this mean the case against Stern will be dismissed?"

"I can't make any predictions, Mr. Peet. I'm sure you realize that." Petersh looked coldly at Ginny. "Shall we be going?"

"Well, that wasn't so bad, was it? How about a celebration feast in Chinatown?" Johnny was smiling at her in the way her mother used to, after a visit to the dentist.

"Sure, I'd love to. Where d'you suggest? I'm so confused, I've lost my bearings. Where exactly are we?"

"At the tip of Manhattan, just below Chinatown. Not that far from Little Italy. Okay, ten-dollar spring rolls or a dollar-and-a-half spaghetti. You choose."

"Spring rolls."

Ginny looked back at the menacing, ugly building they'd just left, and shivered. Thank God, Johnny had convinced her he'd had nothing to do with the detectives' arrival at the loft. Oz must have talked, for who else could it be? Thank God, too, that Johnny had insisted on going with her to the D.A.'s office at 100 Centre Street, where she'd never been more depressed in her life.

Nothing had prepared her for the sight of the D.A.'s office in the Criminal Court Building—ominous, vast, stretching for the length of several city blocks. Nothing had prepared her for its somber interior, either. As they'd followed the detectives along a maze of dreary narrow corridors, Johnny told her it housed in cramped and tiny cubbyholes thousands of toilers in the criminal justice system: judges, assistant district attorneys, legal-aid lawyers, and probation officers.

As long as Johnny was with her she'd managed to feel reasonably calm, but when he was asked to wait in another area and she was escorted to a waiting room with all the charm of a prison cell, panic had set in. She'd been sure she'd never get out; in some way she'd be implicated in the murder and incarcerated in the Tombs—the cells connected to the courthouse at its northern end by the "bridge of sighs."

It hadn't happened. She'd finally given her statement on tape to a bent-over, exhausted-looking assistant district attorney in the Homicide Division, who hadn't hounded her like Petersh and Reever, but who, exceedingly carefully, line by line, had spent an interminable time reading the detectives' lengthy notes.

"You were with Arthur Stern from 8:25 P.M. to approximately 8:45 P.M. on the third floor of the New York Public Library on the night of May second when you both witnessed two men fighting?" He sounded as if he had a terrible cold.

"Yes."

"You both witnessed one man push the other over the balcony, following a gunshot?"

"Yes."

He read on, croaking and wheezing, asking her to repeat how she left the library, then called in a secretary to type up the statement.

When it came back, he switched on the tape again and asked her to swear to its accuracy and then sign it. He seemed so uninterested, she'd had the courage to ask him, "What's going to happen to Mr. Stern now?"

He wouldn't give her an answer. "That decision isn't mine to make," he'd said pompously.

It all seemed perfectly straightforward to her. Her alibi would exonerate Stern and the police would begin their search again.

If Alex didn't convince her when they met that he'd had nothing to do with Svank's death, would she give him away?

The sun suddenly came out, warming her whole body. It seemed like a good omen. Like Scarlett O'Hara, she'd think about it tomorrow.

As she strolled with Johnny in the direction of Mott Street, she realized there hadn't been any sign of the press after all. She wasn't that sorry. She wasn't sure she wanted her identity known, even in order to take credit for the cloak. If it hadn't been Alex in the upper hall, the last thing she wanted was for the real killer to know who she was.

"What are you looking so worried about now?" Johnny seemed concerned, holding her tightly to his side.

An unusual, warm feeling of being safe and loved crept over her. Everything was going to be all right; her living nightmare was about to come to an end.

"Nothing, Johnny, really nothing. I haven't felt so happy in ages." And it was true.

She might not have felt that way if she could have seen the look on Matthew Mossop's face as he finished reading her statement. "What a bitch," he said to nobody in particular.

The assistant district attorney pursed his lips, trying to look in full agreement, although he wasn't sure whether his boss was alluding to the girl or the situation.

Matthew Mossop was chief of the Trial Division, in charge of the several hundred lawyers responsible for all the violent-crime prosecution in the office. He was also one of the few who reported directly to the big chief, the district attorney of New York County.

"I think the girl's covering up something," Petersh snarled.

Mossop looked at the detective as if he wished he'd drop dead. Petersh was his favorite detective in the Homicide Squad, generally as tenacious as a terrier with a bone, helping the prosecution pile up evidence against the accused; but this morning's piece of work was a disastrous setback in their case against Stern, and Petersh knew it.

"It's a classic dilemma; everything has pointed to Stern, except for a few minor details. Now this Brady material is going to ruin everything . . ."

Nobody needed to ask what he meant; in criminal legal circles "Brady material" was part of the language, referring to a textbook case, where a defendant named Brady had been convicted after the prosecution had withheld evidence which might have exonerated him.

Mossop groaned. "I can hear the boss now . . . Stern hasn't been indicted; the case is just sitting there . . . best finish it now . . . we can't be accused of withholding exculpatory evidence. Fuck it. Where does it leave us? With a finger up our ass. I can't bear to think of that fucking self-satisfied look on Caulter's face as we hand everything to him on a plate." He sighed. "Well, I'd better get it over with." He picked up the phone. "I need to see the big man right away. I know he's in town. Tell the D.A. it's an emergency."

The phone was ringing when Ginny let herself into the loft in the late afternoon, Johnny having dropped her off on his way to the office to finish his column.

It was her mother, breathless, nervous, one word falling over another as if she hadn't the time even to construct a sentence. "Your Aunt Lil . . . died this morning. Dad's flying out for the funeral . . . can't stop . . . tried to find Alex . . . a Nurse Dob . . . can't remember her name looking to inform him . . . left a message . . . got to drive Dad to the airport in an hour . . . he doesn't know what to pack . . ."

All the traumatic events of the day paled into insignificance. Ginny felt physically ill, unable to communicate to her mother her shock, her sudden sense of gaping emptiness, thinking of Alex's bereavement. It didn't matter. Her mother hung up before she'd even finished a halting few words.

In a stupor, Ginny still hadn't replaced the receiver when she felt a light touch on her shoulder, a hand over her mouth quickly stopping her scream. Alex's hand.

He knew. She could see the pain on his face, a much loved face, but older, strained.

"That was Mother, Alex. I just heard," she said tearfully. "I'm . . . I'm so sorry . . ."

"I came to say goodbye, Ginny. A friend . . . thank God, a friend with a plane is giving me a lift to the Coast. In case something happens to me I wanted to—"

"Oh, Alex." She flung her arms around him, the cousin who'd taught her everything, who'd tried to turn her into a million-dollar baby like Claudia Schiffer, who'd never given her anything but support. "Oh, Alex," she cried again. "Don't . . . don't say goodbye, I can't stand it."

He was kissing her forehead in the old-fashioned, avuncular way he'd used so often throughout the years to show his approval. He held her out at arm's length, a vestige of his old spirit flaring as he tried to say, "Don't stop pushing the envelope, Ginny. You're going to get there, I know it."

He glanced out of the window, then at his watch, gold and gleaming on his wrist. "I took a risk coming here today. Now I've got to get going.

Don't believe everything you might hear about me, Gin. One day when all this is behind me, you'll understand."

She fiercely held on to his hands. "Look me in the eyes, Alex." She began to sob noisily. "Tell me you didn't push Svank to his death. Tell me you had nothing to do with the murder."

Alex brought his face close to hers, looking deeply into her eyes. "I wish, my Gin, I wish, but no, I didn't do it, that is the truth and nothing but the truth . . ."

So why was he in hiding? Who was he hiding from? Why couldn't he move around openly, normally? Why couldn't he buy a ticket like everybody else to fly to California? Why did he have to have a "lift" in a private plane?

"Who's hunting you down, Alex? Why haven't you been in touch before? What about the jewels?"

"That's another story, Ginny, my darling."

"Please explain, Alex. Don't go, let's talk."

Her entreaties were in vain. He was at the door, blowing her a kiss. "I've got to go, Gin. I'm on the run, but not for much longer. I won't say goodbye, sweet Ginny, just *au revoir*. Don't forget, don't let in any strangers."

She heard him rush down the stairs. She heard the front door bang. She hadn't even told him that only that morning she'd given the police evidence that would lead to Stern's release.

It took a few days of feverish, back-to-back meetings before Caulter was finally, reluctantly called by Mossop and told that based on fresh "Brady material" evidence, the D.A. had instructed him to dismiss all charges against Arthur Stern.

"D.A. Eats Crow" was one headline in the *Post*, which summed up the atmosphere at the press conference called to announce the dismissal of all charges against Stern.

Caulter, Stern's defense attorney, was quoted saying, "The people of New York are happy that justice has been done." He was shown shaking hands with a distinctly unsmiling D.A.

The papers lapped up the behind-the-scenes stories, fastening onto the theme of an overly hasty NYPD, a too-fast arraignment of the wrong man, who also happened to be such a pillar of society. Would Mossop's head fall? Who would take the rap? Few paid much attention to the fact that Caulter used Svank's real name, Vladimir Owzvankigori, for the first time in one of the many interviews he granted.

For the moment the press wanted more about the living than the dead. What new evidence, for instance, had brought about such an embarrassing public reversion from the D.A.'s office?

It didn't take long to find out. Twenty-four hours after the "Eat Crow" headline hit the streets, variations of "The Crasher" detailing Ginny's story were all over the front pages of the tabloids and on the local news.

A couple of Oz's pictures made it into print, although the picture editors were amazed, and delighted, to discover how many pictures they already had of "the mystery crasher" in their files, pictures which showed her in a variety of wild to weird to wonderful designs at all sorts of notable events.

The *Wall Street Journal* devoted its much-read front page center column to famous "crashing" exploits, including some acts of daring during World War II; The Op Ed page of the *New York Times* ran a piece from a prominent psychiatrist explaining and evaluating the psyche of a "crashing" personality.

Ginny was distraught. She felt exposed and alone in the world, although many people phoned to try to comfort her, including, to her added embarrassment, Everard Gosman. Even "Chili," the Indian psychiatrist, offered his services free "during this traumatic time."

It was traumatic all right, particularly when, in response to her anxious questions, her mother told her Alex had not appeared at his mother's funeral.

"But he must have been there," Ginny remonstrated. "He had to have been—"

"I think you mean to say he should have been," her mother snapped, "but unless he came as the invisible man, I can assure you, your father did not see him." She couldn't continue her protestations without her mother becoming suspicious.

She began to receive a series of hang-up calls; then Petersh reappeared to question her again, warning her not to leave town. He reminded her that despite her protestations she couldn't identify anyone, that she was now, along with Stern, a material witness in the case. The nightmare hadn't gone away, it had intensified.

What once upon a time she'd lived for—her name in the papers, big and bold, along with a variety of pictures showing her wearing her own designs—she now had in spades. It meant nothing. She dreaded seeing the papers, feared to go out in case the paparazzi were around, waiting to pounce on "The Crasher" or "Stern's Alibi Girl," as Esme told her she was billed in the *National Enquirer*.

She wrote a four-page letter to her parents, explaining as best she could what had really happened, and Esme sent it by Federal Express.

She felt better—for five minutes—when her mother called and told her they believed in her, and "Why don't you come home for a few days?"

Home? Where was home? Certainly not Florida, with the Walker School of Advanced Learning. All the same, hearing the love and concern in her mother's voice was soothing to the soul.

Johnny tried to tease her out of her depression. "It's your Andy Warhol fifteen minutes of fame. Come on, Ginny, snap out of it. Isn't this what you've always wanted? Walk out the front door with your head held high. Summertime or not, sweat it out with that cloak on your back—"

"The police won't give it back to me."

A month after Svank's death, and three weeks after the charges were dismissed against Stern, Petersh returned to the loft with a new line of inquiry, the one Ginny had been dreading all along.

"Are you acquainted with an Alexander Rossiter?"

"Yes, he's my cousin."

"Do you know where he is now?"

"No . . ." Her mouth was dry with fear.

"Have you heard from him? Has he called you recently?"

She didn't like Petersh. It was easy to lie, to say firmly, coldly, "No, not a word."

"Do you know your cousin uses a number of aliases? Alex Heibron?"

Another one. She felt herself flush with shock. Another name she'd never heard of.

"No, I didn't know that. Why would he do that?"

"What about Angus O'Keeffe? Have you heard that one?"

"I've told you I didn't know. I don't know why he would use another name. Why are you telling me all this? I can't help you."

Petersh came up close, glowering. "I think you're hiding something, Miss Walker. Your cousin is in big trouble. Interpol, the FBI, and now *I'm* looking for him. If you know where he is and aren't telling me, just as you neglected to pass on the information about Mr. Stern, this time you won't walk away from Centre Street so easily."

So he'd seen how frightened she was at the D.A.'s office; he knew how to get her attention now.

She was jumpy and irritable when Johnny arrived an hour later. She'd promised him she'd dress up and risk running into any reporters or photographers still patrolling the street; but after Petersh's visit, she couldn't face it.

"I'm sorry, Johnny, I just don't feel like going out." She had a bump on her chin, her hair was a mess, and she'd been wearing the same T-shirt and jeans for two days.

Johnny had had enough. "You've got to pull yourself together, Ginny. D'you seriously believe there's no life after crashing? What about all that big talk of yours, about being a successful designer? You'll never get anywhere lolling around here." He stared at her steadily. "There's something else on your mind, isn't there? I've been doing some thinking. I don't hear a certain name much anymore, for which I must say I'm thankful. I've added up two and two and think it comes to four."

Her heart started to thump. "I don't know what you mean."

"I think you do. What ever happened to Little Lord Fauntleroy? I never hear you talk about him anymore, I mean your sainted cousin, of course, Alex Rossiter, the man who taught you everything. Can it be this paragon of virtue has dropped you now you've been in this trouble? Where has he been when you needed him most? Has he called? Is that why you've turned into such a limp dishrag?"

She began to steam. He was glad to see it. He went on, "Cousin Alex doesn't come around much anymore, does he, Ginny? I'm sorry to tell you, but I don't think Alex is the sunny little choirboy you've always thought . . . there's something going on, isn't there, Ginny?"

She shut her eyes. First Petersh, now Johnny. She couldn't pretend anymore. She had to confide in someone, and who else but Johnny?

"Well?" Johnny pulled her onto his lap. All the fire went out of her. She didn't resist. "Tell me, baby, tell me what's eating you up? What are you hiding from me?"

And she told him. It just poured out—about her fears when Alex became involved with Svank; about his erratic behavior, his "entailed" gifts, his long absences, his silences; and finally, in a tearful burst, about the hideous discovery of the Villeneva jewels hidden at the bottom of her toilet tank, and their disappearance the night of Svank's death.

Johnny sat in silence, his mind racing, trying to grasp what he'd just been told, never dreaming he'd hear anything like this. He knew from the Art Loss Register and from Trager how hot the Villeneva jewels were. The police suspected that although they were eventually destined for a major drug dealer, they could possibly still be in the U.S., hidden until everything cooled down.

Frankly, he hadn't cared that much. After the shock of learning about Ginny's involvement, persuading her to talk to the police, and Stern's subsequent exoneration, he'd thought he'd put the Svank case behind him.

Now he shook his head in disbelief. It was inconceivable that all this time the precious gems had actually been planted in this down-at-the-heel loft, in a toilet tank of all places. From everything he'd learned about this thief, he knew he was a particularly cool customer, but this was cool enough to freeze the mind.

If Ginny's fabled cousin, Alex Rossiter, really turned out to be the main hand in the Villeneva affair, it wasn't too far-fetched to believe he was responsible for other equally "cool" acts of daring thievery, major thefts which led right back to Svank.

It was ironic. Just when he'd least expected it, just when he was trying to cheer Ginny up, she'd put straight into his hands the identity of the missing person in the Svank puzzle, the "new" man on Svank's team, the one who the FBI knew had dared to disobey the boss and been sent for some tough "orientation" to the back streets of San Juan.

Again Johnny asked himself, was it really possible that Ginny's cousin could be the man the FBI had been after, the small fish in a vast, money-laundering sea of crime, plucked out for bigger things by the biggest fish of all, only to disgrace himself with Svank, the boss, soon after?

Johnny hadn't said a word and Ginny, white, wan, was looking at him in fear. He tightened his arm around her. "Ginny, I can't believe what you've been going through . . . and you never told me." Again he shook his head in disbelief. "Am I such an ogre? Why on earth didn't you tell me?"

"I was afraid . . . I wanted to find out what was going on first." She turned to him, saying earnestly, "I still find it impossible to accept that

Alex is a thief. If you knew him as I do, you'd understand. He's been such an inspiration to me my whole life. If I told you, you'd have had to go to the police. I couldn't let that happen until I heard what Alex had to say—"

"Well, what did he have to say?"

Ginny blinked back tears. "That's the problem. I haven't had enough time to talk to him . . . and Petersh was here this afternoon, asking me questions about Alex. He knows, somehow, that Alex and I are cousins—probably through Oz . . ." Some of her steam came back when she said Oz's name. "Damn him to his metaphysical hell forever . . ."

"What?"

"Oh, nothing, forget it." She jumped up, agitated. "I'm sure Petersh knows what Alex has been up to . . . says he's wanted by Interpol, the FBI. I'm sure Svank is behind all this, that Alex thought he could play in his league and then got out of his depth. Alex isn't a crook. If I could only spend time with him and ask him about everything, I'm sure it could all be explained." She looked at Johnny beseechingly. "Could you help me find him?" She paused, not sure whether to go on, then, "Remember after Esme's wedding, the night when I said I didn't want to go home ever again? I meant it. The jewels were still here in the loft, like something evil . . . when I said I wanted to meet your father, you were so mad, but it was because I thought if he knew the story, he'd know what to do, he'd find Alex and find out the truth. I know it sounds crazy . . ."

He should have been furious, humiliated, but he wasn't. Instead he realized how strong Ginny must be; most women he knew would have broken under the strain of all she'd been through.

"When did you last see him?"

She hesitated. Even now, despite Alex's "the truth and nothing but the truth" avowal, she couldn't tell anyone—not even Johnny—her deepest fear—that Alex was involved in Svank's death.

"I thought I saw him the other day when I went to look at the Barneys cloak. I was sure I saw him with Poppy—you know, Poppy Gan. I jumped out of the cab, nearly got myself killed, but with all the traffic and crowds, I lost them." She bit her lip. "I used to think Alex had a thing for Poppy. Perhaps he does, I don't know."

"Calm down, Ginny. Think. When did you actually see him, talk to him, face-to-face?"

There was a too long silence and finally Ginny whispered, "He called right after I saw him with Poppy. That was the first time in ages. He promised he would come to see me that weekend, to explain everything, that if he didn't call himself to tell me when he was coming, Poppy would—but he didn't come."

Then—another overlong pause—"You know, his mother died, remember I told you, my Aunt Lil? She died the day I went with you to the D.A.'s office. When I got home, Alex came by on his way to the funeral. I haven't heard from him since—or from Poppy. Her phone never answers . . ."

Johnny looked grim. After the decision he'd made in Washington, he'd concentrated on writing about problems where he could make a difference. Goddammit, he didn't want to reenter the Svank cesspool. He'd just received a ton of mail after telling a story that, for once, elevated hope and belief in society. It was based on the news he'd heard from Sister Cochrane, about the redemption of "Madame Sacks to Saks." After his relentless pieces, she'd been taken off the streets and saved by modern medicine and her own renewed faith. He'd been able to report that "Madame Saks," Rosemary, was even teaching again in a school run by caring nuns, one of whom, Sister Cochrane, was determined not to let her slide back into the abyss.

All the same, he knew there was no way he would be able to convince Ginny what a lowlife criminal her cousin Alex Rossiter really was, unless he could present her with undeniable facts. That shouldn't be difficult now, he reckoned, and it would be a pleasure to help Mr. Rossiter get what he deserved.

"I'll help you find him, Ginny," he said slowly. He came over to her and took her in his arms. "No more depression. Put on your glad rags. We're going to hit the town."

A flashbulb went off as they left the loft, she in the sleeveless copper-colored tunic, with sheer dark brown hose.

The ice was broken. She threw back her head and smiled. So she'd get used to being photographed; she'd get backing for her designs; Johnny or his father would find Alex, who would prove his innocence in Svank's death; and everyone would live happily ever after.

They walked hand in hand toward a new bistro, Erica's, where Johnny said the homemade pâté and fresh French bread would make a new woman of her. She tried to shake off the feeling they were being followed. She'd already showed Johnny too much of a sad-sack side and she didn't want to spoil the evening. On the way back to the loft the feeling persisted. She told herself she was being paranoid.

To her surprise, Johnny told her he couldn't stay the night. "Something's come up—I have to go back to Washington at the crack of dawn." Even so, he didn't leave until nearly two A.M., so she was still asleep when her mother woke her with a call around nine the next morning.

"Ginny, have you heard from Alex since we last spoke? Do you know where he is?" Her mother's voice wobbled the way it always did when she was worried.

"No, I wish I did." Ginny was about to tell her mother about Alex's visit, supposedly on the way to the funeral, when there was a loud click on the line.

"Are you still there?"

"Yes, Mother. What about Alex?" Another click, faint this time.

"Someone from the FBI was here," Virginia Walker whispered into the phone. "He wanted to know if we'd seen him. I told him about the last visit—"

"Did you tell him about London, about the story in the—" There was the faint click again. Ginny stopped, frowning, fully awake now, tense. Prickly sweat dripped down her back. "Mums, I've got to go. I'll call you back."

"Oh, Ginny, do you have to? I really need to talk to you now."

"I'll call you back, Mums, really I will," she said softly. "In less than an hour, when I go out. Love you."

Ginny hung up and stared at the phone, which had suddenly become an enemy.

She wasn't being paranoid.

The night before she had been followed and now her phone was being tapped.

Like Alex, she was under somebody's surveillance.

CHAPTER
ELEVEN

7 WEST 43RD STREET, NEW YORK CITY

"Vladamir Owzvankigori . . ." Quentin Peet enunciated each sylla-ble precisely and with relish. "What an absolutely perfect specimen of evil in mankind." He paused dramatically, waiting for Johnny to put down his glass.

"D'you know, Johnny, I have a theory. It can never be proved, of course, but I believe Mr. Owzvankigori attributed the end of the Cold War more to Gorbachev's weakness than to American strategy and tenacity. Around that time—in eighty-eight or eighty-nine—in order not to make a similar mistake and risk the collapse of his own consider-able empire, he began to use the strong-armed methods of another Georgian bandit, Dzhugashvili, or Koba as he also was known between his many arrests and escapes. If Koba had nine lives, Owzvankigori surely had twenty . . ."

Johnny knew better than to interrupt his father. He didn't know what on earth he was talking about, but he did know that in his own good time, QP would come to his point, and it would be a good one.

Meanwhile the evening, which he'd dreaded since receiving his fa-ther's fax, was turning into something he never expected, a warm and wonderful occasion, without one cross word so far. His father was in a rare, expansive mood, encouraging him to talk about himself, seeming genuinely interested in everything he had to say.

He'd summoned up his courage to tell him about the book on mod-ern society he was halfway through; with the help of a young woman, who, he was surprised to find himself saying, "I've become very fond of . . ." So far, he hadn't gone any further.

He hadn't seen his father since the momentous night at the library. Nothing unusual in that. He only had to pick up the paper to know, more or less, where QP was or where he'd been, as usual risking his neck in the world's biggest trouble spots, in and out of Bosnia and, igniting a quickly burned out flash of envy, in Bogotá, Colombia.

Then the fax had arrived, giving him a choice of three dates for dinner, something unusual in itself; his father usually took for granted that he would be free to see him whenever he suggested—or rather commanded—it. The fax had added he had "something important to discuss."

Johnny had been on tenterhooks, waiting for the "something" to drop with the impact of a bomb all through the three courses. Now, mellow and increasingly relaxed with good wine and food, he was actually sorry the evening was drawing to a close.

In the dimly lit, hushed library where they were having coffee and after-dinner drinks, Peet beckoned to the waiter to refill their glasses with the Cockburn reserve port, kept in a special bin for him and a few other connoisseurs, at this, his favorite club.

He settled back against the comfortable old leather armchair, savoring the deep, ruby-red liquid. "Of course, you know who I'm referring to, son, one of the most brilliant minds of the decade, Vladamir Owzvankigori, otherwise known as Svank. He will go down in the annals of the twentieth century as one of the most Machiavellian, brilliant hoods in history."

Johnny nodded dutifully. "And Dzhug . . . whatisname . . . Koba the Greek, where does he come in?"

Quentin Peet let out a great roar of a laugh, which Johnny attributed more to the amount of alcohol his father had consumed than to the wit of his question. "No vacillating Greek, son. Dzhugashvili was born in Georgia, where it's believed Svank came from, Dzhugashvili, who changed his name to Koba and then to Stalin, man of steel. Svank liked that. I think Stalin, the old man of steel, became his role model during the last decade, when—it's just beginning to be understood—Svank did away brutally with anyone he thought stood in his path, old friends, associates, wives, mistresses, you name it. . . ."

His father's tone grew more serious. "My spies tell me you've been on the Svank trail, too. Have to admit, Johnny, I didn't like it much when I first heard about it . . . made me realize"—he swallowed down more of the port—"made me realize I haven't been much of a father, haven't kept in touch as I should, but perhaps I'm not such a swine after all. I was worried, you know, thought you might get hurt." He leaned over and clumsily patted Johnny's knee. "Don't get in too deep, Johnny. Svank's gone, but the cesspool he created is still very much there. . . ."

Johnny flushed. He couldn't remember such a demonstration of affection from his father in years. In fact, he couldn't ever remember his father showing so clearly how he felt. Was it a sign of old age? There was no physical sign of aging. Quentin Peet looked as lean, fit and elegantly handsome as ever, his hair thick and dark with only a trace of silver at the hairline. If only his own hair were as thick. He looked with open admiration at his father, all the old feelings of wanting his love and approbation surging back, stronger than ever before.

"I don't know what you heard, Dad, but yes, I have been following up a few leads. Is that what you wanted to discuss?"

His father nodded somberly. "Yes, that and something else about my own future." He leaned back and shut his eyes; it was an effective and simple way, Johnny remembered from years back, of getting a person's total attention, particularly at home, whenever QP wanted something from his mother.

He shook the thought away and after a minute or so, his father opened his eyes and stared intently at him. "You learn anything from the Art Loss Register?"

Johnny laughed. How could he ever have thought he could tell his father anything! He never missed a trick. "I have to tell you, Dad, not that long ago I came back from Washington pretty pleased with myself, thinking I might actually be able to tell you something you didn't know about the Svank case. How on earth did you know I've been working with the Art Loss guys?"

"I know everything, son. Leave it alone. Svank set up this worldwide network, first to locate and then to steal major works of art and precious stones to use as collateral for massive amounts of currency for drugs and to set up new areas of drug distribution. I've been working with the DEA and the FBI for a long, long time. I tell you it involves some of the most bestial members of the human race. I wouldn't want to see you become the object of their attention. I don't need to tell you what happened to Delchetto, do I?"

Flushed with pride that his father was sharing stories with him and talking to him as an equal, Johnny said excitedly, "I couldn't believe it, that before he got hit, Delchetto had gone over to the other side. It didn't do him any good."

Peet shrugged. "Few lived trying to get the better of Svank."

"Somebody did—the guy who managed to give him the big push. I always knew it couldn't be Stern." Johnny thought about Ginny and made up his mind. "Dad, there's someone I do want to tell you about, someone who could even turn out to be a prime suspect."

"Who?"

Johnny leaned forward. "The girl I mentioned, the one I'm working with on the book, you might as well know now, it's Ginny Walker, the girl described as the crasher, who came forward to back up Stern's alibi and got him off the hook."

"Well, well, well."

Johnny couldn't read his father's expression, but he didn't care. He plunged on.

"I want you to meet her one day. She's a talented dress designer— and that's part of the story behind her crashing. I'm just finishing up a piece for the magazine which explains all that."

"So it was your girlfriend with Stern, who witnessed the murder?"

"Yes, just as it said in the papers. Stern was trying to make out . . . she ran away, left her cloak behind . . ."

"What else did she see?"

Johnny hesitated. "I don't know. I think she's covering up something. Or someone. You're not going to believe this, but it turns out her cousin is Alex Rossiter."

His father raised his eyebrows. "Rossiter?"

"Yep, I thought you might have heard his name. Well, listen to this . . ." Johnny related the whole story that Ginny had told him earlier, about the Villeneva jewels and the probability that Alex had stashed them away in Ginny's loft until the heat was off. "Petersh, on Svank's case from homicide, is looking for Rossiter . . . everyone's looking for him, but he's as slippery as an eel . . ." He paused, his old shyness creeping over him. "I promised Ginny I'd ask if you could help find him." He never thought he'd ever hear himself asking his father for a favor, but he added, "Not surprisingly, she thinks you can do anything, including walk on water."

A heavy silence settled between the two men. Johnny hoped he hadn't blown their newfound camaraderie, but no, to his flushed delight, his father finally said carefully, "I may be able to do just that for your lady friend, Johnny. What did you say her name was? Ginny Walker?"

Johnny nodded proudly.

"An old pal of mine, Patrick O'Neill, may know something he isn't telling me."

"Isn't he the new C.O. of the Major Case Squad?"

"He is indeed, and very anxious to get this Svank case neatly tied up. What Pat doesn't know is, I saved one of his boys' hides a few years back. You know my old pal, Freddy Forrester."

It wasn't a question, and Johnny nodded, embarrassed, sure his father was going to take him to task for contacting Forrester; but leaning forward in a confiding way, Quentin Peet said, "What you don't know, because nobody knows, is Freddy was getting hooked on the fancy little white stuff he was supposed to be reporting to the DEA. When he was supposed to be recovering from a successful prostate cancer operation, I got him admitted into a first-class rehab place. He's never forgotten and because of that I happen to know he's been assigned to help on the Svank case and all its ugly tentacles. I'll make a call to Freddy and we'll go from there."

Should he tell his father now he'd once called on Freddy for help on the Long Island robberies? There was no need.

"Next time you want to check on something, Johnny, call me before you call Freddy." His father's tone was still light, nonthreatening; and as if to show there were no hard feelings, he patted Johnny's knee as he added, "It's embarrassing for Freddy. Can't say 'no' to my son, but it's more ethical if he hears it from me first, okay?"

"Sorry, Dad, you're right. Thanks, Dad." He looked at his father with new confidence. "Once Rossiter is found, I'm sure we'll have a lot of the answers. Right now I'm trying to contact Poppy Gan. Ginny thinks, and so do I, that she may know where Rossiter is."

"I'll pass that on to Freddy. I've no doubt it will soon all come together, including where the Villeneva jewels have ended up." Peet looked Johnny directly in the eyes. "I meant what I said, Johnny. Lay off this case as soon as you can. Concentrate on your book, your column, your girl—and you'd better look after her, too. Somebody in Svank's pay got rid of him, I'm sure of it, and Rossiter could be the one. Cousin or no cousin, Ms. Walker could be in danger. Why don't you take her away somewhere, away from the cesspool."

"Don't worry, Dad. I'm—"

His father interrupted him. "Blood isn't thicker than water in this game, Johnny." He paused as if making up his mind about something. "I read your Delchetto piece; it was good as far as it went," he said slowly. "You can read a sequel by me which, I think, will interest you, in this Sunday's magazine. Delchetto got his hands dirty by accident; he wasn't such a bad guy, just not as brilliant as he thought he was—"

"What d'you mean?"

"Read the piece," his father said in the acerbic tone Johnny was more used to, then his voice softened again. "Delchetto thought he was playing double agent, reporting on some of the bad guys that the drug lords really wanted to get rid of painlessly. There's a lot of intermarriage down there and it was easier to get some deadwood relations put away by the authorities than execute them and have their wives and women give them a hard time over brothers, cousins, sons, whatever. Delchetto got a little payoff—little by Cali standards, not so little for him—and he thinks this is a nice way to earn prizes and start stashing something away for his old age. Then along comes a really bad guy—in the DEA—who regularly comes on shopping trips to Colombia—" Peet gave a short hard laugh, seeing Johnny's startled expression.

"Happens all the time, son, however hard the good guys try to stop it. Delchetto had learned a lot about marijuana; that it's the THC chemical content that determines the potency, only present in the flower and resin of the female plant. He got suspicious when, soon after these shopping trips, the same agent carried out big drug raids, where shipments consisting of stems and male plants, both useless, were seized, while the good stuff arrived untouched later at prearranged destinations, scams involving thousands of tons of pot."

"Is that why he got taken out?"

"Yep," said his father. "It was too good a story for Delchetto to give up on. It's only just coming together, because the bad guy's wife, a heroine in the DEA, suspected her DEA husband was squirreling away millions in a Swiss bank account, but she died—"

"Died in a fire?" Johnny asked woodenly.

"Oh, so you know. Yes, and Mr. Abbott, as my piece on Sunday will relate, is presently in custody, accused of her murder." His father leaned forward anxiously. "Hey, son, you all right? Did you know the wife?"

"Not well." Tears were behind his eyes, in his throat. There had been tears in Ben Abbott's eyes that day after the memorial service. He'd thought they were tears of grief. Had they been tears of regret, or anxiety that his cover was on the way to being blown?

"I'm only telling you all this, son, because with the kind of money involved, more than you could ever dream of, nothing stands in the way of business for these people, cousin or no cousin, wife or no wife, so I repeat, stay away from the cesspool, for your sake, for the girl's sake."

Johnny drank down his glass of port before he could trust himself to speak. When he did his voice was still shaky. "I'm just going to finish up this piece for *Next!* And that will be it, finito, ending with Svank's death—"

"Which could be the beginning, but not for you and"—again Peet summoned the waiter for more port—"not for me either. That brings me to the other thing I want to share with you."

Johnny sat on the edge of the chair, anxious, tense, hoping his sense of building a new relationship with his father wasn't going to change.

"I'm stepping down from the paper, son. I'm getting on, you know. I've been offered a lucrative partnership, not too much work, some travel, an apartment in Europe. Less stress, more freedom." Peet seemed to be talking to himself, staring into space. "I've been thinking about getting away for some time now."

Johnny wasn't that surprised, reminding himself he'd contemplated such a day happening on the plane coming back from Washington. If this was how his father was going to treat him, now that he'd made such a momentous decision, then he would be the happiest, most supportive son in the world.

Johnny jumped up and did something that would have been unthinkable before this evening. He put his arm around his father and kissed him. "Go for it, Dad."

To his surprise he saw tears in the old man's eyes. What an evening. He'd never forget it for as long as he lived.

*   *   *

"Murder, the top homicide count, usually implies that the defendant intended to kill a victim or acted in such a wildly reckless manner that death was predictable.

"Manslaughter, the second category, also has an intentional component, but the defendant is held less responsible, either because he killed in the heat of passion or intended to cause serious injury, but not death. The distinction between the less severe charge of second-degree manslaughter and criminally negligent homicide, the fourth and final homicide category, is so fine that sometimes prosecutors bring both charges for the same crime.

"In criminally negligent homicide the defendant does not even know a risk existed, but the law says he should have known and therefore should have been more cautious."

No one had yet been arrested in connection with Svank's death; but because of all the sensationalism surrounding the "victim," still more conjecture than fact, there continued to be an unusually high number of pieces about the unsolved case. This article in the *New York Times* particularly interested Ginny, because it concentrated on what the charge could finally be, if and when someone was apprehended.

She carefully cut the article out with her pinking shears and put it with all the rest in a folder marked "pending." It was a word that well described her life for the last few months, which she felt she'd literally had to put on hold, despite a vacancy coming up at Calvin Klein, with a job description that fitted her experience and ethos like a glove.

Lee, who'd called to tell her about the job, couldn't understand why she hadn't gone after it immediately.

It was ironic—and heartbreaking—but Ginny knew she wouldn't be able to put what Lee described as her "twenty-first century energy" into the interview, let alone the job. Some mornings she couldn't muster up enough energy to do her hair. Like everything else, her energy was on hold until the mystery of Svank's death was solved and Alex's part in it revealed—or not, as the case might be.

She'd received some consolation from Johnny, who'd recently been able to enlist his father's help in finding Alex. Apparently, the great QP had been in the most wonderful mood, euphoric over a fancy new job offer, and Johnny had told him everything. She was relieved. It was what she'd hoped for since that first night in Johnny's apartment. With the great Quentin Peet on the case, surely Alex would turn up soon.

Until then, she couldn't shake off the feeling that at any minute her world could come tumbling down, that at any time of day or night she might lift up the lid of her toilet and find the Hope Diamond beaming up at her.

Pending or not, her life still had to go on, and there were some things she could do to get prepared for what she referred to in her mind as "the finale." Today's clipping from the *Times*, for instance.

When she wasn't busy reminding herself that Alex had denied having anything to do with Svank's death, she was agonizing over what the consequences would be if Alex had indeed pushed Svank over the balustrade. Could it technically be described as an accident?

In today's story the *Times* reported a few cases of criminally negligent homicide where the accused had been acquitted and walked out of court a free man.

As she often did these days, Ginny put off working to read the article again, when the phone rang.

Another hang-up call? She snatched up the receiver, her voice more hostile than she intended. "Hello?"

"Ginny?" There was only a tiny whisper at the other end, but there was no mistaking that voice.

"Poppy! Oh, thank God. At last." Ginny forgot that somebody might be listening in, forgot everything in her relief. "Where have you been?"

"Away, back home, I went home, Ginny. To New Jersey. Ginny, I have to see you."

New Jersey, that was a surprise. She couldn't visualize Poppy at home in New Jersey.

"Not anything like as much as I want to see you. Where's Alex?"

"That's what I want to talk to you about—Alex. I'm coming back to New York on Saturday. Will you be home?"

"All day, all night if I can see you. Can't you come sooner?"

Perhaps Poppy didn't hear her; perhaps she didn't care. "Saturday, then, count on it. I'll call first, sometime around six."

It was only when she put the phone down that Ginny realized she hadn't conveyed her condolences.

*   *   *

For the rest of her life Ginny would always remember exactly what happened that day. She would go over what she did, running it through her mind like scenes from a film in slow motion.

She went to sit at her drawing board, trying to summon up some enthusiasm for the dress she was finally designing—out of a guilty conscience and at Lee's constant urging—for Marilyn Binez. She was staring at her sketches—different variations on a triangle theme—when the intercom buzzed and the phone rang at the same time. She was humming something from *The Phantom of the Opera* when she picked up the phone to hear Esme's voice, high, hysterical.

"Oh, Ginny, I've just heard the news—"

"What news?"

"On television . . . oh, Ginny."

She would remember feeling irritated with Esme for not getting to the point, which was the reason she snapped at her best friend, "I haven't got television. It's on the blink—" And then she said, "Hang on, Esme, someone's at the door."

It was Johnny, not sounding himself, panting, as if he'd run all the way downtown. "Ginny, are you all right?"

"I've got Esme on the phone."

"Hang up. Don't talk to her now. Something terrible's happened."

She was so sure Johnny had come to tell her that Alex had been arrested for Svank's death and Esme had already heard about it on the news, she forced herself to sound casual and cheerful as she went back to the phone to cut her off with, "Talk to you later, Es. I've got to go. Johnny's here."

She looked at her watch. It was one-twenty. She opened the door and watched Johnny run up the last flight, his face drawn, tired. Because of what she expected him to say, she didn't react when he told her the first time.

"What did you say?"

Johnny tried to put his arms around her, but she was in too much pain. She backed away, warding him off with her hand. "What did you say?" she asked again, panting as if she'd just run up the stairs herself.

She heard herself scream before he was halfway through . . . a body found floating in the East River . . . identified as Alex Rossiter . . . shot once through the back of the head.

"No, no, no, oh God, oh no, not Alex, it can't be true . . . how do you know it's true? It can't be true."

Again Johnny tried to pull her to him, but she couldn't stand anyone touching her, not even him. She held her hands out in front of her, imploring him to tell her it wasn't so.

"My father called me. He heard about it this morning from someone on the job, one of his contacts in Homicide."

She knew she was still screaming, but she somehow couldn't stop. Johnny made her sit down, forced her to let him hold her, rocking her like a baby. "No," she moaned, over and over. "It can't be true, not Alex."

"My father went over to KCH."

"KCH?"

"Kings College Hospital, in Brooklyn." He spoke slowly, hesitantly, as if the words wouldn't hurt so much that way. "The body was taken to the morgue there. It was found on the Brooklyn side of the East River—"

"Who . . . how can they be sure . . . who identified him?"

Again Johnny hesitated. "I'm not sure. Someone had apparently just reported him missing . . . someone he was living with . . ."

Alex living with someone? It had never occurred to her. She had told him everything and he had told her nothing. She started to weep, the pain worse, thinking that Alex hadn't even trusted her with the knowledge there was somebody in his life.

It seemed like hours, but later she realized it wasn't even one hour before the intercom rang again. Johnny picked it up.

"Petersh here."

He covered the receiver with his hand. "Petersh."

"I can't—"

"You have to . . . don't worry. I'll be with you."

When Petersh walked in, Reever was with him.

It was so unreal; she could hardly move, aware of making even the slightest gesture, as if she was acting in a play.

She told them, as she'd been telling them over and over again, that she hadn't seen Alex in weeks, if not months.

"Did he send you anything?"

"Noooo." A low wail.

Couldn't they see she was in mourning, grieving, not for the Alex

Rossiter they were inquiring about; she had never known him. She was in mourning for an Alex they had never known, perhaps an Alex who had only existed in her mind—she wasn't even sure about that anymore—but nonetheless, the only Alex she would allow to exist, as real to her as herself. She was in mourning for a life lost forever, hers, as much as his, a life that would never again be brightened, rescued from any slump of despair, by the cousin who could open Pandora's box, and make her believe anything was possible.

"It isn't only Girl Scouts who have to be prepared, Ginny."

"What you wear says a lot about who you are—or want to be—and so does the way you arrive wearing it."

"Push the envelope, Ginny. Be daring; don't be afraid of what people think." Alex's voice was in her head; she could see the look she loved so much, the wry twist to the mouth, the steady, critical, appraising stare. Oh, no, Alex, you can't be gone; you can't do that to me.

Johnny gently shook her shoulder. Petersh was staring at her. She stared back through her tears. "I repeat, did Alex Rossiter leave anything in your care?"

She shivered as she shook her head. "No."

"At any time?"

"No."

"Did he phone recently to say he was coming to see you?"

She couldn't remember when she'd first wondered if her phone was being tapped; she couldn't think straight about anything. She kept on denying whatever the detectives asked. Why not? Nothing she said was going to change anything now.

"We have reason to believe your cousin Alex Rossiter was working for Svank. Did you know that?"

She tried to keep her voice steady. "I know he knew Svank. I think Svank was a bad influence on him, but I don't know if he was directly working for him. Is that why he was killed?"

"That is what we are trying to find out, Ms. Walker." Reever's voice was still kind, but it didn't mean anything; she didn't expect any kindness from either of them now.

When the detectives finally left Johnny said gently, "Ginny, not now, but soon, very soon, you're going to have to tell the cops the truth about finding the Villeneva jewels in your apartment."

"Why?" she sobbed. "Alex is dead. His name's already ruined. What good would it do? Then they'll never leave me alone."

"Of course they will—"

"No, they won't," she cried. "And I'll never know how it all happened, what trouble Alex was in. All I know now is that he wasn't the murderer . . . that he did tell me the truth, that he wasn't the man I saw fighting with Svank that night."

Johnny paled. "What do you mean the man you saw? I thought you couldn't identify anyone?"

"From a distance he—the man—I was sure it was Alex . . . I even called out his name. From a distance I thought . . ." She started to sob again. "He was as tall as Alex, tall, dark, thin . . . I was sure it was Alex." She wasn't aware of Johnny staring at her in shock. "Now he's dead and I'll never know the truth."

She didn't see Johnny's expression. Only when he spoke did she look up, jolted by the sharpness of his tone. "D'you mean to say all along you could have given the police a description of the man you saw fighting with Svank?"

"I didn't know it was Svank," she said defensively. "When I found out, that made it more important than ever not to mention Alex—"

"You mean all along you suspected it could have been your cousin who pushed Svank to his death?"

"Yes, I was terrified it was him. Even when he told me he didn't do it, I couldn't risk the police going after him . . . putting out a search warrant when Aunt Lil—his mother—had just died."

"Is that the real reason you didn't come forward right from the beginning to support Stern's alibi? If Oz hadn't blackmailed you, would you still be hiding the evidence? Would you have let an innocent man take the rap?" Johnny didn't realize he was shouting. "Were you in love with this cousin of yours? This piece of shit who used you as a dump for the jewels he stole when things got too hot for him?"

He pulled her roughly to her feet, clutching her shoulders. "Just because Alex is dead doesn't make him any less of a suspect in Svank's death. Alex Rossiter was a crook, a small-time crook who thought he could play in the biggest league of all when he hooked the Villeneva jewels. Do yourself a favor, Ginny. Grow up and face the facts about your low-life cousin."

He wrenched her over to the phone. "Call Homicide now. Get yourself out of trouble while you still can, say the shock of Rossiter's death gave you momentary amnesia or insanity or whatever you want to call it." Johnny picked up the receiver and thrust it angrily in her face. "Call them now!"

"I won't," she screamed at him. "I won't, I won't, I won't, not now, not ever. There's no proof Alex stole the jewels. I should never have trusted you, never have told you they were here." Hysterically she went on, "How can Alex be a suspect when somebody pulled a trigger on him? There's a murderer going free out there, somebody who killed Svank and now Alex . . . somebody—"

"—who wants to get his hands on the Villeneva jewels," Johnny screamed back. "Jewels your precious cousin stole as surely as my name's John Q. Peet."

Ginny smashed her fist at the wall. "Get out, get out. Alex hasn't been dead for more than a few hours and you're already trying to pin everything on him."

"Damn right, I am. Your cousin was up to his ass in this and then some—"

Ginny picked up the nearest thing at hand—the Murano glass, once so precious—and hurled it furiously across the room. It hit the wall and smashed into a shower of pieces.

"Get out and don't come back," she cried again. "I've had enough."

"And so have I."

Johnny stormed out of the loft, overturning a chair, slamming the door behind him. "And so have I," she heard him yell again as he ran down the stairs.

Trying to calm down, he walked for a mile or so when he left the loft, not knowing where he was going. He still couldn't believe that Ginny had suspected, right up until the events of the past few hours, that her cousin was responsible for Svank's death.

If she could conceal from him so effortlessly all that was pertinent to the investigation, what else was she hiding?

Of course, he could go straight to Homicide himself now and tell them what he'd just learned, but having Ginny taken into custody wasn't going to help him know the truth.

He'd seen with his own eyes how Ginny could lie straight-faced to the cops. He wouldn't learn anything that way.

He walked until he found a bench, and sank down on it like an old man, trying to think what to do. Slowly a plan emerged. He would hire a car as he'd done in San Juan and start his own surveillance of Ginny. He'd find out where she was going and who she was seeing. He would find out what, if anything, or who, if anyone, Ginny was still covering up. It wasn't only her future at stake. He had to admit to himself, it was now his future, too.

Poppy called the loft about five o'clock on Saturday, her voice still a whisper of its former self. "I'm running late. Is it all right if I drop by about seven?"

Ginny didn't know how she sounded after days of crying. She knew how she looked, like a total wreck, and she hadn't the energy to do much about it. "Seven's fine; anytime. I'll be here."

At least she'd washed and fixed her hair when, to her surprise, the intercom buzzed at about six-twenty.

She was wearing the only thing she felt she could wear during the past few days of suffering, the khaki jacket from the Army and Navy surplus store, its somber color and rough cloth the nearest thing to sackcloth and ashes she owned.

As she quickly looked in the mirror and ran a brown pencil around her lips, the buzzer buzzed twice again. Just like Poppy, as impatient as ever. She picked up the intercom and pressed the release on the front door at the same time. "Come on up. Top floor."

"Coming up."

Oh, my God. She froze. It wasn't Poppy. It was John Q. Peet. "No," she screamed, but it was too late.

Since he'd slammed out of the loft she hadn't heard a word from him. Every hour of every day she'd expected the cops to arrive, but it hadn't happened. Every hour of every day she'd picked up the phone intending to beg his forgiveness, but she hadn't been able to do it. They were poles apart. She couldn't change and neither could he.

Only in the middle of long, sleepless nights had she thought there might be a chance of getting together again one day—when the murders were solved, when the nightmare was finally laid to rest—but by daybreak, despair engulfed her again. There were hundreds of unsolved crimes in New York; what made her think Svank's and Alex's deaths wouldn't join the list?

She'd been aching for him, longing to hear his voice on the phone, but now, with Poppy's arrival imminent, knowing she had something to tell her about Alex, Johnny was the last person, other than Petersh, she wanted to see.

"What are you doing here?" she demanded, full of hostility, from the landing.

Although he was trying to hide it, she knew him too well. He was still angry with her, suspicious, distrusting. If he'd come to urge her to go to the cops about the Villeneva jewels he was still wasting his time.

She kicked the loft door shut behind her. She had to get him out before Poppy arrived. She could feel beads of perspiration on her upper lip.

"I've got a surprise for you." He waved a magazine in the air. "An advance copy of my piece."

He was on the landing facing her now. He had to see that she was highly nervous. So what? What could he do, except call the cops? And so far, for some reason, he hadn't.

"I want you to leave," she said, an unexpected sob catching her breath.

"Why? Don't you want to see it? They liked it so much, it's become the cover story . . . you look fantastic." He shoved *Next!* under her nose. There was a full-length picture of herself on the cover with the headline, READY TO CRASH, THE READY-TO-WEAR TRUE LIFE STORY OF GINNY WALKER.

"Can't I come in, Ginny?"

Her heart was breaking, but she couldn't risk it, couldn't risk him being there when she heard what Poppy had come to tell her about Alex.

"Not now, Johnny."

Tomorrow, she silently pleaded, give me another chance tomorrow.

He shook his head, grim-faced again. "Expecting someone?"

"No, no one. I'm just not ready to see you right now."

He was leaning against the door. She could see the time on his watch. Almost six-thirty. She had to get rid of him. Poppy could appear at any moment.

"Please, Johnny, please go."

He flung the magazine on the floor. "Goodbye, Ginny."

It sounded so final, so cold, she didn't know how she let him leave, watching him trudge down the stairs, his shoulders hunched over, beaten.

"I love you, Johnny," she mouthed, the tears streaming down her face. "I'll always love you."

It wasn't until she heard the front door bang shut that she picked up the magazine and went inside. She was in so much pain she couldn't even open it to read what Johnny had written about her.

She lay down on the bed, motionless like a sick person, staring up at the ceiling. She stayed that way for what seemed like hours, but when she heard the buzzer again it was only seven-thirty; for Poppy, almost on time. She made sure it was Poppy before she opened the front door and they collapsed into each other's arms like long-lost sisters, both crying, wailing, holding each other up.

"Oh, Ginny, I can't believe what's happened, can you? First Svank, now Alex." Poppy threw off a red satin coat and collapsed into a chair. Ginny tried not to wince at the color clash. Underneath the red satin, Poppy was wearing a bright pink dress with a miniskirt, which, as she slumped back, rode up to show off her glorious legs in matching pink hose all the way to her thighs. With a flourish she took off her oversize dark glasses.

Ginny gasped and involuntarily turned her head away, not knowing where to look. Poppy was wearing a lot of makeup, but it still wasn't enough to hide the black-and-blue bruising around her eyes, nor the dark marks and swelling around her cheeks. Poppy looked as if she'd been beaten up.

"What—what happened to you?" Ginny thought quickly. "Were you in a car crash?"

Poppy laughed sardonically. "Come off it, Ginny. You don't have to act Little Miss Innocent with me. You can guess what happened. One of Svank's goons, remember Hugo Humphrey?" She spat the name out. "He beat me up well and good."

"Why, for heaven's sake?"

"Because Svank thought blood's thicker than water, that's why."

"I don't understand. Why weren't you with Svank at the library?"

Again Poppy gave the ugly laugh. "I was in the emergency ward getting my jaw fixed—"

"So what d'you mean? Blood being thicker than water?"

Poppy looked around nervously. "D'you live alone here?"

"Yes, of course, I do. Why?"

"Just wanted to be sure." She got up and looked behind the rattan screen. "Can we lower the lights? I don't want to be seen from the street."

"You can't be, I promise you. Sit down, talk to me. Tell me—"

"Svank found out about my brother and Alex," Poppy blurted out, flopping back into the chair again. "Someone was following Alex and for once Alex didn't know it; he wasn't careful enough . . . someone told Svank everything . . ."

Bewildered, Ginny said, "I don't understand . . . Alex and your brother . . . what d'you mean?"

Poppy looked at her as if she was crazy. "Don't tell me you didn't know Alex was gay? You gotta be kidding me. I thought you of all people would know, although it took me a while to figure it out. What I didn't know until too late was how much a case he had on my kid brother. I introduced them one day and bingo, the next they were holed up together. Svank thought I had something to do with it, that in putting one of his lieutenants"—the sarcastic way Poppy pronounced the word showed Ginny what she thought of him—"together with my next of kin, I was double-crossing him in some way. That's why he sent Hugo over the first time, to teach me a lesson, the fucking animal. The second time was Hugo's own idea—after Svank's death—sort of getting his own payback for me giving him so much trouble while the boss was alive."

Ginny was unable to hide what a bombshell Poppy had just dropped, and yet the minute she'd heard it she'd known there was no way to contest it, to protest. It was as if subconsciously she'd known all along, but why had Alex never told her?

"Have you got anything to drink?" Poppy asked abruptly.

Ginny nodded, trying to recover. There was a bottle of white wine in the fridge. How long it had been there, she couldn't imagine, but there wasn't anything else.

She poured out two glasses. It looked all right. "Why are you telling me all this now?"

"Alex asked me to meet him—"

"I saw you—"

"You saw us?" Poppy's voice showed she was nervous.

"Yes, on East Fifty-fifth Street. I chased after you, but you vanished in the crowds." Ginny didn't care that she was crying again. "That was the day Alex called me, the first time after the murder. Then he came to see me the day his mother died."

Although Ginny sounded heartbroken, Poppy was unperturbed. She looked through a vast crocodile bag for her compact and made a face at what she saw in the mirror. "That animal," she muttered, clicking the compact shut without adding anything to her face.

"Why did he want to see you?" Even now Ginny was ashamed to feel the same old resentment stirring, that Alex had confided in Poppy, and not her.

"My kid brother has AIDS, Ginny," Poppy said in a matter-of-fact voice. "It's in remission. Alex had been paying for all kinds of expensive drugs. He told me that afternoon he was planning to get them both out of the country, but he was scared shitless . . . said someone was after him, although he didn't have what they wanted anymore. Now we know he was right."

Poppy looked at her in a pitying sort of way. "He didn't want me to tell you about Donny, that's my kid brother, he knew you'd get in a panic about the AIDS problem, but once he'd gotten away he wanted me to explain. Wanted me to keep an eye on you, seemed to think you could be in danger, too. That's why I called you." She shook her head from side to side, her curls bobbing vigorously around her head. "It's weird. I call you in the morning and in the evening I hear Alex got hit."

"Why did he think I was in danger?"

"He was just going to tell me—we were in this coffee shop on Madison—when he got into a fucking panic . . . sure someone was watching him. I went to the john and when I came back he'd gone. Left me with the check, the bastard." Poppy nodded reflectively. "Wasn't the first time either."

"Did Alex kill Svank?" There, it was out. There was a long silence. Ginny sat with her fingers crossed, knowing it was ridiculous, but unwilling to uncross them.

Poppy looked around the room. "He could have . . ." she said finally. "He was capable of it, but I don't know." She jumped up to pour herself another glass of wine, drank it down in one gulp, and to Ginny's amazement asked, "What are you making these days? I was sooo sorry not to wear that fab georgette number that night."

After that Ginny couldn't wait to get rid of her. "I can't concentrate on designing much right now . . . you understand, Poppy."

"S'pose I do."

She finished off the wine, and with a promise to "keep in touch" smoothed down her miniskirt and left with her usual sultry glide.

Drained, no more tears left, Ginny hoped she'd never have to see empty-headed Poppy Gan again. How she could mention clothes in the next breath after discussing her lover's murder was beyond her. She felt dirty, soiled by all she'd heard, no nearer the truth, other than to have it confirmed that Alex had been one of Svank's "loo-ten-ents," as Poppy had put it.

On the hall table was the advance copy of *Next!* magazine. How shamefully she'd treated Johnny. He, not Alex, was the man who'd given her real support and love. What had Alex ever really given her? A lifetime of broken promises, culminating in putting her reputation in question and perhaps her very existence in danger.

She took *Next!* back to the armchair, which was still impregnated with Poppy's excess of Shalimar. She began to flip through the pages. Her shame grew as she read Johnny's story about a young girl, brimming with talent and ambition; a story also told in pictures, showing her wearing her clothes at various events. Some of the pictures carried Oz's byline. She sighed. The picture department had to get them from someone, she supposed, and here were some of the best.

It was a love letter in print; a public testimonial to her ability as a designer. It meant she would never again have to apologize for being "the crasher"; and it emphasized an originality that, wrote Johnny, "we must hope will now be recognized." If her phone didn't ring off the hook with offers of financial backing after this, no amount of publicity in the world could do it.

With the magazine in her hand she went over to the phone to call Johnny. The answering service picked up. A message couldn't convey what she had in her heart. She hung up, turning the page to find that the article concluded with two more full-length shots, one of her wearing the blush bridesmaid dress at Esme's wedding, the other of her in the same dress, completely renovated, taken among the crowd at the Literary Lions gala.

As she studied the two photographs, her breath quickened. She felt dizzy. In the background of the library shot was the tiny detail that had eluded her the night of the Lions dinner, the one incriminating piece of evidence she had seen fleetingly at the bottom of the stairwell, but could never remember—or identify—until now.

There was no mistaking it. How could she have blocked it so completely out of her mind?

She stared at the page, seeing again what she had seen on the stairwell. Luminous even in the dim light of the single bulb, she had seen what she was looking at now, a large bronze medallion, the insignia of a Literary Lion, worn around the neck of a tall, dark, slim figure, the man she had mistaken for Alex, the most famous Literary Lion of them all. It was Quentin Peet.

Johnny's father? Johnny's tall, dark, slim father? The shadowy figure in the upper hall, and at the bottom of the stairwell? It wasn't possible. Ginny threw the magazine down and walked around the loft.

Quentin Peet had long been celebrated for his knowledge of the drug world, his exposures of those at the top in Cali. She hadn't read his recent book, *Green Ice*, but she'd read enough about it to know he'd risked his life to write it. Then there had been his most recent scoop. The story she'd read only the other day about the California couple in drug enforcement, the wife who'd perished in a fire, now thought to have been set by the husband, because he knew she'd learned he was getting payoffs from the drug czars.

There were millions and millions of dollars involved in the drug business, Peet had been at pains to point out. Who knew if he wasn't leading a double life and earning some of those millions for himself? Ginny clutched her throat. She felt she was choking with fear, but the more she thought about it, the more certain she became.

From what Johnny had told her about his father, he was an inveterate gambler, always living beyond his considerable means; and as Johnny had said, more than once, "capable of anything." Hadn't Johnny told her only the other day that his father was planning to leave the paper and move to Europe to make a new life?

He was planning his getaway.

Oh, God, what could she do? How could she go to Johnny and tell him what had suddenly opened her eyes, her mind, her memory? Johnny, darling Johnny, living his whole life hoping for his father's approval. What could she do?

There was a rush of rain against the window, a roll of thunder. A late summer storm. It emphasized how alone, how vulnerable she was. Johnny wasn't home, but even if he had been, he was the last person she could call on for help.

Alex hadn't known for sure who'd been hunting him down, but he'd known she might also be in danger. Poppy's words came back to haunt her: "He was scared shitless . . . knew somebody was after him, although he didn't have what they wanted anymore." That had to mean the Villeneva jewels. And now through Johnny, Quentin Peet knew everything about her role in hiding them.

She had been the one to urge Johnny to ask for his father's help in finding Alex. She must have confirmed his suspicion that Alex had the jewels.

And when Peet found out Alex didn't have them anymore, he killed him. She started to shake. Perhaps he thought she still knew where they were. Perhaps he'd been encouraging Johnny over the last few days to distrust her, to taint her with suspicion, so if anything happened to her, it would appear to be all part of the sinister world surrounding Svank. She was the only witness he had left to worry about. He had to be waiting for the right moment to strike.

She crept around the apartment turning out the lights, eerily methodical, with every one of her senses acutely sharp.

Then she sat frantically thinking for several minutes, until she knew what she had to do. What any person in their right mind would have done from the start. She dialed the number on the card that had been left for the second time only a few days before.

"Is Detective Petersh there?"

"Who's calling?"

"Ginny Walker." She was asked to repeat her name slowly.

"Does he know what this is in reference to?"

Fear gave authority to her voice. "Of course he does."

She was put on hold. After a few minutes another voice came on the line. "Yes, miss?"

Be calm, Ginny, be patient; your life's involved here. Again she asked for Petersh, " . . . or Detective Reever, if he's not around."

Another teeth-grinding wait. "They're not in, miss. Neither of 'em. Can you leave a message?"

Hoping she was right and the police, if not also the FBI, were tapping her line, she took a deep breath and said loudly, "Ask one of the detectives to call me urgently. Tell them I know the identity of the man on the third floor with Svank."

"QP? Are you there? Pick up, if you want to know what you've been paying me for."

"Okay, Okay, here I am. What's up?"

Freddy Forrester, on the four P.M.-to-midnight shift, in the highly technical surveillance van parked a couple of blocks south of Chelsea Park, was relieved to hear the voice of the man he called his guardian angel. QP, as he called him to his face, had been paying him well for any extra info on the Svank case and this was the first time he'd been able to deliver anything the old warrior maybe didn't know.

"Maybe nothing, maybe something. The Walker girl just called the precinct a minute ago, looking for Petersh or Reever. She left a message as if she wanted the world to hear it . . ." Forrester spelled it out slowly: ". . . that she knows the identity of the man on the third floor with Svank."

"Good work, Freddy. Over and out."

Since his dinner with Johnny, Peet had been expecting something like this. He was blessed, or was it cursed, with a peculiar sixth sense that had rarely let him down. Ambushes, mines, booby-trap parcels, he'd survived them all, because of his personal antennae. In the last twenty years he could only think of one occasion when he'd been caught totally off guard, when the fucking Russian bastard, Svank, had started to blackmail him about his take from Colombia, and then, when taken to task, man to man at the library, had had the audacity to pull a gun on him.

Stern's arrest had been manna from heaven. It had given him time to plan for his future; to leave the party at the height when his reputation couldn't go any higher and he could make the regal farewell he'd looked forward to making, taking gracefully what the paper thought was such a superb golden handshake.

If they only understood what paupers they all were, in comparison to those in charge of the other world he inhabited, the underworld of Mephistopheles.

He'd known the Stern break was too good to last, but he'd still hoped he'd be able to leave with nothing changed. Perhaps he still could.

Freddy had said the girl made a call a minute ago. Peet looked at his watch. Nine thirty-five on a Saturday night. Knowing the two detectives involved, he was pretty sure one would be at the ball game and the other screwing his black mistress at his favorite hotel off-Broadway.

If he played it cool, he had time to do what he had hoped he would never have to do. How Ms. Walker had suddenly had this revelation he couldn't imagine, but he was not gambling on her making a mistake; he was gambling on getting to her first. He'd give it five to one.

Hearing the rain outside, not for the first time he blessed the midtown building in which he'd kept a one-room pied à terre, for the past fifteen years. The elevator whooshed him down eleven floors to the basement garage. Without encountering a single raindrop, he was on his way downtown less than ten minutes after receiving Freddy's call.

Across the street from Ginny's loft, Johnny, in an Avis Oldsmobile, had already seen Poppy Gan arrive and leave. It hadn't been too much of a surprise. Seeing Ginny earlier that evening in such a nervous state, he'd known something was up. Why hadn't she wanted him to know Gan was coming? What had Gan been delivering?

After an absence of a few days, hoping to move things along and evaluate Ginny's frame of mind, he'd stumbled on Gan's visit by accident, when delivering the advance copy of the magazine. Now, his suspicions newly aroused, he feared it was a coincidence he'd live to regret. He still couldn't believe Ginny was a crook like her cousin, didn't want to accept it; and until this evening had been talking himself out of such a terrible idea.

As he waited and watched, Johnny made up his mind. He wasn't prepared to let another night go by without finding out the truth about Ginny Walker.

It wasn't raining so heavily when Poppy left, so he got out of the car to stand in a doorway, trying to decide exactly when to go back to the loft and take Ginny by surprise.

Shortly after, the lights in the loft went out. At nine-twenty? It was too early for Ginny to go to bed. Was it some kind of signal?

Renewed rain had driven him back into the car just as a dark sedan pulled up. So the lights had been a signal. Who was arriving now?

"Ms. Walker?"

"Yes . . ." A soft, tremulous voice.

"Sergeant O'Neill here . . ." Even at this tense moment, it amused Peet to use the old rank of the now too-big-for-his-boots, high-and-mighty C.O. "I've come to escort you to the precinct."

"Thank God. I'll be right down."

Ginny pulled on her old black raincoat and ran down the stairs, thankful to leave the loft, which had become terrifyingly oppressive. Through the glass panels in the front door, she couldn't see anyone waiting under the porch. She didn't blame the sergeant. Even cops didn't like getting their uniforms wet. She opened the door and saw a dark sedan at the curb, the passenger door half open. She dashed across the pavement—God, it was coming down hard—and bent down to get in. "What a night, I'm—" She screamed one high scream as she saw who was waiting inside. There was a high buzz in her brain and the world went black.

Watching the sedan pull away from the curb with a screech of tires, Johnny heard the scream, Ginny's scream, and he hit the accelerator so violently that the Oldsmobile shot across the street and ricocheted off the pavement. He thought he'd lost them right there because the sedan went through a red light at the corner, but Johnny shortly found himself right behind them.

He was on automatic pilot, not aware of the traffic, not aware of anything except the car in front. He'd been full of suspicion, seeing the sedan arrive and Ginny emerge soon after.

In a second everything had changed. He'd heard her scream. Whoever was driving the car wasn't the person she'd expected to see. God in heaven, she was being abducted.

As he drove he remembered his father saying, "Cousin or no cousin, Ms. Walker could be in danger . . . Svank is gone, but the cesspool he created is still very much there . . . Why don't you take her away from the cesspool?"

Why hadn't he? The cousin was gone, but idiot that he'd been, not trusting his own emotions, he'd transferred his suspicions to her, his own Ginny. God, help him.

At Fourth and East Houston, at the point where the Bowery begins, the sedan swerved madly to avoid by inches a huge Mack truck backing out of a side turning. Although the rain was now torrential, instead of slowing down, the sedan began to pick up speed.

Too late, Johnny saw a car pass him and get between him and his quarry. He drove right up behind the interloper, hooting his horn, shouting, "Move over, you bastard, move over." The car didn't budge, but as long as he could still see where the sedan was headed, he tried to keep his panic down.

He was driving as dangerously as the sedan now, slipping and sliding all over the road. Suddenly, the sedan made a wild swerve to the left in the direction of the Manhattan Bridge. Where were they going? Who was driving the car like a lunatic in this downpour? Whoever it was had to have nerves of steel to keep the car on the road.

Who had made Ginny scream? He would get him; he had to get him, no matter what.

Through the driving rain he saw a sign to Kennedy. He shuddered, thinking of the desolate areas around the outskirts of the airport, the deserted coves in Far Rockaway, the deep waters of Jamaica Bay.

As he followed the sedan onto the bridge he heard a police siren. "Please God," he prayed, "please God make the car in front stop."

The sedan slowed slightly as it went through a giant pool of water, the spray hitting Johnny's windshield and momentarily blocking his view. The police car was flashing him from behind; he moved over expecting it to flash the sedan, but it sped on by, fast ahead.

At the first light across the bridge, Johnny was close enough to get the first few numbers of the registration plate. M 15—but before he could catch the rest, the sedan took off in another sluice of water.

He was gaining on them when he hit another gigantic pool, obscuring everything for a vital few seconds, seconds in which the sedan disappeared from view.

He cursed and screamed. There was a phone booth on the corner. He couldn't do it alone. There was no time to lose.

Johnny's call was put through to Petersh just as he was leaving Ginny's apartment. "Slow, slow . . ." The detective knew the guy was in love with the girl, but he couldn't make out a word he was saying.

"Okay. Now I've got you. Kidnapped, you say. Repeat the car number . . . If you see it again, use this code to get through to me at once." After being beeped at the ballgame, Petersh had rushed over to Ginny's apartment where he got only her answering service when he called.

Now, seconds after crashing the phone down, Petersh put out a general alarm. "Special alert. Calling all cars, intercept a dark sedan, possibly a Pontiac, license plates beginning M 15 . . . traveling southeast on

Bushwick, in the direction of Kennedy Airport. Intercept with caution, driver may be armed."

Johnny drove slowly now through the rain, the poor lighting on the road where he'd lost the sedan making everything more difficult. He thought he heard another siren in the distance. He went in that direction. Ginny, Ginny, Ginny, hang on. I'll find you. I love you.

As he arrived at an intersection, a car flashed across his vision. No two people could be driving as crazily as that in this weather. He swerved to miss a station wagon, made a dangerous U-turn and went after the speeding car.

Whoever was behind the wheel was insane, but he knew how to drive all right. It made him think of . . . wait a minute . . . M 15. His father's license plate M 15 67P, always pronounced in the family as M15 after the British Secret Service . . . and sixes and sevens to show what his father thought of them. M 15 67P.

Johnny gnashed his teeth. What the hell was going on? His father often drove like a madman, like one with nine lives or—what had he said about Svank? More like twenty. What the hell was going on?

It was too much of a coincidence to dismiss. He'd told his father Alex had dumped the jewels on Ginny, then retrieved them the night of Svank's murder. Had he unintentionally given his father the idea that Ginny could be involved? Had he transferred his own subliminal suspicions of her to his father? He groaned. What had he done? Was his father using her as bait? There was nothing his father wouldn't do for his own ends, Johnny knew that. If his father was putting Ginny's life in jeopardy to break the Svank case and be a hero one more time before his retirement from journalism, he would kill him, he would kill him with his own hands. What had he done? What had he done . . . and where were they going?

"D'you pick up the message, Freddy?"

"Sure thing, Pete."

"Did you pass it on to your pal?"

"What d'you mean!"

"You know what I mean. This is serious stuff, Freddy. I want to know now or I won't answer for the consequences."

"Okay, okay. We've all done it. What's the harm?"

"This one's different. The D.A.'s breathing down our necks, the FBI is breathing down his . . . So?"

"Okay, okay, yep, I passed the girl's message on to QP. Thought he'd be in touch with you by now. What's the problem?"

"I'll deal with you later."

"What's the problem?" Forrester repeated plaintively. "He's your buddy, too. Never put a foot wrong yet, only helped us as we've helped him. What's your problem?"

There was no answer. Petersh was on his way.

The weather was getting worse. Johnny couldn't even be sure that the car he was chasing was the same sedan he'd followed from Ginny's apartment. He screamed profanities at the top of his voice to try to keep his panic under control. He was lost; didn't even know which road he was on; straining to hear the police siren, hearing nothing but the moan of the wind, the steady splash as the Oldsmobile dashed through small and big floods.

Now there was more traffic building up. The car he'd seen back at the intersection was three or four cars in front. Where were they going? They'd passed the turnoff for Kennedy.

Out of the mist came the answer. Now he knew for sure it was his father at the wheel. He knew where he was taking Ginny. He didn't know why, but he'd soon find out.

A large sign loomed before him: AQUEDUCT RACETRACK, KEEP RIGHT. One of his father's favorite hangouts, a place he could find blindfolded, a track he knew as intimately as any jockey. It would be deserted at this time of night, but his father would know a way in . . . and so would the police when he told them.

Sure enough Johnny saw the sedan take the right-hand fork. He started to look for a sign for telephones—it came about half a mile down the road. Whoever was planning to rendezvous with his father and Ginny at Aqueduct, Johnny was about to ruin the party.

What wild scheme had his father cooked up, thinking that with his Stallone mentality he could protect Ginny no matter what? This was one time his son was taking charge.

"Put me through to Detective Petersh. This is an xox emergency call," he yelled, using the police code Petersh had given him.

"I can't explain now, but I think my father's with Ginny. He's cooked something up, I'm sure of it. They're heading to Aqueduct, yes, yes, yes, I know it's closed. Take my word for it. That's where he's headed. He knows it like a homing pigeon. I'll meet you there."

Keeping her eyes shut Ginny realized she was in a car, strapped in, traveling at a terrible speed. For a few minutes she couldn't think what had happened. Then she remembered. She wanted to scream again, but she knew if she did the pad that had knocked her out would be clamped over her nostrils and there'd be no way she could escape.

She was in a car with Johnny's father, the man she now knew to be a murderer. She kept her eyes shut, staying motionless, wondering if her hands were bound. Where were they going?

To her horror Peet said, "You can open your eyes, Ms. Walker. I know you're fully awake. The chloroform never lasts more than thirty minutes." In a perfectly normal conversational tone he continued, "D'you know where your charming cousin put the jewels?"

A chill went through her body as she heard him laugh, a short, caustic laugh.

"I do," he said. "He told me before he got shot by some of our mutual friends from South America. In case you think I had anything to do with it, I did not, although I wasn't surprised. I can assure you it's not my style to shoot people in the back. I frightened your cousin into his confession. Unfortunately, he was too much of a big mouth, a show-off. The jewels are supposed to be in a safety deposit box, held, although he doesn't know it, in the name of the honorable young doctor treating your cousin's lover for AIDS. I thought you may also have a key? No?"

"Absolutely not. Where are you taking me?"

"To one of my favorite places—whooa—" The car skidded dangerously through a sudden deep pool of water. "Haven't driven like this in years. Haven't needed to," he added in the same conversational tone. "Pity about you, Ginny. I'm intrigued to know what so suddenly and unfortunately jogged your—" At that moment she heard the police siren; so did he; then another and another.

"Excuse me . . ." Peet crouched over the wheel.

Ginny watched in terror as the speedometer started to climb: 80—85—90 miles an hour.

With a sickening screech of tires, Peet twisted the car off to the right. It bounced off an embankment, miraculously came down on all four wheels, and tore round a corner. Ginny saw a large sign coming up. She couldn't believe it. Aqueduct Racetrack.

Was he going to kill her in a stable, where they'd never think of looking for her body, while he went off to Europe to begin his new life?

The sirens were getting closer—or were they going right by?

As Peet twisted and turned the car, driving in and out of buildings, with a prayer Ginny began to loosen her seat belt. If they hit something, they were both dead. If he had to slow down for any reason, she would try to make a run for it. The sirens were right behind them now, gaining on them.

He was making for the racetrack's exit again. It was too late.

It was blocked by a car, but it wasn't a police car and it wasn't a cop standing in front either.

My God, it was Johnny, standing in the rain, in front of the car. Peet didn't seem to be slowing down.

"It's Johnny, your son," she screamed. "Can't you see? It's your son Johnny."

The unbelievable happened. With only a few feet to spare, Peet slammed on the brakes and Ginny pitched forward against the windshield. It was the last thing she remembered.

1997

Johnny stared at the deep blue screen of his word processor. The cursor had been flickering at him unrelentingly for the past hour, urging him to type at least an opening paragraph. However hard he tried, he couldn't find the words, he just couldn't, deadline or no deadline.

The trial was over at last. The furor over the verdict had started to die down, but he knew it would forever be out there as a journalistic legal football, to be fished out and kicked around whenever somebody thought of another angle, or another big fish got caught in an unexpected net. Still, there was really nothing to stop him writing the inside story as only he could write it.

Absolutely nothing, he told himself firmly. Wasn't it the story he'd been waiting to write all his life?

He stared moodily at the screen, hoping for inspiration. If the umbilical cord hadn't been cut by now, then he didn't need a shrink—he needed a straitjacket.

It had been easy to hate his father before and during the trial, when, of course, the old man had performed so brilliantly.

Half the time he'd sounded like some modern-day King Arthur, helping rid the world of dirty scum like Svank. Only half the time, because from the beginning, the defense's position had been that Peet had been unduly provoked, and that his role in Svank's fatal fall had been nothing but an accident.

Ginny's testimony had merely placed him at the scene of the crime, which he'd admitted. Although it was a miracle she was still alive and her concussion hadn't been worse, the charges relating to her "abduction" hadn't gone anywhere. She hadn't been able to remember anything about the car chase and her final ordeal, and she'd pleaded with Johnny not to testify against his father.

The fact that no weapon or trace of any chloroform pad had been found had supported his father's story, which was that when he learned Ginny was about to be kidnapped by the same drug-related gang who'd murdered her cousin, he'd acted on the spur of the moment to "take her somewhere safe."

It was bullshit, but when the trial finally came to court, week after week, Johnny had been forced to accept that as far as those enforcing law and order were concerned, his father long ago had become "one of us" as opposed to "one of them."

He would forever be amazed by women, because Ginny predicted the verdict, and even after all she'd been through, she didn't appear to be upset, as he certainly was, when the judge ruled, "The prosecution's case has failed to meet the law's narrow criteria for a conviction on a criminally negligent homicide charge."

By then so much of Svank's dirty work had surfaced, there hadn't been much of an outcry that Quentin Peet was going to walk out a free man. He'd lost his job; he'd been publicly reprimanded, if not disgraced, but to Johnny's disgust, his father had been able to see for himself that the pandemonium in the courtroom had been more joyful than anything else.

Their eyes had met. Johnny had turned away. There was nothing more he had to say to a father who had so completely revealed himself that terrible day when he'd stood on the brakes to pull up a scant few feet from running him down.

He would remember for as long as he lived the rueful, disappointed look on his father's face as he'd said, "You win, Johnny," as if in not running his own son down, he'd lost; as if Quentin Peet had discovered to his sorrow that at last there was someone in the world he couldn't bring himself to destroy.

It was Ginny who'd helped him swallow the verdict, pointing out something he knew to be true from his brief experience with the drug world. "Wherever your father goes, however much money he has, he will spend the rest of his life looking over his shoulder."

And now he, John Q. Peet, had the perfect opportunity to set the record straight about Sir Galahad.

Johnny sighed. Not today he couldn't. And maybe he never would. *Next!* was up for a national magazine award in April because of his pieces on Madame Saks, the homeless, and the civil libertarians. He was a blue-eyed boy because of this, so despite a fat *New Yorker* contract being dangled so temptingly before him, he didn't really want to move. One day perhaps, if he ever felt restless, but not now.

There was no point in sitting in front of an empty screen any longer. He picked up the phone. "Ginny," he said, "I've got writer's block. Let's go out to dinner."

At the gala opening of Ginny Walker Fashion, Inc., a few floors up from Donna Karan, Virginia Walker blushed as Ginny introduced her as her greatest asset, "The best fitter and tailor and mother in the world."

She joined in the loud applause as Ginny declared, "Ginny Walker, Incorporated, is now officially open for business."

As Ginny was starting a wonderful new chapter in her life, so was she, "a refugee from Florida," as she'd seen herself described in an interview with Ginny that had already appeared in *Women's Wear Daily*. She was a more than willing refugee. Overriding Graham's moans and groans, she hadn't hesitated to accept her daughter's invitation to be part of her start-up operation—at least for the first few months.

To Virginia's surprise, so far, she hadn't missed Graham at all. If he didn't like it, it was just too bad. She'd spent nearly thirty years as a camp follower. Now it was her turn to kick up her heels.

She waved happily to Ginny as she saw her escape the packed throng in the main showroom and, followed by TV cameras, slip into the all-white, immaculate entrance hall. She was so proud of the way Ginny had soared into the fashion firmament, following her harrowing experiences with Alex and the law. She was bowled over by her own daughter's strength and talent.

Looking back Virginia guessed she'd always had it, remembering the bath towel reefer jacket and her renovated camel hair coat. She may have always had it, but it had taken so long for it to be recognized. There was no looking back now. Ginny was on her way.

In the reception area, where a spectacular print of a Georgia O'Keeffe sunflower hung over the white terrazzo desk, Ginny was pleased to see people were still flooding in. What a wonderful world it was now, with her beloved mother in the next office; Johnny more supportive and loving than ever, arriving any moment to share in her great day; and Esme, radiant in the first maternity dress she'd ever designed, telling anyone who cared to listen how her belief in "Ginny's genius" had never wavered.

Lee Baker Davies, who had been acting as cheerleader for the past few months, had brought along her editor in chief. Not that she'd had to worry about a lack of press coverage. The problem had been fitting everyone in, because everyone wanted to come.

How proud of her Alex, her misguided cousin, would have been. Poor Alex. Ginny shook her sad thoughts away and smiled modestly as a flock of new arrivals dropped effusive compliments on their way into the showroom. She was a lucky woman.

Out in the hallway Ginny noticed one of her two security guards talking seriously to a fragile-looking, strangely dressed young waif.

"Anything wrong, Jim?" she asked.

The waif smiled at her, but Ginny could see she was nervous.

"Her name's not on the list," Jim said gruffly.

"So what," said Ginny, "Come right in, Ms. . . . ?"